San Juanico

★★★

GUY BONNIVIER

ISBN: 978-1-7351771-5-1 (Paperback)
ISBN: 978-1-7351771-1-3 (eBook)

Cover design by Judith S. Nicolas at Judith S. Designs
Editing by Cortni Merritt at SRD Editing Services
Book design by Brianna Davis at Meraki
Design Maps and Illustrations by Jasna Cizler

Printed by Guy Bonnivier, in the United States of America.

First printing edition 2020.

www.guybonnivier.com

For:

The many dedicated Mexican conservationists I met and worked with in Baja California Sur along the way.

TABLE OF CONTENTS

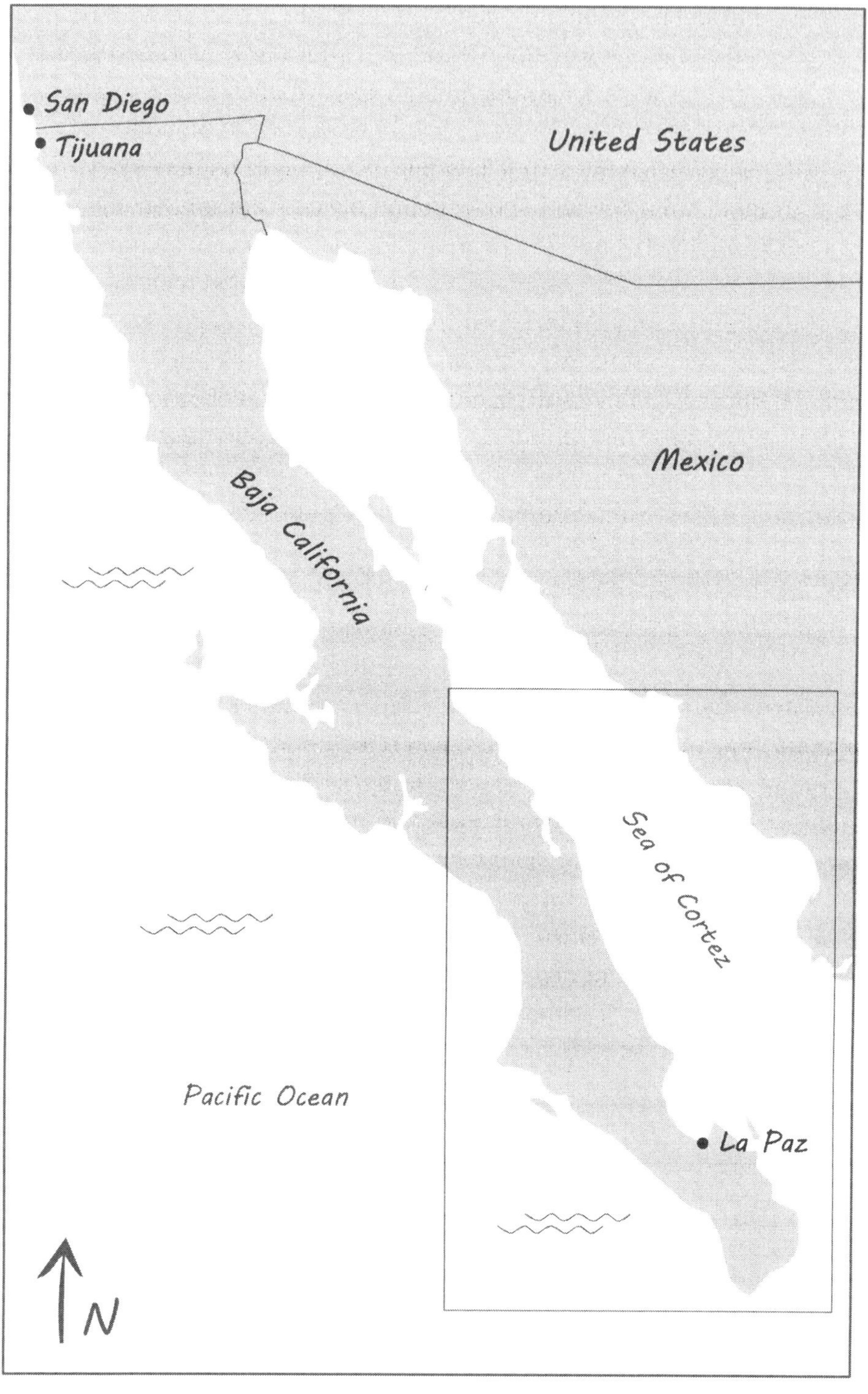
San Diego
Tijuana
United States
Mexico
Baja California
Sea of Cortez
Pacific Ocean
La Paz
N

San Juanico

Guaymas
Santa Rosalía
Sea of Cortez
Sierra Las Gigantas
Loreto
Agua Verde
Santa Marta
San Juanico
Insurgentes
Topolobampo
Timbabichi
Los Dolores
La Paz
Pacific Ocean

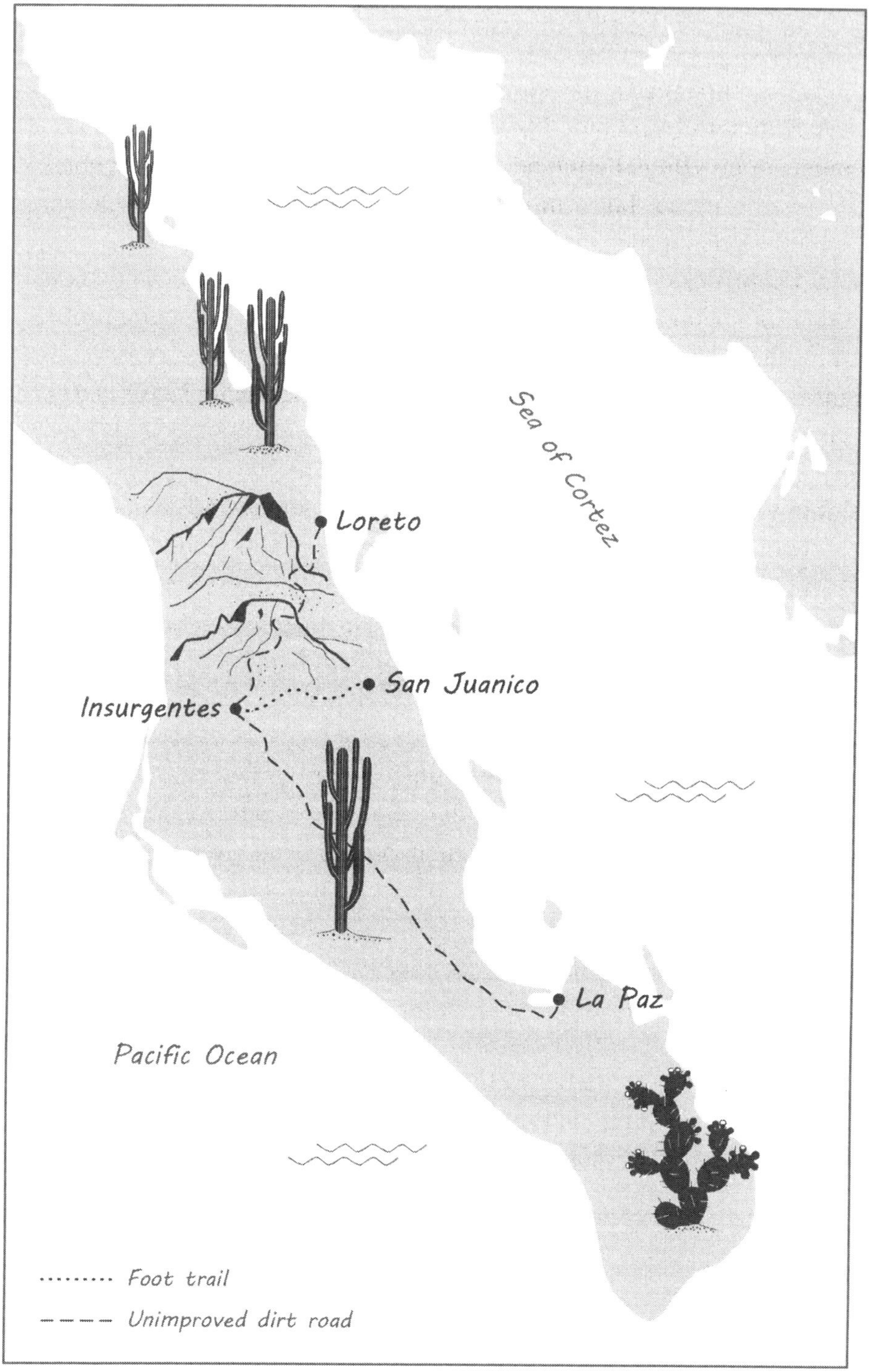
Sea of Cortez
Loreto
San Juanico
Insurgentes
La Paz
Pacific Ocean
Foot trail
Unimproved dirt road

Rancho San Juanico

Ejido San Jose del Norio
Territorio de Baja California Sur

September 1960

Juan Pedro Amador Murillo shuffled slowly along the trail under the mid-day sun in the direction of his shanty. For more than a century, the sharp hooves of domesticated animals seeking water from the spring-fed oasis had followed the same path. On top of the hardened soil, between the scattered rocks, were several inches of pulverized dust. Juan Pedro's nostrils were gray colored from inhaling the fine particles that rose in small clouds with each of his steps. A sweat-stained bandanna hung loosely around his neck, and two weeks of dark stubble shaded his face. His weathered features belied his meager twenty-eight years.

Cactus, mesquite brush, and thickets of impenetrable catclaw blanketed the parched gray-colored landscape as far as the eye could see. To the south, west, and north the horizon was framed by rimrock that crested a thousand feet above the valley floor. To the east lay a broad valley that extended toward the Sea of Cortez, twelve miles away. Dropping down to the sea, there was a thousand-foot vertical wall of craggy rock. Perched on top of the cliff was the high-desert plain Juan Pedro called home. It was the only home he and his extended family had ever known.

As Juan Pedro approached his wretched shanty that day, the sun was directly overhead. The oven-like temperatures of August had given way to the barely-more-temperate days of September. The three village women who greeted him did so from the narrow band of shade that extended from the side wall of the shanty.

"Juan Pedro!" said the smiling, plump woman who was first to speak. Her teeth were crooked but white, brilliant as new eggshell, contrasting sharply against her dark brown, leathery skin.

She embraced Juan Pedro and whispered, "You are a lucky man. You have a son! He is big and healthy with a head of black hair!"

Juan Pedro broke from his sleepy posture and half-smiled. He reached forward and held the woman by her shoulders with his toughened hands and pushed her gently back so he could look into her dark brown eyes. With her reassuring nod, tears welled up in his own dark eyes and fell across his face, leaving slick tracks in the dust and stubble. This was his third child, but only the first to survive childbirth.

"Thank God!" was all he said, and he kissed the woman on the cheek before doing the same to the other two standing by her side. "Can I go in and meet my son?" he asked, but he didn't wait for an answer and turned toward the door-less opening.

In the dim shadows of the shanty, his twenty-three year-old wife, Luisa, was lying on the dirt floor on a mattress made of softened burlap and palm fronds. She was modestly covered with a threadbare cotton sheet as she held the newborn infant to her pale, swollen breast. Her sister, Nora, kneeled beside her on the hard-pan dirt floor with a cup of goat's milk in her hand. She appeared even more serene than Luisa.

"Pedro, we have a son! He looks just like you. Here, hold him and give him his name," Luisa said as she offered up the child.

Juan Pedro studied the infant as he rocked it back and forth. He was speechless, until after a long time he turned to Luisa and said, "Juan Carlos will be his name! I will tell the village and we will have cabrito tonight! I know the animal. I saw a young buck this morning at the water. I'll go find him and build the fires myself. You do nothing, my love. Just lie in the bed and nourish our son. I will return soon with the animal for the fiesta! Here," Pedro said as he carefully handed the infant to Nora.

★★★

The year was 1960. Juan Carlos Amador Murillo was born into wretched poverty in the tiny village known as Rancho San Juanico, in the high desert plateaus and mountains of south-central Baja California Sur, Mexico. The only reason Rancho San Juanico existed was the single spring of fresh water that trickled out of the ground at a rocky crevice on the valley floor. Ancestral natives had constructed a rock wall surrounding the spring to protect it from trampling by their goats and burros, and during more recent generations, a small number of cattle. The amount of water that percolated to the surface was miniscule, about five gallons an hour, but day after day, week after week, the water seeped out and nourished a tiny wetland oasis and an insignificant sparse patch of chilis and beans. The oasis was dominated by a small grove of date palm trees that could be seen for miles when viewed from the distant rimrock that encircled the valley on three sides. A thirty-foot deep, hand-dug well, lined with rock, sat beside the spring and provided for more immediate needs. A bruised and battered, rusty tin bucket knotted up on a length of frayed old rope tied to a mesquite post laid in the dirt. It was used to draw water up from the well.

A dozen or more caves were scattered along the face of the hills surrounding San Juanico. Ancient Indian art etched and painted on the cave walls portrayed bighorn sheep and deer being pursued by stick men with spears and bows. The caves would've been occupied full-time by the local villagers except for their distance to water. When building materials of even the most rudimentary nature became available, the natives found life much easier closer to the water, rather than hauling it in bulky containers made of goat skins or heavy pottery up the side of the mountain. The caves were presently used to store and preserve a small amount of goat cheese, dried meat, and seeds, and as a place to take a siesta in a cool dark place on a sweltering afternoon. Far below the caves and the rimrock, the villagers lived in an odd variety of lean-to shelters, palm frond palapas, shacks and shanties widely spaced over five acres of flat land surrounding the spring. On rare occasions, small planes headed down the peninsula would circle low overhead for a closer inspection of the ramshackle village. The villagers would freeze in place, with eyes fixed on the aircraft in stunned wonderment.

The population of Rancho San Juanico in 1960 was around fifty, mostly related men, women, and children. Cousins commonly married cousins. There were eight families and several solitary widows, widowers, and bachelors. Access to the outside world was limited, and knowledge of the outside world was minimal. Nearly all the men and boys twelve and older had at least seen the Sea of Cortez to the east from the rim of the cliffs. A smaller number of them had actually made the dangerous trek down the rugged trail through the rocks to sea level. In the other direction, a rutted foot trail crossed the desert fifty miles to the west and led to the Magdalena Plain, an irrigated flatland that surrounded the relatively prosperous farming town of Ciudad Insurgentes, a short distance from the Pacific Ocean. It was two days on foot from San Juanico down to the Sea of Cortez, and likewise, two days of steady riding on mules or burros in the opposite direction across the desert to Ciudad Insurgentes.

From Insurgentes, a one lane primitive dirt road went both north and south. To the north the road snaked up and through the raw, rugged Sierra Las Gigantas and reached heights in excess of three-thousand feet above sea level. After a grueling day's journey by truck through dangerous switchbacks and canyons, the road dropped back to sea level, to the small coastal fishing town of Loreto. Loreto was built on a gently sloping alluvial plain, tucked between the foot of the towering Las Gigantas and the Sea of Cortez. Scattered across the alluvial plain were a few isolated springs that fed a limited amount of agriculture, date palm groves, and most importantly, a pipeline that provided a reliable source of precious fresh water to the citizens of Loreto.

The first capital city of California, Loreto was founded by Jesuit missionaries in 1697. They built a magnificent stone mission that same year, which still served the local Catholic parish more than three hundred years later. Loreto, however, never grew and prospered, because it lacked a sheltered port on the Sea of Cortez. Local watercraft were limited to a few dozen banana-shaped pangas owned by fishermen, who left them haphazardly scattered along the local beaches, many of them belly-up in the sand.

Heading south from Insurgentes, in the direction opposite of Loreto, the more-traveled, primitive dirt road crossed rolling desert plains and skirted past solitary mountains, which rose here and there like lonely islands. A long day's journey south by truck brought travelers to the largest city on the southern Baja Peninsula, La Paz. Nearly all commerce supporting the sparse population of the Baja California Sur Territory passed through La Paz. Ships from the Mexican mainland and beyond anchored in the bay, and a semi-weekly ferry provided passage between La Paz and the home country. Oddly, the inhabitants of Baja California Sur referred to the mainland as "Mexico," as if it were another country.

San Juanico

Of the inhabitants of Rancho San Juanico, only a few of the older men had ventured as far south as La Paz. Their stories, and those of rare visitors, along with a few worn copies of old magazines, provided the only information of the outside world. In San Juanico, a lonely cemetery stood by itself between the date palm grove and a small half-circle of low-lying lava rock. The graves were scattered across the parched ground with little thought. A small number of barely legible headstones dated back to the early 1800s. The majority of the graves, however, were marked by decayed wooden crosses or simple piles of hand-sized stones. Most of them were sad little plots indicating an infant or a child. As for the others, fifty years was a very old age.

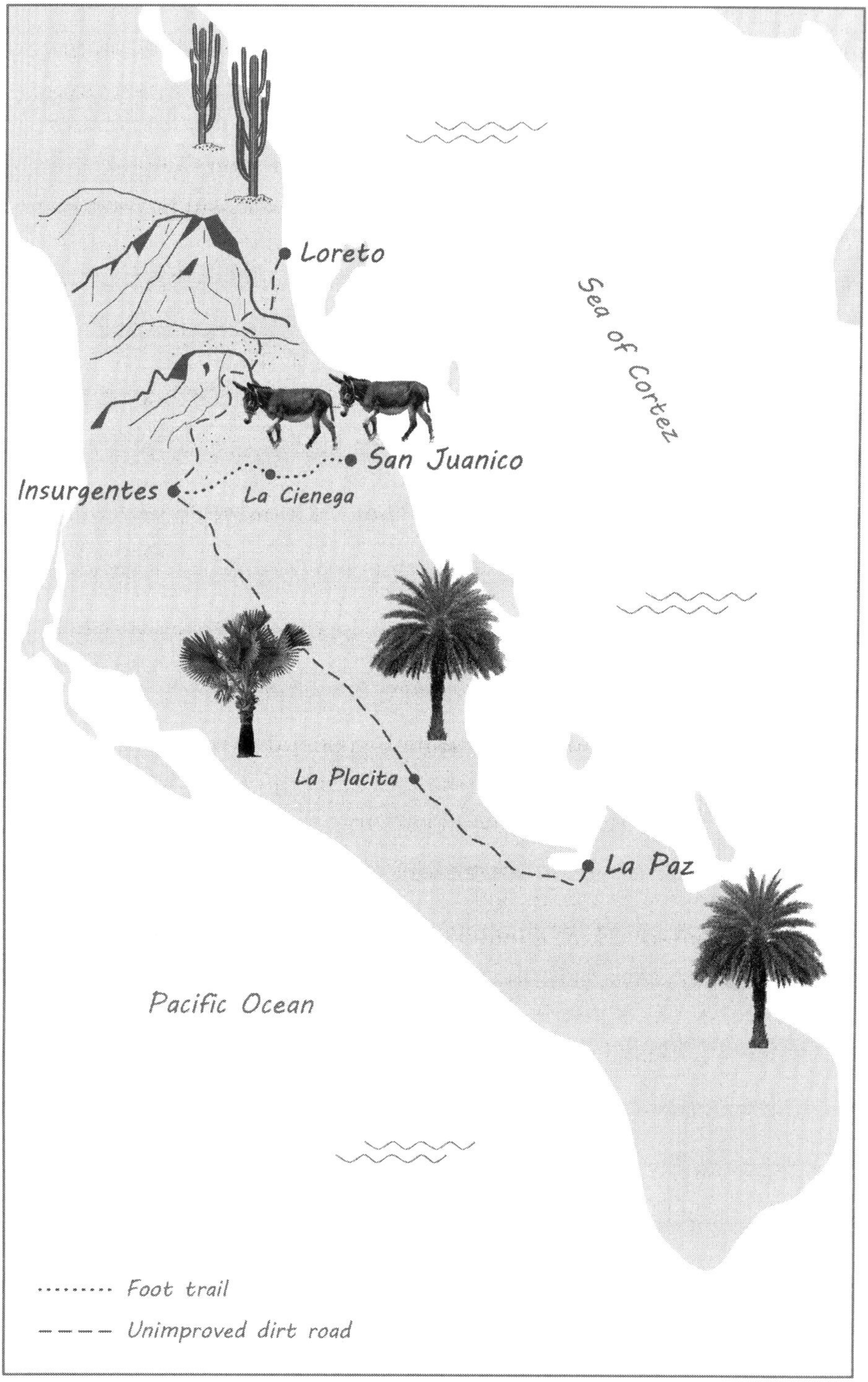
Loreto
Sea of Cortez
San Juanico
Insurgentes
La Cienega
La Placita
La Paz
Pacific Ocean
Foot trail
Unimproved dirt road

Rancho San Juanico

1965

Juan Carlos Amador Murillo was joined by a younger sister, Maricela, in 1961. The little family lived day to day in their pathetic shanty, suffering the brutal poverty that was Rancho San Juanico. The children never laid eyes on a tablet of aspirin or a Band-Aid, nor had they ever tasted any toothpaste. Their diets bordered on nutritional starvation. They were unaware of the hardships, because they knew nothing else. Their smiles, laughter, and antics warmed the hearts of one and all, as most Mexican children did in villages and pueblos in remote, rural parts of the country. They would have been dumbfounded if told they were living in third-world conditions, or that they were not that many miles, as the eagle could easily soar, from places like Los Angeles, California, even Disneyland.

Young Juan Carlos liked to wander off by himself. He might gather a flock of hens and pretend they were goats to be herded, or he might spy on the quail that came during the evenings for water at the spring. He would sometimes surprise a coyote or a group of desert bighorn sheep at the water. One memorable evening, he saw a young bighorn taken down by a mountain lion. The lion had been laying quietly in the date palm thicket, waiting. It could have easily taken Juan Carlos, but its natural prey did not include five-year-old humans.

The intimidatingly large cat ignored the boy, who unwittingly walked directly in front of it as it patiently waited. Mere seconds later, it viciously attacked a group of bighorns that approached the water hole opposite and a few feet to the side. The desperate, agonizing squeals from the stricken animal, the explosion of dust as the other animals turned and fled, and the spray of bright red arterial blood that saturated the lion's terrifyingly primeval face, imprinted immediately in the boy's memory. He never had time to react, because it happened so fast. He simply froze in place, and when he regained his wits, he back-stepped slowly out of the palm grove as the animal hovered over its kill and growled. Only then did Juan Carlos become fearful and begin to vomit as he turned and ran toward the safety of the garden where he huddled in the corner among the chili plants, as he convulsed and cried for most of an hour. Later that evening, after he had recovered, he boastfully told his parents the story of the lion and the bighorn. His father smiled with pride and patted the boy on the shoulder while his mother cringed and tried to put the thought of it out of her mind.

The next day, without a word to anyone, Juan Pedro borrowed a .22 rifle from his neighbor, and he tracked down and shot the lion dead. He knew that it would be only a matter of time before it turned its attention to goats and small children. The villagers all shared in the lion meat that evening for their meal.

Juan Carlos' favorite time of day was the evening, when his father was home discussing the day's events with his mother. His imagination was lively and vivid. When he could no longer stand still, he would pester his parents with questions, but mostly he listened and processed the abstract thoughts in his head. Luisa laughed at him and said his mind was like a jaw trap.

One late summer evening that year, Juan Carlos noticed that his father seemed distracted and restless. Juan Pedro had a pouch of tobacco he saved for special occasions, and this particular evening, he brought it out and carefully rolled a cigarette. Carlos watched as his Papa lit the cigarette, inhaled, and formed his thoughts before speaking to Luisa, who was kneading a mound of tortilla dough on a rickety wooden table across the small room.

"Alonso is sick with the grippe. He asked me to take the mules to Insurgentes this week," Pedro said, as he flicked the ashes from the cigarette off to the side without watching where they settled. That was all he said, watching the smoke rise from the cigarette, he patiently waited for a response.

Luisa looked up, still kneading the dough, thought it over for a moment, and replied, "But you have traveled there only once in your life, and that was with Alonso. God only knows how many years ago. Do you think it's wise for you to make that long journey without him?"

"Why do I need Alonso? A blind man could follow that trail, and those old mules have been to Insurgentes more times than I've had birthdays," he sucked another drag from the cigarette. "They could lead themselves. I would only be along for the ride and to unload the supplies. Besides, Alonso told me that Felix would be going with me."

Luisa looked up again from her kneading and rolled her eyes. She said flatly with a hint of sarcasm, "Felix is just a boy. What help would he be?"

Her response got an immediate rise out of Juan Pedro, and he asserted himself by answering, "He's eighteen years old, and he's been to Insurgentes four times just in the last year. The boy has as much muscle as any one of those mules! Just last week, I watched him wrestle a four-hundred-pound steer to the ground and hog-tie it before the animal knew what happened. Have you looked at him lately? He's as big and strong as any man in this village, except probably for me!"

Luisa stopped her kneading, and her face flushed to stifle a laugh. She responded, "Ahh, there you go. Reminding me that I'm married to the only real man in San Juanico! Please, forgive me Pedro, if sometimes I forget how lucky I am. Maybe I should remind you that I am the smartest and most beautiful woman in all of San Juanico!"

"That you are, Luisa, that you are. I can't argue with you," he replied with a smile. He took a long pull on the cigarette.

After an awkward silence, Luisa asked in a more serious tone, "If you went to Insurgentes, what would I do all those nights here alone, without you? And you, hornier than that Billy goat out there? God only knows where you might end up, after a night drinking too much tequila!"

Pedro smiled again and took another deep pull on his cigarette, as he studied his wife standing at the table, kneading the dough. At twenty-eight, he agreed that she was the most beautiful woman in San Juanico. They had been married for fourteen years, and unlike most women her age, she hadn't grown heavy and round. She was strong and active, and it seemed to him she was always in motion. Her breasts were average size but loose under the thin rag of her blouse. They sagged slightly more than before she bore the children, but they were a perfect size on her wiry frame. She moved with natural grace, although her hips and thighs had widened. As far as he was concerned, she was far more attractive in full womanhood than when they'd married. Her long dark brown hair reached down to her lower back, and she kept it braided in a tail behind or coming forward over her right shoulder. There were strands of silver he had begun to notice. Her eyes always sparkled and faint wrinkles appeared around the edges when she smiled. Unlike many women faced with the challenges of miserable poverty in middle age, Luisa seemed to always be smiling. And to Pedro's unending delight, she had a huge sexual appetite and a brilliant imagination that she shared enthusiastically with him. He knew what a lucky man he was.

"Ahh, but life is so short, Luisa," he finally answered. "You wouldn't deny me a little tequila after such a dangerous journey, would you?" he asked with a chuckle.

Hinting at his mischief, Luisa smiled before she spoke and said, "No, old man. I think you would deserve some tequila, especially after braving such a long, treacherous journey, where you, alone in all your manhood, were in charge of a skinny teenager and some worn-out old mules. Then, maybe one night after you get there, just before you're fallen-down drunk as a fool, before you get sick and puke your guts on the ground, you could taste yourself a young señorita again. I promise you, Juan Pedro Murillo, the next day, before her perfume wore off, you'd wish you were home with the real woman of your dreams! Before this night is through, I'll remind you what that's like!"

"I know. I know," he said a bit sheepishly.

The conversation confused young Juan Carlos.

Following another long silence, as Pedro finished his cigarette, he resumed the conversation from a different angle.

"Really, Luisa, I've been thinking it might be a good time for me to go and do this. Alonso tells me there's serious talk in Insurgentes about building a road from San Juanico to over there. Some people think it might be possible one day for a truck to travel across the desert, all the way back here to San Juanico. Just think, what takes more than a week on a mule would take only one day in a truck. Think about how much more a truck can carry than a mule, and a truck could come two or three times a week. Think about that for a minute, woman, would you just?"

Luisa didn't wait to respond. "There you go dreaming again! No wonder Juan Carlos always thinks of so many strange things. He gets it from you!"

"I could help make this happen! I'd like to see how happy you'd be if a truck full of food and everything else you need drove right here to the front your palapa! What would you think of that, huh?"

"When I see it, I'll believe it. If it's so easy, why hasn't Alonso thought of it already? He's been making the journey to Insurgentes for as long as I can remember, and I've never heard him say a word about it."

"Alonso loves his mules and that way of life, and I think he likes having time away from Julia. He probably doesn't care about a new road. I like Julia, you know I do, but do you ever see her happy? When was the last time you saw her laugh or even make a smile? I think if I was Alonso, I might prefer to spend my time with the mules, too."

Luisa finished kneading and brushed her hands on her threadbare, dull-colored skirt. She studied Pedro for a moment. He was staring at the last of the twilight, and she thought about what a good man he was. He always put her and the children first, and she knew better than anyone how terrible he felt about their hopeless poverty and their decrepit living conditions.

"I've been thinking about this for a long time, Luisa," Pedro began again. "What do you think I do when I'm out there with the goats all day? You think I mindlessly follow them around through the catclaw? I thought we might open a little store. We could sell kerosene, vegetables, lard, flour, and cans of food. We could sell material to make clothes. Everyone always needs clothes around here. Think about it, Luisa. Our lives would never be the same!"

Juan Carlos couldn't resist, and he suddenly spoke up. "Papa, would a truck really come here to the palapa? Can I go with you to Insurgentes? I can ride a mule, you know. You've seen me!"

"No, no, no, Carlos," Luisa responded. "Your Papa is just talking right now. Insurgentes is too far away for a small boy to go. When you're older, you can travel to Insurgentes."

Pedro looked at his son and said, "I believe that before you're as old as Felix is now, you will see a truck drive here to our palapa. I do."

Juan Carlos' face wrinkled in worry, and he asked, "Can you bring a truck back with you?"

"Not this time, but when one finally comes, you can get in and go for a long ride! Right now though, it's time for you and Maricela to go to bed. I want to talk to your mother some more."

Although, it was long into the evening, Juan Pedro was feeling alive. He wanted to think. He stepped across the hard-packed dirt floor and reached for his tobacco pouch wedged between the palm fronds in the ceiling. He couldn't recall when he'd last rolled two cigarettes and smoked them both in one night.

As he inhaled the first drag of his second cigarette, he sat down outside on a wobbly old bench under the edge of the palapa-covered overhang. He could hear Luisa arguing softly with the children behind him. As usual, the Baja stars hovered overhead in a thick, flickering blanket. He was tired. He was tired of herding goats. He was tired of watching Luisa try to feed their small family on dry beans, a precious spoonful of lard, a few tortillas, and maybe a cup of goat's milk. On rare, special occasions, they might have a small block of goat cheese or, far less often, a precious piece of meat. Only about half the time did they have a spoonful of lard.

Pedro noticed one his neighbors a hundred yards away, bending over a small mesquite fire, and heard him clanging some pots and pans together. For some odd reason, it gave him a sinking feeling in his stomach. Their pathetic shanties were at least widely spaced enough across the valley floor that it provided them a small amount of privacy. Even so, they all shared two primitive latrines, and they all bathed behind nearly useless palm frond screens, using buckets of water and coarse sponges. Only a few men who had made the journey to Insurgentes or La Paz had ever seen a bathtub or taken a shower. The women could only dream of such things.

After putting the children down, Luisa joined Pedro on the bench. She placed her hand on his thigh as she sat. Over her shoulder, she looked at him with a crinkly expression and asked, "Two cigarettes tonight? What are we celebrating?" Her eyebrows rose with the question.

Pedro ran his hand back through his long dirty black hair and said, "I want a better life for you and the children. You and I aren't getting any younger, Luisa. Our lives are no different than our parents. My father was dead when he was forty-two! I might have only nine years left if I'm like him. Your father was gone at forty-five. Your mother died the day your brother was born. Is that all we have to look forward to?" Luisa gave his thigh a slight squeeze as she let that thought sink in. She knew it was true.

Pedro blew another lungful of smoke off in the air and continued, "I've decided I'm not going to grow old and die here in San Juanico without trying to make a better life. I've been thinking about this for a long time." He turned and looked at her eyes, they were reflecting the stars.

"I have this chance to go to Insurgentes," he continued, he grasped her hand. "I've decided I'll do more than just lead the mules and trade the cheese. I want to see a road built to Insurgentes. I want to meet the people in Insurgentes who can help us. I might be gone more than a week," he searched her eyes for reassurance.

Luisa pondered for a moment and a layer of creases, one on top of the other, crossed her forehead when she asked, "Are you having what I heard someone call a 'mid-life problem'?"

Pedro didn't answer. He simply sucked harder on the cigarette. His hand shook as he withdrew it from his mouth, and his lungs held still before he exhaled. Luisa noticed his hand trembling.

Luisa collected her thoughts after realizing the serious turn of the conversation, she said, "Even though I give you a hard time, I want a better life too, Pedro. You know that. I make jokes about you dreaming, but that's what I love about you. You know how to dream. Sometimes I forget to tell you, but I have dreams too. I have dreams for our children every day. If that road you want to build could bring us a schoolteacher, it would change our lives forever," she leaned into him as she said it. She smelled the strong tobacco odor on his breath.

"It won't be easy to make the changes you talk about," she went on, "but how easy is it to live in this place with nothing? What food do we ever have? And stupid little things I never talk about – like the one pair of underwear I've owned in my life, a gift from my father on my tenth birthday. I wore them under my skirt until they wore out. They were the only piece of soft girl clothing I've ever had. I want my daughter to know how that feels. Is that too much to ask?" she placed her arm around his shoulder.

They were quiet for a long time when Luisa said softly, "Let's take a bath. I want to give you some love, and I could use some myself." She nudged him and rose from the bench. She pulled gently on his hand for encouragement, in the direction of the palm frond screen.

Under the stars, Pedro and Luisa walked hand in hand without much purpose across the open yard to the screen. They stripped, piece by minimal piece, out of their filthy, ragged sweat-stained clothing. They kicked them off in the dirt. Their bodies smelled of goats and sweat. Luisa picked up the wet sponge and a piece of lye soap from the bucket. She slowly began to wash Pedro, from his filthy hair down to his feet. He did the same to her. He caressed her breasts with the soapy wet sponge and weighed each one in his hands. Her chocolaty nipples hardened with his touch and stood up under the thin film of soap. She ran the sponge over his flat stomach and scrubbed his chest and the pits of his arms. She massaged softly between his legs. She spent more time than needed there, making him clean.

★★★

Early the next morning, Pedro walked down the well-worn path to Alonso's shack, the largest one in the village. Alonso, an overweight man with a bushy head of gray hair, and a noticeable limp was boiling water on a cast-iron grill in the fire pit. A jar of Nescafé sat on a wooden table under the veranda.

"Sit down, Pedro! Have some coffee with me" Alonso ordered as he coughed and spit off to the side. "This is Nescafé," he exclaimed as he held up the jar for Pedro to see. "I call it coffee in a jar. Everyone in Insurgentes is drinking it. You just boil the water and put some of this in the cup. It mixes itself and tastes better than regular coffee, at least I think so!" He started coughing again and turned away as he cleared his throat.

"I spoke to Luisa last night and told her I was going to Insurgentes. I thought we should talk."

"Good, I'm glad you decided to go," he said as he lifted the pot off the grill. "There's so much to tell you and so many instructions. I need to write down all the names, lists, and other things for you, like where to take the cheese, where to find the lard, who to talk to and how much they pay you. I'll put it on paper for you," he explained as he limped back over to the table. "I hope you can read? I never thought. Can you read?" he asked, pouring the coffee. He looked to Pedro for a response.

"A little, but not much," Pedro answered, scratching the stubble on his chin.

"Well, we can figure it out as we go," Alonso said as he handed Pedro his coffee. "Go ahead, taste that and tell me what you think. Julia's jealous, because I make better coffee than she does," he added, chuckling to himself.

Alonso prided himself as being the self-appointed delegado of Rancho San Juanico. Although he was gone much of the time on his many trips, he was the village elder when disputes needed to be settled or decisions made on behalf of the village. At fifty-one years of age, he was the second oldest man in San Juanico, and the villagers looked to him for guidance and authority. Only the sixty-year-old bachelor, Pepe, an old crab, was older, but Pepe spent most of his time alone and didn't mix much with the others.

While Alonso started to scribble his list of instructions, Pedro said, "I wanted to talk to you about the road. You told me there were some men in Insurgentes who wanted to build a road to San Juanico. Is that true?"

"Ah, yes!" he answered, as he began another bout of coughing. When he recovered, he took another sip of his coffee and said, "Damn, I like this! I'm going to put Nescafé here on the list. Buy a full box of it!"

"Alonso, the road?" Pedro reminded him.

"Oh, yeah," Alonso started coughing again, this time so deep and severe he bent over and gagged. He turned, cleared his throat and spit.

When he caught his breath he said, "You ever heard of the man who owns Rancho Santa Marta, down on the beach?"

"Yeah, but not much."

"Well, he's very wealthy, and he also owns some big ranches at Insurgentes, and others down near La Paz somewhere. Anyway, this guy, he wants to see a road not only to San Juanico, but out to the cliffs above Santa Marta," he took a sip of coffee and brought it up to his nose to inhale the aroma.

"What for?" Pedro asked, scratching the stubble on his chin.

"He wants to bring supplies to the top of the cliff. Burros could haul them down to Santa Marta from there on that old trail. Right now, they deliver everything to Santa Marta in pangas. Half the time, the pangas break down or sink. Last year, they lost two pangueros, at least nobody ever saw them again," he added grimly, shaking his bushy head.

"What's the man's name, where can I find him?"

"His name's Oscar Padilla, but he lives in La Paz. You need to go to the Ejido San Jose del Norio office in Insurgentes and talk to a man named Sammy Gonzo. Sammy works for Oscar, and they talk on the telephone every day. Sammy's a good friend of mine."

"Telephone?"

Alonso chuckled, "Yeah, the telephone! You never heard of a telephone?"

"Sure, but I don't know how they work."

He snickered and said "It's like a radio, but the voices are carried on wires. Sammy can talk on one end and hear Oscar talk back from the other. Sammy's had a telephone for three years already," he swatted at a fly and spilled what was left of his coffee. He cussed and shuffled over to the fire and returned with the pot of hot water. He refilled both cups.

As Alonso sat, he continued, "They've had telephones in La Paz for twenty years, but it took them all those years to string the lines north to Insurgentes. If you go out to that two-track La Paz road, you'll see the telephone poles. Far as the eye can see! Makes you wonder what they'll think of next," he shook his head about it.

"Anyway, like I said," Alonso went on, "Oscar and Sammy would like to build a road to San Juanico, then over to Santa Marta, if only they had someone to do the work. All the men from Insurgentes and the Ejido are working on the road to La Paz. They won't be finished with that for two or three more years."

Pedro set his coffee down, "We have fifteen men and boys in San Juanico who do nothing but herd goats once in a while. Why didn't you tell Sammy we could do the work?"

"Oh, you know me, Pedro, I don't care if they ever build a road to San Juanico. I'm old. I don't have too many years left. Besides," he whispered, and looked over his shoulder toward the house, "have you seen Julia lately? She's so fat she can't hardly squat to pee anymore," he belly-laughed, and it led to another fit of coughing.

He added, "If she's not cussing me out, she's throwing pots and pans at me. You've never heard such filth come out of a woman's mouth! No, I don't care about the road," Alonso continued, "I think I'll use what time I have left making trips with the mules. I like to get away. I'll let you in on a little secret," he whispered again, looking over his shoulder. "There's a widow woman at Insurgentes who does a nice job of taking care of me. I might move there and be done with it here."

Pedro raised his eyebrows with surprise. He shook his head as he looked at the old man across the table. He wanted nothing to do with that discussion. "Okay Alonso, I'll get my things ready. I'll tell Felix we'll be leaving before sun-up. Can you have the mules ready?"

"Sure, sure. Don't worry, I'll have two mules for you boys to ride, and I'll string up the rest of em' and have em' packed by sun-up."

"Thanks for the coffee. You're right, that is good!"

Alonso coughed again and smiled at the compliment.

★★★

Three hours before daylight, Luisa was working in her tiny kitchen under the dim light of a kerosene lamp. In a small stone oven, she fed mesquite twigs into a hot blue fire. A pot of refried beans was warming while she heated tortillas over the flames. She spread beans on the tortillas, added chili salsa, rolled them up, and placed them on a flat green palm leaf. When she had seven or eight burritos, she folded the palm leaf, tied it with a thin cotton string, and placed it in a saddlebag. She filled the saddlebag with enough burritos to last two men four days. When she finished, she wiped her hands on her smock, laid the bag on the table and went to check on Pedro.

"Your food is ready."

"Good, I'm ready, except I can't find my machete. I can't see in the dark."

"I have it in the kitchen. I'll put it with the saddle bag. Let's go, I'll help you carry your things."

A few minutes later, they walked up to Alonso's palapa where he had a fire burning in the pit.

"Good morning, good morning! Have some Nescafé, Luisa. Here, put some sugar in it," he took it upon himself to place a spoonful of sugar in her cup. "If you like it, tell Juan Pedro to bring some back for you. Please sit down. Please, right here," he said, pulling out a stool.

"Good morning, Señora," Luisa heard someone with a husky voice say from the shadows behind her. She turned to see a tall solitary figure leaning against a mesquite post with his arms folded in front of him. As her eyes adjusted to the dark, she recognized Felix. She noticed how tall he was, how he moved with fluid ease across the palapa to sit opposite her at the table. She found it difficult to see his face, as the only light was coming from Alonso's fire, directly behind him.

"Good morning, Felix. Nice to see you, if even in the dark. Are you ready for the trip?" she asked.

"Oh yeah, this will be my fifth time to Insurgentes," he said with a hint of pride. "I was there three months ago, in June. It was so hot, we only rode at night. We slept under mesquite trees in the shade during the day, didn't we, Alonso?"

"Yes, we did!" he started coughing, "That's the last time I travel during June. The cheese was soft, like lard gets in the summer, by the time we got there. I couldn't find anybody who wanted to buy that soft cheese. Never again will I go in June. Where is Juan Pedro? He needs to be moving!" he said, looking around.

"Here he comes," Luisa answered. "I think he was packing the mules. Are you ready, Pedro?"

"Yes, the mules are ready. Good morning, Alonso, Felix," Pedro said, as he nodded toward each of them and reached for Luisa's coffee. "It will be a good day for the trail, just like yesterday. Not too hot. Do you have my lists, Alonso?" as he sipped her coffee.

"Yes, yes, right here," he said as he reached into his pocket and pulled out a handful of papers. "Look, here's what you do with the cheese, where to go for lard, and this is Sammy's name, and where you can find him. Felix knows most of the rest, like where you can trade things in the store, and the bank where you can get your pesos. I packed four canteens. Felix knows where the Cienega springs are. You can re-fill them there while you water the mules. I think that's it," he said, scratching his whiskers.

"Thanks," Pedro answered. He took the papers from Alonso and they shook hands. "I'll see you when I return. I might be an extra day or two if things work out with Sammy and the road idea." He turned to Luisa and said, "Say goodbye to the children for me. Be sure to tell them I won't be gone long. Tell them I promised. I don't want them to worry."

Their eyes met in the dim light. There was apprehension. During their fourteen years of marriage, they had rarely been separated overnight.

"Have a safe journey, Pedro. I'll take care of things here." she told him, gripping tight to his hand.

He leaned in, kissing her and holding her hard as he pressed his chest against her breast. "Please don't worry, I'll be back soon, before you even know it. I promise."

Pedro gave her one last kiss. As he turned to leave, he failed to see the tears welling in her eyes.

★★★

As the early hints of dawn broke far off on the eastern horizon, Juan Pedro, Felix, and the string of mules reached the high rimrock that encircled the San Juanico Valley. They stopped, gathered the mules and turned back toward the east to watch the sunrise across the Sea of Cortez. Pedro felt exhilarated, as if he was on top of the world. From their vantage point, they could see a faint sparkle on the water. The first subtle rays of light inched their way up from the depths of the darkness, hundreds of miles away over the Mexican mainland. They watched as if they were the first human beings to ever witness that spectacular scene from that beautiful place, and they probably were.

"We made good time, Felix. The mules have been easy. I hope they stay that way. We might be there by late morning tomorrow. What do you think?"

"We can probably do that. The mules have been following this trail their whole lives, they know every inch of it. I agree, the walking's been easy even in the dark, and you're pushing them harder than Alonso ever does. He's been slowing down."

"I don't know about your idea building a road through here, Pedro," he removed his straw hat and ran his hand through his long black hair. "Tell me what you think after we go through a couple of the canyons up ahead. Remember, you've only made this trip once. I can't picture a road going through there. Look at that," Felix pointed to the east, "the sun's up. Took only a minute for the whole thing to rise! My God, look at that," he exclaimed, as a perfectly round brilliant orange ball ascended over the Gulf of California.

"I see, I see. We're lucky to be alive, Felix!" Feeling invigorated, Pedro asked, "Want to try and reach the Cienega tonight? We could camp there."

"If we don't stop, I think we can make it. We have a place at Palo Blanco where Alonso likes to camp, but two hours more, moving right along, we'd be at the Cienega. There's better feed for the mules there anyway."

"Let's be moving then!" Pedro said, pulling on the reins, he gave his mule a kick. With that, the small caravan turned its back on the Sea of Cortez and headed west in the direction of the Pacific Ocean, fifty miles ahead.

The day passed quickly. Felix went on ahead, leading three mules with loaded pack saddles tethered behind him. Pedro made up the rear with two pack animals behind him. There were seven mules in all. Pedro was impressed with how Felix dodged the rocks and climbed the slopes, keeping a steady gait. He found it a challenge keeping up. His respect for the young man grew with each passing hour and mile. He thought to himself he'd never seen anyone handle mules better than Felix.

As they moved along, Pedro took his time studying the landscape. He tried to imagine riding down a road instead of a narrow trail. He noted that much of the engineering had already been done. The natives who first built the trail knew where to locate the path of least resistance. The trail never went straight up or down. It followed the gentler slopes, inclines, and descents. In many places it was carved into the side hills exactly where it needed to be.

The two men stopped only twice during the day to stretch their legs, eat burritos, and share a canteen of water. Other than that, they pushed on and made steady progress. The desolate country they crossed could easily have made the fifty miles in front of them seem like an endless journey, but Pedro hardly noticed. He marveled at the variety of terrain and the desert life around him. His mind wandered as they moved steadily along.

They passed through surreal forests of stately cardon cactus, relatives of the giant saguaros in the American southwest, some of them standing more than forty feet high. Scrubby, nasty thickets of catclaw blanketed most of the rockier slopes, more than ready to tear at the flesh of any human or beast that mis-stepped off the trail. The mules were familiar with catclaw and never once brushed up against it. The same went for the jumping cholla cactus, a brushy succulent that shed needle-covered segmented joints. The fish-hooked tiny needles on the cholla would cling to bare skin or get so entangled in a mule's tail that it would have to be cut off. In contrast, there were the bright green-barked palo verde trees that helped soften the spine and thorn-infested landscape.

Everything survived on very little rain. Years might pass without a drop of it. When the rain did come, it was often heavy and furious. It would descend in horrid torrents, resulting in flash floods and landslides. Accordingly, most of the plants adapted a shallow web of roots, spread out through the top several inches of rocky soil, enabling them to absorb the moisture quickly before it could run off and be lost. Following a rare heavy deluge, the dull-colored landscape would transform overnight into vibrant shades of green. Next would come the glorious multi-colored flowers, bursting forth for a few brief days of breathtaking splendor.

As they rode on, Pedro felt much like the desert flowers in bloom. Having not left San Juanico for so many years, his senses sharpened, and he became acutely aware of his surroundings. Something remotely familiar deep inside him stirred and made him feel alive again. He came to realize the relentless daily struggles that defined their lives in San

Juanico were slowly strangling the life within him, and he thought, the same could be said of his precious Luisa.

★★★

Toward the end of the long grueling day, as dusk settled in around them, the shadows grew long. The two tired men came upon a flat piece of open, fertile land, surrounded by mesquite and date palm trees. The place was known as the Cienega. A shallow spring seeped to the surface out in the center of the flat, sustaining a broad expanse of meadow. They were surprised to see a campfire burning on the far end of the meadow, and they rode toward the fire.

"Who do you think that is?" Felix asked. "We never see anyone on this trail. There's nothing out here. No reason to be out here. This is strange."

"Let's be friendly, ride over and say hello," Pedro suggested.

"I guess," Felix said with apprehension.

As they approached, before Pedro could shout hello to the two men he saw moving around the fire, two scraggly burros grazing in the grass bellowed out an alarm and greeted the approaching mules. The two men looked up. Pedro and Felix waved.

"Hello," Pedro called when he was within hearing distance. The two men stopped what they were doing. Neither of them acknowledged the visitors. They spoke quietly between themselves.

As they rode in closer Pedro explained, "We're on our way to Insurgentes, we planned to spend the night here. We'll settle in on the other end of the meadow there," he pointed. "We only wanted to come by and say hello."

Pedro climbed down from the mule and stretched his cramped legs. "We come from San Juanico, back over those hills a day or so to the east," he nodded in that direction. Neither of the men said a word.

Sensing their discomfort, Pedro stood still. Felix observed the strange scene from his seat on the mule. Pedro glanced at the fire. There was a desert bighorn sheep carcass roasting on the spit. He saw a .22 caliber lever-action rifle leaning against the trunk of a tree.

"Looks like you got you a nice desert sheep there. A young animal like that can be some good eating!"

There was still no reaction from either of the men. They looked at one another. The older of the two finally broke the silence with a smile and said, "We didn't mean to be rude, it's just you surprised us. We didn't expect to see anyone this late in the day. Come have a piece of goat. There's more than we can eat, it's best to eat fresh. Come on, come on now," he said, waving his arm. Felix dismounted, the roasted bighorn smelled delicious.

Both men wore loosely clung, ragged, filthy clothes. Neither had shaved for what looked like months. The older man's beard and stringy hair were greasy and streaked with gray. When he smiled, Pedro noticed his mouth was full of gold teeth. Pedro also noted their camp was primitive. There were no pots, pans, or bedrolls. Both men had machetes strapped to their thighs in leather sheaths.

"They call me, Guapo" the older man chuckled. "That one," he said, looking at his even-uglier partner, "is el Gato. He isn't much to look at, but he's the only company I got," he chuckled at his joke. "We're from Santa Rosalia. We worked in the mine. We're going to La Paz to find some work in the new mines there. We got that sheep in the Gigantas yesterday. Thought we'd stop here, roast it up, and spend the night."

"Thanks, Guapo. My name's Pedro, that's Felix," he nodded toward Felix who was quietly watching the exchange. "I can't remember the last time I had a piece of fresh meat. What do you think, Felix? I say we take him up on his offer and have us a bite."

Felix shrugged. It sure smelled good, he thought.

Guapo walked over to the fire and cut a hunk off the hind quarter with his finely-honed machete. He offered it to Pedro, saying simply, "Here." After he passed the dripping piece of meat to Pedro with his filthy blackened hands, he licked his fingers. When he came close, his body odor turned Pedro's stomach. Pedro guessed the man hadn't bathed in a month or more. Guapo passed more meat to Felix and Gato, before cutting a piece for himself.

"Damned good, I'd say" Guapo remarked after swallowing a piece and licking his fingers again. Juice from the meat dribbled across his chin and down through his beard. "I'll have to shoot me another one of these the next time I run across one. What do you think, Gato?"

Gato grunted and looked at Guapo with dark shifty eyes.

By this time the sun had fully set and there came a chill in the air. Standing around the fire felt good. They all inched up closer to the flames and sat down.

"So, what's all that you got there on those mules, Señor?" Guapo asked between bites. "Looks like you got quite a load there. Here, have a snort of this with your goat," he added, passing Pedro a pint bottle of tequila he pulled out of his back pocket.

"Thanks," Pedro said, reaching for the bottle. "I bet it's been more than a year since I've had a sip of tequila," he mouthed the bottle. "Mmmmm, fresh goat meat and tequila. This trip is paying off already, wouldn't you say Felix?"

Felix nodded, barely raising his eyes as he chewed on a mouthful of the juicy meat. He examined what remained of it in his hand.

Pedro started to pass the bottle to Felix after he'd taken a gulp and pulled his hand back, "Wait, maybe you ought to get the canteen and have some water. We don't want anyone thinking I corrupted you on this trip, do we?" he grinned.

Felix rolled his eyes, spit out a piece of gristle and said, "If you spend any more time around me, you'll soon learn I've done a lot worse things than drink a little tequila, Juan Pedro. Hand it here," he demanded, reaching for the bottle.

"Suit yourself, kid," he snickered and passed the bottle.

"Don't call me 'kid,'" Felix took a long pull on the bottle and wiped his face with the side of his arm.

"Pedro, you didn't answer me. What is it you have packed on those mules? What's so important you need to haul it across this damned desert to Insurgentes? Huh?"

Without giving it much thought he answered, "Let's see, there's goat cheese, some braided leather lariats, quite a few of them in fact. The women tan the hides and weave the braids. The cowboys in Insurgentes pay good money for them. We got a few bags of sweet dates, some goat jerky, empty kerosene cans and some other odds and ends. We trade for lard and whatever else we need. These mules make four or five trips a year. The man who usually runs them to Insurgentes is sick, and I'm filling in for him."

Felix shifted his posture and became more alert when Pedro began describing the contents on the pack saddles. Guapo noticed.

"Those are some good-looking mules. They belong to the other guy?"

"Yeah, they're the other guy's. He says people in Insurgentes have offered him three hundred pesos each for them, but he wouldn't think of selling any of them."

Felix wiped his hands on his pants and fixed his gaze on the man asking all the questions.

"I wouldn't think so" said Guapo. "He'd be a fool to part with those fine animals."

A thin sliver of moon rose in the dark sky. There wasn't enough moonlight to cast a shadow. The men ate their fill of sheep and finished a second bottle of tequila as the fire burned down. Felix was light-headed, and Pedro was slurring his words. During the evening, Pedro told Guapo about life in San Juanico, Luisa, young Juan Carlos, and Maricela. They learned nothing about the two men from Santa Rosalia.

During a pause in the conversation, Pedro stood up and turned away to pee. He stretched his arms and said, "It's been a long day. I don't think I'm gonna have any trouble sleeping tonight. How about you, Felix?"

"I don't think so, but we should call it a night," Felix said rising to his feet. "Without any moon, it's so dark I can't see a thing out there, and I need to hobble those mules. I should've done that before we sat down."

"Yeah, should've thought about that earlier," Pedro slurred. He turned and said, "Thanks for the goat and the tequila, Guapo. I don't get to talk much to folks from outside San Juanico. I enjoyed that. I wish you well on your journey to La Paz," he offered his hand and they shook.

Guapo nodded and said, "Nice to have you men come by. You have yourselves a restful night."

Felix and Pedro made their way a quarter mile across the meadow in the pitch-dark blackness. They left the pack saddles on the mules, and Felix hobbled them in the grass as Pedro laid out their bedrolls, side by side.

"I think that long day took all the spunk out of em," Felix said as he laid down. "I don't think we have to worry about em wandering off on the hobbles tonight."

"They'll be fine. There's so much grass here, they'll think they've died and gone to heaven! It's so thick, it'll be softer than my bed at home!"

They laid back, looking at the brilliant stars contrasted across the inky black sky. Felix said, "I don't like those guys, Pedro. Something's not right with them. Should've asked em' why they weren't following the road to La Paz. That's the only way to travel north and south in this country. You have any idea how hard it is to cross the Gigantas on game trails, or breaking your own trail through there?"

"I hadn't thought about that. I was too interested in eating that goat. Come to think of it, they weren't much prepared either. They had no bed rolls or much else in their camp. They were riding those two scrawny burros, too. I wouldn't travel across this rough country on a little burro like that. I'd rather walk, for God's sake!"

"I think we'd better get out of here early, well before sun-up. Put some distance between us and them tomorrow. I'm not sure I'll even be able to sleep tonight, I'll keep one eye open," Felix said.

"I think you're right, but let's get us a few hours of sleep. The first one to stir should get up and gather the mules real quiet-like. The trail out of here is right behind these trees. We'll slip out while they're still asleep. They won't hear a thing."

Felix mumbled, "I'll gather the mules," then fell into a deep tequila-induced slumber, dead to the world.

★★★

Felix felt it first. He yelled, "Goddamn motherfucker, get off me!"

"Wha, wha, what's goin on?" Pedro stuttered as he tried to focus. The night was far too dark to see much. His hands instinctively reached up for his neck. He pushed against the machete pressing down against his throat.

"Either one of you boys move so much as an inch, we'll kill you," Guapo growled as the machete caused Pedro to choke. "Got it? Tell me you get it, or we'll kill you right now. You don't mean shit to us! It'd be easier just to cut you, so don't push your luck!"

Gato straddled Felix and held a razor-sharp knife across his throat just below his chin. With his other hand, he held Felix's head in place by pulling down on his hair. He held Felix's arms down with his knees, from a sitting position on his chest. Felix strained with every ounce of strength he had, trying to overcome the ugly brute on top of him, but he was helpless. Gato wanted more than anything to sever Felix's head, but Guapo warned him not to.

"Do you get it?" Guapo yelled one more time. Pedro couldn't help from inhaling Gato's rancid breath, and he forced himself not to gag while the machete was pressing down on his throat.

"Yes. We get it, we get it," Pedro mumbled as best he could. "Don't fight it, Felix! Do what he says!"

"What the fuck you want?" Felix snarled as he brought up his knees, arched his back, and lifted his own and Gatos' body a foot off the ground. Gato was surprised by the young man's strength and growled angrily, before slamming Felix's head down against the ground three times by yanking on his hair.

Guapo ordered, "I want you boys to roll over on your stomachs. I want you to put your arms behind you. Real easy, or we start cutting. Do you get it?"

Stunned by the blows to his head, Felix hesitated. Gato rolled him over and ground his face in the dirt and began slamming his forehead down hard on the ground. Felix lost consciousness for a moment.

"Gato, strip off his clothes and hog-tie him up with these," Guapo reached over and handed him several pieces of leather reins he'd taken off the burros. When you're finished with him, come over here and do the same to my friend Pedro here."

"You got a problem, Pedro? If you do, let me know and I'll take care of your problem for you right now."

"Do what you want," Pedro muttered. "Just don't kill us."

Guapo laughed, "Why would you think that?"

Gato had Felix tied up and helpless in no time, then he did the same to Pedro. "Okay, I got em," he said.

"Good, double check your knots and pull em' up tight as you can. We don't want them getting loose. I want em' to cook and shrivel real slow-like in the sun today. Maybe the vultures will show up real hungry this afternoon when they're half-delirious and start feeding on them. That'd be fun to see, wouldn't it?"

Guapo stood up and said, "That was easier than I thought. By God, they didn't even put up a fight! A couple of real dumb ones from the rancho, wouldn't you say, Gato?"

Gato made a guttural sound, spit on Felix, and kicked dirt in his face before he walked away.

★★★

Pedro's mind was racing, trying to make sense of what happened. If he wasn't bound up so tight, his hands would've been shaking uncontrollably. Felix was seething with anger. Surrendering went against every fiber in his body, but the beating to his head had saved his life. He twisted and struggled against his restraints, but he was too bound up to move.

"Gato, we've got work to do," Guapo said as they stood off to the side of the two men on the ground. "Lead the mules over and tie them at our camp. Pick up their clothes and bring them. They're a lot better than what we're wearing. Get those bed rolls too. We're gonna be set up just fine for the rest of our trip down to La Paz. Who'd of thought we'd have such a stroke of luck?"

An hour later, the only sign that Guapo and Gato had been in the Cienega were the smoldering embers of their fire and two content little burros with full bellies dozing across the meadow under a mesquite tree.

★★★

"What are we gonna do?" Felix asked from where he laid on his side in the dark. They were both naked and bound up like hog carcasses ready for the fire spit. They shivered in the crisp night air and the brittle dry grass and gravelly soil under them grated their skin each time they moved.

"Damned if I know. One of us has to get loose, but I don't know how in the hell we're gonna do that. I'm tied so tight I can't even feel my hands."

"Me too. Every time I pull, it gets tighter."

"Let's think this through," Pedro said. "We'll fry if we lay out here very long in the sun."

For twenty minutes they laid quietly, each of them testing the leather reins that bound them. They remained that way until the song-birds started chirping in the surrounding shrubs. A horned owl hooted one last time as it settled in the palm trees to roost for the day.

"I can see hints of daylight over there to the east," Pedro remarked. "We'll be able to see in a few minutes. One thing I'm sure of, we can't count on getting anyone to help us. Weeks probably go by without anyone passing by here. But it's like I said yesterday when we watched the sun come up, 'We sure are lucky to be alive to see it again."

"Yeah, we're real lucky, Pedro. I don't get how you think."

A moment later the sun rose, and the light broke through the palm and mesquite trees on the far side of the meadow. The temperature began to climb along with the sun. Pedro lifted his head so he could see above the grass.

"I can't see very much from down here, how about you? Are you able to roll over?"

They were faced in opposite directions.

"Let's see … yep, I think I can roll."

Felix started rocking his body, slowly bending in contortions until he built up the momentum to flip over to a position where he faced Pedro's back side.

"There!" he said as he came down behind Pedro. He wiggled into place as the coarse grass sliced his skin, causing it to burn.

"Can you get behind me to where you can chew on this strap or whatever it is around my wrist? I think it's just leather. You should be able to chew through it, don't you think?"

"I can try, but you have to get turned around just right. I'll wiggle in behind you. Don't make me do everything, scoot up would you?"

"There's a sharp rock under me and cholla thorns pressing against my ribs," Pedro moaned.

"Don't complain to me, I'm all cut up and your butt's right in my face. You fart, and I quit."

"Just get your mouth down there and start chewing, would you?"

Felix' found the leather rein on Pedro's wrists and started gnawing like a dog on a bone. The one side of his face was in the dirt and he had to keep his lower eye shut tight. Not long after getting started, the skin on his lower cheek down against the ground was scratched raw from the chewing motion.

An hour later, Felix groaned, "My jaw's sore! I can't get the angle right, and I've got a mouthful of dirt. Pull your hands up higher off the ground. Help me, would you?"

"Dammit, that piece of cactus is still under me. There, does that help?" Pedro asked, straining to lift his wrists.

"Yeah it does, but my mouth is full of dirt. It's too dry to spit it out. Tastes like shit and makes it hard to chew!"

Four hours passed, and the mid-day rays of the sun beat straight down on them. Felix continued to twist his neck, trying to get his mouth at the right angle. Partly from the tequila but mostly from his raw gums, strained jaw muscles and loosened front teeth, his head pounded like it was an anvil beneath a sledgehammer. Their bodies burned and started to blister on the sides exposed to the sun.

Felix coughed more dirt and said in a scratchy voice, "Ok, pull! Go ahead, pull hard! Harder, dammit!"

"I'm pulling, I'm pulling! I don't have any leverage!"

"I said pull! I've done all the work, don't whine! Just Pull!"

"Wait, wait, oh my God! I think I got it! I think it broke! There!" Pedro gasped, losing his breath. "You did it! My hands are free!" he said, straightening and stretching his arms. His hands were chalky white from the lack of circulation. He shook them and rubbed them together until he felt the tingling go away. He untied his ankles and crawled stiffly over to Felix. His legs were cramping and hard to move.

"There!" Pedro said as he pulled the last knot free on Felix's wrists.

"I can't move! I have no feeling in my hands or feet. I have to piss! Help me up, would you?" Felix muttered through a mouthful of dirt. Pedro was in a kneeling position next to him and Felix placed a hand on his shoulder and propelled himself up to a standing position. As soon as he was erect, he let loose a powerful stream of dark brown urine that arced high in the air in front of him.

"Ahh, that tequila, I've been holding it all day! I can't piss when I'm lying down, and I sure wasn't gonna piss all over myself." He tried to spit but his mouth was still full of dirt. "I'm going to bury my face in that spring," he said as he started to turn and fell flat on the ground. "Shit, I forgot the ankles, I can't feel them." he moaned and nearly cried.

Pedro took baby steps back and forth, as if learning to walk again. He stretched his arms and legs and got his blood circulating. Felix raised his face, covered in mud from the spring. He asked, "Now what?"

"Don't know. They took everything. Let's see if they left anything in their camp."

They limped and shuffled across the meadow, stopping every few yards to remove thorns from their feet.

"There's nothing here, not a damned thing!" Pedro groaned as they looked around the empty camp.

"No, look there!" Felix pointed to a cluster of mesquite trees on the edge of the meadow. "They left the burros!"

"Well I'll be, they did! They're just standing there in the shade. They should be easy to catch. Look at that, they're still wearing halters, and they have the lead ropes tied around their necks! I told you we were lucky!"

When they had the burros tied up, Pedro ran his hand over the stubble on his chin and said, "I think we already know which way we have to go. It'd be two days back to San Juanico on these burros. We could probably make it to Insurgentes from here in one long day. It's already late, but if we stop for the night somewhere, we'd be in Insurgentes tomorrow afternoon. That's the way we go."

"What are they going to think when we show up naked like this?" Felix asked looking down at himself with a concerned expression on his face.

"For God's sake Felix, I had no idea you were so modest! Who's ever going to care? Break off a palm frond over there and take it with you. You can hold it over yourself, and you can swat flies with it along the way."

Felix sighed, "It's just the way I am about things like that," he walked over to a small palm tree and broke off a limb.

★★★

The burros were half the size of the mules, so their short stubby legs made for a slow, rough ride. Both men were burnt a blistering red on their back sides from the sun, and the sweat stung like sharp daggers as it dripped down their bodies and pooled on the burro's back. The burros were also sweating profusely as they labored under the afternoon sun. The soaking wet, coarse hair on the burros' backs chafed them raw in no time and burned like fire down below in their privates. Although they had their fill of water at the Cienega, they had no way of carrying any, and they were dehydrated a few hours later. Each and every step became more painful than the last, but they endured, and the sturdy little burros moved steadily onward.

The sun moved west, and the shadows grew longer as the day came to a close. The two men hardly spoke a word; talking would waste energy they didn't have. The blinding pain and discomfort led to grim thoughts of doom and despair, which were kept in check only by their determination to survive. Where the day before, Pedro was awed by the landscape, causing his spirit to soar, he barely noticed it this day. Everything was dismal and gray.

As the last of the twilight gave way to another black moonless night, Felix said, "I can't see the trail, and the burro keeps stumbling on rocks. We need to find somewhere to spend the night. This is too dangerous."

"Okay, let's look for a good place to stop. I can't see a thing back here, how about you?" Pedro asked.

"Can't see much but looks like a big flat rock here in front of me. We can sit on the rock. Let's wait out the night here. Hold tight to your lead rope, if the burros get away, we're dead," Felix said through his utter and complete exhaustion.

"A rock would be far better to sit on than this burro. How far are we from Insurgentes?"

"Not sure. Probably another four or five hours. The first sign we're getting close will be a camp where the farm workers stay. The farm is a mile past the camp. They have a well there."

★★★

Neither of them slept. They cat-napped in a sitting position with the lead ropes tied around their wrists. The burros were content standing in one position. The night dragged on forever and first light found them back on the trail in the cool, early morning air. Hardly a word passed between the two sunburned, dehydrated, raw-skinned men. They knew what they had to do, and they simply got up and did it without saying so much as a word.

The closer they got to Insurgentes, the lower they were in elevation. The town was only fifty feet above sea level. It made a huge difference in the vegetation and the landscape. The land was flat as a tabletop and received a tiny fraction of the meager rainfall that was common in the mountains. Vegetation was sparse and unhealthy – a wasteland, except for the fresh water that pooled unseen in an ancient aquifer, hundreds of feet below the surface.

The first sign of approaching civilization was the trash. The westerly winds off the Pacific blew the lighter trash from the migrant camp west to east, where it got hung up in the spiny branches of dwarfed mesquite and low-lying cactus. Toilet paper and newsprint used for the same purpose were predominant among the first batches of litter they found. After they passed through this "paper zone," they started to see cardboard, much of it the remnants of temporary shelters. After the scattered cardboard, they started to see heavier trash the wind was unable to move – it laid on the ground where it had been discarded – bottles, cans, wire, and such a variety of things that much of it was difficult to identify. Shallow, open latrines, filled and over-flowing with dried human waste, were everywhere they turned. Not a living thing stirred anywhere on the desolate landscape as far as they could see. The sparse, sickly vegetation, still composed mostly of stunted mesquite and cactus, barely grew any higher than their ankles. The first unobstructed early afternoon winds were starting to blow in from the Pacific, heating the air. The winds were exposed to miles of bare, sunbaked sandy soil surrounding them.

"My God, Felix. How many people did you say were here?" Pedro asked.

"I don't know, a hundred, maybe two hundred, it was impossible to count. There were people everywhere, mostly women and children. I remember thinking they made San Juanico look rich. They were as poor as anyone I'd ever seen. Many of them were living under sheets of cardboard, the only shelter they had. They wore tattered rags to protect them from the sun, and they were all barefoot. The kids were skinny, I remember that. I could see ribs on most of them."

"I had no idea. There was none of this the last time I was here, but that was ten years ago. No, it was a longer than that."

"This is all here because of the groundwater they found, and the diesel pumps they brought in. Most of this all came about in the last five years, at least that's what I was told. I only made my first trip here last year."

"How far until we find some water?"

"We'll be coming to some tractor sheds and a couple of houses in another mile. That's where the well is."

The empty camp gave way to dry fields covered with rows of withered chili plants, stretching as far as the eye could see. In the distance, on the horizon a mile ahead of them, they saw the farm buildings. They kicked the exhausted little burros and picked up the pace, although the pain of riding was nearly too much to bear.

★★★

Late that afternoon, they arrived at the farm. Felix yelled "Hello there," waving to three young girls. They were carrying schoolbooks, dressed in crisp white blouses and navy-blue pleated skirts. They were walking along a two-track dirt road toward one of the small turquoise-colored farmhouses. They started to wave back but stopped abruptly and covered their eyes when they saw the two naked, sunburned, filthy men on the burros. Felix was holding a palm frond firmly over his crotch, Pedro was far too exhausted and dehydrated to care any less.

Felix spoke up so they could hear him clearly, "We've been robbed! Bandits took our clothes! Help us, please! We need water!"

The eldest of the three girls slowly lowered her hand from her eyes and answered, "I'll get my mother. She's in the house. She will help you. Wait there," she held up a halting hand re-enforcing her command for the two men to stay put.

The girls ran to the first house and disappeared through the door. A few moments later a middle-aged woman stepped out, shaded her eyes, and looked in the men's direction. They were about one hundred yards from the house. After taking in what she could see from that distance, she went back in the house and came out a few minutes later carrying a canteen.

"Hola, Señora," Pedro said. The woman walked up to Pedro and handed him the canteen, looking up and down the length of his sunburned, filthy nakedness. He remained on the burro and brought the canteen to his lips. He took three long, noisy gulps, and with water dripping down his chin through the thick black stubble, he passed the canteen to Felix.

"We were traveling from Rancho San Juanico to Insurgentes. Bandits robbed us yesterday. Can you help us? We need some clothes," he stated the obvious.

The woman paused for a moment and said, "Take your burros over there to the barn." She pointed to a large tractor shed. "There's water in those corrals. You can wash up there. I'll bring you some food and clothes." She turned and walked slowly under the late afternoon sun back to the house.

There was a trough of water in the corrals, and the burros smelled it. They went directly to it. The men splashed it on their faces, and despite the pain, they stepped slowly in, and soaked their parched, burned and bruised, wounded bodies. It felt both wonderful and painful at the same time. After five minutes they could tolerate the soaking on their damaged flesh no longer. They stood in the shade of the barn and let the dry desert breeze bring them small relief.

A few minutes later, the woman returned, carrying an armload of clothes and a basket of food. "Put these on," she commanded, handing them the clothes. "I don't like talking to naked strangers. There's burritos in the basket and a jar of aloe. Spread the aloe on those burns and wounds. You can keep the jar. You'll be needing all of it. You say you're from San Juanico? I know the old man Alonso – he stops here to water his mules. I saw you riding with him once, didn't I?" she asked, looking at Felix.

Felix nodded and said, "Yes, Señora. You did."

"My name's Leonora, what's yours?"

"I'm Felix, that's Pedro," he nodded in Pedro's direction.

Pedro spoke up, "We were packing Alonso's mules, when the bandits robbed us. About twenty miles from here, out at the Cienega, if you know where that is. They jumped us while we were sleeping. I thought they were going to kill us, but they tied us up and left us for dead. We broke free and found these burros. They took the mules with the pack saddles on them."

Leonora got a concerned look on her face, and the three of them were quiet as they thought through the consequences of the stolen mules for a moment.

Leonora asked, "The mules carry the food for San Juanico, what will you do?"

"I'm not sure, we haven't had time to think about it," Pedro replied. Changing the subject, "Do you know where we can find a man named Sammy Gonzo? I need to talk to him about this."

She nodded, "Of course, everyone knows Sammy. He's the delegado of Insurgentes. He owns some of the bigger farms you pass on the way into town. The man has his fingers in everything. You can find him in the Ejido San Jose del Norio office, on El Centro. Just look for the sign, and I'm sure you'll find him in there, or they'll know where he is. You can be there in an hour if you ride the burros, but you're more than welcome to spend the night here in the barn if you'd like, it's getting late," she looked up at the receding sun. "I've got more food and some blankets. Looks to me like you could use the rest. You could get a fresh start in the morning. Up to you."

"Thank you, Leonora," Pedro answered and turned to Felix, who nodded, "I think we'll take you up on that. We need the rest. We haven't slept much the last two nights. We'll repay you for your trouble soon as we're able."

"Never mind that, I'm happy to help. You're my closest neighbors, if I was to go off in that direction," she nodded her head east and laughed. "Maybe I'll show up at your door all naked one day and need help myself. Never know!"

They laughed and it felt good to smile.

★★★

The following morning, back on the burros, Pedro and Felix approached Insurgentes. Felix pointed out El Centro, the small town's main street, and they followed it through the business district. El Centro was about a quarter mile long and ran straight as an arrow north and south. All the stucco buildings along the street were single-story structures painted white or any of a variety of bright colors that contrasted with the dullness of the desert. There were fish taco stands on every block. A fresh, white, concrete double curb, ran down the center of the street and it served as both a divider and a planter. It was filled with healthy, young fan palm trees and beautiful red, white, and pink flowered Bougainvillea shrubs. Pickup trucks, flat-beds, and automobiles lined the orderly street in front of the buildings. Pedro had never seen anything so prosperous looking in his life and his head was spinning as he tried to take it all in. Felix barely seemed to notice; he'd seen it all before.

"The town looks different," Pedro said as their burros continued down El Centro.

"It always looked like this, at least since I've been coming here. The men who own the new farms are rich, and the government pays for all the diesel fuel. There's a lot of money here. Look, there's the sign for the Ejido office. Let's tie the burros over there," Felix nodded at a hitching rack in front of the building.

They secured the burros, climbed three short steps up from street level and passed through the open door of the bright, airy office. An attractive young woman with long, shiny auburn-colored hair, conservatively dressed in white slacks and a flowered blouse, welcomed them with a wide smile. Pedro smiled back and said, "We'd like to see Sammy Gonzo. Is he here today?"

"Yes, he is. Can I tell him who wants to see him, and what it's about?"

"My name is Juan Pedro Murillo, and this is Felix," he gestured. "We're from Rancho San Juanico. Alonso Garcia, who packs the mules for San Juanico, suggested that I speak with Señor Gonzo."

The woman smiled again, displaying her perfect pearly white teeth highlighted by her bright red lips and replied, "Please wait for just a moment. I'll tell Señor Gonzo you're here, as soon as he's off the telephone. You can have a seat over there if you'd like." She pointed to several yellow vinyl chairs under the front window.

Pedro looked around the room at the clean white stucco walls, the colorful tiles on the floor and the heavy wooden polished doors and window frames. He'd never been inside a building like it.

Pedro and Felix sat down. They could hear a man talking in the room behind the woman's desk. Pedro felt out of place. They were dressed in hand-me-down farm clothes with worn-out old sandals on their feet, but he tried to reassure himself that at least the clothes were clean and properly mended. He took a deep breath and turned his thoughts again to the mules and their predicament.

Pedro was rattled out of his daydream when he looked up to see a well-dressed, middle-aged man come out of the back office. As the man approached, he extended his hand and said, "Hello, my name is Sammy Gonzo. Would you like to step back into my office? I understand you'd like to discuss something with me."

They stood and shook Sammy's hand. Pedro spoke up first, "Yes, Señor. Thank you for seeing us. My name is Juan Pedro Murillo, and this is Felix," he turned slightly to acknowledge Felix. "We're from Rancho San Juanico. Alonso Garcia told us that we should speak with you."

"Ahh, my good friend Alonso! How is that old goat? Haven't seen him in months," he commented, entering his office.

Sammy sat down behind a large, olive green, government-issued metal desk. Pedro and Felix sat on two yellow vinyl chairs across from him. Pedro noticed neat stacks of paper, notebooks, pens, pencils, and a black rotary-dial telephone sitting on the desk. Sammy had one prominent gold tooth in front that flashed when he smiled and slick black hair, combed back, worn longish, reaching nearly down to his collar. A heavy gold chain hung around his neck, past the top three open buttons on his shirt, down across his hairy chest. He was warm and friendly, quick to smile, but all business.

He asked, “So tell me, Juan Pedro – or can I call you Pedro? – What is it you think I might help you with?”

“Yes,” he nodded. “Please, call me Pedro. Everyone does. I wanted to speak with you about building a road to San Juanico, but on our way here, we had some trouble,” he looked down at his hands for a moment. “Two days ago, we were tied up, robbed, and left for dead. The bandits rode off with Alonso’s mules and the pack saddles. I’m not sure what we should do. I thought it would be a good idea to ask for your advice.”

Sammy’s face flashed instantly from pleasant to serious. His dark eyes stared hard directly at Pedro, like a predator. He said, “That explains your sunburn and all the injuries then,” he turned to look at Felix, then back to Pedro. “Tell me exactly what happened. How many men? Where were you? What did they look like? Tell me everything.”

Pedro told Sammy the story from beginning to end, and Felix added a few comments of his own. Sammy listened intently and didn’t say a word to interrupt them. When they were finished, he ran his hands through his hair and took a deep breath as he gathered his thoughts. He opened the top drawer on his desk without saying a word. He reached for a pack of cigarettes and lit one.

Exhaling, he asked, “Would you care for something to drink? Ice water? Coffee?

“Yes, please,” Pedro and Felix both answered.

“Water please, we’re dehydrated,” Pedro added.

“Anna, bring these men some ice water please,” he said loud enough for the woman in front to hear.

“Just be a moment,” she answered.

Sammy got back to business, “The two men you describe, this Guapo and Gato, I suspect they may be escaped inmates from the federal prison up in Santa Rosalia. There was a riot a couple months ago, more than twenty men escaped and the last I heard, only about half of them were re-captured. The prison in Santa Rosalia is high-security and houses only the most dangerous men – murderers, rapists, narcos, and the such. I'll call the federales as soon as we're finished here, and give them the description of the two men who robbed you. I'll inform them they're on their way to La Paz. I'm near certain that's who they were."

Sammy thought for a moment and added, "But that doesn't help you with your problem does it?"

"No, Señor. San Juanico depends on those mules. The village will starve. Alonso spent his whole life raising those mules. Is there anything you can do to help?"

"I have no simple answers for you, but let's think about it for a moment. San Juanico's part of the Ejido. We desperately need more men from the Ejido to work on the new road to La Paz. Too many of the men we employ are migrants who come and go. Our Ejido workers tend to stay. Perhaps, if you help me, I could help you. I have a government contract to provide workers for the road project."

"How do we help you?" Pedro asked.

Right then Anna walked in with a brilliant smile on her face and two glasses of ice water. She handed each man a glass. Felix had a hard time taking his eyes off her shapely body, and his gaze followed her backside as she turned around and left the room.

Pedro raised the glass of water to his lips, and for the first time in his life, he tasted ice. He found it a surprising, pleasant sensation as it melted in his mouth. He lost complete track of time and place for a moment.

Sammy resumed the conversation and brought the two of them abruptly back to the present, "As I was saying, I need men from the Ejido to work on the road."

"I'm just a poor man who herds goats, how would I be of any help to you building a road?" Pedro asked with uncertainty.

"We can train you. You're not too old to learn, are you?" Looking at Felix he added, "You're certainly not too old."

"I suppose so," Pedro responded, still uncertain. He shifted from side to side in the chair.

"Sure, you can learn, and you can earn enough money to feed your family. When you have some experience, you could lead a crew building that road you want over to San Juanico. Think about it, with a road to San Juanico, you wouldn't need the mules. It makes perfect sense, it'll just take some time. What do you think?"

Before Pedro could respond, Felix set his glass down on Sammy's desk and spoke up, "I think we should do it. I'd like to work on the road and make some money!"

Pedro was uncomfortable with how quickly things unfolded beyond his control. He turned to Felix, "That's easy for you to say. You don't have a family to worry about. What would my family do without me, while I'm out building roads?"

"Jesus," Felix slammed the palm of his hand against his forehead and looked up at the ceiling. He turned to Pedro, "You're the one who wanted a road to San Juanico! How'd you expect the road would get built if everyone stayed home with the goats? We're being offered an opportunity here. We'd be fools not to take it. You have any better ideas?"

Pedro looked at Sammy and back at Felix. He gave a half-hearted shrug and said, "Maybe you're right." He didn't sound convincing. He looked past Sammy out the open window behind the desk and wished he was somewhere else.

"Good!" Sammy said quickly, not wasting any time. "We have more details to work out, but I'll talk to my foreman and see to it he gets you started. There's a camp on the edge of town where you can stay until the next truck is ready to go to the work site. That'll probably be three or four days from now."

Pedro's head was spinning. All he could think about was Luisa and the children. He was just a simple man, terribly ill-prepared for the rapid pace of Sammy's decision making.

★★★

Pedro and Felix spent four nights with a dozen other men in a tent camp on the outskirts of Insurgentes. Two women came by each day to cook their meals and do their laundry. There was a central water tank, a latrine, and a small palapa with hot water for private showers. Pedro took the first shower of his life, and it lifted his spirits. He went on a long walk down a nearby arroyo where he filled his pockets with tiny seashells. He found some discarded fishing line and spent two days drilling holes and stringing the shells together into a beautiful necklace. He hadn't thought how he'd get it to Luisa, but it made him feel good just to have made it. When it was completed, he tucked it away in an empty tobacco pouch and carefully placed it under his pillow.

Pedro thought about Luisa constantly. He married her when she turned fourteen. All those years ago. He ached for her. The poor woman had no idea he wouldn't be returning as he'd promised. She'd be getting by on next to nothing, as she always did. He pictured her going about her days, smiling and humming melodies to herself, as she thought about their reunion. It made him physically ill to be abandoning her. He was haunted by it.

Around the cooking fire on their last night in the camp, Felix was watching him, "You don't look so good, what's going on?"

Pedro sighed, "We haven't even left yet, and I can't bear the thought I've abandoned my family. They have no food, nothing. They're expecting me back any day, and here I am about to leave for who-knows-where, for who-knows-how-long, without even telling them. It's not right, it's just not right. Sammy was talking so fast my head was spinning. I was confused when I agreed to do this. It's my fault. I can't be doing this. I need to get back to San Juanico."

Felix thought for a moment, "It's not all your fault. I was so anxious, I didn't think what it meant for you. I'm sorry. Let's think about this a minute."

"What's to think about? I can't be doing this."

"What would you do, ride the burro back? Then what?"

Pedro was confused, he placed his head in his hands.

"We don't have a single peso between us. You know that. You go back and your family still has nothing to eat. Then what?"

"I don't know. I just don't know," he looked up with a lost expression.

Felix was determined, "Here's what we do," he paused to gather his thoughts. He stood and paced short steps back and forth. "We go see Sammy in the morning, before the truck leaves. We ask him for a month's wages, upfront. We give him a list of the food we want. You know, the normal stuff – lard, beans, rice, tortilla flour, coffee. Then all he needs to do is find someone with a mule to haul it out to San

Juanico. Whoever does that can tell Luisa, Alonso and the others what's happened. If Sammy's not willing to do that, we still have the burros. We quit, we ride back to San Juanico," he watched Pedro come back to life.

"You think he'll do it?"

"He'll agree. He needs us."

Pedro smiled for the first time in four days.

They were drinking coffee with Sammy at daybreak. Felix did the talking. Sammy agreed and told them he had just the man he could send to San Juanico with a pack mule, as soon as he could make the arrangements. Before leaving, Pedro entrusted Sammy with Luisa's shell necklace. Sammy promised to have his hired man hand it to Luisa personally.

Three hours later, Pedro and Felix were on their way, down the road in the direction of La Paz.

★★★

Two ancient flatbed trucks, coughing and spewing thick, oily, black diesel fumes, departed Insurgentes at mid-morning. One carried tools and supplies, the other had a canvas cover providing shade for fifteen men on the rear platform. At ten or fifteen miles per hour, there wasn't enough wind to clear away the exhaust as it mixed with the thick clouds of dust. The toxic fumes billowed up and under the canvas; hovering inseparably above the truck, it hung around them in the hot dead air as they bounced down the road. The men all wore bandannas over their faces, leaving exposed only their vacant owl-like eyes. They sucked in the toxic fumes behind their bandannas, as they braced themselves the best they could for the ten-hour trip.

The truck rattled down the rutted, rock-cluttered dirt road. It twisted and turned to avoid the holes. The driver downshifted each time he dropped down into one of the hundreds of rock-filled arroyos. The men stopped talking among themselves only fifteen minutes into the trip. A few of the more fortunate passengers stood where they could hold on to the upright stakes that held up the canvas cover, while the others were forced to sit on the hard floor, recoiling with each jarring rock, pothole, and rut.

There were very few signs of civilization as they traveled south. They passed a few trucks and buses heading north toward Insurgentes and they drove past a few isolated shacks with goat herds standing blankly around empty water troughs. At one dusty spot, an old man stood watch over a few skinny goats from the shade of a fallen-down palapa. He waved his frail hand at the truck as it went by and watched until it faded away in the trail of dust. He was the only human being they passed in the first two hours after leaving the outskirts of Insurgentes.

Toward mid-afternoon, the trucks came to a stop in front of a weathered shack made of rusted tin and ragged sheets of loose tar paper. Amid moans, groans, and fits of coughing, the fifteen men climbed out of the truck, and stepped into the blazing sun. Several gnarly mesquite trees provided a meager bit of shade, and the men gathered beneath their extended branches. There was a fifty-five-gallon drum of scummy, warm, green water, with three tin cups hanging along the rim of the barrel. Because none of them had canteens, each of them stepped up and took a few swallows. One by one, they walked over to a latrine that was half-hidden behind a date palm shrub, but they were so utterly dehydrated, very few of them could bring themselves to make water. An obese woman in her forties, with calves and ankles the diameter of small melons, laid out stale burritos on a table under a palapa shade. Flies buzzed noisily around the food. Nobody spoke more than a few words. The silence was welcome, after the monotonous six hours of muffler-less engine noise and the endless rattling. The woman watched the men eat but offered nothing more than a grunt or a shrug when she was spoken to.

"How much longer?" Felix asked the truck driver who walked up and helped himself to a burrito.

The driver smiled, "Are you getting tired of traveling already? Don't worry, we should be there in three or four more hours. We're going to a brand-new camp, a place called La Placita. You'll like it. There's cold, fresh well water, plenty of shade, and some pretty women who will take care of everything for you. And I do mean everything! It's better than you probably have it at home!"

Felix smiled, he asked, "Do we have time for a siesta?"

"No, no, no, amigo, we want to hurry down to La Placita. We don't want to be on this road in the dark!"

Felix laughed, "You call that a road?" After that short exchange, the men were quiet again, until they were told to load back up.

They arrived at La Placita at dusk. The fifteen weary men hauled themselves slowly down from the flatbed and stretched their stiffened limbs. There were a dozen canvas tents scattered around on the hard-packed ground, under a grove of tall, healthy date palm trees. Another dozen or so men and a few women could be seen moving about. One large palapa with open walls was set up as a kitchen, with long tables off to one side where the crews would sit for their meals. A mesquite fire blazed in a brick hearth, and two perspiring women busied themselves with pots and pans. A white-haired man with a thick, bushy mustache looked up from one of the tables where he was working on papers. He stood, twisted the ends of his mustache and walked over to greet the new arrivals.

"Hello, there. Welcome to La Placita," the man said as he greeted the dazed group of travelers. "My name is Francisco Talamentes, but you can call me Cisco. I'm the boss here. You must be exhausted after that long drive, so please come and sit down, have something to drink. There's cold well water in those pitchers" he motioned toward the tables.

"Listen up," he stepped to the head of the front table. "I'll tell you about the rules of the camp, and some of the work you'll be doing. After that, we'll have dinner," he glanced at the women. "The ladies have been working on a special meal for you all day. I'm sure you're hungry after your journey."

Cisco waited a moment for the men to settle in and he cleared his throat. He began, "We've been here in La Placita for only a week. We started work two years ago down near La Paz. That's eighty miles south of here. We've completed the new road from La Paz all the way to here," he pointed to their location on a map. "I'll leave this map on the table. You can take a closer look at it after dinner if you like.

"The finished road is hard-packed earth and rock, topped with graded material. Every ten miles we move to a new camp, so we don't waste time traveling. La Placita is probably the best camp we've had since we got started," he smiled and waved his arm, "with all this shade, and unlimited water. We'll be here for three months before we move again. In another two years, if we keep up this pace, we'll have a new road all the way up to Insurgentes."

Pots and pans were clanging in the background, Cisco paused to glance in the direction of the busy women in the kitchen.

"Before you start working on the road tomorrow, I'll take you south a few miles so you can see what the finished product looks like. It's a lot different from what you drove on today. We have dozers, graders, and diesel-powered shovels to shape the roadbed," he paused to watch as a cheerful young woman placed fresh warm tortillas, wrapped in bright red cloths, on each of the tables. The pretty woman and the pleasant aroma caught the men's attention.

"Thank you, Liliana," he said to the woman. She smiled, nodded, and brushed the loose hair from her face.

Cisco continued, "You men will be responsible for the finish work and building the cement crossings through the arroyos. As you know, there's more arroyos out there than a man can count. When we're done, each one of them is going to have a rock foundation and a cement surface," he held up an engineer's drawing of a crossing structure for them to see. He placed it on the table with the map.

"It's hard, hot, dirty work, fourteen hours a day, seven days a week, but we'll feed you well and you'll earn five pesos a day. We'll pay you once a month, but you won't need any money out here. We'll give you a bank note like this one to help you keep track," he took one out of his pocket and showed it to the men. "You can cash your notes at the bank in Insurgentes after every three-month shift. Are there any questions?"

Among themselves the men discussed their wages, none of them had ever made thirty-five pesos in a week. Three women seemed to enjoy serving them their first camp meal of refried beans, tortillas, and spicy beef fajitas. They joked and chatted with the men. Afterward, Cisco brought out a bag of moist aromatic tobacco. Most of the men rolled cigarettes, an unexpected pleasure that greatly lifted their spirits. Exhausted and content, they drifted off in small groups to their assigned tents. Pedro and Felix shared a tent with two men from another rancho, somewhere in the Ejido they had never heard of. They spoke about their lives back home as they laid down on their cots. In a matter of minutes, they fell into a deep well-deserved sleep.

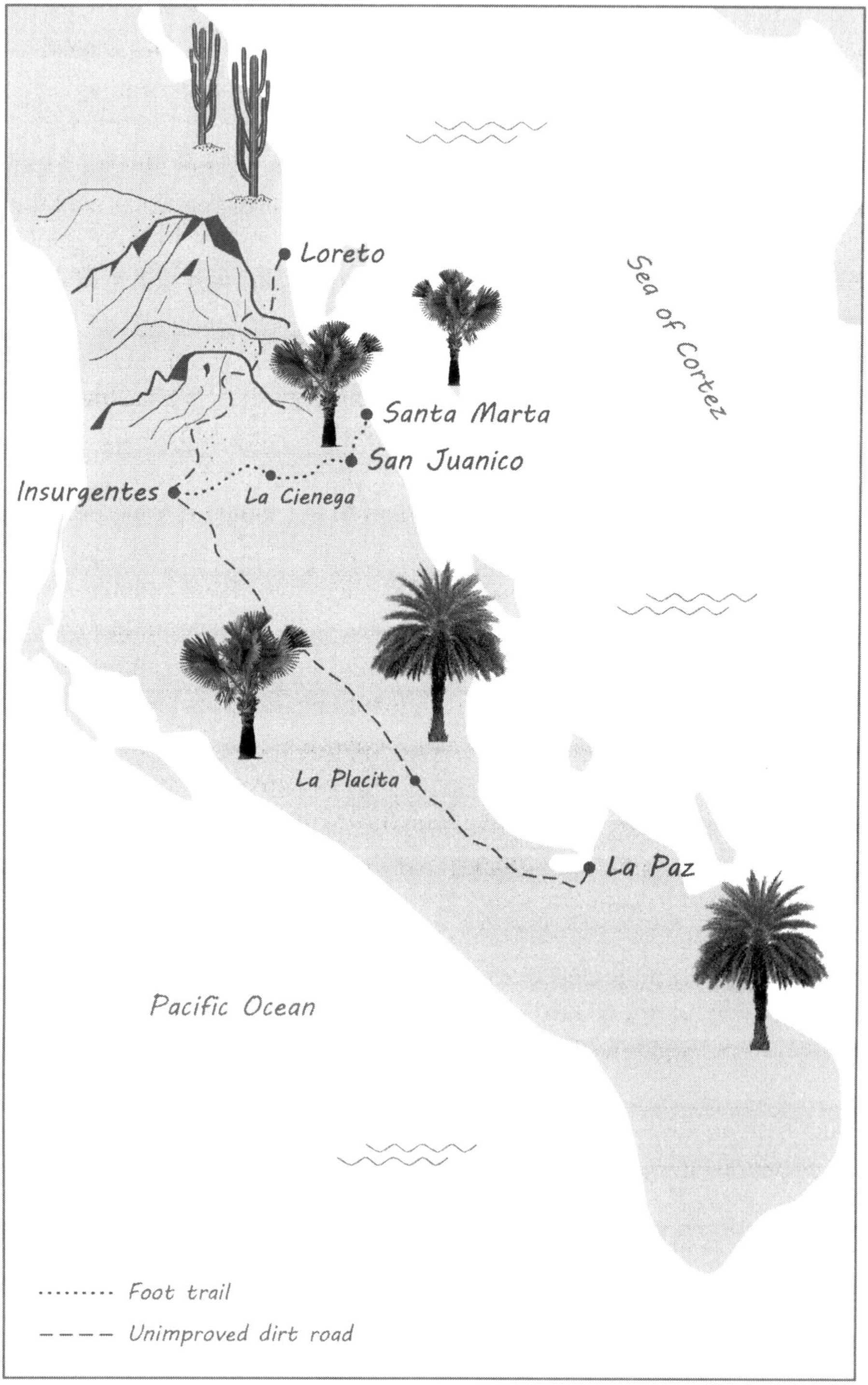
Loreto
Sea of Cortez
Santa Marta
San Juanico
Insurgentes
La Cienega
La Placita
La Paz
Pacific Ocean
Foot trail
Unimproved dirt road

Santa Marta

Antonio Sanchez Ruiz, at forty-seven years of age, was too set in his ways to be of much good on the road crews or the farms. He was thin, wiry, tough and weathered from a ranching life lived hard outside under the brutal Mexican sun. He had a twinkle in his eye, a quick wit, and an easy smile that caused his handsome face to crease and wrinkle around his mouth and eyes. His longish hair, salt-and-peppered, perfectly matched the color of his mustache.

Antonio had never married, and he'd worked for Oscar Padilla's family on their many ranches in Baja California Sur for most of his adult life. Oscar Padilla had long ago recognized his talents, and in turn, treated Antonio with trust and respect. Antonio, or Tonio as close friends sometimes called him, enjoyed traveling on horses and mules, and he was a master at packing animals, as well as nearly everything else he set his mind to.

Among other things, Antonio was Sammy Gonzo's right-hand man, and Sammy asked him to make the trip to Rancho San Juanico to bring the news of Pedro and Felix, and deliver the food they had requested. Antonio told Sammy he was happy to ride over to San Juanico, but he was going to take an extra week to visit his cousin who lived beyond San Juanico on the beach down at Rancho Santa Marta. Sammy, who was always plotting and planning, asked Antonio to have a look and advise him of the challenges they might encounter building a road to San Juanico, and beyond there, to the cliffs above Santa Marta.

Antonio left Insurgentes two weeks after Pedro and Felix departed for Las Placita. The two men had been gone from San Juanico for a month by then, and the now-anxious villagers were desperate with worry. Luisa went about her daily chores and cared for the children, but she laid awake at night, feeling haunted. She slept restlessly, or not at all, yearning for the feel of Pedro by her side, dreaming about a new life with a road, trucks carrying food, a small store, and sewing clothes for the people of San Juanico. She even dreamed they had a teacher who came in a truck to instruct the children in a new village schoolhouse. She imagined in her dreams a wonderful new life for them all, but night after night, she bolted upright to the cold, harsh reality of the empty bed beside her, with an ominous feeling in her stomach.

On the morning of his third day traveling, Antonio came to the rim of the mountain, and he looked down on the small palm grove at Rancho San Juanico. He remembered the view from a trip he'd made twenty years before. To his measured eye, nothing much had changed. The same parched desert spread out far and wide, and the turquoise blue of the Sea of Cortez, a marvelous contrast off in the distance. He found it pleasing to lay his eyes on that magnificent vista again.

★★★

Two young boys playing in the date palm grove were the first to see Antonio as he approached San Juanico on the trail. Visitors were rare, and the boys excitedly ran as quickly as they could to announce the news. One by one men, women and children dropped what they were doing and gathered in the center of the village to greet their unexpected visitor. Of the twenty or so people in the group, only Alonso knew Antonio by sight.

"Antonio!" Alonso waved. "Amigo, what brings you to San Juanico? Antonio is my good friend from Insurgentes," he proudly explained to a few of the villagers standing near his side.

"Hello, Alonso," Antonio waved as he drew his horse to a stop in front of them. Coming right to the point, Antonio started, "Sammy asked me to bring you some news of Pedro and Felix, who came to Insurgentes three or four weeks back."

Sensing a problem, Alonso's smile faded, and Luisa, who was standing nearby, became tense and rigid. She twisted a wash rag into a knot as she listened for what might come next. Juan Carlos and Maricela both sensing their mother's uneasiness, each grasped her tightly around her thighs.

"What is it? Did something happen to Felix and Pedro? We were expecting them back before now," Alonso asked with concern in his voice.

"I'm afraid they ran into some trouble. Banditos robbed them while they were camped at the Cienega, and they took the mules, along with the pack saddles. They left Pedro and Felix tied up, naked, but they broke free and made it to Insurgentes on a couple of burros." Noting the fear on their faces he added, "Don't worry, they're unharmed, but they did lose the mules and everything else they had with them."

The crowd became deathly quiet. They were in shock. They felt violated, as if they'd been raped. They seethed with anger as they tried to make sense of it. They knew the mules were their lifeline to the world. They glanced at one another with looks of uncertainty. Life as they'd long known it was about to change. Alonso was the first to speak.

"My God, how are we going to survive?" he said, looking up at Antonio. His words of despair drifted off in the hot, dead-calm air. The moment resembled a funeral. Alonso took off his wide-brimmed hat and ran his hands through his bushy, white hair. He looked around at the faces of the villagers for an answer, but he saw only downcast eyes or grim expressions.

Luisa stepped forward, with the two small children clinging to her thighs, and said with a stern angry voice, "Where is Pedro, now? Why isn't he with you if he's unharmed?" she glared at Antonio.

Startled, Antonio replied, "Sammy Gonzo gave Pedro and Felix jobs on the new road to La Paz. They'll be gone for three or four months, I don't really know how long. With their wages, they bought some food for the village. I have it there on that mule," he gestured toward the pack animal. "Would you show me where I can water my animals? Then maybe someone could help me unload?"

"Yes, of course," said Alonso. "Come with me to my palapa. We can take care of everything there."

The group followed the two men to Alonso's palapa. The villagers dragged their feet, forming a sad, slow procession. Alonso and Antonio spoke softly between themselves as they walked, but nobody else uttered a word. Antonio hitched his horse and the pack mule to the fence after they drank their fill at the trough. He untied the lacing that held the packs in place. One by one, three men, Luisa, and one of the older boys stepped forward, unloaded the food, and placed it on a table under the palapa. Alonso took charge of dividing the food up among the families. They each thanked Antonio and quietly dispersed.

Luisa was left standing next to Antonio, "I'm sorry I was angry with you. You're very kind to have traveled so far to bring us this food, and the news of my husband. The least I can do is feed you. I have a young goat tied up; I was waiting for Pedro to return. I'll butcher it, if you'd please come for dinner." She glanced at Alonso, "Please join us and bring Julia." Both men accepted and graciously thanked her for the invitation.

Later that afternoon, following their meal, Antonio stayed on. He was seated outside Luisa's palapa, drinking coffee. When Luisa finished clearing the table, she sat down next to him.

Antonio reached inside his vest pocket and said, "Pedro left this with Sammy. He asked that I deliver it to you. I waited until we were alone. It's something Pedro made for you," he handed her the tobacco pouch.

Luisa's eyes watered as she opened the pouch and removed the necklace. She held it in her hand to study its intricate beauty. She pressed it against her chest, "Thank you, you don't know how much this means to me, thank you. Will you be going back to Insurgentes in the morning?" she asked, placing the necklace back in the pouch.

"No, Señora," he replied. "My cousin lives down at Santa Marta. I haven't seen him in many years. I'm going down there for a visit. I'll be staying a few days. Sammy Gonzo also asked me to look at the trail down that way. He wants to know what I think about building a road through here, on out that way."

"Will you be stopping here when you return?" she asked.

"Yes, it's on the way," he sipped his coffee.

Luisa thought for a moment, "I may want to send something back with you, if you wouldn't mind."

"Not at all, Señora, I'll stop and visit with you when I come back."

"Thank you, Antonio. Please, call me Luisa?" she looked him in the eye.

Antonio smiled, winked, tipped his hat, "Yes, Señora. I'll be sure to do that."

As he walked back to Alonso's that evening, Antonio thought about the fate of the villagers in San Juanico. He saw how they were living on the edge.

★★★

Antonio soon learned that nothing much had changed on the cliff trail that dropped precipitously down to Santa Marta. It remained a treacherous, steep, narrow path, through rotten, crumbling rock where his horse and the mule had to be led the entire way. Even with extreme care, boulders jarred loose and fell a thousand feet, rumbling down the cliff face until they came to rest on the flat ground at the base of the rock wall. Turkey vultures, frigates, and other large birds soared on thermals below him, and he gazed down on them as they spun their aerial circles. Seemingly endless switchbacks first turned south before turning back north, each level acting as a stair-step down, bringing him and his two animals closer to sea level. Twelve hours after leaving San Juanico, he reached the bottom. He sat on a large rock to rest in the afternoon shade of the cliff. "I'm getting too old for this" he thought, and he dreaded the thought of having to climb back up only a few days later.

Rancho Santa Marta, a lush oasis by the sea, had been established by the natives, nobody really knew how many years earlier. The ranch nestled on a mile-wide flat bench between the toe of the cliffs and the beach. Several steep fissured canyons on the cliff face merged as they reached the bottom, forming one large, wide arroyo that crossed the flat, draining into the sea a mile downstream. Along the arroyo's course, groundwater collected unseen just below the surface. Artesian pressure caused several spring seeps to form in low spots, resulting in small freshwater pools. The high water table nourished a thick forest of date and fan palm trees that lined both sides of the arroyo. The first adobe and stone structure ever built in Santa Marta could still be seen on the fringe of the palm forest, but all that was left was a mound of crumbling remains. Shards of broken pottery and arrowheads were scattered across the ground surrounding the ruins.

Rancho Santa Marta was an island of private land within the vast sprawling Ejido San Jose del Norio. The ranch, along with its abundant freshwater resources, had been filed on and claimed as private land more than one hundred years before the Ejido was established. Santa Marta was a small, insignificant part of the immense private holdings of the wealthy Padilla family, whose home base was Mexico City. The day-to-day ranch operation was overseen by Antonio's cousin, Leonardo. Leonardo worked for Sammy Gonzo, although Leonardo hadn't spoken to Sammy in five years. There was no way to communicate between Santa Marta and Insurgentes. With the livestock, vegetable gardens, fruit trees and unlimited seafood, the inhabitants of Santa Marta were largely self-sufficient.

Sammy Gonzo split his duties working for the Padilla family, the ejido, and as delegado for the town of Insurgentes. He owned a number of large ranches and farms surrounding Insurgentes as well. Oscar and Sammy's interests often overlapped, though nobody seemed to pay much attention or care. Antonio served the multiple entities as if they were all one and the same and did whatever he wanted anyway, so Sammy and Oscar left him mostly alone, trusting his good judgement.

As Antonio was finishing his last burrito, he heard a bell in the distance. He knew it was a herd of Santa Marta goats, so he rose from his seat on the rock, tweaked his stiff joints, and climbed up on the horse. It felt good to ride again, after leading the animals down the trail for so many hours. He rode toward the sound of the bell, and the trail slowly became worn and well-traveled. As he came around a sharp bend, he ran into the goat herd. It was being pushed along down the trail toward the ranch by his cousin Leonardo.

"Leo, Leo," Antonio yelled. "Hey, it's me!"

Leo turned and searched for the source of the voice. He spotted Antonio on the horse and didn't recognize him.

"I wonder who that might be, coming down off the cliff," he thought. Very few people ever came down the cliff trail.

Antonio continued riding toward Leo and yelled again, "Leo! It's me, Antonio!" He took off his hat and waved it in the air.

With that gesture, Leo recognized his cousin and waved back, "Antonio! I thought somebody had hung you dead, a jealous boyfriend or a pissed-off husband! What brings you down here?"

"I was taking a ride and thought I'd come drop in on you," he pulled up on the reins and stopped the horse. "It's been ten years! I was moving cattle somewhere the last time you were up in the big city. Good to see you, old boy, but you're showing your age, all that gray hair," he climbed off the horse, took a few steps and embraced his cousin.

The two men hugged and held each other at arm's length, taking in their familiar but aged faces. Leo, two years younger than Antonio, was cut out of the same mold. Trim and lanky, he was taller than the average Mexican. Decades of life on the ranch had toughened his body. He moved with the stiff joints of a cowboy, but with easy-going assuredness. Like Antonio, he was a ruggedly handsome man. When the two of them were young, they chased girls, drank tequila, and raised hell together. Leo eventually settled down and married, but Antonio kept up his free-spirited ways.

"I'm glad I decided to take this little journey, Leo. Coming down that cliff isn't for old men, is it?" he stretched his back. "Good thing I did it while I'm still able. Here," he handed Leo the reins to the mule, "get yourself up on that mule. Let's ride down to the ranch. We've got some catching up to do."

Leo mounted the mule with a smooth swing of his leg, and they rode toward the ranch. It was a mile down the trail, through the palm trees, just a stone's throw from where the flat ground dropped off to the beach.

In Antonio's eyes, Santa Marta was the closest thing there was to heaven on earth. Even for an old, wandering cowboy who'd seen so many beautiful places in his life, he found the tranquility at Santa Marta overwhelming. From the veranda on the front of the hundred-year-old rock ranch house, he could hear and see the waves along the beach. To one side there was a small bluff with a hot spring at its base, on the other was a crescent-shaped white sand beach where pelicans and swarms of sea birds dove on schools of baitfish in the warm, placid waters of a small bay. Most days a pleasant breeze came off the water and moderated the temperature along the beach. Only a few hundred yards back in the desert from the house it was twenty degrees warmer on a sunny day, and rare was the day that wasn't sunny. Monsoons might come in late summer, but they would slam the coast for a day and not return for another year or more. The Sea of Cortez side of the Baja Peninsula was calm and temperate, compared to the cold brisk winds and wild surf on the Pacific, only sixty miles away as the turkey vulture soared.

When the two cousins arrived at the ranch house, they tied their animals to a hitching rail in front of the house, and Leo called to his wife, “Carmen, Carmen! Come see who’s here!”

An attractive woman in her mid-forties came to the open door with a dish rag in her hand and looked out at the two men. When she recognized Antonio, she broke into a wide grin and exclaimed, “My Lord Jesus, almighty. Antonio! Is that you? My Lord, my Lord,” she repeated as she swept her long hair back over her shoulder and made an attempt to straighten her wrinkled smock. She rushed down the steps.

“You old scoundrel, if I’d known you were coming, I would’ve dressed up in my finest and had dinner ready! It’s so good to see you,” she said as they came together. She leaned up on her toes and pulled Antonio down. She kissed him hard on the mouth. After they separated, Antonio blushed and tried but failed to compose himself. He self-consciously straightened the bandanna around his neck and removed his hat.

They both had wet eyes following the kiss. As a young man, Antonio had courted Carmen, but in the end, she wouldn’t have him. She’d said he was too wild for her, he’d never settle down and raise a family. He had too much of an eye for the ladies. He liked his tequila more than he did her. She’d given him dozens of chances, but he failed her every time. They both realized it wasn’t meant to be. They licked their wounds and got over it, remained friends, and along came Leo, who knew a good woman when he saw one. Leo and Carmen married, and came to Santa Marta as a young couple, had three children together, and stayed for twenty years. They hoped to have another twenty before old age got the best of them.

“Well, well, I didn’t expect such a warm welcome as that!” Antonio said, blushing as he brought his hand up across his mouth, covering his self-conscious smile. Changing the awkward subject, he said, “I brought you a little something, Carmela,” he reached over to his saddle bag. He removed a package wrapped in heavy brown paper. “This here is the prettiest dress I could find up in Insurgentes. I’d like it if you went back in the house and put in on for us. Maybe then, as a way to thank me, you might make us one of those fine dinners you were just talking about." Turning to look at his cousin he said, "Now Leo, since I know you don't keep any tequila around here, I brought plenty of it with me. It's in my pack there," he gestured in that direction. "But first, before we start drinking, I'd like go sit in the hot springs for a little while. It's been a long time since I've had a hot bath. After that, you and I can open one of those bottles under that veranda over there and have us a good long talk about how life's been treating us."

Antonio soaked his tired bones in what he was sure was the finest bathtub in all of Mexico. The hot water percolated up from coarse gravel at the base of a large rock bluff, just inches above the high-tide line along the beach. The natives had built the oval-shaped stone pool two feet deep and twelve feet across. It was so perfect nobody had changed a thing in over a century. Feeling suddenly content, he laid back, pulled his hat down over his eyes, and dozed off into a calming deep sleep, as he listened to the chattering sea birds and the soft gentle lapping of the waves.

★★★

That evening, Antonio and Leo sipped their first tequila under the veranda, while the stunning orange glow of the setting sun was beyond description, as it crept behind the jagged mysterious peaks of the Gigantas, forming a magnificent backdrop above them. Carmen and Leo hardly noticed, but Antonio thought not even a great artist could have painted the scene. It robbed him of his breath and caused him to pause and ask himself where the last twenty years had gone. It had been that long since he'd witnessed a Santa Marta sunset.

Carmen spoke up and brought Antonio back to the present, "Antonio. Leo. Come, dinner's ready."

The two cousins walked over to the table and sat. Carmen brought out a few more things then settled in to join them. Laid out in front of them was a platter overflowing with mesquite-roasted chicken, a bowlful of steaming rice, warm green beans, bright red slices of succulent tomato with goat cheese, a bowl of fresh chili salsa, and warm flour tortillas wrapped in a bright yellow cloth. Carmen blessed herself and said, "Help yourself, Tonio. We've missed you."

"I don't know what I've done to deserve this, but this is the best-looking dinner I've had in front of me in years! And that new dress doesn't have much to do with it, but you are the most beautiful woman I've had dinner with in as many years as I can remember. My compliments all the way around, Señora." He raised his glass.

Carmen blushed, a bright crimson color, looked down at her plate and said, "Thank you, Tonio. So good to see you again."

As they were finishing dinner, Leo leaned back in his chair and asked, "So, what's the news from Insurgentes, Tonio?"

"Where do I begin?" he pushed his empty plate to the side. "Insurgentes is growing by the day. I hardly recognize it anymore. Even with that poor excuse of a road, more trucks and buses than ever are coming up from La Paz, bringing more people," he shook his head at the thought of it. "A few of them are going all the way through up to Loreto."

"Are you finished?" Carmen asked as she reached for Antonio's plate.

"Yes, I am. That was delicious, well worth the trip down that cliff! Thank you."

Antonio turned back to Leo, "I hear they've somehow tied that old goat trail north of Loreto together all the way up to Concepcion Bay and Santa Rosalia. They say a truck can get through there now. I don't know how they did it. Used to be hard just getting a mule through there. You know, you've done it."

Leo chuckled, "Yeah, sold a horse to a man up at Rosalia, took me two weeks to lead the animal up there. Only made ten pesos on the deal. I was young and stupid," he shook his head.

Antonio started again, "They're breaking ground for more farms in the desert every time I turn around. And they're building that whole new town, Ciudad Constitucion. Hard to know where it begins and Insurgentes ends," Antonio twisted his mustache as he thought about it.

He went on, "I saw a thousand migrant farm workers camped out between the two places a few months ago. I didn't think there was that much humanity on the planet. I do my best to stay out on the ranch or up in the mountains when I can anymore."

Leo pushed his chair back and stood, "Let's take that bottle out to the veranda, there's a nice moon coming up and a fresh breeze," he reached for the tequila and a handful of limes.

They settled into two comfortable chairs looking out over the water, and Antonio asked, "You know what's funny? The reason I came on this trip was Sammy asked me to ride over to San Juanico. He wanted me to tell those folks two of their men were robbed on their way to Insurgentes. As you know, Sammy doesn't miss a trick, he put them to work out on the new road to La Paz. Nobody in San Juanico had any idea what happened to the men, so I got the job of going over there and telling them."

"Leo said, "I'm glad he sent you and that bottle. I haven't had a sip of tequila in a year," he laughed.

Antonio emptied his glass and kept going, "The funny part of the story is that Sammy wants to build a road from Insurgentes all the way over here to the top of that cliff," he pointed. "He wants me to look at it and advise him how to do it. So here I am, an old cowhand who never drove a car or a truck in my life, helping Sammy engineer his road project. The things I get asked to do sometimes," he chuckled about it as he reached for the bottle.

Carmen stepped out of the kitchen and interrupted them as she carried a chair across the opposite side of the veranda. "I won't bother you if I sit out here in the breeze for a little bit, will I? The kitchen feels like an oven."

"You can sit with us all night if you like," Antonio answered.

"Just until I start to doze off. Won't be long."

Leo was itching to ask, "What good is a road going to do anyone up there at the top of that cliff? I don't understand," Leo scratched the back of his head and looked up that way.

"He says he wants to make Santa Marta a little easier to get to. I'm gonna tell him not to bother with the road unless he does something with the trail down the cliff first. It needs to be made safe before he sends anybody near it," Antonio set the bottle down and took a sip.

Both men paused to drink while they thought about the trail and the road to the cliff. Leo re-filled his glass and squeezed a lime over it.

After a few minutes Antonio changed the subject, "Sammy wanted me to talk to you about the cattle. It's been five years since you've driven any cattle home to Insurgentes. You used to trail the yearling steers and the worn-out old cows every year south through Los Dolores, and up to Insurgentes. I didn't know about the problem with the neighbors until the other day. Sammy tells me they want to charge you to trail the cattle across their land?"

Leo set his glass down and angrily answered, "Yep, and I'm not willing to pay the sons of bitches! I've just left all the cattle down there on their own the last five years. I'm not sure what else to do," he looked at Antonio as if he might answer the question.

Antonio twisted his mustache and asked, "How many head you have down there?"

"Sure to be quite a herd by now, but I haven't been down there to count for several years. It's in the hundreds, maybe three hundred by now. They're spread out across more than twenty miles of canyons north, south and west of Timbabichi. Most of them were on the old Quintanna Ranch, the last I knew."

"You sure there's no way to work out a deal with the neighbors? I mean, offer them a small sum?"

Leo set his glass down hard on the small table between the two chairs, "No, they want about half as much as the cows are worth. We'd be losing money. I'm not going to pay them, that's all there is to it! They're trying to put me out of business so they can graze all that country themselves."

"I see," Antonio thought things over.

After a long pause Antonio spoke up, "I'm gonna tell Sammy he'd better get to work and widen the trail on the cliff, it's the only other way out to Insurgentes. If he's serious about building that road up there, he'll have to work on the trail anyway. Better he get started sooner rather than later. We'll take the cattle out this way."

Leo looked at Antonio curious, "How would you widen that trail? It's a thousand-foot high wall of rock."

Antonio cracked a smile, "Dynamite. He'd have to put a blasting crew together. I've seen them do it on the road to Loreto up in the Gigantas."

"When does Sammy want the cows back at Insurgentes?"

"Come spring."

"That gives him fall and winter, not a lot of time."

"Knowing him, he'll figure out a way. We should plan for a spring round-up. I'll get back down here in late winter. Think you can you have them sorted and gathered in one place somewhere by then?"

"Sure, it'll take me a couple of months," Leo paused to think. "I'll need to hire a couple extra hands. There's two boys up in Agua Verde I can get to help."

"Good, you have the herd ready first of March, and I'll be back down with a few cowboys to trail them home. Everything will depend on having the trail widened by then, but that's Sammy's problem."

Leo drained the last of the bottle and held it up, "You have another one of these?

"Sure, more than one," Antonio rose from his chair to retrieve a second bottle.

Leo stood up and leaned against the railing around the veranda as he waited for Antonio to return. The moon was near full and the crescent-shaped beach edging the bay stood in bright contrast against the water. "Beautiful evening isn't it?"

"I was thinking the same thing. I enjoy listening to you and Antonio. Reminds me of old times," Carmen said as Antonio returned with the bottle.

"This will be it for tonight, cousin. We'll need to ration things if I'm here two or three more nights."

"I think that bottle will do us tonight," Leo smiled.

Leo changed the subject again when he sat back down and poured another drink, "I was thinking about that new road up there. Quite a few boats from La Paz and the mainland, friends of Padilla, have stopped by here over the last couple years. They stay down in the guest house. It never fails, they always ask where the road out of here takes you. When I tell them there's no road, they ask why we don't build one. I don't know why they'd care."

"Who knows? Most of those people from over in Mexico think about nothing but driving everywhere. Just lately I heard they want to turn that dirt track from La Paz to Insurgentes into what they call a 'highway.' And they want to take it all the way north to Tijuana! They're talking about covering the whole damned thing with cement. I'll believe that when I see it!"

"I like things the way they are."

"Well, you're good down here for as long as you're alive, Leo. They won't be building any roads through here any time soon. In fact, I thought more than once that I'd like to have me a little casita over there in the palm trees, when the time comes for me to sit back and put my feet up. I haven't stumbled across any place I've ever been that's better than this. Not even some of those canyons I like so much up in the Gigantas.

"In the Gigantas, as much as I love it," Antonio went on, "you're always down in the canyons, and you can't see very far unless you climb out. The older I get, the more I like to see long distances and the less I like to climb. Like, sitting here right now," he waved his arm toward the ocean, "you can see someone coming from five miles out there on the water. I like that. I can see out there all those miles, and I'm in this comfortable chair on this veranda feeling the cool breeze with a glass of tequila, and there's a beautiful woman sitting right over there," he looked at Carmen. "That's my idea of living well. I want it to be just like this in my old age."

"You know you'd be welcome here, Tonio. We grew up together on the ranch. Might be fitting for us to spend what time's left for us right here. This place has just about everything a man could want. That's my plan."

"You let me know if you ever learn how to make tequila out of all that agave you have growing out there. If you could do that, I doubt I'd ever leave. Of course, I'd need to find me a good woman to be down here with me. I'm still working on that."

Carmen, who'd been quietly listening to the men, laughed out loud when she heard his comment about women. "You've been working on that since you were twelve years old, Antonio. That's more than thirty-five years. Good luck with that if you haven't found one by now. Maybe you're the problem, not the number of good women out there!"

"You got me there, Carmela. I never looked at it that way," he said, twisting the end of his mustache, pausing in thought. "But seeing as I have all that valuable time already invested, I'd be a fool to quit now. Think I'll work on it a little while longer."

"God pity the woman if you do happen to find her!" Carmen rose from her chair, "I'm headed for bed, I'm dead tired," she leaned down and pecked Leo on the cheek. "Don't let him have too much more of that bottle, Tonio. He's out of practice."

Carmen wished them goodnight and stepped away through the shadows. The men clinked their glasses in a toast.

★★★

It was early evening, and a small group of men were drinking coffee under Alonso's veranda when Antonio rode back into San Juanico four days later. Alonso called to Antonio when he saw him coming and said, "Come join us. We're talking about mules. I was thinking there must be some for sale over around Insurgentes. What do you think, Antonio?"

"Don't know," he answered. "Ever since they brought cars and trucks to town, you see fewer mules, much less any good ones. People are all getting lazy, riding around in their trucks. The only place you see a mule any more is out on the ranches, and those animals usually spend their whole lives living right where they were born. And you know as well as anyone, good mules are never for sale."

"How about Sammy? Think he could find us a few mules, if even just for a year or two? Loan us a few, I mean. He must have some mules somewhere on all those ranches and farms he has. I was gonna ask you, could I ride back with you, so I could talk to him?"

"That'd be fine. You can ride with me in the morning. That mule there," Antonio nodded at his pack animal, "only has that small saddle bag on his back. There's plenty of room up there for you."

"Good, good! I'll go with you in the morning. You can sleep there in that palapa if you'd like, same place you slept the other day," he pointed at a thatched casita where his children stayed when they visited.

Antonio said, "Thanks. I'll put my pack in there, but I need to go visit Luisa before it gets dark. I'll be back."

Antonio asked a young boy to lead his animals to water and find somewhere they could be hobbled and left to feed overnight, then walked across the village to Pedro's shack.

Juan Carlos saw him coming and said, "Mama, Mama. Señor Antonio is coming!"

Luisa came out of the palapa, wiping her hands on her skirt as she watched him approach. "Hello, Antonio. I've been expecting you. Please, sit down. How was your visit to Santa Marta? Would you like some coffee?"

"Just fine, just fine, Señora," Antonio sat a small table outside under a palm frond overhang. "No coffee for now but thank you."

Juan Carlos and Maricela were peeking around the corner in the shadows from inside the palapa absorbing every word of the conversation. Very seldom did they have a guest from outside the village. They were excited to witness it.

Antonio removed his hat and placed it on his knee as Luisa sat opposite of him. "Took me twice as long to climb that cliff than the last time, but then, most things take me a lot longer anymore. It was well worth the effort, though. Santa Marta's just about the prettiest place on earth. You need to do yourself a favor and go see it. My cousin and his wife live there. Tell them I sent you, and they'll welcome you like family. That's the way they are."

Luisa smiled nervously and fidgeted with her hands, "It's funny, I've lived right here my whole life. I went to the top of the cliff just once. That was with my father on my birthday, when I was a young girl. I remember looking down at the beach, so many years ago, and seeing all the palm trees and the water. It was such a beautiful view. I can only imagine what it's like when you're down there. Maybe one day, I'll be lucky enough to see it up close," she looked at Antonio and he tried to interpret what he saw in her eyes but found himself unable.

Antonio kidded, "Get that husband of yours to take you down there when he gets back. Have you a little honeymoon," he winked. "The both of you could soak in the hot springs, that alone is worth the trip."

Luisa blushed and looked down at her hands as she wrung them together. The children didn't make a sound. They were frozen in place as they peered around the corner.

For the first time, Antonio studied her up close and saw how truly beautiful she was. The evening light was soft, and it reflected perfectly on her flawless complexion. Her cheekbones were high and rounded, her eyes, nose and mouth were set perfectly on her face. Her lips turned up naturally on their outside edge as if ready to smile, though he saw there was sadness about her.

"I'm worried about Pedro," she started. Wrinkles appeared out of nowhere and formed across her forehead. "This is the first time he's been away from us, and who knows how long it might be before we see him again. You said it could be three or four months, but even you didn't know how long it would be. I have no idea what it's like out there building that road. I've heard stories that it can be very dangerous," she looked away over her shoulder as if to escape.

Abruptly, she said, "I have something in the palapa. Please, just a moment," she stood and went around the corner through the opening.

He watched her move. She was graceful. He saw that in the few steps it took her to reach the door-less opening. He could see she was strong by the way she rose from the chair. When she turned through the door. she pivoted on her toes. He saw clearly because her feet were bare. She surprised him. He found that he respected her, liked her, yet he barely knew her.

She returned to the table with a piece of folded paper in her hand. "You told me you would take something back to Insurgentes for me," she looked up at him through wide dark brown eyes.

"Yes, I did."

"Here," she said, offering him the paper. "I can't write well, but one of the other women helped me. I wrote this for Pedro. I'd like for you to find him and be sure he gets it. Please, if you can, hand it to him yourself, so it stays private. It's the only thing I've ever written to him. It would mean so much to me if you would do this."

He was touched, and he paused before he reached for the paper. He thought about the responsibility he was accepting. He placed the neatly folded paper in his shirt pocket. He said, "Señora, you have my word. Wherever he might be, I'll find him, and I'll hand him your letter directly. I promise you that."

Antonio rose from his seat and stepped around the table. He leaned down, placed his arm around her shoulder and kissed her softly on the top of her head. There was a pleasant fragrance in her hair. He stood erect, tipped his hat and nodded in respect before walking away.

★★★

Pedro and Felix were on a crew building a rock crossing through a wide arroyo about two miles north of the base camp. They were settling into life at La Placita and growing accustomed to the work and the schedule. They were up and ready for breakfast each morning an hour before first light, and by the time the sun had risen, they were on the road with six other men on the back of a flatbed.

Cisco wanted the rock foundation across the arroyo completed within five days. Following the rock bed, he wanted them to mix cement in wheelbarrows until a finished concrete surface with a spillway spanned the arroyo. The crossing was designed to withstand the worst of the flash floods, a common occurrence during the monsoon season. There were dozens more crossings to complete just like the one they were building in the immediate miles ahead.

The crew was taking a short siesta after lunch during the heat of the day, when Pedro got up to relieve himself. He walked up the dry creek bed, well away from the others, and climbed the bank, where he could see out across the endless desert. As he was squatting and leaning against a large rock, he thought he saw a flicker of movement about a mile away, near a cluster of mesquite trees.

"Perhaps it was my imagination," he thought. But his curiosity got the best of him. After he was finished with his business, he stood and propped himself against the side of a boulder to steady his gaze. He shaded his eyes from the sun's mid-day glare with his hand.

After watching for a long time, he saw it again. For sure this time. He was convinced he saw something move, but ever so slightly. He forced himself to concentrate, to focus, then he gasped in disbelief when he realized what he was looking at. His heart started to race. It pounded in his chest. Adrenaline pulsed through his veins, and his hands started to tremble.

"I'll be damned!" he muttered to himself. He was seeing a mule's tail casually swishing from side to side. He looked more carefully, and he counted seven mules tethered in a line under the trees. He stared until his eyes grew weary and lost their focus. He rubbed them until they watered and recovered. He measured and surveyed the lay of the land with his eye. He mentally recorded every detail in the landscape until it was etched indelibly in his memory, before he forced himself to return to the work site.

Back at work that afternoon, Pedro was lost in thought. Other men spoke to him, but he barely acknowledged them. Nobody thought it unusual, because they all sometimes acted that way as they toiled at the back-breaking labor under the glaring sun. When they took a water break later in the afternoon, Pedro motioned for Felix to join him off to the side.

"You won't believe what I saw out in the desert."

"What?" Felix asked, only half interested, fanning the hot air in front of his face with his hat.

"I saw our mules, tied up under some mesquite trees. I didn't see them, but I'm sure Guapo and Gato are out there, too, probably sleeping under the trees. They must be following the road now but staying back and away out of sight. Looks to me like they're traveling at night and laying low during the day. I want to get those mules back, and I want to make those ugly cocksuckers pay for what they did to us. I want to leave them stranded just like they did to us."

"Where are they exactly?" Felix asked, suddenly excited and fully recovered from his heat exhaustion.

"They're about a mile from here, in the general direction of La Placita but about a half mile out from the road. If we plan it right, I think we can sneak right in on them."

"What do you mean 'we'? Just you and me?"

"Yeah, there's no reason to involve anyone else. The more people, the harder it would be to sneak in on them. Remember, they have that rifle. We need to be careful. I want to do it real quiet-like and surprise them. Do you think you can get your hands on a couple of machetes?"

"Sure, I know where they keep all the tools."

"Good. As soon as we get back to camp, we should finish up here for the day pretty soon, you get the machetes and meet me on the other side of the palm trees. I'll be over there making a plan."

On schedule, the crew rode back to La Placita on the flatbed. After they arrived, all the men wandered off in the direction of their tents to clean up and rest before dinner. Felix slipped out and went after the machetes. Pedro walked over to tell Cisco he and Felix were going for a walk, so they wouldn't be missed. They met on the edge of the palm grove. The first shadows of early evening were emerging in the late afternoon light.

"With any luck, they won't be moving out until it's good and dark," Pedro said. "There's a scattered boulder field right up against their camp that will give us good cover. Let's hustle out there and get in position. We can figure out how to move in on them from there, if we're not too late."

"OK, let's go," Felix was anxious and ready for a fight. His face was tight and determined. His knuckles were white, his fingers curled around the handle of his machete. There was an air of youthful confidence about him.

Thirty minutes later, they were crouched behind a granite boulder less than one hundred yards from the camp. They could see the mules still tethered to the trees and heard the muffled voices of the two men talking to one another. They couldn't make out what was being said.

"We're in luck," Pedro whispered. "They haven't left yet. Let's crawl in closer, slow-like, come on now."

They slithered on their bellies like snakes across the ground, behind and between the scattered boulders, until they were only twenty-five yards from the men. The shadows were fading fast, and twilight was setting in. Their timing was perfect.

They were lying side by side behind a dense, bushy, cholla cactus, and Pedro whispered, "You go right, I'll go left. Get between them and the mules. Try to get out of there without a fight, but if we have to use the machetes, so be it. Remember, they left us for dead not long ago."

"Don't worry about me. I'll be all over them," Felix said as he stared straight ahead with venom in his eyes, gritting his teeth, seething with anger.

"Okay, when I say three."

Pedro took a deep breath and tightened his grip on his machete.

"One, two, three!"

They exploded from behind the cactus and sprinted into the camp. Guapo had his back turned and was walking away from his mule. An instant later, Pedro stood between him and the mule with a machete raised above his head yelling, "Stay back! You son of a bitch!"

Felix let out a blood-curdling howl, like a ferocious animal, and headed straight toward Gato, who was strapping a canteen on his mule's saddle. Gato reacted with the cool instincts of a fierce predator, afraid of nothing, as if this was an everyday occurrence. In one smooth motion, he brought his hand down from the saddle to his waist and pulled the knife from his belt; it was the same menacing knife he'd once held against Felix's throat.

In the blink of an eye, Felix realized he had no choice. With tremendous momentum already propelling him forward, he went airborne. Simultaneously, he brought the machete up in a full swing from behind, and he brought the heavy blade down with a sickening thud, in a deadly stroke across El Gato's arm. Gato's knife went spinning through the air, and he wailed like a gravely wounded animal. Felix crashed head-on into him, before the man even had time to stagger. They rolled and collapsed, as if they were one person, together down to the ground.

Twenty feet away, without missing a beat, Guapo turned the tables on Pedro, swung around, and charged right back. It was completely unexpected, and Pedro was thrown off balance. Guapo hit him with a full body blow that sent them both spinning into one of the mules. The frightened mule reared up on its hind legs, and the two men hit the ground in a tangled brawl as they slid down under the animal. The mule came down hard on its front hooves and immediately reared up again, higher and even more frantic than the first time. The two men were growling like savages, the mule snorted in terror, and its eyes rolled back in their sockets. In such a close hand-to-hand fight, the machete was worthless, and Pedro let it drop from his hand. Guapo moved in for the kill and wrapped both of his hands around Pedro's throat. Pedro started to choke. He brought his hands up in a desperate attempt to pry Guapo from his neck.

When they hit the ground, Felix's head slammed into a rock, and his body went limp. Gato's forearm was severed, except for some silky, white tendons, causing his lower arm to dangle grotesquely as he flopped around in the dirt. He screamed like a mad man as he watched his life's blood pulsing from his arm just below the elbow. It saturated the lower half of his body, as well as Felix's face, as he lay unconscious amid the carnage.

Guapo's mule came down with even more force the second time. One of its front hooves landed squarely on Pedro's face, just above where Guapo's hands had closed off his throat. Guapo continued to choke Pedro, until he realized there was no more fight in the man. He loosened his grip as he gagged. He backed slowly away. He saw that Pedro's skull had been crushed. He dry-heaved until he vomited on the ground, right up against the side of Pedro's body.

It all happened so fast. A matter of seconds, not minutes. There was a sudden death-like silence in the air, except for the sound of Guapo's raspy breathing and a few husky snorts from the mule. Both faded away. The dust settled. An owl hooted softly from its perch somewhere in the mesquite trees. The mules resumed swishing their long, feathery tails.

★★★

In the middle of the night, Felix cracked open his eyes. He had no idea where he was. He laid stunned and still for a long time, until a sharp pain in his head forced him more fully awake. He brought his hand up to his forehead, where he felt a lump the size of a small hen's egg. He felt the crusted blood covering his face and most of his upper body. He recalled nothing about the fight or El Gato's severed arm.

The moon that night was nearly full, bright enough to cast shadows. Felix could easily make out the mule standing off to his side, and he could see that it was tied to a tree. He looked at El Gato's body lying next to him in the dirt. He rolled over, sucked up, and gathered all the strength he could muster to rise on his knees. His head throbbed and spun in circles, forcing him to remain on his knees with his hands planted firmly on the ground in front of him until it subsided. Another deep breath, and he forced himself to stand. The dizziness overwhelmed him, and he fell back to the ground. He rested for a long time before he tried to get up again. He failed for a second time, collapsing down in the dirt. On his third attempt, he stood, and he placed his hand on the mule's side to help steady himself.

"Pedro!" he called. He called again, but there was no response. There was no other sound except for the swishing of the tails and the soft buzzing of nocturnal insects.

He staggered over to a rock and sat down to gather himself and let his eyes better adjust to the moonlight. He looked over at Gato on the ground and was sure he was dead, not that he cared. He saw another body in the dirt, thirty feet away. He forced himself back up on his feet and shuffled over to have a closer look.

He kneeled next to the body. There was no face. It was mangled beyond recognition, but he knew the clothes, the old work boots and the thin wedding band on the finger. He checked for a pulse, although he already knew Pedro was gone. Holding tight to Pedro's cold wrist, he choked and sobbed from the depths of his body, from a place so deep he didn't know it existed.

At only eighteen years of age, he had just killed a man who he had truly hated, and he was holding the lifeless hand of his old friend. He had hardly any wits about him to collect, but he numbly crossed Pedro's hands and placed them over his chest. He held them there for a moment and patted them softly.

"Goodbye, Pedro" was all he could find the words to say. Tears flooded his eyes, and he lost complete track of time and place as he bowed his head and cried.

★★★

The few hours leading toward morning were a blur. The moon crept one way, followed by the sun rising from the other. From what Felix could piece together, it appeared Guapo had gotten the best of Pedro and overpowered him. He wasn't sure how Guapo had done all that damage to Pedro's face, but it didn't matter. There were six mules still in the camp. He assumed Guapo left on the other one.

Moving slowly but deliberately, Felix dragged El Gato's body, tied by one foot, across the rocky ground behind one of the mules a short distance across the desert. He hauled it up and dumped the body on a flat rock, so that it was fully exposed to the sun and easy for the vultures and coyotes to find. He kicked dirt on Gato's gray-colored face and spit on the corpse. He cursed Gato to hell and walked away, leading the mule back to where Pedro was lying on the ground.

He laid an open bed roll next to Pedro and carefully rolled him over, then tied it securely, mummy-like around the body. It was already stiff, and an unpleasant odor rose to fill his nostrils. He lifted Pedro up and over his shoulder and laid him across the pack saddle on the back of one of the mules. Then he went about lining the mules up in a string, tying them all together, and he climbed up on the lead animal. An hour later, he arrived in La Placita. The only people left in the camp at that time of the morning were Cisco and the kitchen help.

Cisco saw Felix coming. He'd been keeping an eye out for Pedro and Felix since the night before. When they were still gone in the morning, he was near certain they'd taken to homesickness and deserted the crew, which was not uncommon. Now he was confused as he watched Felix riding into camp with six mules and what looked like a body laid over one of the pack saddles. When Felix arrived, Cisco saw that he was covered in dry, crusted blood. A cold chill ran down Cisco's spine when he saw the feral expression on the young man's face.

"My God, Felix. What's happened to you? Where is Pedro? Where did you find these mules?"

Felix raised his hand for Cisco to shut up and stop with the questions. He said, "Help me with Pedro. That's him back there."

Juan Pedro Murillo, thirty-three years old, husband, father of two, of Rancho San Juanico, Baja California Sur, Mexico, was buried later that day, on the edge of the palm grove that surrounded the work camp.

No one knew his grave would mark the future location of a cemetery for a small pueblo named La Placita, which would soon be established in that very place. The cemetery would lay less than one hundred yards back from the future location of an oily black strip of asphalt that would become known as Mexico Federal Highway 1. A small pile of hand-sized stones marked his grave.

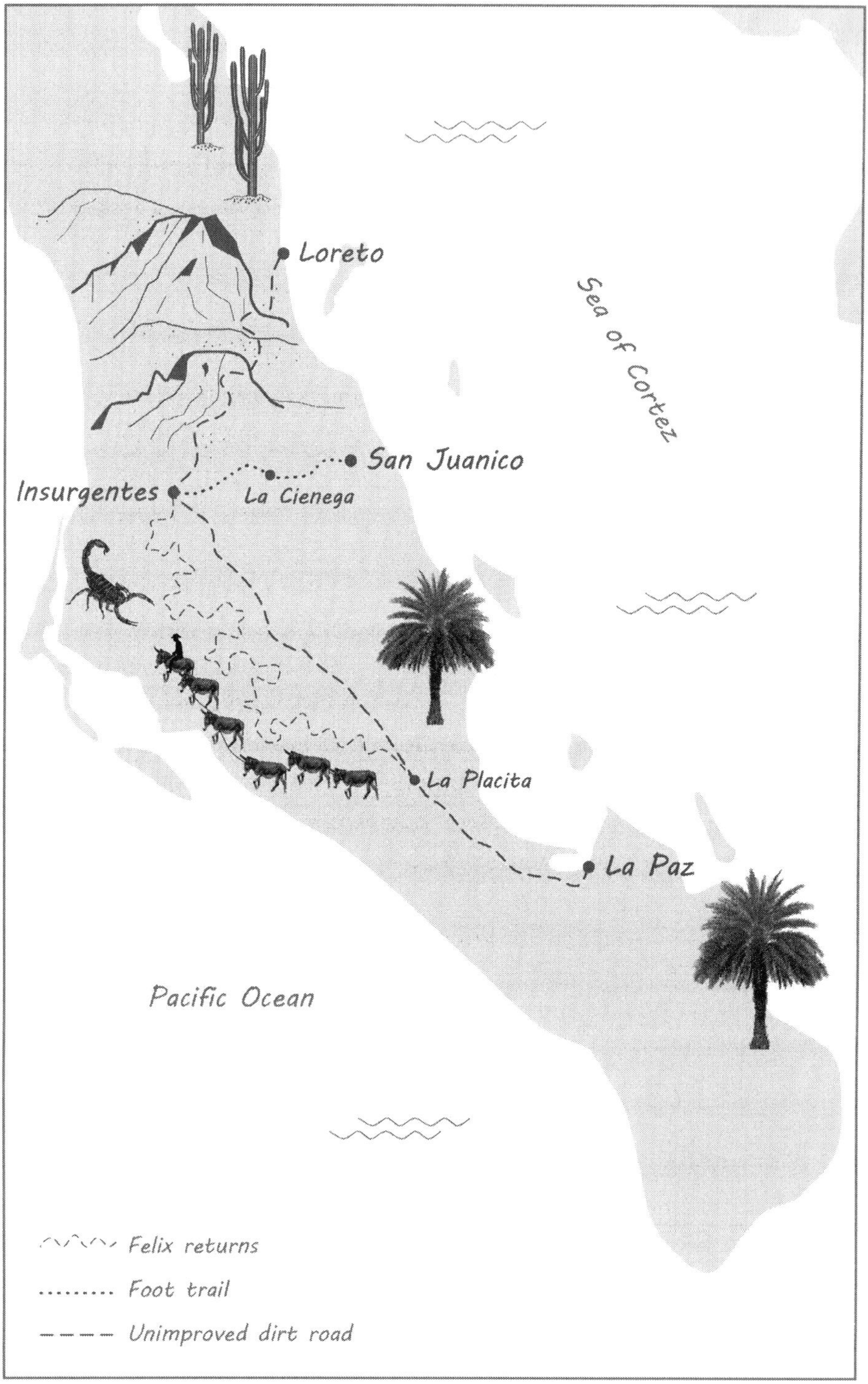
Loreto
Sea of Cortez
San Juanico
Insurgentes
La Cienega
La Placita
La Paz
Pacific Ocean
Felix returns
Foot trail
Unimproved dirt road

Vision Quest

Before the sun came up the following morning, Felix announced he would be leaving immediately for Insurgentes and San Juanico. Cisco and many of the other men encouraged him to wait until someone was free to travel with him, but he insisted on going alone. He dismissed all further discussion, and the matter was settled. Cisco asked the cooks to prepare enough food to see Felix through the five or six days he thought it would take him to reach Insurgentes.

Felix rode north, leading the string of mules in the direction of Insurgentes. He traveled miles back from and away from the road, but he followed a mostly parallel path. During the first day, he heard several trucks or buses without mufflers far off in the distance, and it caused him to drift further west until he heard them no more. He spoke only to the mules, and he slept on the ground among them. He drank with the animals at infrequent water holes, usually stagnant green puddles that he found in low depressions in the bedrock within deep arroyos. He ate prickly pears and dates, when he could find them, and rattlesnakes every time he came across them. He contemplated life and the small number of things that seemed to matter. The fierce sun, the dusty dry wind, and the constant squinting as he scanned the hazy horizons, aged his face, giving him the appearance of a far older man. He saw not another soul, and that was exactly how he wanted it.

Sixteen days later, still leading the mules, Felix rode down El Centro. People along the street paused and took notice, but none of them waved. They seemed to sense the young man's desire to be left alone. The story of Pedro, Felix, and the stolen mules of San Juanico had been a subject of great interest among the locals for many weeks, and here appeared a young man leading just such a caravan through the middle of town. Felix stared straight ahead; the mules' heads were hanging low, just above the ground. Their ribs were prominent and protruding, and they were all covered in a thick layer of gray trail dust. Felix brought the caravan to a halt directly in front of the Ejido San Jose del Norio office, and he slid stiffly down off the mule.

He paused for a moment to survey his surroundings and gather his thoughts. He secured all the mules to a seldom-used hitching rail, brushed off some dust, and took his hat in his hand. He climbed three short steps up and walked through the open door.

He was greeted by Sammy's pleasant young assistant, who looked up from her desk with a cheery smile. She gasped, lost her breath, and brought her hand up to cover her mouth, but she failed to conceal the shock in her eyes.

"Felix?" she remembered his name.

Holding his hat over his chest to help disguise his shameful condition, he nodded and responded, "Yes, Señora. I'm Felix, we met here a month or two ago. I don't remember how long ago it was. I was here with Juan Pedro Murillo from San Juanico."

"Yes, I remember you. What's happened? Are you hurt? Are you all right?" she stood up and came around from behind her desk.

"Yes, yes, I'm fine. At least, I am now. I've been riding for a long time. I'd like to speak with Señor Gonzo, if he's here?"

"He's not, but he'll be back soon. There's a chair in his office where you can wait for him." When she stepped up close to assist him, she gagged from the foul odor. She placed her hand on his arm to help him along. She saw that he was not to be led when he politely removed her hand. He moved far more quickly than she'd expected, and he passed through the door ahead of her.

"Would you like some ice water?"

"Yes, please Señora. Water but no ice."

"Where have you been?" she asked as she poured the water.

"I've been with a road crew at a place called La Placita, north of La Paz somewhere, but I'm on my way back to San Juanico. I wanted to speak with Señor Gonzo on my way through here."

Right behind them without any warning, Sammy walked through the door. He'd seen the mules out front and didn't know what to expect once he got inside the office. The look on his face went from bewilderment to surprise to a half-smile when he saw Felix sitting in front of his desk. He stepped forward and offered his hand. Felix stood up and extended his own. They shook hard without saying a word.

When Sammy gained his composure, he said, "This is a surprise! Are those Alonso's mules out there?"

"Yes, Señor," Felix responded. "All of them but the one Guapo got away with. I'd like to talk to you, if I could, before I leave for San Juanico."

"Certainly, of course." Sammy smiled. Felix stared at his gold tooth.

Knowing the answer before he asked the question, Sammy said, "Have you had anything to eat? I was on my way to the cantina when I saw the mules. Would you like to join me?"

"I haven't eaten anything today. I'd like that. Thank you."

Sammy and Felix walked up El Centro and entered a cool, dark building where a sign out front read "Cantina del Aguila." Sammy chose an empty table under the front window that offered both privacy and light. In his weakened state, the organic smell of beer, fried food, and cigarettes nearly overwhelmed him. He glanced from side to side and noted two wealthy-looking ranchers at one table and a middle-aged man holding the hand of a pretty, much younger, woman at another. He felt out of place, but he was determined to talk business. He'd had plenty enough time out on the trail to prepare.

"Please, Felix. Tell me what's happened. I have so many questions, I don't know where to start. It's probably best that you begin."

Felix told Sammy about the work camp at La Placita, and how he and Pedro confronted Guapo and El Gato. Sammy listened carefully to every word with a silent intensity that Felix was not accustomed to. His piercing eyes seemed as if they might penetrate his soul, but Felix did not falter. Felix spoke with an assuredness not common among the rural, uneducated people Sammy had known, especially someone so young. Felix was relieved when he finished his story, telling Sammy about his long journey back to Insurgentes with the mules.

Sammy sat quiet, as if he was trying to put all the pieces together in his head. He looked across the room and waved to a young woman who was standing behind the bar. "We would like to order lunch," he told her when she stepped up to their table.

"I'm going to have a steak. Would you like one?" Sammy asked.

Felix shifted awkwardly in his seat, "Yes."

"Good," Sammy said turning back to the girl, "We'll have steak and eggs, and could we get some coffee? Cream and sugar for me. Felix?"

"Black."

Sammy turned his attention back to Felix and asked, "You're certain the men you fought with at La Placita were the ones who stole the mules?'

"Yes, I'm sure. I got a good look at the dead guy's face."

"I confirmed that they were two of the escaped prisoners from Santa Rosalia. I was told they were a couple of the worst ones in the place. Oscar Padilla has actually crossed paths with Guapo, and he tells me he's a very dangerous man, with close ties to the Sinaloa narcos. You're lucky to be alive, Felix."

Felix's face flushed red through the sunburn, and he said, "Pedro always used to say that. Do I look lucky to you?" His charcoal-colored eyes glared at Sammy from across the table.

Sammy smiled nervously, held his hands up in defense, and said, "No, no you don't. I'm sorry, I didn't mean it that way. I'm sorry." He went on, "Is there something other than that story you wanted to talk to me about?"

"Yes," Felix answered looking down at his blistered hands in front of him. "Pedro wanted to see a road built to San Juanico. I didn't agree with him, but that was before I saw the road being built to La Paz. I've had a lot of time to think about what it would mean for the people of San Juanico, and I'm here to ask for your help."

Sammy thought for a moment before he replied, "I don't know what to tell you Felix. You saw that we have a hundred miles of road to build from La Placita all the way up here to Insurgentes. That's a long way, as you know from having just crossed that country with the mules. What you didn't see was the hundred miles of new road we need through the mountains from here up to Loreto, and three different roads we need to build over to the Pacific. This is not to say that I that don't want to help you, because I do."

The girl brought their plates, fully covered with steak, eggs, refried beans, rice and tortillas. Felix felt his stomach roll at the overpowering smell of the food and didn't think he'd come close finishing it all.

Sammy sliced his steak as he continued, "Tell you what, why don't you give me a little time to work on it. I'll be going down to La Paz tomorrow, where I'll be having meetings with Oscar Padilla. Maybe he and I can put our heads together and come up with something. What I haven't told you is Alonso is here in town. He's asked me to find him some mules, but now since you've solved that problem, why don't you go tell him? Then, the two of you can come back and see me when I return from La Paz a week from now. We can talk more about the road then."

Felix asked, "Alonso is here? Where is he?"

"He's staying with a widow woman about a mile north of town. I can give you directions how to find him. Please tell him we met and what I said about talking in a week. He should join us. As for you, my ranch is not very far from here, and it has a bunkhouse. You're welcome to stay there. I'll have Anna Marie help you get settled in. There's a corral for the mules, and all the alfalfa they'd ever want. It looked to me like they could use a little something to eat too!"

"Thank you, Señor. That's very kind of you. I'd like to go see Alonso today, if that's alright with you."

"From now on, please call me 'Sammy.' And yes, go see Alonso after you and Anna Marie get out to the ranch. I wish I could be there to see Alonso's face when you ride up on one of his mules!"

They finished their meal mostly in silence, as they each thought more about the conversation they just had.

★★★

Felix followed Sammy's directions out to the widow's ranch. As he approached, he saw a scattering of collapsed wooden buildings and an old stone ranch house. The land was flat as a pancake, covered in scraggly dry brush and stunted cactus. The fences had all collapsed from neglect. A few under-nourished cows and a small herd of goats stood vacantly next to an empty trough. Alonso was relaxing in a rocking chair on the porch of the stone house when he saw Felix coming from a mile away. He rose, leaned up against a post that supported the veranda, and used his hand to shade his eyes as he watched the mule come closer. He grinned like a child on Christmas morning when he recognized Felix on the mule.

"By God!" he beamed, slapping his thigh and punching his fist in the air. "Where on God's parched brown earth did you find that mule, son?"

Reserved with a half-smile on his face, Felix responded, "Long story, Alonso. A really long story."

They swayed forth and back on side-by-side rocking chairs as Felix told the story. Happy as he was to have his mules back, Alonso was grief stricken, and the tears welled in his eyes when Felix told him about Pedro.

Alonso wiped his face with the inside of his arm, as Felix told him about the ride back to Insurgentes and his meeting with Sammy Gonzo.

"That's it," Felix concluded.

"Well, I guess this means you and I will be riding back to San Juanico in a week or so. Is that what you're thinking?"

Felix nodded, "Yep."

There was suddenly a new dynamic between them. Felix had always been the kid responsible for the grunt work after Alonso enlisted him to ride and help with the caravan, but Alonso's indebtedness and new-found respect for the boy was powerful. Without a word passing between them, they became equals. They were quiet for a time, and they let it settle in.

Felix broke the silence and said, "You know what the worst part of this is? I lay awake at night dreading the awful thought of facing Luisa. I have no idea what I'm going to say to her. How do you tell a woman something like this?"

Alonso looked down, avoiding Felix's eyes, and said, "I don't know, but when the time comes, may God have mercy on you and help you to find the words."

Felix pinched the bridge of his nose as if it might help him think, and he changed the subject. "I'm staying out at Sammy's ranch. It's a great place for those sorry-looking mules of yours. They were about to bloat on that green alfalfa, so I found them some dry old grass hay. For their own good, they'll have to do with that. Still, it won't be easy when it's time to go back to San Juanico where there's nothing but mesquite to eat." He managed to smile.

Alonso chuckled and said, "I'll meet you in town in a week, and we'll see what Sammy has to say."

Felix later departed on his mule, waving back over his shoulder at the old man on the porch.

★★★

Felix took his time riding back to Sammy's ranch. It was three miles from where Alonso was staying, and he used the time to think about his future. Everything seemed a blur in the young man's head.

Sammy's ranch was unlike anything he'd ever seen before. The main house, a sprawling rock and adobe structure with a clay tile roof, supported by massive log vigas, was shaded by towering eucalyptus trees. In the center of an open courtyard was a powerful diesel generator and a deep well with a pump feeding twelve-inch steel water lines, which led out to the surrounding fields. A dozen different trucks and tractors were parked in an orderly line next to a two-story barn with sliding doors large enough for the trucks and tractors to pass. The second floor was stacked full of fresh green alfalfa hay. Three lower profile buildings with spacious covered porches were used as bunkhouses. Most of the remaining space in the immediate vicinity was taken up by several acres of shipping corrals, large enough to hold hundreds of cattle. Alonso's mules were in a small corral on one end of the complex, their faces buried in bunkers full of fluffy grass hay.

Felix rode straight into the courtyard and stopped at the pump where his mule drank thirstily from a galvanized trough. He dismounted and was loosening the saddle when Anna Marie came up behind him.

"Are you finished traveling for the day?" she asked.

Startled, Felix turned and said, "Yeah, but I think I'd better jump in this trough. I'm ashamed to say it's been a few weeks since I've washed up any."

"I have just what you need," she said. "Over there, where I'm staying," she side-nodded her head toward the first bunkhouse, "there's a tub I can fill with all the hot water you'd ever want. We don't ever share it with the cowboys, but after what you've been through, I think I can make an exception."

Felix couldn't believe his good fortune. He blushed at the thought of taking a bath in the young woman's house. "I'd be a fool to turn that down, Señora."

"Call me 'Anna.' After you get your mule put up, come over to that red door right there," she pointed toward the bunkhouse. "I'll have everything ready for you."

Thirty minutes later, carrying a clean change of clothes, Felix knocked on Anna's door. She greeted him, "Follow me."

She led him through a spacious kitchen and down a long narrow hallway with bedrooms on each side. At the end of the hall she showed him through a door into a perfect little bathroom with a sink, toilet and a free-standing tub full of hot water, topped with a thick layer of sudsy bubbles. A white cotton towel was neatly folded on a wood bench next to the tub.

"The cowboys never had a bathroom, but we told Sammy if he wanted us girls from La Paz to stay for very long, he'd better get us one. So, here it is," she said spreading her arms, "It's all yours!"

"Um, I'm not sure what to say, I've never been in a bathtub before."

She rolled her eyes, "Don't tell me I have to teach you how to bathe yourself. That might be embarrassing," she hinted a little mischief.

Blushing Felix stuttered, "No, I didn't mean that I didn't know how to use it. It's just this is my first time."

"Well, there's a first time for everything, isn't there?" she smiled. "Enjoy yourself. I'll be in the kitchen if you need anything. I'll have dinner ready in half an hour."

"Last night I was sleeping in the dirt with the mules, and now this. Thank you, Señora."

"I told you, call me Anna. I'll leave you to your bath. I'll be down the hall. Call me if you need anything"

Felix felt like a new man when he returned to the kitchen. He was clean and relaxed for the first time in as long as he could remember. Anna was busy working over a sink and a cook stove. Propane lights brightened the room. She'd changed out of her office clothes into a pair of skin-tight yellow cotton shorts and a white blouse that stood in stunning contrast to her olive-toned skin. She was barefoot, pivoting on her toes as she moved from counter to sink to stove. He noticed how easily she moved. As hard as he tried to guess her age, he was unable to do so.

"That felt good," he said as he stepped up to a chopping block covered with fresh vegetables. He helped himself to a slice of tomato, and he savored the sweet juice. Delicious aromas spread through the room coming from the stove top.

"I'd say you needed that bath probably more than anyone I've ever seen before." Then she added with a quick laugh, "I should've said 'anyone I've ever smelled before.'"

Changing the subject, sounding more serious, she said, "Sammy told me what happened. I'm sorry about your friend. He seemed like a nice man."

"Yeah," he said looking down at the floor. "He was like an older brother to me. I knew him my whole life. The worst part will be telling his wife. They have two young children, a boy and a girl."

Without a word, Anna crossed the room and placed her arms around him. He didn't resist. He saw that her eyes were moist and full of compassion. He buried his face against her neck. The smell of her hair reminded him of cactus flowers.

When she broke the embrace, she took a deep breath and said, "Come and sit down." She motioned toward the table. "I have some tequila I've been saving for a special occasion. Share it with me."

"Sure."

Anna poured them each a shot over ice and added a squeeze of lime. She returned to her kitchen duties and asked over her shoulder, "You live in San Juanico your whole life?"

"I did. Looking at it now, things were pretty simple. There were five kids in my family. I'm in the middle. My two older brothers left San Juanico when I was young, and I never knew them much. They're both fishermen down in Agua Verde. My two younger sisters help out around the village, taking care of the smaller children. My mother died after my youngest sister was born, and my father herds goats. My sisters take care of him," he paused and drank down his shot of tequila, savoring the powerful flavor.

He set the glass down and continued, "I built a little palapa out on the edge of the village about a year ago. I was tired of living with my sisters, and I was never close to my father. He and I don't talk much. I help them with food when I can. You said you came from La Paz? How long you been here?"

"Six months" she answered, washing the vegetables for their salad. "I was working for the Padilla family in La Paz. Sammy had business with Oscar Padilla, so I would see him when he came by the office. One day he offered me a job up here. He hired a few other girls from La Paz, too. They do his housework. He has four or five houses around Insurgentes on different ranches. The other girls live here part-time, but I don't see them much. They work six days a week and are only here for a night or two at a time."

She placed a pitcher of water and two glasses on the table, and Felix asked, "Do you miss your family and your life in La Paz?"

"Sure, I miss La Paz, but it's not easy for a woman to make money in Mexico. If you don't get married and have a family by the time you're my age, there aren't many options. I was lucky when I met Señor Padilla, he got me out of the cantinas. A lot of the girls I knew in the cantinas don't have it so good. I feel bad for them."

She looked around and said, "I think we're ready. Let's serve ourselves at the counter and then we can sit down."

Felix was hungry again, he thought whatever it was she was cooking smelled delicious. He filled his plate for the second time that day. There was fried cabrilla, beans, rice, and a fresh garden salad. Anna re-filled his drink and sat down across from him at the small square table. Seeing her close up, he noticed for the first time she wasn't much older than he was, but she'd obviously seen much more of the world than he had. He wanted to know her better.

"I'd like to go to La Paz," he said, "Alonso is the only person I know who's ever been there, and I think he was only there for a few days. I really don't know anything about it."

"You should go there. I'd like to show it to you. It's a big city with thousands of people. I love going to the Malecón on Saturday nights.

There's always music, dancing and wonderful food. The ferry from Topolobampo comes in twice a week, and bigger ships come and go from all over the world. There are old hotels along the Malecón with beautiful gardens. That's where I worked in the cantinas, so I got to meet all sorts of different people."

He noticed her eyes sparkle and her mouth turn up in a smile as she talked about La Paz.

She became so involved in her description of the city, she held a fork-full of salad in mid-air, "I think the best time I ever had was Semana Santa last year. Nobody slept for three days! There was so much music and good food, I'll never forget it. Right after that, Sammy offered me this job. I've had to get used to how quiet it is here, but I like it," she finally brought the salad to her mouth.

Felix picked up his tequila and drank his second shot.

Anna watched him and reached for her drink as she said, "Since Sammy's down in La Paz, I have a few days off," she downed her shot without missing a beat. "Would you like to go with me over to the Pacific tomorrow? We can take one of Sammy's pick-ups. The ranch has a fish camp there where we can stay. Want to go?"

The invitation took him by surprise, and he fidgeted in his seat as he thought about it, then said, "Why not? I'd love to go. I've never been to the ocean. I've never even ridden in a truck before either, at least not in the front seat. You know how to drive?"

Her eyes rolled, "I drove that same truck all the way up here from La Paz, and everyone in it with me survived! I think I can drive it over to the Pacific from here. It's only about ten miles down a dirt track."

"Okay, I was just asking," he grimaced inside, wishing he hadn't asked the question. "When do you want to leave?"

"I'll make the food tonight, enough for three days. Let's get an early start, but not too early," she thought about it. "I like sleeping in on my days off."

"I'm good with that, I haven't slept much lately, being with the mules and all. In fact, I should probably be turning in," he said as he rose from his chair. "Thanks for the dinner and the bath. I can't thank you enough…"

"I was happy to do it," she got up and kissed him on the cheek. "Rest up, vaquero, I'll see you in the morning."

With a light head, Felix ambled across the open yard to the bunkhouse where he was staying. A light was burning in the kitchen window. When he stepped through the door, he came upon two men and a woman playing cards at the table. All three looked up as he entered.

"Hello there," said the older man in a cowboy hat who was gathering cards. "You must be Felix. Anna Marie told me you'd be staying here for a few days. My name's Antonio. This here's Gilberto, and that's Juanita," he nodded toward each of them. "Have a seat and pour yourself a shot. Can I deal you in?"

Felix pulled out a chair and said, "I'll have a drink, but I really need to get some sleep." The two men looked like genuine rancheros. Their hands were well muscled and thickly calloused, their skin was leathery, and they had prominent lines across their foreheads from wearing their hats in the sun. The woman was all dolled up, like the whores he'd seen in the cantinas.

"I guess you probably do need to catch up on your sleep," Antonio said as he shuffled the deck. "I saw those mules out there, and I heard about your journey up from La Placita. I was in San Juanico not long ago, telling those folks the mules were gone and not to expect you and Pedro back any time soon. I brought them that food you asked for. They were grateful," he glanced at the cards in his hand. "That's a tough deal about Pedro. I met his wife. She gave me a letter she wanted me to bring him. Seeing as what happened, I think I'll just hold on to it until I make it over there and hand it back to her in person. We're gonna have us a cattle drive over that way in the spring," he started dealing.

"Pay attention, dammit, if you insist on dealing the cards!" Juanita glared. "We can't hardly trust you to get it right as it is, much less while you're carrying on with him." She glared at Felix.

Antonio chuckled and continued dealing, "Settle down, sweetheart. I can deal and talk at the same time. You know that."

"I'm not sure what I know about you anymore. It's late, let's make this the last hand so you and I can get on with it. I'm sure Gilberto doesn't need our help draining any more of that bottle."

"Juanita, dear. I only see you about once a year, so it's easy to forget how bossy you can be."

"You show up once in a blue moon and expect me to be nice and sweet?"

"Come on, now. You know I love you, girl," he reached over and pinched her butt.

She laughed and swept his hand away. "You old fool. You just wait!"

"See what you've got to look forward to in your old age?" he said to Felix. "I wish you luck in finding a gal as spunky as this one! They don't make many of them like her anymore!"

Felix blushed and said, "I can see that." He raised his glass and finished his drink. "Like I said, I need to get some sleep. It was good meeting all of you. I'll see you in the morning."

"Sleep well, son. That was a good piece of work getting those mules back for San Juanico. You should be proud. Have yourself a good night." Antonio raised his glass as Felix turned away toward his room.

★★★

Felix had no idea what time it was, but he found Anna Marie standing outside next to a green 1956 Chevy pickup. She had it packed and ready with a cooler, a pile of bedding tied in a bundle with some twine, and an overnight bag.

"Climb in," she ordered.

The more he observed her, the more intrigued he was. He'd never known a woman like her. He watched as she pressed down hard on the gas with her right foot and let up on the clutch with her left. She had perfect coordination. He was fascinated by it. In the confines of the cab he could smell her hair. He got dreamy, looking at her.

The old pickup shimmied and shook as it lurched forward. She pulled up to an iron gate and jarred him out of his trance, "Hop out and open that would you? Close it up tight after I pull through."

He jumped out to get the gate and climbed back in after she passed through.

Bouncing along the rutted trail, Anna was smiling as she gripped the wheel. “I love driving!” she said.

He fixed on how perfect her teeth were when she smiled. He watched as she ran her tongue across her thick red lips.

He forced himself out of the trance, “How long have you known how to drive?” he asked.

“I had a boyfriend with a car when I was thirteen or fourteen. He taught me. Cars and trucks are pretty much the same. Trucks are just a little bigger. If you want, on the way back I’ll give you a lesson,” she said looking over at him, still smiling.

“I’d like that.” He paused, “So if you learned when you were fourteen, how many years have you been driving?”

“You’re funny. You could’ve just asked how old I was, I wouldn’t care. I’m twenty-three. I’ve been driving for ten years already. How old are you?”

“I’m eighteen.”

“I would’ve guessed you were older than me. You act older, not that it matters. I liked you right away back when you first came to the office, however long ago that was.”

She made him self-conscious by saying that, and he turned to look out the window to collect his thoughts.

He turned back toward her, “You know, a lot’s happened to me in the last few months. Some good, but a lot not so much. Being here with you is one of the best parts. I like you.”

She smiled again and looked him up and down before turning her attention back to the ruts in the road.

Following a pause in the conversation, Felix asked, “You think it’s about two hours to the beach from here?”

“Uh, huh, almost that much. It’s only ten miles, but the road doesn’t get any better than this, so it’s slow going. Beats walking though doesn’t it?”

She reached for the glove box, opened it with one hand, and pulled out a bright red package of Pall Malls. “See if you can find some matches in there would you?”

He looked through and under some papers and came up with a book of matches. “Here’s some right here,” he said. “Want me to light that for you?”

“Sure. Pack it first, and light one for yourself, if you want,” she handed him the pack.

He lit two cigarettes and passed one back to Anna Marie. She took a deep drag and exhaled out the side of her mouth, as if she’d been smoking for years. “I like to smoke while I drive. Really though, I like to smoke any time. It’s more fun while I’m driving, though. Settles the nerves.” She glanced over at him and asked, “You smoke much?”

“We don’t often have cigarettes in San Juanico. Pedro and a few of the others roll their own, and they share with me once in a while. Never had a store-bought cigarette though. This is good.” He exhaled.

The desert passed by the open window, barren and dead, there wasn’t much to see. The vegetation, what little there was of it, was sparse, low-lying withered gray shrubs with tufts of coarse scattered dune grass here and there. Nothing seemed to be alive, not a bird or a rabbit anywhere. Far ahead in the distance, large rounded sand dunes rose through a blanket of fog on the horizon.

Felix couldn’t help but watch the fascinating woman sitting next to him. He thought she was physical perfection. Her long dark hair shone with hints of red auburn when the sun reflected across it just right. She had it tied in a loose knot, but the wind through the window blew wisps of it across her face. She brushed it away from her eyes from time to time. She had incredibly strong arms with well-formed muscles, and he wondered how that was. She was wearing a white t-shirt tucked into a pair of tight-fitting khaki shorts. Her calves were hard muscled, he noticed when she pressed on the pedals. For such a trim, compact woman, she had generous breasts that were tightly confined in an uplifting bra. He became aroused and self-conscious watching her and turned his attention back out the window.

Before long, they drove under the fog bank and entered the dunes. The road twisted and weaved its way through the wind-swept sand formations. The dunes towered above them as they followed an arroyo, as it sliced a path through the sandy hills. “We’re getting close. Just a few more minutes," Anna said in anticipation. Felix was busy taking in the sudden, surprising transition.

As they rounded a sharp turn, the fog broke and gave way to a brilliant blue sky with puffy round cumulous clouds. They came to a stop in front of a primitive shack made in part of an amusing variety of materials that had drifted in off the ocean. The shack was perched on a low dune and looked out over an expanse of flat sand beach as far as the eye could see both left and right. A foamy white surf crashed with aggression upon the shore. The crisp sea breeze cleared the dust from their sinuses. Felix inhaled the ocean for the first time in his life. Sea gulls, pelicans, terns, and hundreds of birds he'd never seen before dove in the shallows between the waves. Shore birds scampered and danced along the surf's rising and receding edge. Felix felt the magic.

"Look at that!" he spread his arms and turned to Anna.

"I love it here. I'm glad you came," she said.

Felix turned to look at the shack more closely. He saw the building was nothing more than a shelter. It had a sand floor and a rusty tin roof. The windows and the door were simply openings. There were two over-turned pangas resting along one outside wall. A large pile of driftwood stood next to a stone fire ring. Two hammocks hung side by side under a narrow over-hang.

"What more could you want? It's perfect!" Felix said as he stepped down out of the truck.

"Kick off those boots, chico. You won't be needing them."

They unloaded the truck and ate lunch at a small table under the over-hang. They chatted for several hours, and before they knew what had become of the day, it was mid-afternoon. They settled into the hammocks for siestas. Felix noticed that she had removed her bra and untucked her t-shirt. The sight of her was soothing and their long easy conversation caused him to relax. He drifted peacefully into a restful needy sleep. He'd forgotten how exhausted he was.

He woke up slowly an hour later and looked over at Anna who was asleep next to him in the other hammock. One of her arms hung off in the air, and she snored softly. Her lips were parted in a smile. Her hair had fallen over half of her face. He got up and stepped quietly off in the direction of the beach.

He took off his shirt and laid it across the pile of firewood. He rolled up his loose pants to his knees and followed the trail down to the water, where he sat barely above the tide line. The sun was approaching the far horizon and the birds had settled down for the day. As he soaked in the scene and inhaled the pure humid air, the rhythm of the waves brought him to a place he'd never been before. He let his mind wander as he often did during his journey with the mules. He felt at peace.

So much had happened. For now, the only thing he knew for sure was he wanted to return to San Juanico. He thought his presence there would be important as the villagers adjusted to the loss of Juan Pedro. He thought the people of San Juanico should be his first priority. After that, his mind drifted into a meditative state. He grew weary trying to sort it all out.

Anna Marie surprised him when she collapsed to her knees behind him and wrapped her arms around his body. He could smell her hair as the breeze blew strands of it in his face. She whispered in his ear, "Let's walk down the beach. It's so beautiful this time of day."

"Okay."

They started to walk and didn't feel the need to talk. Their hands met and became entwined. They walked for twenty minutes, all the while holding hands, perfectly relaxed.

He asked, "What was it like growing up in La Paz?"

She paused, "I love La Paz, but I don't like talking about me so much."

"Please, I'd like to know more about you."

She waited again as she thought it over and said, "Alright, but there are parts I'd rather leave out."

"Tell me whatever you're comfortable with."

"Okay," she paused again. "I never knew my parents. I was left at an orphanage when I was a day-old infant. There were a hundred girls of different ages who came and went, and we all lived in a large dark dormitory. There were nuns living with us. Most of them were angry old women, and we were afraid of them." He gripped her hand.

She looked out over the water. "The older girls were all we had for parents, but they were only twelve or so years old themselves. A child might get adopted once in a while, but not many ever did. The rest of us just struggled to survive."

"Please, go on," he said after she paused again. They continued walking, but more slowly.

"I left, rather, I escaped, when I was thirteen. I learned how to live on the streets. I'm ashamed of what I did, but it was better than living with those nuns. I was a prisoner there. They abused me in many terrible ways. I started working in the cantinas. It was better than starving."

She stopped walking and looked down at her feet, "A lot of men would pay me to be with them. I shared an apartment with some other girls, and we learned to stick together, just like in the orphanage. We were family. Some of the girls got hurt, but I was lucky. I never got beat up bad like some of the others did." Her voice trailed off.

She turned around and they began walking back, "About three years ago, Oscar Padilla rented a hotel for a week. He had businessmen from Mexico, Colombia, Panama, and wherever else, for a convention. He hired some women to get things ready. One of those women was a friend of mine, and she asked me to help. She introduced me to Oscar, and one thing led to another. He started looking out for me. He offered me a job in his office. I met Sammy there, and that's how I ended up in Insurgentes."

"I grew up in a shack with a dirt floor without much to eat, but it sounds a lot easier than what you've been through."

"Maybe it was, but we're not much different in many ways. We both came from less than nothing, but here we are. Look around. This isn't so bad is it?" She waved her arm.

They stopped, and both of them turned inward. He wrapped his arms around her. She felt precious to him. She looked up in his eyes and melted. He leaned in, and their lips met. She opened her mouth, and they shared a first kiss. They lingered there before continuing their walk.

As the sun sank on the Pacific horizon, they stopped again to embrace. Felix reached under her shirt and found her breast loose and heavy in his hand. She moaned, and her tongue probed his ear. "Yes," she whispered.

Felix was gentle. He never wanted anything more than he wanted her at that moment. He pressed against her, and she climbed up on his body. She pulled back and reached down to unfasten his pants. She slid her hand over him. In the glow of the setting sun she pulled her shirt up over her head. She dropped it in the sand and stepped out of her shorts.

She was, by far, the most beautiful thing he'd seen in his life. She was looking up at him with a sense of need. Her eyes were wet. Her breasts were far larger than they'd appeared under her bra. Her belly was hard and flat, a rich, creamy bronze color. He'd had sex with three different girls in his life, but nothing compared to the beautiful woman offering herself to him at that moment.

Anna picked up their clothes and spread them on the sand. She pulled him to her as she laid back and spread her legs. He knelt in front of her, and she guided him. He felt her warmth as she wrapped her legs around him and pulled him closer. They worked themselves into a frenzy. They lost all sense of time. It may have been five minutes or an hour, neither of them knew or cared.

They laid together until the last trace of the sun dropped below the horizon. He remained inside her, not wanting to leave.

Walking back to the camp, he draped his arm around her. Anna broke the quiet by saying, "You know what I want to do?

"What?"

"I want to build a fire and set that old bed frame out there. I want to lie with you under a blanket. I want to look up at the moon, and I want to listen to the waves. And I want to make love to you over and over and over again."

"Me too."

And that's what they did, all three nights on the beach.

★★★

Four days following his and Anna's return to Insurgentes, Felix met Alonso at a taco stand in the town square. Alonso bought coffee for them both and seemed anxious to see his mules and return to his routine.

"I don't know, Felix," he started. "When I'm in San Juanico, I think about Insurgentes. When I'm in Insurgentes, I think about San

Juanico. You know, women are funny. One day I can't live with them, and the next day I can't live without them. When there's two of them, it's twice as bad!"

"It's you who's funny, Alonso. They both want the same thing. It's you who always wants something different. Even I can see that."

"I know, I know. To be honest, I don't think I'll ever be able to decide which woman or which place."

Felix shrugged, "I'm not sure what to tell you. I can see why you like your time with the mules. Are you ready to go see Sammy?"

Alonso nodded, with a troubled look on his face, he set down his cup.

They walked down El Centro to the Ejido office. The door was open, and they stepped in to see Anna sorting through stacks of paper on her desk.

"Hi," she beamed when she saw them. It had only been a few hours since she and Felix had woken up in bed together. He looked at her and was struck by the thought she was just as beautiful behind the desk in her office clothes as she was lying naked next to him in bed.

"I see you found each other in the big city."

"I can spot one of my mules from a mile away," Alonso answered. "Felix had it tied up over in the square."

She smiled, "I'll tell Sammy you're here."

Sammy came out and shook each of their hands and gestured toward his office. "Go in and take a seat, I'll have Anna get us some coffee."

As they settled in, Sammy winked and asked Felix, "Did you find the bunkhouse comfortable?"

Felix didn't expect the question and blushed before he could answer. He recovered his wits and responded, "I did. I hope you'll invite me back, if I find myself in Insurgentes again."

"You're more than welcome, any time. All you have to do is ask, and it's yours."

Anna served them coffee, and Sammy got down to business.

"As you both know, I met with Oscar Padilla in La Paz. I told him how the people of San Juanico would like to see a road built. He also wants to see a road to San Juanico, but he'd like it to continue past there to the cliffs above Santa Marta. Antonio was out there looking things over. As it turns out, before we build the road, we'll need to improve the trail that drops down the cliff," he waited for their reaction. They seemed to be fine with it.

Sammy continued, "We're having a cattle drive this spring along the coast, and we need to bring the herd out that way. The trail needs to be widened and made safe before we can do that," After the trail is finished, we can start the road."

Sammy sipped his coffee before he continued.

Felix thought how organized and determined Sammy was when discussing business.

"Here's how it would work. We'll need every able-bodied man in San Juanico on the crew. I recall Pedro saying there were fifteen of you in the village. Is that right?" he looked to Felix for a response.

Felix answered, "Yes, counting the boys who are old enough to work."

"Good, let's say we have a crew of fifteen. We'll need a foreman who can supervise the others and be responsible for reporting back to me. Obviously, the foreman must have experience working on a construction crew and traveling between the job site and Insurgentes. That narrows it down to you," he looked straight at Felix. "Are you up to it?"

Felix shifted uneasily and looked across the room at nothing in particular as he thought.

Sammy, experienced negotiator that he was, decided not to let Felix think too long, "I realize that most of the crew are older than you and may have a problem taking orders from someone younger. On the other hand, not many men I know would take a one-hundred-mile journey on their own with a caravan of mules. My instincts tell me you're up to the job. Plus, don't forget, we wouldn't be having this conversation if you hadn't approached me about building the road. What do you think?" he stared hard at Felix with his intense dark eyes.

"Whoa," Felix took off his hat and set it on his knee. That's a lot to think through," he ran his hand through his hair. He glanced at Alonso then back at Sammy, "I did come to you and asked you for a road."

Sammy was quick, "Yes, you did."

Alonso reached over and placed a reassuring hand on Felix' shoulder. "Every single person in San Juanico is going to respect you when we ride into the village on those mules, and they learn how you made that possible. Take the job, Felix. You'd be damned good at it."

Felix was humbled and unsure. He looked at Sammy, who nodded and said, "He's right. I wouldn't ask you to do it if I didn't have confidence in you. What do you think?"

The butterflies churned around in his stomach, but he answered, "Okay, I'll do it, and I'll tell you this much: I'll treat each man on the crew with respect. I'll do everything I can to earn their trust. I can't offer you any more than that."

"That's good, Felix. That's what I was hoping you'd say," Sammy replied.

Sammy added, "Antonio advised me you'll need a lot of dynamite in addition to the hand labor. I'll provide a couple of men with blasting experience, plus all the dynamite you'll need. We'll be paying your crew the going wage, just like we do for the laborers on the La Paz road. You provide me the records, and we'll have their wages deposited in the bank here in Insurgentes. They can draw on it with notes I'll be providing you."

"When would you like to get started?" Felix asked.

"I'll have the dynamite and two men experienced with explosives ready in two weeks, I'll need to borrow them from the La Paz crew. You go out to San Juanico and get your crew organized. Go down and have a good look at the trail. Plot it out and make a plan for what tools and supplies you'll need. Alonso can turn around and come back here with the mules and begin hauling what you need. Any questions?"

"Would you make us loan? I want to pack some food and supplies back to San Juanico. I'd like to get an early start and leave tomorrow morning."

"I can do that," Sammy answered.

Felix and Alonso spent the day gathering supplies. By the time they returned to the ranch that evening, it was dark. They put the mules up for the night, and Felix walked over to Anna's. She answered the door with a tentative smile.

"You'll be gone in the morning," she said. "I wasn't ready for that. We've been together for over a week, and I've grown really close to you. From the things you've said I know you feel the same way," she wiped a tear from her eye. "I knew the day would come when you'd have to go back to San Juanico, but I was hoping we'd have more time before that happened, that's all."

"I told you before I left the office this afternoon."

"I know, but I didn't have time to think about it until now. Can I go with you?"

"Not now, Anna. This is the best place for you. I have so much to do that I can hardly think straight. It wouldn't be fair to you. When the time comes for us to be together, I want to do it right. I'll be making trips back and forth, so we'll still see each other all the time."

"I don't know. This doesn't feel right. I know things happened fast, but I just want to be with you. I want to know you better. Is that so hard to understand?"

"No, but it won't work right now. I won't even be living in one place. One day, I'll be in San Juanico, then two weeks on the trail, then back here. It's best if I see you here. Besides, you have a good thing here. I know a lot of people who would give anything to have your job and live in a beautiful place like this," he looked around the room and noticed she had fresh flowers in a vase on the table.

She looked defeated and his heart went out to her. He wrapped his arms around her and squeezed.

"Alright, we can try it for a while. It's just that all my life I've wanted what I feel right now with you. But I have this way-too-familiar feeling that what I most want is slipping away again. All my life, I've had to live with this terrible sense of impending doom. I try my best to rise above it, but I promise you, Felix, it's always out there. I'm fighting it really bad right now."

She began to cry, and he kissed her.

★★★

Luisa lifted the bucketful of water up from the bottom of the well by pulling hand over hand on the knotted old rope. When the bucket reached the top of the thirty-foot well, she lifted it out and poured the water into one of the many empty buckets behind her. Her four-year-old daughter Maricela stood next to her chatting. The little girl stepped forward to look down the dark hole.

"Get back from there!" Luisa said. "I don't want you to fall in. You'd never get out!"

Maricela retreated with a frightened look on her small face.

It was noon on a typical early autumn day in San Juanico. The cloudless sky was a pale blue, the sun beat down relentlessly, and there wasn't a hint of a breeze in the flat calm air. The villagers had all retired for their mid-day siestas due to the intense heat. Luisa kept on and toiled through the day, because with Pedro gone, she could never keep up. The sweat dripped down her forehead and across her face. She continually lifted the lower end of her loose t-shirt up from her waist and used it to wipe her brow. She hummed softly as she worked to lessen the drudgery.

As Luisa dropped the second bucket down the well, her younger sister Nora walked up from behind and surprised her. Nora was in many ways her lifeline. She checked in with her sister two or three times a day to help with whatever Luisa was doing and to simply keep her spirits up.

"Let me help you, Luisa. Fill two buckets for me, and I'll carry them for you."

"Thanks, Nora. That'll save me a trip. We've been using eight or ten buckets a day. Hauling this water reminds me of Pedro. I think he liked carrying water, because he'd never complain and he might carry up twenty buckets a day, which was way more than we'd ever need."

"Seems like he's been gone forever sometimes. What's it been? Over two months now?"

"Something like that. I try not to count days or weeks anymore. Who would've known he'd be gone this long?"

As Nora lifted the buckets she said, "Never knowing must be the hard part. He might show up tomorrow, next week, or next year!"

"Don't say that! It's hard enough to hold out hope without thinking of him being gone for a year. I don't think I'd survive that," she looked behind to be sure Maricela was following them.

Luisa talked as they trudged along with the heavy buckets. "Do you know what we had for dinner last night?"

"No, but I can guess."

"Beans and tortillas! I traded Lynda some tortillas for the beans! I'm so tired of this. We had beans and tortillas for breakfast today, and now we're out of beans again! I've also got to catch a goat, so we can get some milk. I'm no good at that. Sometimes it takes me four or five hours to find and catch a goat. Even then, the goat might be nearly dry! Pedro always caught the goats."

"I can help you with that. I'll get one of the boys to go with us. We should be able to catch a goat pretty quick. The boys can usually tell which goats are good and wet from a distance. I'll go and see if I can find Pepino as soon as we get this water up there." Luisa's shack was on the far end of the village perched up on a small rise. The two women were both drenched with sweat when they reached their destination.

"Here," Luisa said as she handed Nora a tin can she'd dipped in one of the buckets. They drank their fill of the warm green water.

After sitting for a few minutes Nora rose from her chair and said, "I'll go find Pepino, he's most likely home taking a siesta. I'll be back."

Pepino had recently been orphaned after his mother came down sick and died rather suddenly. His younger sister was adopted by the neighbors but twelve-year old Pepino remained living in the family's palapa. He often shared meals with his sister and the neighbors, but he was an independent young boy who never had a father. He learned at an early age to help provide for his mother and it served him well after she passed. The villagers all admired the boy and they collectively kept an eye on him, helping him out when he needed it.

An hour later Luisa, Nora, and Pepino were walking up the trail in search of one of the dozen goat herds that browsed freely in the surrounding desert. Each herd had at least one old nanny fitted with a tin bell around her neck. The clanging noise helped to locate the herd out in the scrub.

After walking a half hour, Pepino heard the bell and pointed "That way!" The two women hadn't heard anything.

They walked another ten minutes and saw he was right. They came upon a herd of forty goats browsing in a narrow, scrub-filled canyon.

"Let's watch for a minute and find a good doe," Pepino said. "When we see the one we want, get your ropes ready, and we'll go in real slow." Each of them carried a short lasso. "They'll let you get right up close, if you're careful not to spook them."

"See that rusty-colored one over there?" he pointed to a goat standing on the outside edge of the herd. "She's got a good bag. I'll take the lead and go straight in. You guys come at her from the side. Go slow and don't look directly at the goat."

With the skill of a master goat herder, the boy inched steadily closer toward the rust-colored doe. Luisa watched as he appeared to be looking at two other goats on his opposite side. Those animals were wary of the approaching boy, but the one he was after didn't feel threatened, and it continued to browse.

As Nora crept closer to the rusty doe, it raised its head and took a few steps away from her in the boy's direction. Pepino easily encircled the doe's neck with his braided lasso. "Got her!" he said excitedly as he leaned over and felt her teat. He squeezed and a stream of milk squirted six feet through the air to where it landed in the dirt.

"She's about as full as a tit can get!" he said through a brilliant smile. "That should take care of you for a few days Luisa!"

"Pepino, that was wonderful! It might've taken me half the day to do that, and I doubt I would've found one so full of milk. I can't thank you enough! Come by later and share some creamed honey dates with us. You'll have to tell Juan Carlos how you did that!"

Pepino beamed with pride as he led the goat away from the herd.

★★★

High above on the rimrock, Felix and Alonso paused to rest the mules and enjoy the view out over the Gulf of California in the distance. Felix noticed the two women and the boy with the goat herd about a mile away and a thousand feet below. He pointed them out to Alonso and said, "That looks like two women and a boy. I wonder why the women are out there with the goats?"

"We'll find out soon," Alonso replied as he removed his hat and ran a bandanna across his wet brow.

Luisa, Nora and Pepino leading the goat on a short rope, walked down the canyon until they reached the trail leading back to San Juanico. The goat's comical twin day-old kids wobbled and struggled to remain close behind their mother. Luisa's spirits soared after capturing the goat. It did her a world of good to have that little bit of time away from her ever-more-challenging life in San Juanico. She thought about how it was all catching up with her. She tried to remind herself not to lose touch with her cheerful spirit, and to always remain strong for the children. She went over things in her head and became lost in thought as they meandered down the trail.

Pepino stopped and held up one of his hands. He turned around and tapped his ear with his finger to indicate he heard something. "Someone's coming on mules. Listen!"

The women looked at one another because they heard nothing. Luisa said, "What?"

"I hear mules, more than one. They're coming. Listen! Maybe Alonso is back!"

They stood in the middle of the trail. The goat turned to look behind them, and its ears perked up. "Look, the goat hears them," Pepino pointed.

As Pepino spoke, Felix came from behind a mesquite tree on the lead mule. They saw him, before he noticed them standing on the trail. Luisa's heart skipped a beat. It could only mean that Pedro was home. She smiled and tears of pure joy fell across her face. She wiped her cheek with a brush of her hand and waited for him to appear from around the same tree.

Felix was exhausted, slumping forward in the saddle, when he looked up and saw the three people standing on the trail in front of him. Before he recognized who it was, he raised a weary hand in a greeting, but his smile faded fast when he recognized Luisa. He lowered his hand to his side and failed to conceal the sudden look of despair on his face.

So hopeful, she critically watched Felix's every move, Luisa reacted instantly. Her smile turned to a cold, hard stare. Her lips became tightly drawn. She may have been only twenty-eight years old, but she was all-too-familiar with the cruel twists and turns of life. Her senses deadened.

Two heavily loaded mules were tethered behind Felix and came into view as he continued down the trail. Next came Alonso, who appeared with two mules trailing behind him. Luisa saw nothing more. The caravan stopped in front of the three people.

Pepino excitedly said, “Heh, Felix! Alonso! You’re back!” he raised his hand and waved with youthful enthusiasm.

Alonso raised his hand and waved without much heart.

“Where is Pedro?” Luisa demanded. “Why isn’t he with you?”

Felix turned toward Alonso in hopes the other man would answer her question. Alonso’s eyes were filled with dread. Felix slowly dismounted. He removed the straw hat that was shading his face, took three unsure steps toward Luisa, and stopped six feet in front of her. Her dark eyes penetrated his soul.

“He’s gone, Luisa,” he began to cry. He was holding his hat in his hands.

“Goddamn you, Felix! Where is he?” she demanded again. She made a fist with each of her hands, as if she was prepared to hit him. “Tell me where he is! Goddamn you!”

Still crying, he forced himself to say it again. “He’s gone, Luisa. He won’t be coming home. He’s gone.”

Luisa brought one of her balled up fists to her mouth and bit down hard on the knuckle. It began to bleed.

“Don’t you say that, Felix! Just don’t you say that! Don’t you fucking say that, again!” she began to convulse. The upper half of her body collapsed forward, and she spread both hands across her face and started to scream incoherently.

Nora and Pepino were dumbstruck, momentarily unable to move or speak. The only sound was Luisa’s dreadful screaming. The air was dead calm around them.

Felix dropped his hat in the dirt and stepped forward. He held his arms out to her, but she collapsed to the ground before he could reach her. He went down on his knees, cradling her suddenly frail body. He held her, while she choked, unable to catch her breath. He cried, as did Alonso, Nora, and Pepino.

Luisa lifted her head and from a few inches away she looked into his eyes. Her lips were trembling as she tried but failed to speak. She balled up her fists again and started beating Felix in the center of his chest. He just let her hit him, over, and over, and over again.

Nora recovered first and came forward. She knelt down and held Luisa's head in her hands. She whispered, "Come here. Come here now. Won't do any good to be hitting Felix. Come here, let me hold you."

Luisa went still and stopped beating on Felix. She hung her head. Her hair had broken free of its ribbon and fell across her face. She turned into Nora and buried her face against her sister's breast.

"There, just hold still." Nora looked at Felix and asked through grief-stricken questioning eyes. "What happened?"

"He was killed by one of the men who robbed us. There was a fight. Pedro was killed."

"Oh, Goddamnit to hell," she swore and looked down at her sister.

Luisa's body went limp in her arms.

"We have to get her back to San Juanico. She needs to be in bed. Luisa, listen. Can you hear me? Listen now," she said as she shook her gently by her shoulders. "We need to get you up on that mule. Felix, here, help me get her up. Let's put her up on your mule. You get on behind her and hold her up. Alonso, I'm going to climb up and ride with you."

Twenty minutes later, they rode into San Juanico. Luisa was slumped over in the saddle in front of Felix. He had one arm around her and his other hand held the reins. The entire village came out to greet the caravan, but they held back when they saw Luisa. Their faces were suddenly horror-stricken at the sight.

Nora ordered, "Go to my palapa. Don't stop for anything!"

Nora shared her small palapa with her husband and two daughters, ages ten and twelve. Both of her daughters stepped out when the mules walked up. They immediately sensed the seriousness of the moment, with their big round terrified eyes.

Nora commanded, "Girls, prepare my bed for Luisa. She needs to lie down!"

A few minutes later, Luisa succumbed to a coma-like sleep. Nora stepped out with a distraught look about her. Every man, woman, and child from the village was huddled about in a group, watching from a respectful distance. Alonso was with them. He answered their questions the best he could. Six tired mules were tied off to a hitching rail. Nobody thought to unpack their heavy loads. Visibly shaken and pale as a ghost, Felix sat at a table under Nora's palapa shade, staring at an empty coffee cup in his hands.

Through saddened eyes, he asked the question of Nora without saying a word.

"She's asleep. You'd better tell me the whole story. I'll know best how and when to share it with her. I'll get some coffee."

During the days that followed, the entire population of Rancho San Juanico experienced a dreadful state of mourning. Even the children were affected. Many of the villagers wore black clothing in the awful heat, at least the ones who owned any. People whispered among themselves. The village lacked a chapel, but there was a small stone grotto under the palm trees that sheltered a statue of the Mother Mary, draped in a light blue gown, spreading her arms. There was a candle flickering in a jar on a ledge, sheltered from the breeze. One by one, every person in the village, young and old, knelt on the stone step in front of the statue and prayed. They never failed to keep the candle lit. Young Juan Carlos, five years old, went there alone and kneeled. He thought about his father. He tried but failed to make sense of it all.

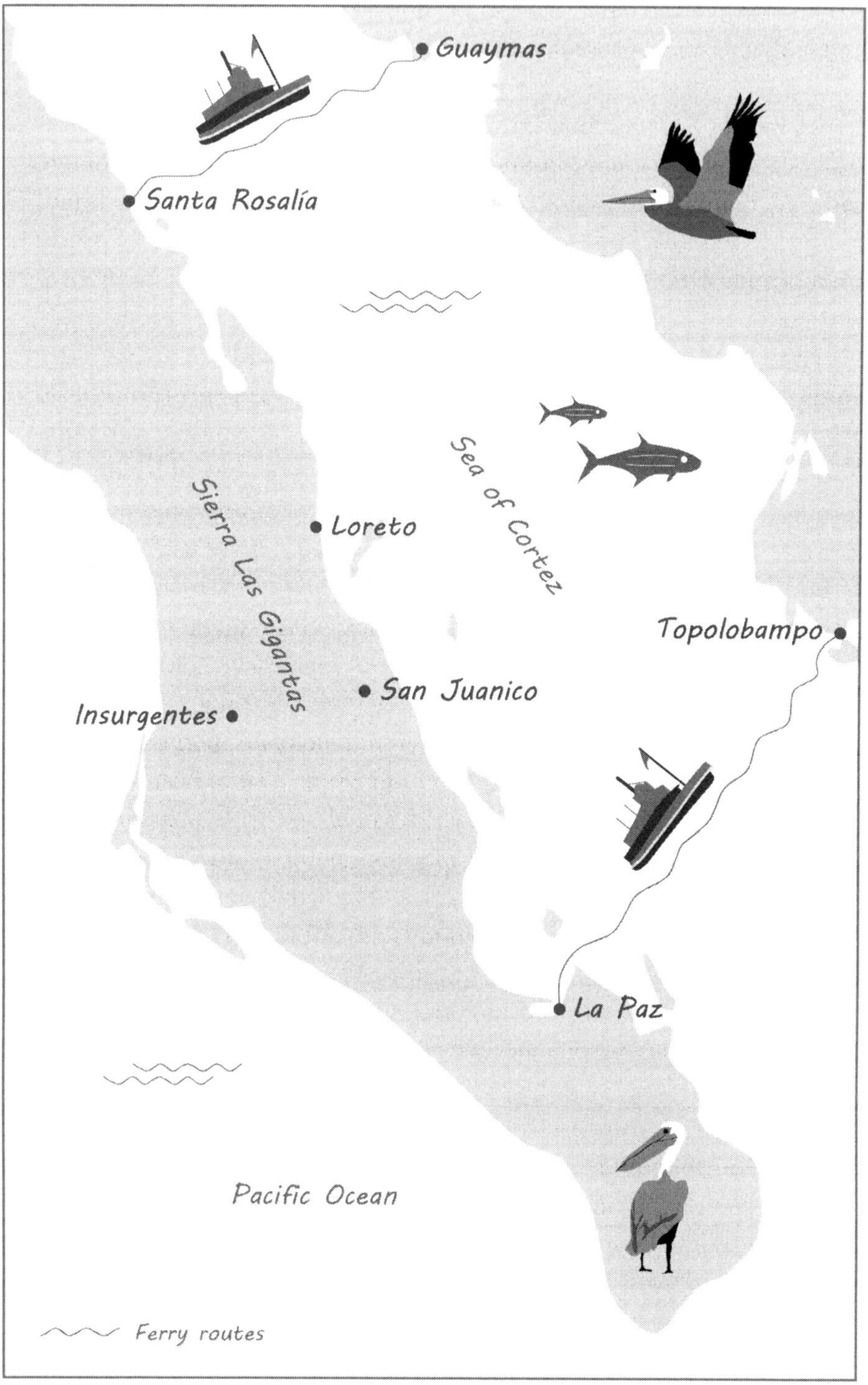
Guaymas
Santa Rosalía
Sea of Cortez
Sierra Las Gigantas
Loreto
Topolobampo
San Juanico
Insurgentes
La Paz
Pacific Ocean
Ferry routes

Sea of Cortez

Leo and Carmen were sharing coffee early one morning on the veranda overlooking the sea, when they heard an outboard motor to the south. Fishing boats from Agua Verde were common in the waters off Santa Marta, but very few boats approached from the south that early in the morning. When the boat came closer, Leo noticed that it sounded more powerful than a fisherman's panga. When he heard it slow down, he slipped into his sandals.

"I'm going to see who that is," he said as he started down the path to the beach.

Unconcerned, Carmen answered, "I'll be in the garden."

A small bluff rose from the beach on Santa Marta's south side and blocked Leo's view. What he saw when he reached the water was not one, but two, large super pangas, each of them fitted with dual outboard Evinrudes. Each panga had four passengers, and they slowed to an idle as they prepared to land. They shut down for their final glide. One man in each boat stepped up on the bow with a lead rope and jumped off when they drifted into knee-deep water. The men in the sterns dropped anchors.

Leo noticed that neither boat had a registration number on their sterns nor a name on their bows. Local fishermen never registered their pangas, but all of them named their boats after their wives, daughters, or girlfriends. It was unusual to see larger boats with no identification. Leo's level of curiosity rose.

After they came over the side, all eight men began shuffling to shore, avoiding the stingrays as they stirred the sand with their feet. As they neared, Leo recognized the oldest man in the group as his employer. He stepped into the shallows and extended his hand to Oscar Padilla. Oscar grinned, shook hands, and placed his left hand on Leo's shoulder, giving it a friendly squeeze.

Padilla was a distinguished looking man in his late sixties, fit, of medium height with olive-shaded skin. His thinning, graying hair was combed straight back. He wore khaki pants rolled up to his knees and a white dress shirt open at the collar, revealing a thin gold chain draped across his chest. Six of the other men were all in their twenties and wore identical tight black pants and black t-shirts that failed to conceal their muscular physiques. They all wore large gold rings on multiple fingers and heavy gold chains around their necks. None of them smiled. The last man was middle-aged and dressed identical to Oscar.

"It's been a long time, Leo. So good to see you!" Oscar said as they continued to shake hands.

"Yes, sir. I can't remember how many years. Welcome ashore!"

"Thank you, I'm afraid old age makes the trip a bit more trying. We left La Paz two hours before first light. We had flat water all the way, and we made superb time. Of course, these new boats make a hell of a difference. I think I'm ready to stretch my legs on solid ground for a while," he said as they stepped out of the water up on the beach.

"How is life treating you, Leo? You look fit!" he looked Leo up and down.

"Life is good sir. It's just Carmen and me here now. The kids have moved on and scattered to who-knows-where. I haven't been up to Insurgentes in five years, so I feel a little out of touch with the world, but that's the way I like it." Leo slipped back into his sandals.

"I know you well, so I can understand that. I was hoping we could spend the night in the beach house, if that's okay," he glanced up at the rustic building they used as guest quarters.

"Of course, it is. It's just as you left it last time you were here. I put a new roof on it after a monsoon took the old one off."

"Good, good. I'll have the men unload and carry our things up. Let me introduce you to my partner in my new airline business," he said as he turned to the middle-aged man standing next to him.

"Sergio Suarez, this is Leo Sanchez Ruiz. Sergio is the president of the airline as well as a damn good pilot in his own right. He's flown me all over Central America and over to Mexico more times than I can count. We're scouting the coast for a few places where we might put in some landing strips." He used his hand to shade his eyes as he scanned down the beach. "I was hoping we could fit one in here, but now that I see it again up close, there's just not enough flat land. I think we'll take a look around up at Agua Verde."

Leo shook hands with Sergio and asked Oscar, "Why would you want to build a landing strip here?"

"We'll be flying up and down the coast a lot more in the future, and it's always good to have a few places where you can touch down in this God-awful terrain. I don't care much for water landings. I also thought about building a sport fishing lodge up this way, but if we can't land a plane here, that kills that idea."

Leo kicked at a dead sea urchin that had washed up and said, "I like this place just the way it is. If you don't build an airstrip here, it won't hurt my feelings any."

"I'm not surprised. I know how you feel." Oscar took out a white handkerchief and wiped his brow. I'd like to have a look around Agua Verde this afternoon, however. Sergio says he's seen some promising locations up there from the air when he's flown over. Would you care to join us?"

"I would, in fact." He turned to see two of Oscar's men pass by, carrying a large cooler. "I was going to ride up there next week to hire a couple of boys to help with the roundup. If you'd leave me at the beach in front of the village, it'd save me three or four days of riding."

"Fine then." He turned, and they started walking up to the beach house. "We'll get settled in, have ourselves a bite and a short siesta. Meet us down here in a couple of hours, and we'll motor up there for a look around."

Leo walked up to the ranch house, where he had a late breakfast with Carmen. Two hours later, he met Oscar on the beach, where five of them boarded one of the pangas. The four other men seemed content to remain behind.

Leo was awestruck when the twin outboards propelled them out into the open water. The forward thrust as they accelerated pressed him back into the seat. His body had never experienced such a feeling of power and speed. He grabbed for his hat before he lost it, and the wind whipped wildly through his hair, making him feel alive in a way he never had before. He grinned like a kid who'd just kissed his first pretty girl.

The towering cliffs along the coast passed by faster than he imagined they ever could. At full throttle, they cruised head-on into a feeding frenzy, where hundreds, perhaps thousands of pelicans, gulls, boobies, and frigates were diving on a dense school of sardines driven up from the depths by hordes of ravenous yellowtail. The swarm of diving birds parted barely inches in front of the panga, as it sliced through the chaotic scene at full speed. Over the roar of the motors and the shrieking of the birds, Leo could hear Oscar and Sergio belly-laughing at the spectacle. He laughed along with them, sharing their sheer enjoyment.

A half hour later, the panga slowed as they came around a break in the cliffs and entered the flat, calm waters of Bahia Agua Verde. Along the horseshoe-shaped beach was Agua Verde, a small fishing village nestled beneath the backdrop of the three-thousand-foot Sierra Las Gigantas. The village consisted of a dozen shacks and palapas occupied by a handful of fishermen and their families. Transients who came and went with the seasons left various primitive shelters scattered about under the dense stands of date palm trees. A dozen weathered old pangas lay side by side, where a bone-dry arroyo met the water.

"Ahh, Agua Verde. What a beautiful place!" Oscar said as he spread his arms, and they idled toward shore. "We should bring the Doña Guadalupe up here and spend some time, Sergio," he said, referring to his yacht. "What a waste we don't find more time to enjoy that beautiful boat in places like this." He inhaled the magnificent scenery.

They edged the panga up to the sand, and the five of them climbed out. A fisherman was sorting his lines in the shade of the palm trees and watched the men approach. He yelled, "Heh Leonardo, where did you get that panga? You sell the cows and buy a boat?"

Leo grinned at the fisherman, "No, no, no, Gayo. That is Señor Padilla's panga. I'm along for the ride. How are you, amigo?" he stepped forward and embraced his old friend in a man-hug.

Gayo was a jolly, round, heavyset thirty-five-year-old fisherman, born and raised in Puerto Agua Verde. He'd married his cousin, Paloma, at a very young age, and they lived in one of the palapas back a short distance from the beach under some palms with their seventeen-year-old son Christian and two young daughters. His biceps were the size of a normal man's thigh, and he moved with the brute force of a Brahman bull. In a surprising contrast, his handshake was limp as a dead fish, and his eyes twinkled when he spoke. His voice was high-pitched for such an enormous man. He'd been fishing the Cortez coast his entire life, and he often shared his catch with Leo's family when he passed by Santa Marta.

"You found me on a good day, Leonardo! The calamari run started this morning! Very soon, I will have all those racks covered with squid, drying in the sun!" he gestured toward row after row of neatly netted frames. "I'll make enough money to buy a panga like that one!" he said eyeing the fancy boat, laughing. "I'll be rich!"

Leo laughed along with him and said, "I want you to meet Señors Oscar Padilla and Sergio Suarez. They're up from La Paz. Señor Padilla owns Santa Marta. He's looking for a place to build an airstrip."

Gayo shook hands with the two men and seemed unconcerned with landing airplanes. A moment later he said, "You won't be landing airplanes here so close to that mountain." He looked in that direction. "You'll have to go up to Playa Aguja."

Oscar and Sergio were taken by Gayo's comment, and Oscar asked, "Where is Playa Aguja?"

"Around past Solitaire, there," he pointed at a needle-like pinnacle of rock covered with pure white guano, out in the blue water, "over there up the coast a mile. There's a beach with a salt flat behind it, perfect for landing airplanes. A guy was here looking at it a couple years ago. He talked to me about clearing it for him, but I never heard from him again. Just another narco, talking such as they do."

Oscar asked, "Would you mind showing us the place?"

"No, I'd like a ride in that panga while it's here, anyway."

"Let's go then," Oscar replied. "Leo, we'll pick you up here on our way back."

"Fine, I'll go find the boys I need to talk to."

Leo walked inland toward the main village while the others launched the panga.

The panga entered the blue water and turned north. It sliced through the afternoon chop and passed below the vertical pinnacle of rock that Gayo had pointed at from the beach. Oscar looked up at the pure white narrow spire covered with cliff-nesting sea birds, rising three hundred feet straight up from the water, and thought it would make a perfect landmark for a pilot unfamiliar with the area.

They pulled around the next rocky point and saw a flat beach nearly two miles long. It was unlike any other beach Oscar had seen along the mountainous coast. Low dunes concealed what appeared to be a flat plain between the water and the toe of the mountain, a mile inland.

"Pull over," Gayo commanded as he pointed toward a lone mesquite tree up against the boulders. "We'll walk in from here."

Behind the dunes was a salt flat more than a mile long and a half-mile wide. If a piece of it was cleared of the knee-high salt scrub, there would be more than enough room to land an airplane. The ground was hard as asphalt, with spider-webbed cracks from long-ago standing water.

"Perfect," said Oscar. "This is better than what I'd hoped to find! From out on the water, you don't even know it's here. This is perfect!"

Gayo puffed up his chest and said, "I told you!"

"Who owns this land, Gayo?"

Gayo chuckled, "Nobody, it's just wasteland. You know it's worthless if they didn't bother to include it in the Ejido."

"That makes it easy," Oscar commented.

They walked the salt flats long enough for Oscar to explain what he wanted, and he hired Gayo to clear the airstrip.

★★★

Leo walked through the village waving and saying hello to those he passed, until he came to a small palapa off by itself where he knew the two cowboys lived. They were from the ranch country up in the Gigantas but decided to try their hand at fishing and came down to Agua Verde two years before. They were taking siestas in a couple of hammocks when Leo walked up.

"Charro. Paco. Wake up, you bums!" They raised their groggy heads. "Hey, it's me. Leonardo!"

"What?" Charro grumbled.

"It's me, Leo!"

"Okay, okay. Give me a second," Charro swung his feet down off the hammock.

"Come on. You don't see me for a year, and you won't even get out of bed? Where's your manners?"

They were in bare feet, dressed in shorts without shirts. They were bachelors, which seemed to suit them just fine. Charro was twenty-nine and Paco was twenty-seven. Both were handsome young men who had settled nicely into their lives as fishermen.

The boys dragged themselves off the hammocks, and the three of them settled in at a table to catch up on news of the past year. After thirty minutes of chit-chat, Leo sensed it was time to mention the roundup.

"I need to gather the Santa Marta cattle over the next couple months and bring them home, Leo started, glancing back and forth at the two men. I've never laid eyes on many of the animals, as I haven't been down there in more than four years. They're spread out down at Timbabichi, across twenty miles of country. I won't know for sure where they all are until we get out there and find them."

"We?" Charro asked raising his eyebrows.

"That's why I'm here talking to you. I can't gather them by myself."

Charro glanced over at Paco, who was still half-asleep, not paying attention.

"I don't know, Leo. Timing's not so good. Calamari started running yesterday. We're real busy all of a sudden."

"What you think, Paco?"

Paco shrugged, "I don't know. I kind of miss cowboyin. I'm gettin tired of this fishing. Smells bad."

"Hmphh," Charro snorted. "How come you never said anything about that before now?"

"You didn't ask."

Charro shrugged, turning back to Leo. "You'd pay us a good wage?"

"Yeah, and I'd cover room and board."

"Now what does that mean? Last time we worked cows with you, I recall 'room and board' was no more than sleeping on the ground and eating your nasty beans."

"Yeah, but you can stay in the bunkhouse, and Carmen will cook for us when we're there."

"Don't bullshit me, Leo. I know what to expect if we have to gather cows all the way down to Timbabichi."

Charro thought for a moment and said, "If we agree to do it, when would we have to start?"

"About a month. I need to have all those cattle gathered up, sorted and in one place later this winter. I figure it will take us a few months. Antonio will be coming down to drive the herd up to Insurgentes. You still have your horses?"

"They're up in the box canyon somewhere. Easy enough to find."

"Well, what do you think?"

"Tell you what. Give us six weeks. I want to put up a few hundred kilos of squid. If we fish hard, we can do that. Then we'll need a little time to get things ready. Will that work?"

"Works for me. How about you, Paco?" Leo asked. "You're awfully quiet over there."

"Three hundred kilos is a lot of machaca, Charro. I don't know." He yawned.

"We put up more than three hundred last year. Let me worry about the calamari, would you just?"

Paco shrugged and looked away uninterested.

They were quiet for a moment when Charro asked, "How many animals you figure you got down there? I never liked it there in Timbabichi. Nasty place, nothing but banditos, as I remember it."

"God knows. Must be a few hundred head spread out around that country. Depends how well they've done on their own these past five years."

"That's a lot of animals, and you say you haven't laid eyes on most of them? I take that to mean you haven't cut the bull calves. Jesus Christ, Leo. I gave you more credit than that. You probably have a hundred or more bulls down there, all full of piss and vinegar. They aren't going to like your relocation plans one bit. Not to mention those ornery old cows, all dead set in their ways after all those years. Jesus, Leo …" Charro shook his head, letting the thought sink in.

"That's why I need you boys to help."

"You'll be needing more than us."

"Sounds like an adventure," Paco perked up. "I'm getting bored with fishing. I'm up for something different."

"Figures," Charro muttered, looking at his partner.

Just then, Leo heard the big panga returning. He settled matters with the boys and walked down to the beach. He found Oscar and Gayo finalizing their plans for the airstrip, and five minutes later, the big panga was headed south to Santa Marta.

★★★

Carmen prepared dinner for ten, just like old times, when she had three children at home, several ranch hands, and guests staying in the beach house. Guests always marveled at how she prepared such delicious meals without refrigeration, on a two-burner gas stove, with no running water. Oscar thought the meal that evening was better than many he'd recently had at restaurants in the city.

"Thank you, Carmen. We never expected to have such a wonderful dinner tonight!" Oscar exclaimed. "Please help Carmen with the clean-up," he said to two of his men who were seated at the table.

"Leo, Sergio. I have some Cuban cigars and brandy at the beach house. Why don't we walk down there and have a nightcap?"

Leo built a small mesquite fire in the pit, while Oscar poured shots of brandy at a small outdoor table. Sergio came out of the beach house with three Cuban cigars. They sat down on three chairs Leo placed around the fire.

The beach house sat on a flat dune on the edge of the palm forest, overlooking the water. It was shaped like an octagon. Eight treated palm log posts formed the corners. Slats of rough-sawn lumber from the mainland covered the walls. The upper half of each wall raised up on hinges on the inside, and latched to the ceiling, creating expansive windows, wide open to the sea breezes and ocean views. Inside the house was one open spacious room with a massive vertical post in the center, surrounded by eight cots, two large tables, and chairs. The roof was thickly thatched palm ojas, which formed a circular ceiling. Oscar had the building constructed twenty years earlier to accommodate his guests. It hadn't seen much use in recent years.

"I haven't had a cigar since the last time you were here, or any brandy for that matter," Leo said, raising his glass. "If I may ask," he continued, "What's this talk about building a road from San Juanico over here to the cliff?" He looked up at the mountain. "Is that true, or was Antonio pulling my leg?"

"It's true. I've always wanted to make Santa Marta more accessible, and it seems the time is right. Sammy tells me we need to bring our cattle out this way, so we need to improve the trail for that as well. He's hired a crew from San Juanico, and I understand they've started."

"Yes, they have. They started at the top. We hear their dynamite charges all the time, and their foreman has been down here several times. Who are you wanting to make Santa Marta more accessible for?"

Oscar sipped his brandy and pulled on his cigar as he thought about whether he should say more. The rich aroma of the cigars hung in the dead calm evening air, slowly mixing with the mesquite smoke from the fire. Oscar leaned forward in his chair and began unlacing his shoes.

"Please allow me to explain, because it's a very small part of a much larger plan. We are building a new highway from Los Cabos, all the way up to Guerrero Negro, which as you may or may not know, is on the State of Baja Norte's southern line. The government of Baja Norte is well on their way, building a new highway from Guerro Negro up to Tijuana. When the two highways are combined, they will be one thousand miles long, spanning the entire Baja peninsula. We expect the road will be completed no later than 1975, ten years from now," Oscar pulled off both shoes and socks. He buried his bare feet in the sand.

He continued, "The new road, upon completion, will be formally named Mexico Federal Highway One. At that same time, the Territory of Baja California Sur will become Mexico's thirty-first state, and La Paz will be named its capital city. We have met with the highest of PRI officials in Mexico City as well as Presidents Mateos and Ordaz on the matter. We have their full support, including some generous federal funding for the project.

"How is your brandy?" Oscar asked, offering the bottle to Leo. Leo refilled his glass and passed the bottle to Sergio. They were thoughtful for a moment, admiring their cigars, letting what Oscar described sink in.

Leo asked, "What's that got to do with a road on the top of that cliff?"

"Let's just say that in the rush to modernize Baja California, I don't want to see my little piece of it left behind. I know that it sounds selfish, but I'm in the position to pull the money strings, so be it. I've been working on this for twenty years, and it's about to pay off. The Baja Peninsula will never be the same."

The discussion went on past midnight as the three men finished their cigars and drained two bottles of brandy. They watched the fire burn down to bright orange embers and slowly fade away. Oscar and Sergio found their way to their cots in the beach house. Leo, tipsy with his head spinning, somehow kept from stumbling as he walked up to the house. He found Carmen asleep on their spare bed in the yard under a palm tree, where she could catch a breeze. On warm nights they often slept there.

He sat down on the side of the bed and listened to Carmen snoring softly under the moonlight. He took off his clothes and laid down beside her. He kissed her on the neck, stroked her shoulder with his finger. He thought about their life together, the children gone, both of them approaching fifty years of age. With the heaviness of the brandy weighing on him, he rested his head on the pillow next to hers and faded away, his breathing in perfect sync with hers.

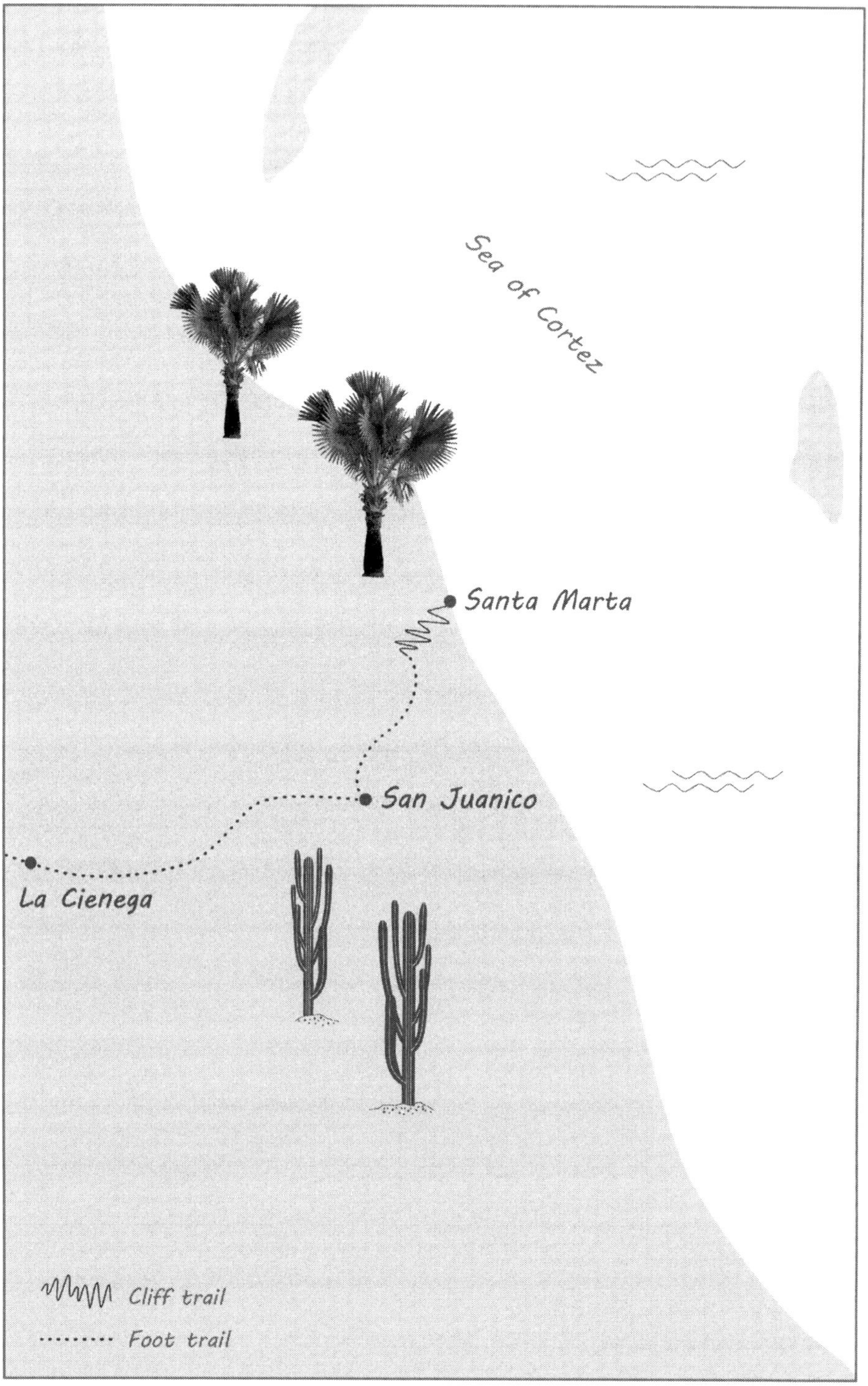
Sea of Cortez
Santa Marta
San Juanico
La Cienega
Cliff trail
Foot trail

The Cliff Trail

A crew of fifteen men and boys from San Juanico had begun working on the trail six weeks earlier. There were two men from La Paz trained in the use of explosives. A base camp consisting of six canvas tents and a palapa shelter were set on the rim of the cliff in a place that offered a spectacular view of the ocean. Far below, at the foot of the cliff, they could see the palm forest and Rancho Santa Marta, nestled up against the broad expanse of blue water.

Felix was growing in his new role and learning to become an effective leader. He showed the crew respect and openly valued their thoughts and opinions. He never asked anyone to do a job he wasn't willing to do himself, with the exception of working with the dynamite. He'd heard gruesome stories about accidents on the road to La Paz, and he wanted no part of handling explosives.

During the brief time before the crew arrived, Felix made three trips up and down the trail to evaluate and prepare for the project. He counted twenty-one switchbacks spread over what he estimated to be a one thousand-foot vertical drop, covering nearly one mile of trail. The original trail had been scratched and carved into the rotten rock face, and was nothing more than a narrow-slanted ledge throughout most of its length. Loose rocks dislodged by his or his mule's footsteps sailed through the air, bouncing off the lower cliff on their quick descent to the flat ground at the bottom. He suffered paralyzing bouts of vertigo that left him crying like a baby, face-down on the ledge, in puddles of vomit. He was only able to overcome his fear, and that horrid reaction, by teaching himself to never, ever look down past his feet.

The crew accomplished wonders in their first six weeks. They widened a half mile of trail to a width of eight feet. Thunderous dynamite charges sliced through walls of rock, sending showers of dangerous debris down the vertical face to sea level. Puffy gray clouds of dust rose hundreds of feet above their heads in towering plumes. The brown-skinned men returned to camp each evening, appearing as pale, clown-like ghosts, their eye slats, rounded nostrils, and open breathing mouths the only visible signs of the human beings beneath the layers of dust. The peace and serenity at Santa Marta were marred by the unnerving sounds and sights of the human-caused earthquakes up above, day after day, from dawn to dusk.

Felix kept a close eye on the precious supplies of food, water, and dynamite. Two young boys made continuous water deliveries, leading four sturdy little burros back and forth between San Juanico and the camp, providing fifty gallons of fresh water every two days. Felix saw, after six weeks, they were running dangerously low on food and explosives. Although he hated to leave the crew, he decided the time had come to re-supply. He'd also promised Sammy he would report back to Insurgentes on a regular basis, and that obligation was on his mind. Over dinner, a time designated to discuss camp business, Felix announced he would be leaving for Insurgentes in the morning, hoping for a ten-day return.

Felix set out at dawn on his mule for the twelve-mile ride to San Juanico, his first trip back to the village in six weeks. He felt good to be traveling again. As he relaxed on the back of the mule, his thoughts turned to Anna Marie. He longed to see her smile, smell her hair, and feel her soft, delicate skin. He dreamed of the moment when they embraced again. It seemed to him like a lifetime. Thoughts of her raw beauty caused him to smile and his mind to drift as he crossed the monotonous desert. The hours passed in a blur, and his dreams came to an abrupt end, the moment he looked up and saw the silhouette of the date palm grove at San Juanico on the horizon.

He arrived late in the afternoon, as the heat was letting up, and he found the village to be eerily quiet. A few children waved half-heartedly to greet him, and the two women he did see barely acknowledged him, as they labored up the path with heavy buckets of water. The stale smell of old mesquite fires hung in the air. He found Alonso at his palapa, appearing tired and depressed. His spirits rose when Felix asked him to have the mules ready for a trip to Insurgentes in the morning. When he heard that, the chubby old man sprung to life and quickly assumed the determined role of a man on a mission. Felix chuckled to himself at the sight of him.

Felix's palapa was off by itself on the outer fringe, across, on the opposite side of the village from Alonso's. He'd built it himself a year earlier when he decided he no longer cared to live in cramped close quarters with his father and young sisters. He had no building materials, so the small frame was made entirely of mesquite posts planted solidly in the ground. They and the roof were covered with date palm ojas. Outside, a handmade table stood next to a fire ring encircled by stones. The palapa was minimal, but it was home, and he cherished his quiet time there.

After he left Alonso, he passed through the village on the way to his palapa. He stopped and chatted with those he met along the way. They were anxious to hear the latest news of their loved ones and curious about progress on the trail. They yearned to learn more about what life was like in that faraway place, although it was only twelve miles away, at the end of a well-worn trail. He patiently filled in those he met with the latest news, and before long, darkness had set in.

Dead tired and relieved to finally settle into his palapa, he built a fire in the fire ring. He sat in the dirt and watched the match catch a twig. As the flames caught and flickered, he heard a soft whistle off to the side, just beyond the firelight. He turned to see who was there. As his eyes adjusted to the shadows, he saw Luisa step reluctantly into the dim light. She hesitated, as if asking permission to come further.

"Felix, can we talk?" she tentatively asked.

"Hi, Luisa. Of course. Sit down. Are the children with you?" He looked behind her, then gestured at the ground on the opposite side of the small fire.

"No, they're with Nora."

Luisa squatted, cross-legged on the other side of the fire. She twisted her hands together in a knot. She looked down, then away. She hadn't spoken to Felix since the day on the trail when he'd told her about Pedro's death. She looked up, and he saw her lip tremble, as she attempted but failed to smile. She was gaunt, far thinner than before. Her normally perfect, beautiful hair was a tangled mess. In the firelight he could make out dark circles under her eyes. Even in the dim light, he could see how much she'd aged. There was no hint of the self-confident, cheerful woman he'd known. He saw she wanted to speak but couldn't seem to find the words, or he thought, perhaps she didn't know where to begin.

Following a long awkward silence, Felix spoke first with the words he had agonized over ever since that fateful day on the trail.

"I never expected to run into you out there like I did. That wasn't how I'd planned to tell you about Pedro. It was the hardest thing I've ever had to do, and I'd spent all those long weeks thinking about how best to tell you. Then, there you were, standing in front of me with that wonderful smile on your face. I lost it. I had all that time to figure out what to say and how to say it, but when the time came, I wasn't able to say it. I'm so sorry. It was pathetic the way I did that. You deserved to hear the news in a more compassionate way. I'm sorrier than you'll ever know. I pray you'll let me make it up to you."

A long pause. Silence, except for the crackling fire and a pack of coyotes howling and yipping in the distance.

Luisa looked down, slowly shaking her head back and forth. The fire light flickered across her grief-stricken face. Still, more silence.

Then, "Oh, Felix. Don't. It's me who's sorry," she blurted, as she continued wringing her hands. She looked up. "I should've never screamed at you, or hit you like that. Can we just forget it happened? Life either moves on, or it doesn't. From what I hear, you've moved on. I'm happy for you. It wasn't long ago I thought of you as just a cocky punk kid. I know now how wrong I was. You're a wonderful young man, and I never saw it coming. I'm so sorry. I'm the one who needs to get it together. I'm the one who has to learn how to get on with life."

Silence again, except for the hushed sounds of the fire crackling and nocturnal insects buzzing in the dead air.

Felix sensed that she wanted to keep going, to say more, but all she did was continue to twist her hands and look from the ground in front of her to the fire and back again. She didn't bother to brush aside the thick strands of hair that had fallen across her face. He thought perhaps she was trying to hide.

Felix ached to hold her, to comfort her, but he held back the urge and asked, "Is there anything I can do to help you? I'm the only man besides Alonso who will be in San Juanico in the coming months. I know you don't care much for him. I'd like it if you'd talk to me, Luisa. Please confide in me. Pedro was my friend. You have no idea how often I thought of you when I was alone out in the desert with the mules.

Pedro would want me to help you. I'll carry water for you tomorrow, before I leave. Anything. I want to help you."

She looked away, out at the darkness. He hoped she didn't take what he said the wrong way. He poked at the embers in the fire with a stick and watched the sparks spiral up.

She looked back at him, "Pedro thought the world of you."

He thought she might cry. He waited for her to say more, and when nothing came of it, he asked, "What's on your mind, Luisa? Please, share it with me."

Nothing but more silence.

Luisa stared down at the thin knotted-up hands in her lap, as if they didn't belong to her.

Without any warning she looked up at him and let go. "I don't know what to do anymore!" She choked as she said it.

The tears gushed out from her eyes and drenched her face, flowing around gaunt cheekbones. She pleaded with her sad eyes. Her once-beautiful face morphed into a twisted contortion that he didn't recognize.

"I've never in my life felt like this. I need to get away from here. It's so fucking hard being here, when I know that Pedro is never coming back. I feel stuck. It's like I've fallen down in the fucking well. It's so dark in there. The walls are slippery and slimy, and I can't climb out. It does no good to scream, because nobody's out there who can hear me. I'm confused, and I'm afraid, and I have two children to think of. It'd be bad enough, if it was just me. If it was just me, I'd say fuck it all, but I can't do that. I just can't do that. Do you understand?"

"I do, Luisa, I do. I felt that way the whole time I was alone in the desert coming back from La Placita. I know exactly what you're saying. I really do."

She nodded and wrapped her arms around herself in a hug, rocked back and forth and choked again. She started to gag and heave.

It was more than he could take. He crawled around to her side of the fire and wrapped his arms around her quivering body. She buried her face in his neck and sobbed. Every trace of tension, terror, doubt, and fear came to the surface and racked her body, until she was completely and utterly spent. He held her as the convulsions faded away and became nothing more than a heartbreaking series of whimpers. They remained embraced.

After a long time, neither of them knew exactly how long, she broke free of him and wiped her face. As she did, she said, “Thank you, I needed that. I’m sorry.”

“Please don’t ever say you’re sorry for that, again. I’m going to remember this time with you for the rest of my life. I’m here for you. Remember that.”

Felix got up, retrieved some wood and put it on the fire. He went into the palapa and returned with a tin coffee pot and placed it on a flat rock on the edge of the flames.

“Where would you go if you left San Juanico? Insurgentes?” he asked as he sat back down on her side of the fire, both their knees crossed, barely touching.

“I thought about it, but I’m not ready for that. At least, not yet. I’ve lived my whole life here. There are too many people in Insurgentes. I don’t think I could make that adjustment. Not now. I’m too fragile. I’m not afraid to admit it.”

“So, what else is there?”

“I want to go to Santa Marta. I think it might be a good place for me and the children. I’ve only seen it once, many years ago, from the top of the mountain, but I remember how it made me feel good looking at it. I remember hearing the sea birds and the waves when the wind blew just right. My father and I ate lunch there, just him and me. It was my birthday, and it was all so beautiful. That’s what I need right now. I need some beauty in my life again. I’m afraid that I’m dying here, Felix. I can’t explain how that feels.”

“You already did.”

Felix looked her deep in the eye for the first time, and they said nothing as each of them studied the other. Their eyes were only inches apart. Luisa felt good for the first time in many long weeks. She needed his eye contact and his presence. She felt a sense of security. She stopped twisting her hands and stared right back at him, prolonging the moment.

She looked away, over her shoulder, “Do you think I’m crazy, wanting to go somewhere I’ve never been before at a time like this?”

"Not at all. Santa Marta is just like you say. It's a beautiful place. I've stayed there three times, and I've gotten to know Leo and Carmen. They're nice people, and they have plenty of room. There's three empty bedrooms where their kids used to stay, an empty bunkhouse and even a beach house they use for guests. That's where I stay when I'm there. They have a garden like nothing you've ever seen before – chickens, pigs, goats – and a hot spring big enough for five or six people to take a bath in at the same time. Carmen was telling me how she could use some help now that she and Leo are down there alone. I don't think it's a crazy idea at all."

"Would you take me there? It's not far out of your way is it?"

Felix thought for a moment, "I could do that. I'll be back in a week. You could ride with us back to the camp. From there, I'll take a few days off, bring you down to the ranch and introduce you to Carmen and Leo." He reached for the coffee pot and poured hot water into a cup of Nescafé. He sipped it and offered it to Luisa.

"Do you think so?" she took the cup and shared his coffee.

"I do. It wouldn't be any trouble. All you'd need to do is have your things ready to go when I get back from Insurgentes. Can you do that?"

"Oh, dear God. Yes Felix. Thank you!" She spilled the cup, leaned over, wrapped her arms around him and kissed him so hard on the cheek that it shocked him.

He blushed. He couldn't remember feeling so good about anything in a long time. He held her as the fire burned down, and she slowly started to relax.

★★★

Two days later, sunburned and covered in trail dirt, Felix stepped through the front door of the Ejido office. Anna Marie looked up from her desk and cracked a smile. "Well, look who's back," she said as she rose from her chair.

"Hi, chiquita," Felix removed his hat. His long, filthy black hair was matted to the sides of his head, but his smile was bright. He stepped around her desk with his arms open, and she reached up to kiss him. She folded her arms neatly around his neck.

"Mmm, it's been a long time."

"Way too long. You smell wonderful."

"You smell like something a dog would roll in," she laughed.

"Nice to see you. You have no idea how many times I've thought about kissing you again."

"Me too, you beautiful hunk of a man. How about some lemonade?"

"Lots of ice."

"Have a seat," she said with a wave of her hand as she crossed the room to a small refrigerator.

"Is the boss here?" he asked.

"He's somewhere in town at a meeting. I expect him back soon. Tell me all about what's going on. Are you building the trail? And things in San Juanico. How is that? How long will you be here?" she fired off the questions as she handed him the lemonade.

He wasn't used to someone talking so fast. He took a long drink and finished the whole glass in a series of uninterrupted swallows. He tried to think.

"I have to turn around and go back tomorrow," he answered, unsure of himself.

"What do you mean? We have one night together? That's it?" She stopped where she stood, with an angry look on her face. "I thought you were going to try a little harder than that."

"I'll be gone for ten days as it is. Its four days just to get here, four days going back, and a day each here and in San Juanico. The crew hasn't had a day off since we started. It's not like I can take a vacation while they're out there working their asses off." He hadn't thought this part through very well.

As she was about to respond, Sammy came through the door.

"Heh, Felix my boy. Good to see you!" he said. "We've got to talk. Tell me, how's it going out there? Should we go down to the cantina for something to eat?"

Felix glanced at Anna, then back at Sammy, "Sure, I haven't eaten anything today."

"Let's go then. You can finish up with things here later."

Felix saw Anna's lips tighten into an ugly straight line before she turned her back to them. Sammy draped one arm around Felix's shoulder and said, "You're looking well. The new job must be agreeing with you." And they were out the door.

"I've got good news," Sammy began as they sat down in the cantina. "Oscar came up with more money for the San Juanico road, and I'm going to buy some new equipment for that project. There'll be a dozer, a grader, a loader, and a couple of dump trucks. That's more than enough to start. I'll need to find a few men to operate it, so it'll be a month or two before it's all in place. What we really need is for you to finish up the trail down to Santa Marta. How's that going?"

"We're ahead of schedule, at least the way I'd planned it. I think we might be able to finish it in a month, maybe six weeks."

"Wonderful! Oscar was there at Santa Marta not long ago, and he's all fired up. So, everything's working in our favor."

"I want to turn around and go back first thing in the morning. Alonso is gathering supplies as we speak. I'll give Anna all the paperwork, and you might not see me again until the trail's finished."

"Great. You have no idea what a relief that is. Is there anything special you need from me?"

"There is. I'd like to give the guys a little bonus to help keep their spirits up."

"What are you thinking? A couple of professional gals from La Paz?" he joked.

"How about two cases of Nescafé and a kilo of fresh tobacco?"

Sammy thought for a moment. "I'll do you one better on the tobacco. We have a new shipment of American cigarettes in the warehouse. I'll call over there and tell them to load up four cases of Pall Malls along with the Nescafé. That should keep them happy for a while!"

Felix grinned, "They aren't going to believe it when I show up with store-bought cigarettes. I can't thank you enough!"

He still had a grin on his face when the waitress laid a plateful of steak in front of him.

★★★

Felix and Anna took a walk down the lonely ranch road that evening. They needed to clear the air in the short time they had together, but neither of them knew where to begin. They made small talk and avoided the subject until Anna stopped, turned toward him and said, “Seeing you for a night every few months isn’t going to cut it, Felix. At this stage of my life, I’m looking for more than that. You already told me it wouldn’t work for me to go with you, so where does that leave us? Or is there an ‘us’ anymore? I don’t think so. You tell me.”

Felix suddenly faced a serious dilemma. He’d been totally consumed, adjusting to his new role in the working world. He’d done little more than think about Anna in a dreamy, boyish sort of way. He hadn’t given any thought to relationships or commitments. He was being confronted unexpectedly by a woman far more experienced in life than he. He looked up at the blanket of stars for an answer. He started to say something, but he wasn’t sure what it was, and he stuttered.

He looked down at his feet and said, “I-I don’t know. I’m sorry. As hard as I try, I can’t figure out how to do this.”

“Goddammit, I did it again!” she said, put her hands on her hips and kicked at the dirt. “I let myself dream and want something I can’t have.” The two of them stood on the deserted road under the stars looking at each other.

She blinked a few times and reached into her back pocket for her cigarettes and shook one out. She handed him the pack. “Go ahead, you might as well have one too.”

They lit their smokes and resumed walking. There were tears dripping down across her face.

That night, they made love only once. Neither of them said much. A feeling of finality lingered in the air. Felix left her at the door in the morning with a peck of a kiss on her cheek. She stared straight ahead with ice-cold eyes, clenching her jaw.

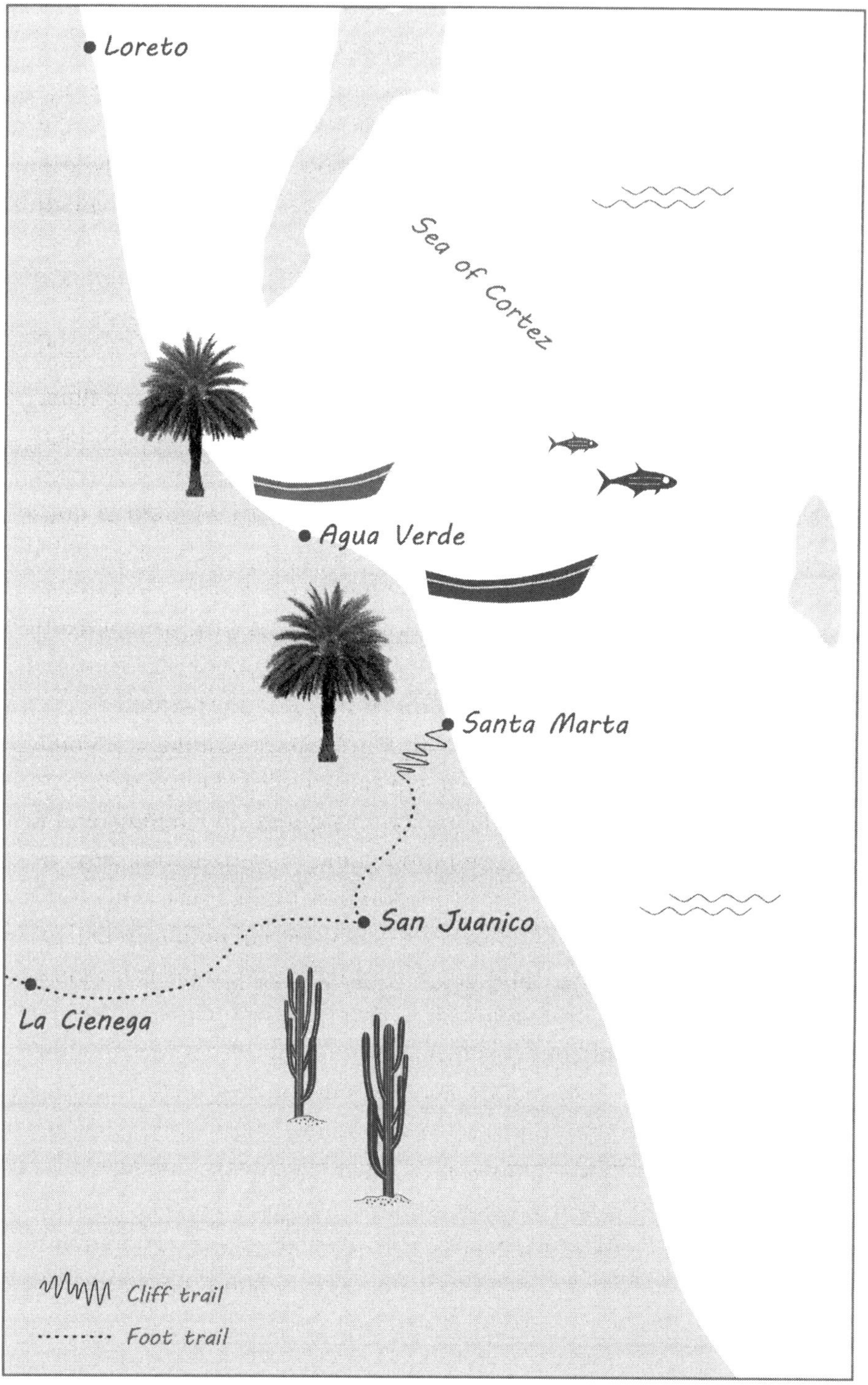
Loreto
Sea of Cortez
Agua Verde
Santa Marta
San Juanico
La Cienega
Cliff trail
Foot trail

Agua Verde

The squid were running hard and fast each night in the deep waters outside Bahia Agua Verde. The drying racks were filling up with kilo after kilo of sweet, salted calamari meat. Four young boys were building more racks out of mesquite posts and old fishing nets. The women cleaned, sliced, and salted the meat, and laid out a steady new supply of steaks on the racks each day. A rancid stench from several tons of guts and discarded tentacles and other body parts rose from the placid waters of the bay, where the men field-dressed their catch each morning. Seabirds by the tens of thousands feasted on the spoils and lazed around on every cliff, rock, and square foot of beach to be had during the heat of the day. Nobody cared about the oppressive smell, because it reminded them of money. There were very few ways to earn money in Agua Verde, and the seasonal squid, when and if they came, were a God send.

Gayo, the heavyset fisherman who agreed to build the airstrip for Oscar, was the de-facto leader of the small group of men and boys who launched their pangas each evening. He took the others out to where he'd discovered a massive concentration of squid. The half-dozen banana-shaped old pangas with two men or boys in each fished within sight of one another, just off a submerged shallow rock shelf that dropped off vertically into three hundred feet of water. Each panga had two or more kerosene lamps mounted on their bow and stern. The light attracted schools of squid from a mile or more away. The squid remained in the deep water, but as they migrated across the sandy bottom toward the light, they ran into the three hundred-foot wall of rock. They milled about by the thousands, directly below the pangas at the base of the wall. The fishermen anchored their pangas on top of the shelf above and dropped their baited hooks into the voracious mass of thirty to forty pound octopus-looking creatures. Spirits were high, for a change, in Agua Verde.

Gayo not only led the fishermen, he fished hard himself. His son Christian was by his side every waking moment. Day in and day out, the father-son team caught twice as much calamari as the other pangas.

They were so successful they towed an empty panga behind them each night and filled both boats with their catch. Gayo trained all the men in the quickest and most efficient techniques of field-dressing the squid. When he finished with the cleaning, he supervised the boys building the new racks and the women preparing the meat. By midday, Gayo and Christian might make it home for a meal and a few hours of sleep before doing it all over again. The calamari run would last no longer than a month. Gayo pushed the others hard and told them they could catch up on their sleep after the calamari were gone.

Among the fishermen were Charro and Paco, the two transplanted cowboys. They came to start new lives and learn how to fish for a living. The villagers of Agua Verde were mostly accepting of migrant fishermen, who came and went with the seasons, and welcomed the two young men into their small village. They gave the boys their first panga and sold them an old motor for next to nothing. The villagers helped them acquire all the tools of the trade and patiently taught them the skills required of fishermen. Within a matter of days after arriving in Agua Verde, the boys built themselves a palapa off by itself on a far end of the village. Charro and Paco were now in their second calamari season. They had proven themselves as fishermen, as well as being valued members of the community, which led the villagers to look beyond their differences.

The sun was tipping past the western edge of the high Gigantas, one blistering hot late afternoon at the height of the calamari season. Charro and Paco were sprawled naked across their elevated bed in the dark shadows of their palapa. Charro woke first and laid his arm across his eyes to block the light. Two hard weeks of squid fishing every night was beginning to catch up with him. He groaned as he stirred. He turned and put his feet on the ground. He ran his strong, calloused hands through his tangled hair and hopped off the bed, slipping his bare feet into a pair of canvas shorts. He walked outside a good distance over to the base of a date palm tree and relieved himself. Stretching, he looked around beyond the camp and walked stiffly back under the palapa canopy, then he picked up a coffee pot, filled it, and placed it on a small gas flame. He went back in the palapa and saw that Paco hadn't moved. Sitting on the side of the bed, Charro shook Paco by the shoulder.

"Wake up. Time to get with it!" There was no response. He shook Paco again and brushed his hair to the side from over his face. When there was still no response, he started rubbing Paco's back. "Come on, coffee's on. I wanted to sleep, too, but it's time."

Paco stirred and turned his head to Charro, who smiled at him. "Keep rubbing my back, and I'll think about getting up."

"I'll keep it up for a minute, but then you're out of there, even if I have to drag you!"

"Um-hmm." He closed his eyes again.

When Charro smelled the coffee, he took Paco by the arm and pulled until he was in a sitting position. He walked across the room, picked up Paco's shorts, and threw them at him, hitting him in the chest. "Put those on, and I'll make some dinner. It's gonna be another long night."

Paco slowly rose, clutching his pants in his hand, and walked across the palapa and out to the palm trees, where he stood and relieved himself. "Is there any water in those wash buckets?"

"Yeah, they're full. You're the only damned fisherman I know who takes a bath before going fishing. An hour from now, you'll be cutting rotten bait and wiping your hands all over yourself. What good is a bath gonna do you?"

"It's gonna make me clean. I like to be clean, and I like to smell good, if you haven't noticed."

"How could I not notice? I live with you!"

"So, lay off. It's what I do," Paco said as he walked over to the three buckets full of clean, fresh water that sat under a low-hanging palm branch. He leaned over, picked up an empty tin can, filled it, and dumped it over his head. He repeated this three times, then lathered up with a bar of soap.

While Paco was busy with his bath, Charro was pouring coffee and looking through the food they had on a shelf on the outside wall of the palapa. A rusty red Coca-Cola cooler sat on the ground next to the table. He opened the lid to see their precious block of ice had shrunk down to nothing.

"Fuck me. No ice!" He turned to Paco and asked, "What do you want to eat? We don't have much."

"Anything but squid," Paco said, while rinsing off, pouring a can of water over his head. "I'd rather wither away before touching another piece of calamari! What else we got?"

"Eggs and machaca. We got four eggs."

"That machaca have squid in it?"

"No, it's cabrilla. Paloma gave it to me. She knows we don't have time to cook," referring to Gayo's wife.

"That'd be good then," Paco said as he poured himself a coffee.

"Put your pants on. The neighbor kids might come by. Doesn't look right when you walk around naked all the time."

"I'm gonna be glad when this calamari run is over," Paco said, slipping into his pants. "I keep thinking about getting the horses and going after those cows for Leo. That'll be a good change of pace. No more stinking fish guts for a while. I'll smell a lot better."

"Yeah, you'll smell like cow shit, horse piss, and sweat. Out there on the trail you won't have a bar of soap and a bucket of fresh water to pour over your head every morning. I won't want to listen to you bitchin about it when we get on with the round-up. I'll remind you how good you had it when we were fishing."

Paco shook his head and walked over to the small mirror hanging on the wall. He ran a nylon comb through his shiny black hair and admired himself as he patted the last stray hairs into place. "Hurry and finish up with that food. I'm ready to go fish!"

★★★

Gayo sucked a breath into his huge barreled chest as he straightened up from sorting his fishing lines in the bow of his panga. He looked around and saw the six other pangas were anchored in the shallows with two men in each, ready to launch. As the long dusky shadows spread across the idyllic crescent-shaped beach, Gayo took a moment to study the sky out over the open water beyond the bay. As was his custom, he stopped what he was doing and gathered his thoughts before saying a few words to the men.

"The last two days have been the best! Every panga was full this morning. That never happens. You did good!" He looked over his shoulder. "I don't like the looks of that sky off to the south," he continued. "We might see a storm tonight, so we need to be ready to get back inside the bay if we see one coming. I'll shout a warning if need be. Keep your eyes and ears open out there, and let me know if you see something I missed." He glanced around for acknowledgment.

Looking to the south, one of the older fishermen spoke up, "Maybe we should hold off and see what comes of that dark spot down there." A few of the others nodded in agreement.

"What are you thinking, Santo?" Gayo asked him. "You're just tired, like the rest of us. You want an excuse for a night off? We can't afford to pass up a run like we had last night. We'll all keep our heads up and our ears to the wind. At the first sign of trouble, we're back in the bay. It's only five minutes out."

"If you say so," a hesitant Santo answered with uncertainty. "I promise I won't be waiting for your orders. If I don't like the looks of things, I'll be the first one to pull anchor. The rest of you would be wise to follow my lead on this one. Gayo's a helluva a good fisherman, but he takes too many chances. A panga full of smelly old squid isn't worth drowning over."

"I'm no fool, Santo. You know that. If I see trouble coming, I'll cut and run just as soon as the rest of you. Until then, I'm going after them. Starting now," he said as he motioned for his son, Christian, to climb up in the bow. In his left hand, he held the bowline of the empty panga floating alongside, and with his right hand he pulled on the starter rope. It kicked in on the first pull, he shifted into forward and slowly motored out from the beach, towing the empty boat. One by one, the other six pangas followed.

Twenty minutes later, all seven of the small vessels were anchored on the same rock shelf as they had every other night for the past two weeks. The skies to the south were black as coal dust. The skies to the west were glowing orange, highlighted by the dark ragged shadowy peaks of the Gigantas in the foreground. Nobody knew which way the storm might be headed, but they all hoped it would drift west toward the Pacific, or east to the mainland, just not to the north in their direction. At the time they anchored, the storm appeared to be stationary and remained well off to the south. The small group of hopeful fishermen lowered their baited hooks and immediately began jigging their three-hundred-foot lines.

A repeat of the night before seemed likely. In less than a minute of each baited hook reaching the bottom, all fourteen fishermen had squid on. The squid were in the thirty to forty-pound range and fought well beyond their weight. Each of the voracious animals had multiple three-foot-long tentacles that waved in unison, creating an enormous downward force. The fishermen's arms bulged and swelled with an effort that rocked the pangas back and forth on their anchors. On occasion, one of them would shriek with joy or excitement at the strength or size of their catch.

They clung to their lines with their thickly calloused hands, allowing the huge squid to run while the line slipped through their fingers. So many miles of line had passed through each of their hands their skin was hardened like saddle leather. The nylon line that would burn through normal human flesh only made a soft whirring sound through their fingers, as the squid made repeated fifty-foot desperate runs. The men hung on and wore the formidable creatures down through sheer exhaustion, and only then were they able to lift them to the surface. Once alongside the panga, they would gaff the heavy animal with a wood-handled sharpened hook and lift them into the boat. With a forceful whack of a club to the head, the lifeless animals were thrown onto the bloodstained floors of the wooden boats. The stench in each of the boats was overwhelming. It would cause the average person to puke.

An eerie calm enveloped the fishermen this night as they went about their intense efforts to boat as many squid as humanly possible. The rippled water around them turned abnormally flat and placid, as the dead squid piled up in the bottoms of their pangas. The flat water made for an easy rhythm, but something wasn't right. It falsely reassured the fishermen, and they let down their guard. Over their shoulders and behind them to the south, the blackness crept closer.

After landing yet another squid and tossing it in the bottom of his panga, old Santo was the first of the fishermen to pause and study the southern sky. He saw a layer of light sky blanketing the black. He smelled rain. He didn't bait his hook but held it in his hand while he pondered what he was seeing. A single puff of wind crossed over his face before the thick air went still again.

"Thick air, this isn't good," he thought.

Gayo bellowed, "Christian, pull up. Cut your line, now!" He took out a knife and sliced his own line while yelling "Chubasco! Pull anchor. Go for the bay! Go for the bay! Now! Go for the bay!" He pulled on his starter rope and set his motor in neutral on an idle. He lifted his thirty-foot anchor line hand-over-hand up from the rock shelf and yelled again. "Pull up! Pull up! Pull anchor! Stop fishing, head for the bay! Chubasco! Now!" he kept screaming.

Each of the men stopped fishing. Knives came out and each man cut his line as the first of the cold raindrops hit, followed closely by the waves. The pangas began to rock dangerously in the sudden turbulence. The waves were small at first but grew into a chaotic chop, some of them six feet high in the blink of an eye. Each engine started, and each anchor was raised. Each motor was shifted into gear, and all of the pangas, heavy with squid, turned to face the bay at the same time. All of their throttles were fully opened, and they retreated just ahead of the worsening, treacherous waves. All but one.

Charro's heart skipped a beat, and his stomach rolled in his gut when he hit the throttle too hard and his old motor flooded. Monster wave after monster wave crashed down and across his panga. He frantically pulled on the starter rope, but he knew the sound and feel of a flooded carburetor. He looked over his shoulder to see Paco gripping the rails with every ounce of strength he had in his thick arms. He screamed over the crashing waves, "Hold on, don't let go! Stay with the boat!"

Paco's face contorted in horror and turned unnaturally white. He screamed incoherently. He started crying. Neither he nor Charro knew how to swim. There were no safety rings or life preservers in the panga. There was nothing they could do but hold on and let fate take its course. With the huge pile of thirty and forty-pound squid in the bottom of the heavy old boat, they were doomed. Two different waves hit them at bad angles. The panga rolled. Top side down.

The other six pangas reached the mouth of the bay where the water, at least for the moment, remained placid and still. As he eased back on the throttle to take measure of the group, Gayo was the first to notice there was one panga missing. He counted once, then again, as they all glided side by side toward temporary safety.

"Charro! Where's Charro?" he yelled. He turned and looked behind him, to see nothing but violent waves. "Son of a bitch!" he yelled as he whipped his panga around and headed back into the storm at full throttle.

"Throw out the squid!" he yelled at Christian. He only had to say it once. Christian was all over the boat, tossing squid left and right into the surf as if they weighed no more than a feather. In less than a minute, Christian was standing on the bow platform with one of his arms wrapped tightly around the bow-rope, as if riding a ferocious bull, watching for any sign of the lost panga in the frothing mess. They came to the rock shelf where they'd all been anchored a moment before, but there was no sign of the missing panga. Gayo somehow circled the rock shelf as the waves crashed over him. He knew it was only a matter of one rogue wave before he took on a fatal amount of water.

"There! Over there!" Christian screamed as he pointed with his free hand. Gayo looked and saw the overturned panga with one man clinging to the bow. "Christian, take the motor!"

Christian flew across the panga with the speed and grace of a gazelle and took hold of the tiller, steering it the best he could toward the other boat. Gayo cut the anchor off its line and tied the line around his waist.

"Pull up close!" he yelled as he dove head-first over the side, just as another monster crashed down on the over-turned panga and obscured it from sight.

The besieged panga never came back up. Christian managed to keep his panga upright in a trough. Gayo's head and arms broke surface where the other panga had been mere seconds before. He went under twice, three times more, and Christian gritted his teeth. Split seconds seemed like forever. They were one badly angled wave away from an untimely end, when Gayo surfaced with a limp body under his arm. With his free arm, he pulled himself along the anchor rope back to the side of the panga. Christian had no choice but to pull the shift lever up to neutral, let go of the tiller, and reach over the side. He risked being thrown into the surf where they'd all perish, but he gave it not a thought.

Christian extended his arm as far as he could reach. A huge wave brought Gayo right up alongside the boat, and Christian grabbed ahold of the belt around the waist of the lifeless body. He pulled with every bit of strength he had, and he watched as Charro spilled over the side onto the flooded floor of the panga. He looked back at the water, just in time to see Gayo dive again.

Christian bent over and pulled Charro up to a slouched sitting position to keep his head above the water on the floor. He fingered Charro's mouth and gave him a desperate quick series of hard slaps on the center of his back until Charro coughed and spit out sea water. He turned his attention back to Gayo and saw him struggling to climb back into the panga. He reached over and latched on to Gayo's two-hundred-seventy-pound frame and miraculously pulled him aboard. Gayo flopped on the floor like a beached whale in a puddle, and his eyes rolled up in his head.

Christian flew back around and grabbed the tiller at the same time that he threw the shifting arm down to forward position. He had to somehow steer and guide the half-submerged panga back inside the bay. With a glance, he calculated the timing and the rhythm of the surf. He was able to turn the heavy lumbering boat in the direction of the prevailing waves, as if he was on a surfboard, even though he'd never surfed in his life. Instead of taking on the waves, he worked with them. After what seemed like forever, Christian reached the bay. He was still standing, with an iron grip on the tiller stick, when he saw a panga ahead of him, circling in thick sheets of pounding cold rain.

Old Santo, with his fishing partner in the bow, brought his panga over to Christian's side. They couldn't see the two men lying on the bottom of Christian's panga, but he tossed over a line to hold them together. "What can I do?" Santo yelled.

"Take these two men. They're drowning in here. I've got to bail, or I'll sink. Hurry!"

Seconds later, Charro and Gayo were in Santo's panga, where he and his partner went to work. Both men regained consciousness and were sitting upright on the floor by the time Christian finished bailing. Both pangas motored slowly back to the beach, where the entire village was waiting in the ferocious wind and thick sheets of pounding rain. They resembled a pathetic mass of half-drowned rodents as they came forward to help Christian and Santo beach their boats.

"Paco is gone," was all Christian could say through his clenched jaw when he was close enough for them to hear above the crashing surf. His tears were unseen through the treacherous sheets of rain. The villagers stared ahead with saddened eyes. They lost another one of their own to the depths of the sea.

★★★

The rain and the wind were relentless. For hours, the violent torrent plummeted the flimsy shacks and palapas that were the village of Agua Verde. The entire population of the village sought shelter under the rocky overhanging ledge on the side of a bluff behind the arroyo, as their homes were blown away by the wind and crushed by collapsing palm trees. The normally dry arroyo in the center of the village became a deluge of chocolaty water rushing toward the sea. Palm logs floated by like match sticks. The run-off would continue for days as the high Gigantas above the village shed vast volumes of water from across the slopes and canyons. The noise was deafening. Everyone, young and old alike, hunkered down under the ledge and waited.

Six hours later, the storm passed, just as the first rays of light appeared from the east across the Sea of Cortez. The dull, heavy clouds drifted away, almost as quickly as they had come. The crude shelters the villagers called home were gone. Only three pangas were anywhere to be seen, and they were washed up well above the beach, in what was left of the tangled palm groves. Even in the normally peaceful bay, the waves broke and crashed high above the beach. The women consoled and spoke softly to frightened children. One by one, the men appeared and walked quietly about to survey their losses. Everywhere they looked was devastation and total destruction. Nothing had been spared. The beach was cluttered with unimaginable trash.

Christian, Santo, and Gayo met on the beach. For a few moments, they said nothing and simply stood dumbfounded in the pale dawn light.

"In all my years, I've never seen anything like this," Santo whispered, shaking his head. "There's nothing left!"

"We're still alive," Gayo said as he scanned the destruction.

"Not Paco. He isn't alive," Christian was quick to say with a hint of anger. "He's gone, and we won't know about the rest of us until the sun comes up and we start counting."

Gayo turned to look at his son. It was his first chance to study the boy after the harrowing rescue out in the sea. He saw not a seventeen-year-old boy, but the young man he had become. He looked at the wise old Santo off to his other side and said, "We have to rebuild Agua Verde. It's up to us. The women, the children, the others, they need us. When the sun comes up, we need to gather the village and start working together like we never have before."

Christian nodded. "I'm going to go find Charro. I want to partner up with him."

Wise old Santo said, "Let's begin by gathering everyone together and finding something to feed the people. Then we start to work."

Gayo looked down the beach to his right. There was no trace of the drying racks, which held thousands of kilos of calamari only hours before. The good fortunes of Agua Verde were completely lost in the storm.

★★★

A week following the hurricane, which only brushed up against Santa Marta as it passed out on the open water, Leo set out to locate his small herd of horses somewhere out in the surrounding canyons. He'd decided to head out on his own, ahead of the round-up, to locate and count the Santa Marta cattle herd, at least that part of it he could find across the many miles of open desert range to the south. He needed to find his two best horses and prepare them for the trip. He sought a tall bay gelding he'd broken and trained five years before, along with a ten-year-old pale spotted mare. He knew both horses well and had spent many months working with each of them.

Leo rode a burro out to the canyons where he knew he'd find the horse herd sooner or later. He led a second burro that carried his saddle and tack. He left Santa Marta at daylight and reached the canyon he thought the horses would be in at midday. The canyon smelled like heaven. Flowers had followed the rain, and they blanketed the rock-strewn slopes in their colorful splendor. He inhaled the over-powering aroma and couldn't get enough of it into his lungs. The sweet scent gave him a sense of well-being and caused him to smile. He pulled back on the halter lead and held the burro back to absorb the moment.

He found the eleven-horse herd he was after, scattered loosely across a half mile of wide, rugged canyon, just where he'd thought they'd be. He spotted the bay gelding up high on a slope, grazing in a patch of Palo Verde trees. He got off the burro, tied both of them to a tree, and took a halter with a lead rope out of the pack saddle. He slung it over his shoulder. He walked up to the gelding, speaking softly, haltered him easily, and led him back to where he'd left the burros.

Leo brushed the embedded cactus needles and mesquite thorns from the horse's back. The gelding stood without moving, his head lowered. For them, it was as if the years had never passed and they were back at Santa Marta, both several years younger. Leo couldn't stop smiling and talking to his old friend. He saddled the horse and fitted it with a brilliant silver bridle, a gift from his father. The gelding never flinched when Leo tightened the cinch and climbed up on its back. He laid a stiff, coiled rawhide rope across the horn and nudged the gelding forward in the direction of the main herd, where he hoped to find the pale spotted mare.

As the afternoon light faded, Leo rode into the ranch yard, where Carmen saw him approaching from the veranda.

"You found your horses and brought them back in a nice neat package! I almost forgot what a good-looking animal that gelding is. I raised that horse from a foal right there in the corral." She glanced at the enclosure. "I wonder if he remembers me." She came forward and stroked its snout. The horse closed its eyes in pleasure.

"You plan to leave in the morning?" she asked, looking over her shoulder at her husband.

"I do."

"There's a big moon tonight. Why don't we go down and soak in the springs? It'll be your last hot bath for a while."

"Let me put these animals up, have something to eat, and we can walk down there after it gets dark."

Following a meal of bean burritos and tomato green bean salad, Carmen and Leo walked down to the beach and over to the hot springs, just after the moon had risen. The moon was a day from full and caused them to cast distinctly clear shadows as they approached the spring. A great horned owl watched from a ledge on the bluff not far above them. They took off their clothes and laid them on the stone bench that sat off to the side of the pool. Carmen untied the ribbon behind her neck and ran her hands through her long hair, causing it to tumble across her shoulders. The streaks of gray had become more prominent in the last few years, but Leo often remarked how it only complimented her beautiful face and shapely body. With a contented smile, she lowered herself into the warm water next to where Leo was already seated.

"All these years, Leo. Where did they go?" she asked, settling in beside him.

Leo sighed, "Leave it to you to remind me. As if these aches and pains weren't enough of a reminder. Do you realize how lucky we are? How many people have anything like this life we have here?"

"We are lucky. We've been lucky ever since the day we met. Lucky to live here at Santa Marta all these years. Lucky to have raised three wonderful children. And now that we're getting old, we're lucky to have each other, and to be as healthy as we are. Not many can say that. So many folks pass on before they reach our age."

"Good living, Carmela. It comes from good living, and I've got you to thank for so much of it." He slid a little closer and their bodies touched. He reached back and laid his arm around her shoulders.

"How long will you be gone?" she asked as she gazed across the ocean and watched the moonlight sparkling on the water.

"Hard to say. Its two long days, maybe more, just straight through to Timbabichi. Fifty miles of up, down, back and forth with only a goat trail here and there. That's why I never made the effort to get down that way. It's not worth checking on those scattered-out old cows when they don't have anywhere to go."

"So, what do you think? A week? More?"

"I'd say two or three. There's about a dozen different springs spread out over twenty miles around Timbabichi where those animals have to go to water every day. I've got to visit every one of them and see which springs are being used and how many head at each one of them. If they've done any good at all these past five years, there could be more than three hundred animals, counting cows, calves, yearlings, and bulls." He leaned into her and nuzzled her neck.

He went on after taking a moment to inhale her fragrance. "The bulls are going to be the biggest pain in the ass. I don't even want to think about it. I wish I'd rounded them up every year like a normal operation and cut them while they were young. I can't blame anyone but me, I should've told Sammy I needed help with the herd. But I didn't, and now I'm gonna have to live with it. I'm lucky to have Charro and Paco coming. As good as they are though, I'm not sure I won't need more help than that. If I had a way of getting word over to Insurgentes, I'd ask Antonio to bring a couple extra hands with him and come a little sooner."

"On this trip, will you be moving cows by yourself?" she turned to study his features in the bright moonlight.

"No, I doubt I'll be working any cattle. If I find a spring with just a few animals, I might push them over to a larger group, but I'm more interested in getting a count and finding out where they are."

They were quiet for a moment. He stroked her neck with the hand he had rested on her shoulder, then said, "To hell with those cows, I want to spend my last night here, enjoying you."

He reached for her breast and cupped it in his hand. He bent down and covered it with his mouth. Carmen leaned back and sighed. She ran her fingers through his hair and held him in place. Her body arched as his other hand brushed across her belly and found the place between her legs. She buried her tongue in his mouth. They enjoyed each other for most of an hour in the pleasing hot water. They walked back up to the ranch house, where they made love on their bed, out in the yard, under the big bright moon.

★★★

Felix was in a foul mood when he and Alonso reached Rancho San Juanico with their overloaded string of mules. He went straight to his palapa and built a cooking fire. He searched for food he thought he had but didn't. He became angry and threw his hat across the palapa down on the dirt floor. He couldn't erase the image of Anna's face as she watched him leave her house two days before. He felt like punching someone, so he made two fists with his hands and gritted his teeth.

She barely said goodbye, and she didn't even bother to hide the angry look on her face. As difficult as it was for him, he tried to convince himself not to take it personally. She'd had a hard life long before he came along. He tried his best, over and over again, to remind himself of that fact. In the end, as he rode away from her door, he turned one last time to look back and wave. She didn't even bother to raise her hand. He felt foolish holding his hand in the air. He nodded his head at her and fought to hold back the tears. He was hurt when he saw her eyes open, dry, and hard. He turned his back and rode away.

★★★

"Welcome home!" Luisa said with a radiant smile as she, Juan Carlos, and Maricela walked up to his cooking fire. She looked like a different person from the distraught woman who visited him at this same place five days before.

She startled him out of his ugly funk, and he said, "Luisa! I just got back. I was thinking about you," he lied. He would've rather been thinking about Luisa, and he surprised himself when he realized it.

"The children are excited! Are you still taking us with you?"

"Yes, I'm planning on it. I'll get organized here this evening, and we'll set out first thing in the morning. Alonso will be going with us as far as the camp tomorrow. All the mules are packed heavy, so I'll find a couple of burros for you and the children to ride. We'll give Juan Carlos his own burro, you and Maricela share the other one. Okay?"

"Yes, of course!" Luisa replied through a beautiful smile.

Felix caught himself staring at her sparkling teeth and her tongue as she unconsciously ran it across her lower lip, in what appeared to be excitement.

When he recovered his line of thought, he said, "I'm sure you have a lot of things to take with you, so we'll come to your palapa to pick you up in the morning. We'll pack whatever it is you need to take on the mules. All you need to do is be ready for us at first light."

Luisa took a few steps toward Felix and hugged him for all she was worth. He blushed from the unexpected burst of affection. When she saw this, she pulled him back a second time, wrapped him in her arms and whispered, "I can't thank you enough. You don't know what this means to me."

"I guess I didn't," Felix answered as he brought his hand up to wipe the embarrassment from his face. "I've been so busy coming and going, here and there, that I don't give myself time to think things through anymore. We'll spend tomorrow night in the camp, and I'll have you down at Santa Marta the next day. I can't wait to see your face when you see it up close for the first time. It'll be a big change from what you're used to."

Luisa watched Felix, listened closely, and glowed as she took each child's hand in her own and said, "Let's go pack our things for the big journey."

He watched them walk away hand in hand, and for a moment, they made him feel good, and he forgot about Anna.

★★★

Alonso and Felix arrived at Luisa's shack just as the sun was coming up. Felix arranged a blanket on one of the burros and lifted Juan Carlos up in place on the animal's back. The boy was anxious to get moving. He beamed with pride when Felix handed him the reins.

"What's my burros name?" the boy asked through his excitement. "I'll need to talk to him, won't I?"

Felix chuckled as he came up with a proper name, "Chapo. His name's Chapo."

Juan Carlos scratched the back of the burro's head and said, "Hi, Chapo. I'm Carlos." He grinned.

"Is that all you have?" Felix questioned Luisa when he looked down to see a small, mostly empty burlap bag lying at her feet.

"That's all, we don't have much," she replied, touching the delicate shell necklace around her neck.

Felix picked up the bag, tied the top in a knot, and secured it on one of the mules. He turned back to Luisa.

"Ok, put your foot right here, and step up," he said as he joined his hands about knee-level in front of her. She placed her foot in his hands and one hand on his shoulder. She bounced up on the burro with a lightness that surprised him. He took Maricela in his arms and swung her up in one smooth motion, placing her in front of her mother on the burro's back. Both had grins on their faces, as if he'd just granted them a life-long wish.

Luisa and the children waved goodbye, as a dozen women and children lined up along the path to wish them well. Luisa's sister, Nora, wiped a tear as they went by. Luisa waved excitedly and blew her a kiss. At twenty-eight years of age, Luisa had spent every single day of her life right there in Rancho San Juanico. Since the day she was born on the dirt floor of her parents' shack, she had never spent a single night anywhere else. She'd married Juan Pedro at fourteen and bore him four children on that same bare dirt, only two of which survived. She never had the chance to bury her husband, because he died in a faraway place. He was laid to rest by strangers. Every night since she had learned of Pedro's fate, she had laid alone on the ground in her bed, unable to sleep through the night. She'd thought of the dreams they shared. She knew that it was up to her to be strong now, for all three of them, as the future unfolded. As she rode away on the burro that morning, she held her head high and promised herself she would never return to live in Rancho San Juanico, not ever again.

★★★

"Good morning, sweetheart! You smell just like the cactus flowers after a rain!" Antonio exclaimed, as he kissed Anna Marie on the cheek after stepping into the Ejido office.

"Oh, Tonio. I do love you!" she blushed.

"Well, thank you, dear. You know how to make a man feel good. What do you think, can we get back together without screwing things up again?"

She nodded and smiled at him through happy eyes.

"I was out breaking a stubborn young horse this morning, and one of the boys came out to tell me Sammy wanted to see me. Is he here?"

Anna looked over toward Sammy's closed door and said, "Let me tell him you're here. He's been on the telephone with Oscar most of the morning. Just a moment," she knocked softly and hesitated before she entered his office.

"I'll just serve me a cup of that coffee over there while I'm waiting," Antonio said to himself. He filled a cup and sat down in a chair next to Anna's desk.

Anna returned. "He'll be with you in just a minute. He's still on the telephone."

"I'm sure glad I don't have one of those things. Seems to me like a piss-poor way to spend your time – talking to someone you can't even see!" he snickered.

Anna smiled and replied, "Must be something going on. Oscar's called three times already this morning."

"I suspect we'll soon find out," Antonio replied, sipping his coffee. "Must be serious if he doesn't want me to finish breaking that horse."

Just then, Sammy emerged from his office with a wrinkled look about him. He walked over to the coffeepot. "Hello, Antonio," he said, pouring the coffee. "Thanks for coming in. Let's step into my office. I need to go over some things with you."

Antonio winked at Anna as he rose from his chair. "See you tonight?"

She nodded discreetly and tried to hold back her smile in front of Sammy.

Antonio followed Sammy into the office, closing the door behind them.

He sat down in one of the yellow vinyl chairs in front of the desk. He noticed that Sammy's hair was wild and uncombed, as the man placed his head in his hands.

When Sammy looked up, Antonio was surprised by the dark circles under his eyes and the expression on his face.

"What is it? What's wrong? Why'd you call me in here?" He set his coffee on the desk and waited.

The normally flamboyant Sammy said nothing. He rose from his chair and walked over to the single window behind his desk. He opened it to let the fresh air enter the stuffy room. He walked back to the desk, opened a drawer, took out a pack of Camels, and shook one out. He brought it up to his lip and lit it, then waved the match and threw it on the floor without watching where it landed. He sat back down, drew deeply on the cigarette, and blew a lungful of smoke toward the ceiling.

"I'm fucked!"

With a questioning expression, Antonio asked, "What does that mean?"

Sammy sucked harder on the cigarette and blew the smoke off to the side. "I've been fucked, Antonio. Really, really fucked over! That Goddamned Don Jose Osuna!"

Antonio's eyebrows went up, curiously.

"Do you remember, two years ago I spoke to you about how I might buy the Los Dolores and Timbabichi ranches?"

"I do," Antonio replied, pushing the rim of his hat a little higher on his forehead.

As he took another hard pull on the cigarette, Sammy rose from the chair again. He began to pace back and forth behind the desk.

"Well?" Antonio asked.

"Well, you know the Quintannas own both of those ranches. They're cousins of the other Quintannas from the Loreto mountains. Up in the Gigantas, our cattle mix it up all the time with theirs. As you know we always sort things out. You've stayed at their ranch. You're friends with them."

Antonio laughed, "You don't remember I was pretty serious with Francesca Quintanna there for a while? It didn't work out, but I've still got a sweet spot for her. I wonder if she ever married that scoundrel up in Loreto," he added.

"Never mind about the Goddamned woman!" Sammy scolded. "I assumed that I could trust the other branch of the Quintanna family. I found out too late they use a bank down in La Paz owned by Don Jose Osuna. Jose Osuna and Oscar Padilla are sworn enemies."

"I know."

"Last year, Rafael, the oldest of the Quintanna brothers came down sick and asked me if I was still interested in buying those ranches."

Still pacing, he continued, "I thought I'd buy them, slice off a piece for myself, and let Oscar buy the rest."

"That makes sense," Antonio said. "We've been running our cows down there for years. I never understood why the Quintannas owned those places; they had no interest in cattle."

Anna Marie tapped on the door and stuck her head through the crack. "I'm sorry, the men from the ejido are here for their meeting. What should I tell them?"

Sammy stepped back to the window without answering. He placed his elbows on the sill and cradled his chin in his hands with his back to her. Anna looked at Antonio who shrugged his shoulders.

"Sammy?" she asked.

He continued to stare out the window. Anna stepped through the door and closed it behind her. She took a seat in the empty chair next to Antonio. He motioned with his hands for her to hold back. She folded her hands in her lap and they waited.

When he turned around, he went straight for his desk and took out his cigarettes. Standing behind the desk he lit another one and threw the pack back in the drawer before he slammed it shut.

"Tell them something has come up, and we'll have to postpone the meeting."

Anna's eyebrows rose, "Okay, should I reschedule?"

"We can do that later. I have no idea right now what my plans are. Tell them, I'm sorry."

She saw the distraught look about him and the desperation in his eyes. "I'll take care of it." She rose from the chair and left the room.

Sammy sat back down and sucked on the cigarette.

"I cut a deal to buy those ranches from Rafael. We shook hands on it, and I borrowed 400,000 pesos from the bank here in Insurgentes. When I was last down in La Paz, Rafael deposited the money into an escrow – in an Osuna-owned bank, it turns out."

"So, what's the problem?" He took off his hat and set it on the desk.

"The money's gone," he groaned. "No trace," he closed his eyes and massaged them. He pinched the bridge of his nose. "My receipt is worthless." He looked defeated, beaten, almost suicidal. His voice rose in a pitch Antonio had never heard before, "I've got a worthless one-page handwritten letter signed by Rafael. Osuna's high-powered law firm sent me a fancy letter and copies of documents yesterday informing me they bought the ranches. Said all the livestock were included. They're about to brand all of our cattle as their own. Now do you see why I'm fucked?" he stared at Antonio.

Antonio listened and started to get angry.

Sammy threw the cigarette down on the floor and crushed it with his foot. "I've not only lost 400,000 pesos but the cattle too. It'll break me! I'll be ruined! The bank will end up with everything I own!"

"Jesus almighty, Sammy! You did dig you a hole this time. What does Oscar say?"

"He says don't even bother taking it to court. Osuna's paid off all the judges."

"So, what'll you do?"

"We need to get those cattle out of there. If Osuna gets to them first, I'm finished. We can deal with the land I thought I bought later."

"I was planning to have a cattle drive. We'll just get started a little sooner than expected. We might have to pick a fight, but I'll prepare for that."

"So, do it!" Sammy snapped.

Twisting the end of his mustache, Antonio asked, "What's Osuna's interest in those worthless old ranches? There's hardly a drop of water anywhere, and the cattle live on nothing but prickly pear and mesquite. Osuna's not even in the ranching business. Why the hell would he want them?"

Sammy stepped back to his desk and sat down. He reached for another cigarette and offered one to Antonio, who politely declined. "No thanks, those things make you impotent."

Sammy rolled his eyes and ran his hand through his hair. "Drugs, he wants those ranches because of the drugs."

"What drugs? If I'm going down there for those cows, I deserve to know what I'm getting into."

"They plan to use the ranches as a drop-off point for their South American shipments. With the new highway, Baja Sur is about to become a preferred route for drug runners heading north. Mexico's become too risky."

"I had no idea."

"Antonio, we have to go get those cows out of there. Now."

"I can do that. Give me two days to gather up supplies and find a couple good hands, and I'll be on my way. I'll be needing some guns."

"Come out to the ranch tonight. We'll look through what I have. Anything else you can think of?"

"Not for the moment, except I'll be needing some tequila. You have plenty of that, don't you?"

"I do. More than you can pack on a mule!"

Sammy looked relieved for the first time that day.

★★★

The determined villagers of Agua Verde made steady progress rebuilding their homes in the weeks following the hurricane. The remains of their old shacks and palapas lay drying in burn piles the size of small mountains. The men and older boys labored side by side for sixteen hours a day building palapas, while the women managed a primitive outdoor kitchen. The younger boys provided a steady supply of fresh trigger fish, cabrilla, clams, scallops and lobsters for them all to eat, and the girls cared for the young children. They worked together, one and all, and the village rose, almost like magic, from the rubble.

Santos scavenged the remains of the nine village pangas and rebuilt two of them. He would be taking them to Santa Marta to harvest fan palm ojas for the roofs on the new palapas.

Charro and Christian cut the palm and mesquite logs that were needed for the frames of the new palapas. They stacked logs at each new palapa site as a team of men came along behind and planted the them in the ground. Gayo kept everyone organized as he labored alongside.

One afternoon, after they cut their last log, Charro and Christian hiked four miles up a remote canyon in the Gigantas and returned that evening with two lively cow ponies. The young animals needed nothing more than a little human contact before departing on the vigorous journey to Timbabichi.

★★★

Santos and three teenage boys landed their two pangas on the beach at Santa Marta early, as the sun was rising behind them over the Gulf. They gathered their few meager belongings and walked up to the ranch house, where they found Carmen scattering scraps to a few anxious hens at her feet.

"Good morning, Santos. You're out and about early today," she said through a beaming smile.

"Hello, Carmen! We've come to cut some of your ojas. The hurricane flattened Agua Verde – not one palapa was left standing." He looked around and saw no signs of damage. "Looks like it missed you."

"We saw the worst of it pass by out on the water," she glanced out toward Isla Catalan. "It did rain pretty hard for a while there. Sorry to hear about Agua Verde."

"This one made the storm of '55 look like nothing," Santo said, shaking his head.

"You're welcome to cut as many ojas as you need," Carmen said waving her hand at the palm forest. "Leo's gone off to Timbabichi looking for cows, so I'll enjoy having your company. We can gather some fruit and vegetables out of the garden to send back with you." She threw the last of the scraps to the chickens. "I can't hardly keep up with the garden anymore."

"Thank you, we could always use the food," he said with a smile. "It may take us a week to cut what we need." He looked over at the palm trees. "I heard there might be a roundup. Leo's getting started early, huh?"

"He is." She nodded. "He started thinking about moving all those cows, and he couldn't sit still. He rode down there to count the herd. Said he wanted to see what they'd be getting into."

Santo hesitated and looked away for a moment. He looked back at Carmen with a serious expression, "Leo hired Charro and Paco to help him, but I'm afraid there's been a terrible accident. We got caught out on the water, fishing for calamari in that storm. Charro's panga sunk.

We lost Paco," he looked down at the ground, afraid to meet her eyes. The three boys were uncomfortable and looked away.

"Oh, my God," Carmen gasped. She brought her hand up and covered her mouth. "Paco and Charro hired on with us a few years ago." Her forehead wrinkled. "I'm so sorry. How is Charro taking it? Those two boys were so close."

"He's doing the best he can. He's keeping busy putting Agua Verde back together. He wanted me to tell you, he still plans to help with the roundup."

"That's just terrible." Her voice trailed away. "Well, come along." She turned toward the bunkhouse. "Let's get you settled. Then we'll find you a thicket of ojas."

As they turned to follow Carmen, there was an explosion and a thunderous rumbling from high above on the cliff. They looked up to see a thick cloud of dust rising from high up on the face of the rock.

"What the…?" Santos muttered, shading his eyes to see more clearly.

Carmen shook her head, "That's the men from San Juanico. They're widening the trail. Every hour or so you'll hear a blast like that. Funny, I'm getting used to it. Don't even notice anymore."

"I'll be," wondered Santos. "Seems like a lot of trouble. For what?"

"They're planning to move the cattle up that way. They needed to widen the old trail."

Santos watched as the dust cleared and he could see the men, appearing to be about the size of ants, rolling rocks off the trail.

★★★

Late in the day, Felix, Alonso, Luisa, and the children arrived at the camp on the rim of the cliff. The mules had been traveling for more than a week without much food or rest. Their heads were hanging low to the ground when they came to a stop. The crew was down on the trail, so they were met by just the ornery old cook, Pepe, and young, energetic Pepino.

The boy waved excitedly as Pepe shrugged and turned back toward the kitchen. Felix said, "Pepino, would you chop some prickly pear for these animals?"

"I'll get them all they can eat! There's water in the trough."

Felix looked over his shoulder at Luisa and the children. They were frozen in place on their little burros, staring at the mountainous coastline, stretching out on the horizon as far as the eye could see. Lonely islands to the north and south rose mysteriously from the haze-covered ocean. The faint calls of sea birds echoed in the background on the soft breeze, as it brushed across the cliff.

"What do you think, Juan Carlos?" Felix asked. For once, the boy was speechless. Felix shrugged and said, "Let's get off these animals and get them get a drink. Come on, now. We have all day to watch the ocean. It's not going anywhere."

Felix and Alonso went about removing saddles and packs while Luisa and the children walked over to the cliff's edge. Pepe grunted something, and Pepino ran by with an armload of chopped cactus. The mules shook vigorously as soon as their burdens were removed. Two of them rolled in the dirt scratching their backs. Felix thought about how far he'd traveled in the last ten days. How his life had been turned completely upside-down. Thoughts of Anna Marie were still haunting him. He simply couldn't shake the thought of her. They hadn't been together for very long, but it was his first serious relationship with a woman. He was slowly learning an important lesson.

The sun was hovering low on the horizon when the exhausted men dragged themselves one by one up the trail and over the canyon rim. They were in low spirits, filthy, and in desperate need of nourishment, having survived on plain corn tortillas for five full days. The moment they saw the mules, Luisa, and the children, everything changed. There was a sudden festiveness in the air. Luisa's brother, Fausto, cried tears of joy as he hugged and kissed the three of them. All the men and boys gathered around for hugs and greetings as if it were a long-lost family reunion. The fresh food and the presence of the little family made for a festive and memorable evening. Every person in the camp was happy and excited to learn of their new life down below at Santa Marta.

Not long after a dinner unlike any other they'd had in weeks, the men drifted off to their tents and bed rolls, many of them with fresh packs of Pall Malls in their pockets. Luisa and her brother, Fausto, were the only ones left at the campfire. Fausto was excited his sister had left San Juanico, but he struggled over the fact she was on her own with two small children.

"What will you do there?" he asked.

Luisa shrugged, "I don't know. I need to be in a new place. I had to get away from San Juanico. There's nothing for me there."

Fausto looked hard at his sister in the firelight. He saw how the years had aged her. She'd lost the youthful shape to her face. There were new wrinkles about her eyes. He saw a middle-aged woman. A determined woman. He was proud of her.

He said, "Santa Marta won't be so far away after we get the trail finished. I'll come see you as often as I can."

"Thanks, that means a lot to me. I'm afraid, but I'm alright. We'll be okay."

Fausto wiped his eye, "I love you, Luisa."

The fire faded, and Luisa laid down to sleep next to her children in Fausto's tent, the first time in her life she would sleep somewhere other than San Juanico.

★★★

Late in the afternoon, during his second day of riding, Leo came across the first signs of cattle on his journey to Timbabichi. He smelled the pungent odor of fresh cow pies before he saw their tracks. He scanned the country for a water source and saw a long arroyo snaking its way down the rocky slope toward the sea, two miles away. He was certain he'd find a spring seep, down below in that drainage. He nudged the bay horse in that direction, and the pale spotted mare followed along behind them on a lead rope, as they made their way through the rocks and cactus.

In a day and a half, Leo had ridden thirty-five miles south through mountains and canyons so rugged that there were no continuous trails. Here and there, he followed trails made over the centuries by wild burros, deer, and bighorn sheep, but they were all short-lived and led nowhere. He'd come across three wet seeps, but none amounted to more than a puddle of warm stagnant water, hardly enough to water the horses. There were reasons, throughout history, humans had avoided this place.

The La Giganta range receded the farther south he traveled. The 3,000-foot spiny peaks near Agua Verde, north of Santa Marta were no higher than 1,500 feet, up and behind him now, and the terrain continued to flatten as he neared Timbabichi. A powdery gray trail dust lined his nostrils, but he could smell the ocean when the breeze blew just right. The lower hills and canyons, although they made for easier traveling, became more desolate to his eye. When he thought of crossing this country with three hundred head of cattle, it made him uneasy.

Leo came to the uppermost reach of the arroyo and found a scattering of palo verde trees, a few patches of mesquite, and thickets of prickly pear, cholla, and catclaw. On the deeper soils along the arroyo, he also saw tufts of dry grass and more fresh sign of cattle. He continued down the arroyo and found himself on a well-worn trail. It entered a deep, narrow ravine as it wound down toward the ocean, a mile farther ahead.

The rock walls rose much higher on both sides the farther he rode. The vegetation grew thick, and the cattle trail meandered through tangles of thorny brush in the narrowing canyon. He stopped when he heard an animal bellow. He thought it must have heard the horses approaching. He rode around a blind corner and came upon four cows and an enormous old bull he recognized from years ago. In a cloud of dust, the group all snorted and stampeded down the ravine.

Leo asked himself aloud, "What have I gotten myself into?"

He could hear waves crashing on rocks not far ahead. When he came around the next bend in the trail, he rode right into a primitive camp nestled under a few scraggly date palm trees, growing out of a crevice at the base of the rock wall. There was a sheltered overhang in the wall, and under it sat two men, a woman, and a child, around a small cooking fire.

The four people looked up in shock as Leo approached. They were barefoot, dressed in flimsy ragged shorts, with nothing more. They were gnawing on hunks of lobster, throwing the shells on the ground on a pile of old fish bones. A rotten odor hung in the stifling afternoon air and mingled with the smoke from the fire. One of the men stood as Leo got down off his horse.

"Hello, stranger," the man said with an apprehensive smile. Leo counted four visible teeth in the front of his mouth. "Where in the world did you come from? We been here three years, and you're the first person to ever visit us from up there!" he nodded up in that direction. "My name's Mondo. Come," he motioned, "sit down, and have some lobster. We got more than enough!"

Leo glanced left then right and took in the scene.

"Primitive," he thought, "is an understatement." All four were a dark bronze color from living under the sun without the benefit of clothing. The woman was topless, and her enormous breasts sagged half-way down to her waist. They all stared at him as if he was an oddity.

"Him," Mondo said pointing to the other man at the fire, "that's my brother, Beto. And her," pointing at the woman, "that's our wife, Martina. We call her Tina. The kid over there, that's Efrain. He's out of Beto, I think, but hard to say. Pay him no mind. He's a little off."

Leo walked stiffly over to the fire and extended his hand to Mondo.

"My name's Leonardo. Nice to meet you, Mondo. I'm from Santa Marta. That's a little ranch thirty-five or forty miles up the coast. I'm out looking for cows. I have a bunch of them to round up in a month or two. I'm trying to locate them and get a count. How many have you seen here in the canyon?"

"Oh them," he said, glancing toward the beach. "There's just the five of them. They were here when we came. That's been three years. There'd be a few more of them, but we eat the calves when they're born. Good and tender at that age. The three of us can almost finish a newborn calf before the meat spoils," he broke off a piece of lobster tail and offered it to Leo.

Leo accepted the lobster and said, "Thanks. Two days on the trail eating tortillas makes me hungry for a piece of meat. Even if it is lobster!"

"Tortillas? I'd kill for a tortilla! Haven't had one in six months! We don't have fixings for them here as you can see." He looked around the bare camp.

Leo walked over to his horse and opened the saddle bag. He brought out a stack of tortillas wrapped neatly in a yellow flowered cloth and returned to the fire.

"Here you go. There's a healthy stack of em' for you." He handed it to Mondo.

With that gift, Mondo became a friend for life.

The other three people around the fire stood to get a closer look at the tortillas. Mondo held on tight and appeared undecided whether to run with his prize or share it. Tina made the decision for him, when she tore the package from his hand.

"I'll be in charge of the tortillas, if you don't mind!" she demanded.

Leo saw that she was a large woman and outweighed Mondo by probably fifty pounds. She unwrapped the cloth and brought the tortillas up to her nose inhaling their aroma. She moaned as if experiencing a powerful orgasm, and her knees went weak. Her body swayed and her huge pendulous breasts quivered and rolled from side to side. Efrain watched everything around him and appeared to be clueless.

Leo joined the friendly family around their fire and made their day even more memorable when he brought out a jar of hot chili salsa. They became far too busy eating lobster tacos to say very much. They just made different, mostly pleasant, noises expressing their contentment.

"Efrain hasn't had many tortillas in his life, look at that boy eat!" Tina said with her mouth full.

Leo looked over at the boy and noticed his eyes were a little bit crossed. He guessed the boy's age to be around four.

When they were finished, Mondo rolled a cigarette. Leo wondered how they happened to have tobacco. Mondo inhaled and passed it over to Tina, who took a deep pull before passing it to Beto. As Beto passed it to Leo, he recognized the earthy aroma of marijuana. Leo took the joint but passed it back to Mondo, he didn't care to get stoned right then. Tina got up and walked about thirty feet, dropped her shorts, squatted and took a pee. Nobody but Leo seemed to notice.

Leo asked Mondo, “Where’d you get the marijuana?”

“A panga washed up on the beach in that big storm,” he exhaled. “It was full of this stuff, all wrapped up tight in canvas bundles?” he made it sound like a question. “There was a dead man in the panga, too. I think somebody shot him. I don’t think he drowned. Hard to say, he had a big hole in his chest. We floated him out to the deep water and sunk him, because he smelled bad.”

“Is the panga still down there on the beach?” Leo asked.

“Yeah, but it’s empty. Three men came in another big panga and took all the marijuana. I watched them do it. They didn’t even know I was there.”

Leo was thinking that over, when he looked over at Efrain. The boy had a dead bird on the end of a string. He was twirling it in circles above his head, as he danced in front of Tina. She smiled at the boy with obvious pride. He stepped closer to her and opened his mouth, still dancing and twirling. He pointed at his mouth with the index finger from his other hand. Tina lifted one of her huge boobs and took careful aim.

Using both hands for accuracy, Tina caused her tit to squirt a perfect stream of milk nearly three feet through the air, directly at Efrain’s wide-open mouth. About half the milk found its way into Efrain’s mouth, while the rest of it splattered over his delighted face and down onto his protruding belly.

Tina shrieked while Mondo and Beto stood and applauded. For the finale, Efrain swung the fluttering, lifeless bird, and let it fly over their heads to land up on the rocks behind them.

Efrain said, “Whew!” as he wiped his brow.

“Nice work,” Tina said with admiration.

Efrain stepped up and collapsed on his mother’s lap, where he began sucking on her tit in earnest.

Leo chuckled and joined in the applause. He wanted to be polite. When things settled down, he asked Mondo, “Can you show me where the cattle water?”

Mondo was happy to please his guest and rose right up on his feet. “There’s a spring down below where we get our water, right over there,” he pointed. “It puts out a lot of water.”

They walked a short distance over to the spring. Leo knelt and took a drink out of the small pool. "That's a lot of water, cold and sweet, too."

Leo thought for a moment and asked, "Down there on the beach, can the cows wander away, or is there something to keep them from running off?"

"There's bluffs on both ends of the beach. The cows are trapped. A man can climb around the bluffs at low tide, but a cow sure can't. They wouldn't want to anyway, they like staying close to the spring."

"That's interesting," Leo thought out loud.

Leo and Mondo walked a little further to the beach where Mondo said, "That wrecked panga is right over there in the rocks. Want to see it?"

"I do."

Leo saw the beach was a quarter mile long, blocked on each end by steep bluffs rising two hundred feet high on the water's edge. Waves crashed into the rocks at the base of both bluffs and caused a white froth.

"You're right," he said. "No cow is gonna go around either one of those bluffs. This is just like a corral." He noticed the five head of cattle huddled down at one end of the beach, watching them warily.

"Look at those ornery sons-a-bitches staring at us," Leo commented. "I don't think they're gonna like what I have planned for them one bit," he chuckled.

"That panga is right there behind that rock," Mondo pointed as they walked.

The men stepped around the rocks and a battered, broken panga, a similar model to Oscar's super pangas, laid half-buried in the sand. Leo noticed there were no registration numbers. The boat had been nearly new. The twin fifty-five-horsepower Johnsons were beat-up and bent. They appeared to be worthless, except perhaps for parts.

"Hmm," Leo mumbled. "I'd heard rumors that they were hauling drugs up the Gulf. I never paid it much attention. Maybe I should." He scratched the whiskers on his chin. "This place, does it have a name?" he asked.

"What do you mean? What, the beach?"

"Well, I mean this place, the beach, the canyon, here where you live. This place in general. Does it have a name?"

"The local fishermen who come by every now and then call it Cajón Bonito."

"Hmm, I've heard of that, never knew exactly where it was. I've ridden past here up above a dozen times. Never came down the arroyo, didn't have a need to. How did you end up here?"

"We'd been scallop-diving up and down the coast for years, but our old motor finally gave out. We floated up right here and found this place full of scallops, clam beds, lobsters, and all the fish we could ever want out there on the reef. And there's all that spring water. Why leave?"

Leo liked Cajón Bonito and the strange little family. Sunset was only a couple hours away, so he decided to spend the night on the beach. He chased the cows back up past Mondo's camp and laid his bedroll down on the sand. He was out cold shortly after the sun went down.

★★★

"Go slow, take short steps," Felix told Luisa as they set off down the cliff early in the morning. He'd crafted a rope harness and had Maricela secure on his back, while he led the one mule and two burros behind him. Luisa walked ahead of him, holding on firmly to Juan Carlos with a rope she'd tied around his waist. She lectured the boy to watch his feet and not the ocean down below.

"This will be good practice for what we run into up ahead," Felix said. "We've got this first part of the trail widened up, and it's easy. The next part, where we haven't done anything is a different story. You'll see when we get there, but right now, get in the habit of moving steady but slow."

"How long do you think it will take to reach the bottom?" Luisa asked.

"Depends how often we stop, but I'd say we'll be at the bottom early afternoon, four or five hours," he said. "From there, we'll ride to the ranch. That's less than an hour, so I think we'll be there by mid-afternoon, if nothing slows us down."

"I don't like looking down," Luisa said, placing the palm of her hand on her forehead. "It makes me dizzy."

Felix smiled, "It does more than make me dizzy. The first time I came down here, I made the mistake of eating before I started. That was before we did any work on the trail. I also made the mistake of looking down. I puked up burritos and had to lie down to keep my head from spinning. I ended up crawling for a while. After that I promised myself, I'd never look down there again. When I do look down now, it's only to watch where I put my feet."

"I've already learned not to look down, if only I could get Juan Carlos to stop doing it."

"He probably has a stronger stomach than we do, and better balance. He's closer to the ground than we are. He should be alright."

An hour later, they reached the end of the improved trail. Luisa gasped and went pale when she saw the narrow, slanted trail ahead of her for the first time. She asked to move behind Felix and the animals. He insisted she stay right where she was, a step in front of him, where he could keep an eye on her.

"It's no wider than my feet!" Luisa exclaimed. "Look there," she said pointing at the ledge. "It's covered with loose rocks, and it slopes down! I want to crawl!" she attempted to kneel.

"No, you don't!" He stepped behind her and placed his free hand around her waist. "You need to stay on your feet and keep moving, or we'll never make it. We don't want to spend the night up here. The worst part is the first few steps. Keep moving and don't look down," he reminded her. "Go! Move it! Take baby steps. Don't look down!" he said again.

They repeated the terrifying exercise dozens of times as they descended. They stopped at each switchback, where there was a wide place to catch their breath and steady their nerves. Luisa's hands kept trembling. He covered them with his own and held them until they calmed. The entire way down, he coached her. He spoke to her and the children reassuringly. They were dripping with sweat in the mid-day heat. The sea breeze died when morning passed, and afternoon wore on. The powerful rays of the sun reflecting off the rock nearly blinded them. Rocks broke loose and tumbled down the cliff, making ominous sounds as they bounced along. Five grueling hours later, they reached the bottom. Drenched in sweat, Luisa sighed, and smiled nervously as she looked up at the near vertical rock wall rising a thousand feet above them.

She shuddered and said, "We did it!"

Felix laughed, "I know grown men who would never do that. They would've cried like babies and begged to turn around. I knew you could do it. Let's get up on these animals and ride over to Santa Marta!"

The well-worn flat trail was relaxing, compared to what they'd just been through. They soon came to the edge of the date palm forest lining the wide arroyo for nearly a mile on its way to the ocean. Luisa had never seen so many trees. She tried to imagine what it was like inside, under the dark mysterious canopy. She heard songbirds making beautiful music that was foreign to her ears. A group of twenty grotesque turkey vultures were sunning out in the open, next to a spring-fed seep, with their wings spread open. They paid no mind to the mule and the burros walking past them. She smelled the musky decay of the forest floor mixed with the odor of salt, seaweed, and fish drifting up from the ocean. For the first time in her life, she clearly heard the ocean. She was surprised that it made so much noise. She'd never thought about water making noise. Little did she know she was hearing only the soft sounds of a calm, restful sea.

The short ride to the ranch went by like a motion picture. Everything was moving as Luisa rode through it in awe on her little burro. Her head twisted and turned on her slender neck, and her face was fixed with a brilliant, wide smile. Her pearly white teeth reflected the sun, and her dark brown eyes sparkled. Felix watched her and chose to say nothing. He took pleasure in her pleasure. Juan Carlos was chattering and asking one question after another, but he didn't seem to care when nobody responded.

The date palm trees gave way to fan palms as they came to a patch of deep, sandy soil. Felix heard voices as they rounded a bend in the trail and slowed his mule when he saw two people stacking ojas on the side of the trail.

"Hi there!" Felix waved, greeting an old man and a boy.

The man, with a sun-worn face and a white mustache under a wide sombrero waved and said, "Heh, you surprised me. I didn't hear you coming. Where'd you come from?" He took off his sweat-stained hat and scratched his snowy head of hair, as he thought about what he was seeing.

Felix heard a noise high above them in the tops of the palm trees and looked up to see two teenage boys moving around like monkeys, with no apparent fear of the deadly height. Luisa came out of her trance and waved to the men.

"We came down the trail from San Juanico. We've come to visit Leo and Carmen," Felix answered.

"I'll be," Santos responded, running his knotted-up fingers through his hair again, and wiping the sweat from his face with a bandanna. "The looks of that cliff made me think people didn't really use that trail. I know Leo goes up there once every few years, but that's his job, and he's probably used to it. But seeing a young family coming down like it's a Sunday afternoon visit to the neighbors? Well, I'll be. We're from Agua Verde." He glanced up at the boys in the tree. "We came down here to cut ojas."

"I have two brothers in Agua Verde. Enrique and Bernardo from San Juanico? My name's Felix, and that's Luisa," he said gestured in her direction.

"Hi!" Luisa waved for a second time.

"Sure, I know your brothers, they married those two sisters. I always thought that was funny, two brothers marrying two sisters all on the same day. But I sure had a good time at their weddings. Turned into a three-day fiesta!" he laughed.

Felix chuckled at the thought, "Tell them 'hello' for me, would you? I'm part of the crew working on the trail up there. You've probably heard the dynamite."

"Oh yeah, you're making quite the ruckus. Rocks falling every which way!"

"Are Leo and Carmen at the ranch?"

"Carmen is, but Leo's down to Timbabichi after some cows. Don't know when he'll be back."

"Hmm, well, we better keep moving. It's been a long couple of days getting here."

"Nice to meet you, Felix, and you too, Señora." He tipped his hat at Luisa.

As they started to ride, Luisa said, "He thought we were a family. Did you hear him?"

"I heard him." Felix chuckled and nudged his mule on.

Luisa gave her burro a kick to keep up with Felix, and they passed through the palm forest and approached the ranch.

Carmen was hanging clothes on a line as they rode up. She paused with a bed sheet in one hand when she saw them and brushed the hair from her face with the other. When she recognized Felix, she threw the sheet over the line, straightened her loose-fitting smock, and stepped out to greet them.

"My God, there's no end to the surprises," she said as they met in front of the house. "I thought I might be lonely with Leo gone. Welcome back, Felix. Who's that lovely gal you have there with you, and those two darling children? I can't remember the last time there were any little ones running around here!"

"Nice to see you, Carmen! These are friends from San Juanico. Let me get off this mule, and I'll introduce you." They climbed down.

"You must be thirsty. I'll get some lemonade. Hitch your animals there," she waved at the rail. "Have a seat on the veranda, and I'll be right with you."

Luisa and the children were in awe of the surroundings as they sat down at the massive ironwood table looking out at the ocean.

"Here, you two better sit up on these, or I won't be able to see your faces," Carmen said as she placed folded saddle blankets under the children's bottoms.

"Now, that's better! I bet you like sugar in your lemonade, don't you?" she asked looking first at Juan Carlos then Maricela.

"Yes, Señora," Juan Carlos answered. "She does too." He nodded at his sister. Maricela was too shy to speak.

The children finished their lemonade in short order and started fidgeting in their seats.

"Carlos," Luisa spoke up softly, "please take Maricela for a walk down on the beach, so we can talk here."

The children got excited and jumped out of their chairs. Carlos held out his hand to Maricela, "Hold on, let's go," he ordered. They broke into a run.

Carmen laughed, "I love children at that age." She looked at Felix, "What'd you do? Decide to come down the hill and take a vacation? I haven't heard any dynamite today."

"They took a day off, so we could make it down the trail. They'll be back working tomorrow and the next day. Then they'll take another break so I can climb back up. I've got three days to rest up here, if that's alright with you. I got back from Insurgentes yesterday, and I'm dead tired of traveling."

"You know that's fine. You can stay down in the beach house." She glanced at Luisa. "Santos, a friend from Agua Verde, and three boys are in the bunkhouse. They're back somewhere in the grove, cutting ojas."

"We met them on the trail. He knows my brothers who live in Agua Verde." He turned to Luisa. "This is my friend, Luisa, from San Juanico." He gestured toward Carmen. "Luisa, meet Carmen."

"Nice to meet you, and to have you visit, Luisa. You have two darling children there," she turned to look at them down on the beach. "I raised three of my own right here. They're all grown and off on their own. Happens so fast. Enjoy the young ones while you can," she said nostalgically.

"You have a beautiful home here, and such a beautiful place, the ocean, all the trees. Your cousin Antonio told me about it. He said I should come see it." Luisa smiled.

"Actually, Antonio's my husband's cousin, but I consider him family. I've known him most of my life. He introduced me to my husband, Leonardo." She smiled as she thought back to the time. "I'm glad he talked you into coming for a visit. I enjoy having woman company. Doesn't happen very often."

Felix folded his hands together on the table and said, "Luisa lost her husband in an accident out on the road to La Paz not long ago. He was a friend of mine. I was with him when it happened." He paused and looked down at his hands for a moment. Nobody spoke as they waited for him. He looked back up and continued, "Like she said, Antonio told her about Santa Marta, and she asked me to bring her down here. I'd appreciate it if you might let her and the children stay for a bit of time. She could use a fresh start. I'm sure she'd be a big help to you. She's a good person and a hard worker. I've known her my whole life." He turned and looked at Luisa sitting next to him. She folded her own hands in front of her on the table exactly like Felix and looked down at them.

Carmen became thoughtful. A faint smile cracked across her face. Her eyes took on a shine as she studied Luisa and looked out to the beach at the children playing.

Luisa raised her eyes from her hands and looked across the table at Carmen, "I work hard at whatever I do, and I can do almost anything. It'd be only until I sort things out," Luisa said, then looked down again, as if she may have said something out of line. She twisted her hands around.

Carmen looked at Felix and thought she saw something more than Felix simply doing Luisa a favor. Something, perhaps more than just a casual friendship.

Silence hung in the air, until Carmen took an audible breath and said, "I was thinking the other day I need to find some help. Leo's started on the roundup, and I don't know how many cowboys will be passing through that we'll have to feed. I've got a garden that's way too big for me, thirty chickens, three herds of goats, a couple families of pigs, then there's the horses and burros that come and go. Besides all that, there's the other chores. I can't keep up with it anymore."

All three of them were quiet again. Luisa looked at Carmen, and their eyes held. Carmen smiled and broke the silence a second time. "If you'd be willing to work for room, board, and a small wage, I'd be happy to have you here at Santa Marta, for as long as it makes sense for the both of us. God knows I need the help, and as I said earlier, it's been a lot of years since I've had any little ones around to boss!"

Luisa placed her hand over her mouth and started to cry. The tears flowed down her face and dripped off her chin. Felix reached his arm around her shoulder and hugged her. She buried her face against his neck and cried out of pure joy. She gripped the front of his shirt and clung to him until she composed herself. Her face was a bright scarlet color as she turned back to Carmen and said, "I can't tell you how grateful I am. I promise you won't be sorry for giving us a chance. I promise you that."

Carmen wiped a tear from her own eye with a single finger and said, "I believe you, Luisa. I only met you thirty minutes ago, but I believe you, dear," she turned, and watched the children dipping their toes in the ocean.

★★★

"Julio, buy a round of whatever they're drinking," Antonio said to the bartender, waving his hand in a circle as he stepped into the dark cantina. A dozen cowboys and locals were mixing it up late in the afternoon. Two young women flirted from table to table and were drawn toward Antonio when they saw him come in. The west wind off the Pacific had turned blustery that afternoon, and the men were seeking shelter as much as they were the drink or the women.

"You still got the pickup and that old horse trailer, Benito?" Antonio asked the cowboy sitting at the bar.

"I do. The pickup's outside, the trailer's at home. Haven't hauled a horse in it in months. It just sits there, doing nothing."

"How'd you like to earn yourself fifty pesos today?"

"Doing what?"

"I want you to hook up your trailer and drive up the Gigantas to El Coronado Ranch. It's on the back road about halfway to San Javier. You know where that is?"

"I have an idea. That's a long haul on a bad road, especially if I'm dragging a horse trailer. What do you want me to do when I get there? That is, if I go?" He had a beer bottle in his hand and brought it up to his mouth.

"I want you to find an old boy named Naco," Antonio laid ten pesos down for the bartender. "He works for El Coronado. Tell him I need him down here, fast. Like tomorrow. Tell him to load up his two best horses, along with what he needs on the trail for a couple months. He'll know that I'll pay him well. He's done it before. I'm sure he'll drop whatever nonsense he's up to and get on with it. Think you can do that?"

The bartender stepped up and put a shot of tequila in front of Antonio. He downed it in one swallow, "Ahhh." He wiped his mouth with his arm and set the empty shot glass down on the bar and pointed at it. "One more."

"Yeah, I could probably do that, but I want the fifty pesos up front to pay for the gas. It isn't cheap, but you wouldn't know anything about that, since you don't drive."

"Don't you worry about what I do or don't do. You'll worry yourself into an early grave if you knew the half of it. Here's the money, and you'd better get moving. Drive all night if you have to and get back as soon as you can tomorrow. Bring Naco out to Sammy's ranch. I'll be there." The bartender set another shot down on the bar.

"You doing a roundup?"

He nodded, "You have any interest?"

"I've been looking for something to do since I came back from Rosalia."

"Well, bring two horses of your own and whatever else you'll need out to Sammy's tomorrow. We'll leave bright and early the next morning. Now you better be moving. It'll be dark in a few hours, and that's a helluva bad road, as you say, even in the daylight."

Benito finished his beer and turned to leave as the two whores approached.

"Girls, girls, girls!" Antonio said, soon as Benito left and the two women cozied up, one on each side. "I wish it wasn't so," he put an arm around each of their waists, "but I've got way too much work to do, getting ready for a roundup right now. Might be a couple of months, but the day I get back, I'll look you up first thing, and we'll make up for it." He kissed each one on the cheek, "How does that sound?"

"Julio, here's some more pesos, anything these girls want tonight, make sure they get it. Would you do that?"

"Whatever you say, Tonio, I'll take good care of them!"

The girls giggled and hugged him again before he could get away. He squeezed them both on the butt and shrugged his shoulders with regret.

★★★

Antonio arrived at Sammy's ranch shortly before dark. He was turning his horse into the corral, when he saw a shiny, black 1959 Chevy pickup truck pulling away from the bunkhouse. There were four people in the front seat, and the windows were drawn up against the brisk wind. The truck swerved and pulled a donut in a dust cloud before leaving the open yard and coming to a stop next to him. The driver's window came down. From the middle seat, Anna Marie leaned around the driver so she could speak to Antonio. The driver looked to be in his early thirties and was adorned with thick gold chains around his neck and gaudy rings on his fingers. He had a cocky smirk on his face, as he sized up the old cowboy.

"Antonio! I'm glad I saw you. I'm sorry, but I won't be able to meet up with you tonight. Rosario – he's an old friend from La Paz," she paused and glanced at the driver. "He came by on his way to Loreto and asked me to go with him. I've never been to Loreto, so Sammy gave me some time off. Can we get together when I get back? It'll only be a few days." Her eyes were questioning.

Antonio stepped up to the window, where he was six inches from the other man's face, and looking past him to Anna, he replied, "Sorry, sweetheart. I'm about to leave on a roundup over to the Gulf. I might be gone a couple months. Looks like we missed our chance again. I was hoping we'd patch things up before I left. Too bad." He glared at the man in the window, spit off to the side and started to walk off.

He only took three steps when he stopped, turned, and met Anna's eyes for a fleeting moment, as the truck spun its tires in the dirt. He thought she looked confused.

★★★

Sammy looked across the dining room at all the rifles and pistols laid out on the sofa. "That's a lot of guns for three men," he said, sipping a brandy over steak dinner with Antonio.

"No. There's me, Naco, and Benito up here, but there's Leo too, and he'll have a couple hands helping out down there. That's six. What I don't want to do is run out of guns or bullets. Whatever we don't use,

I'll bring back. You don't go into something like this half-baked. That'd be stupid." He took a bite of steak.

"I guess you're right."

"I am right. There's way too much on the line to get caught with our pants down on this." Antonio sliced another piece of steak and paused before he put it in his mouth. "What do you hear about that trail down to Santa Marta? If that's not fixed, we'd have all those cows bunched up down there, with nowhere to go."

A young woman stepped out from the kitchen with a bottle in her hand and asked, "More brandy?" Antonio nodded and held up his glass. Sammy waved her off; his glass was near full.

"Felix was here a few weeks back and said they were ahead of schedule."

"That's not good enough," Antonio answered, as he stared hard at Sammy. "If there's no trail this whole thing's off."

"Well, you'll be there soon enough to see for yourself." He sipped his brandy. "He promised me they'd have it finished."

"I'm just warning you. I'll call it off if there's no trail."

Sammy shook his head and left it at that. His nerves were on edge. They continued eating in silence.

Antonio finished with his steak and set his fork down. "Who was that jerk Anna took off to Loreto with?"

Surprised by the question, Sammy replied, "What do you care? I thought the two of you were over and done with."

"We're working things out," he said curtly and stood up to retrieve the bottle of brandy from the side table.

Sammy shook his head. "Sorry if I'm unable to keep up with your love life."

Pouring the brandy, Antonio looked up and said. "He looked like a narco."

"I wouldn't know, he didn't come in and introduce himself."

"I got a bad feeling about it. I know a narco when I see one. I care for that girl. I should've dragged her ass out of that truck. She does some pretty stupid things sometimes." He raised his glass and took a gulp. "I want you to do me a favor, since I'm about to go off to bail your ass out."

"What would that be?" He shoved his empty plate to the side.

"I want you to keep an eye on her for me when she gets back. I'll be working things out with her when I get back, but I've got this dammed roundup to go off on now. You owe me that much."

"I'm not sure how I do that. She's just an employee. Pass the brandy would you?"

"Just do it, would you? Keep her busy and try not to let her do anything stupid."

"Whatever you say," he shook his head. "She did tell me where she'd be staying. If it makes you feel any better, I'll call up there and check on her. I'll make it sound work related."

"Thank you, I'd appreciate that. I'll be leaving soon as the men get here. I'll load up the guns tonight." Antonio finished his brandy, set his glass down, got up and left without another word.

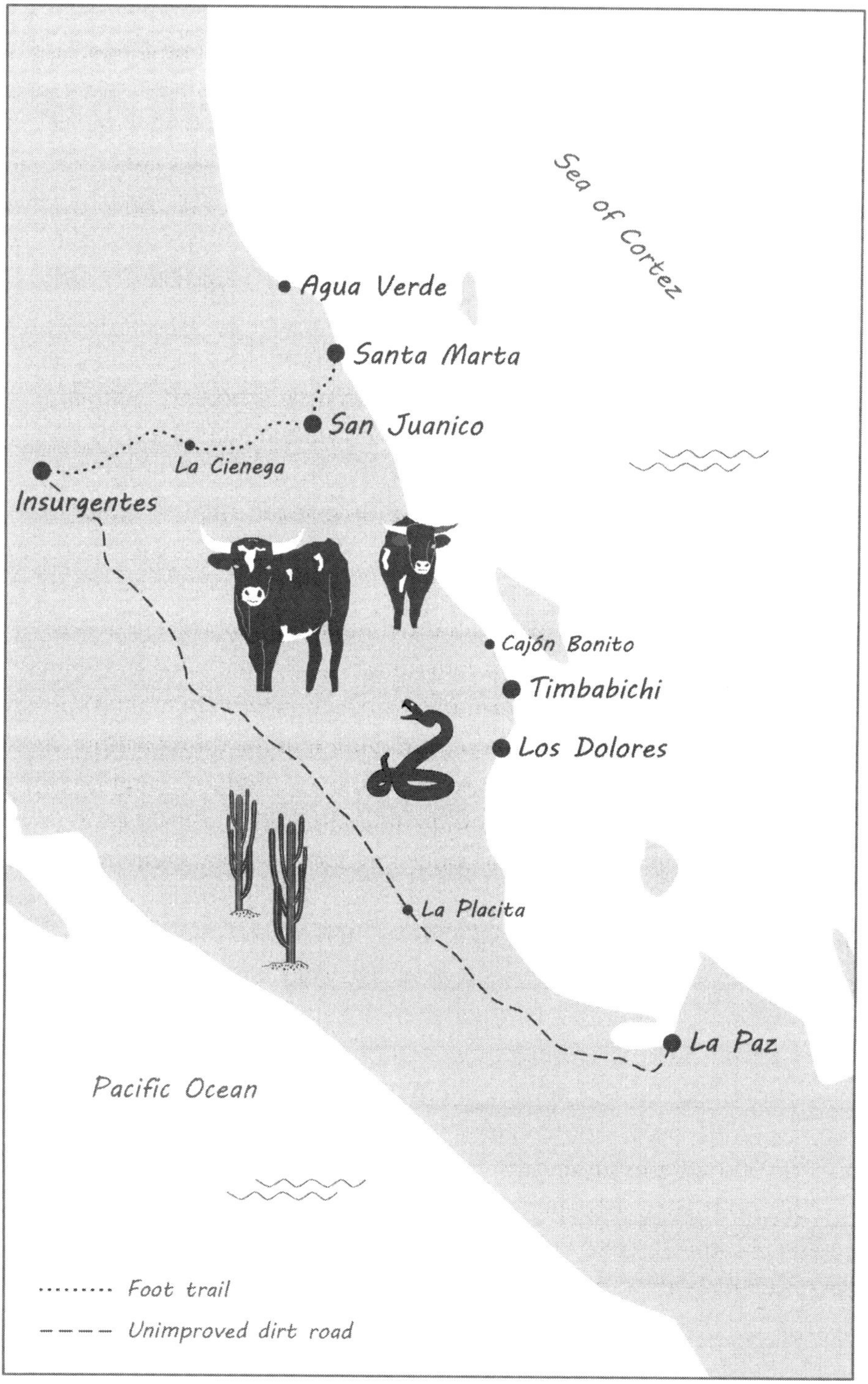
Sea of Cortez
Agua Verde
Santa Marta
San Juanico
La Cienega
Insurgentes
Cajón Bonito
Timbabichi
Los Dolores
La Placita
La Paz
Pacific Ocean
Foot trail
Unimproved dirt road

Timbabichi

Leo was confused. He was sitting on the gelding, looking down at the Timbabichi arroyo from the barren solitary ridge. He'd ridden to three different springs that day on his way to Timbabichi, after spending the night with Mondo and his family at Cajón Bonito. At each spring, the cattle sign was fresh, but every cattle track he saw, including those of several horses, were all headed in the direction of Timbabichi. He couldn't find a single cow, not even a straggler in the hills and canyons where they'd been living undisturbed for the last five years. Somebody had gathered all the animals, and he had no idea who that might be.

A good distance up the broad Timbabichi draw near a cluster of scraggly mesquite trees was a sprawling complex of rustic old palapas, where Leo's long-time friend Coco had been living for many years. Leo noticed a thin plume of smoke rising from the outdoor hearth, and he turned the horse, nudged him with a soft kick, and headed in that direction.

Coco appeared as ancient as the hills, but Leo had never asked his age or even tried to guess. Leo wasn't surprised to see the old man still hobbling around on his gimped-up leg as he rode up. Coco's eyesight was apparently fading, because he squinted and didn't recognize Leo until he slowed the horse and said hello.

"Well, I'll be," croaked Coco in his scratchy voice, "it's about due for you to come by! I thought you'd maybe died somewhere. What's it been? Four, five years?"

"Something like that. Good to see you, old man! You look about the same. Life must be good, heh?" Leo slid down from his horse and the two men embraced. Leo noticed Coco felt like skin and bones.

"Looks can be deceiving, Leo. I think I turned seventy, but I'm not sure. I never counted any years since I was a boy. I never bothered with it, being just me to do the counting. Never seemed important enough to worry about, so I lost track," he bent down and lifted a coffee pot from the iron fire grill. "Now that I'd like to know how old I am, there's no way of telling, so I just live day to day, and don't even know for certain what year it is here," he handed Leo a tin cup and poured it full of coffee.

"Thanks, haven't had any coffee since I left Santa Marta."

"It's probably a good thing you chose right about now to show up again. Seems there's some boys around here who have an interest in those cows of yours." He set the pot back on the fire.

"That's what's got me curious, Coco. I see the tracks where somebody's herding them south. I know it's been a long time since I've paid any attention to them, but those are still my cows. I don't intend to let any rustlers run off with them." Leo eyed the water trough thirty feet to his left. "I need to water these animals." He set his coffee down and led the horses to the trough.

Limping alongside, Coco said, "No, the men gathering the cows aren't rustlers. They work for the new owner of the Los Dolores and Timbabichi ranches."

"What?" Leo looked up from watching the horses quench their thirst. "New owner?"

"Yeah, the men who took the cows said a guy named Don Jose Osuna from La Paz bought them." Coco scratched the sparse white stubble on his chin.

"I'll be." Leo looked south in the direction of the ranches.

"I know, sounded funny to me, cause I heard a rumor that your guys Gonzo and Padilla bought them. Of course, by the time word finds its way down here to me, it's all old news. I don't keep up with all the goings-on." He shrugged.

Leo started walking the horses to a hitching rail and Coco followed, "So, you talked to them? What all did they tell you?" Leo asked as he loosely tied the horses.

"Well, they rode right through here with all those cows, as you can see by the tracks over there," he pointed. "That was a week ago. A couple of the boys stopped here for water, and we shot the shit over there by the well for a bit." He nodded toward the well. "The guys I talked to were out of Sinaloa, of all places, like there aren't any cowboys around here who know how to move a cow."

"Sinaloa? And they're working for the owner who's in La Paz?" Leo took off his hat and ran his hand through his hair as he thought it over. He walked back over to the trough, untied the bandanna around his neck and dipped it in the water. He used it to scrub the trail dust off his face.

"That's what they told me. They said Osuna bought the ranches from Quintanna, and the cows were part of the deal." Coco shifted from one leg to the other, watching Leo for his reaction. "I didn't say anything, cause who am I to know whose cows they are? As far as I knew, they were your cows. But five years is a long time, Leo. You shouldn't a gone and not checked on em' that long." He looked away afraid he may have offended Leo.

"It's a good thing I came along just now," Leo said as he pondered the news. "Did they say where they were taking them?"

"Well yeah. They did." Coco shifted legs again as a pain shot through his bad knee. "They spent three months building corrals up behind the old Mission. They floated a barge-full of alfalfa hay in there to the beach, and they're gathering every cow they can find and holding them there." He grimaced and bent down to rub his knee. "After they gather all of them, they'll be driving em' down to La Paz."

Leo became visibly angry, "What the fuck?"

"That's not the half of it, they're building a landing strip and a road all the way out of there, and you can buy yourself a drink or rent a whore in the old mission." He chuckled. "They put a new roof on the place and turned the former house of God into a cantina. I guess there aren't no rules anymore!" He shook his head.

Leo muttered, "I'll be," as he looked south again and thought it over. He turned back to Coco. "That's good to know. I think I need to take a ride over that way and see things for myself. I'd offer to buy you a drink in the new cantina, but it might be best if you're not seen in my company. I might be causing them some serious trouble."

"That's what I thought." With a concerned look on his face, he said, "You need to be careful. The two boys I spoke to had some serious weapons with them. Lots more than what you'd need to kill a rattlesnake now and then."

"Thanks, but I think I'll ride over that way and play the part of a local cowboy."

"I know you can handle yourself, but just be careful. There's a whole bunch of them over there."

Leo smiled and changed the subject, "I know I've said this to you before, old man," he placed a hand on Coco's frail shoulder, "but I'll say it again. I think it's about time you find yourself a woman to share the good life here. Might add ten years to it. Just me saying, don't take offense."

"No offense taken, Leo. I wouldn't know where to begin looking even if I had a mind to. Be good to have the company. All these years, I haven't come across many women. At least none that wanted to live here." He waved his hand at one of the fallen down palapas.

"My cousin, Antonio – you remember him, don't you?"

Coco nodded, "Sure."

"He tells me there was a thousand of em' up in a camp at Insurgentes, working the chili patch. Every one of them barefoot and probably wishing for a better life. Maybe after I get these cows taken care of, you and I can ride up there and have a look around."

"Don't tempt me unless you mean it, Leo. I'm ready when you are. Be careful around those boys over there. I didn't trust none of em' that I've met."

Leo offered his hand, and he was surprised at the strength of the old man's grip. They held the handshake longer than either of them expected. Leo stepped over to the pale spotted mare and opened the pack on her back. He removed a colt pistol in a weathered leather holster. He strapped it around his waist and climbed up on the gelding. He tipped his hat to Coco as he turned to ride off.

★★★

Late in the afternoon, Carmen, Luisa and the children were soaking in the hot springs at Santa Marta. Luisa felt like she was in heaven. It was the first warm bath she'd had in her life.

"What do you think of that bathtub, Juan Carlos?" Carmen asked the boy as he raised his head up from the pool of sparkling warm water.

"I like it!" he exclaimed before taking a quick breath and going under again.

Carmen and Luisa sat off to the side and enjoyed watching the children swim around like frogs in the shallows.

"I never in my life imagined something like this could exist," Luisa commented. "Fresh, clean hot water bubbling up from the earth. I've never even sat in tub of water, much less something like this. I can't tell you how happy I am to be here. Thank you, Carmen!"

"No thanks necessary, dear. Soak it up and enjoy yourself." Reaching behind her, Carmen picked up a large woven bag off the stone bench and began rummaging through it. "I have a gift for you in here somewhere." She dug deeper. "Ah, here it is," she lifted a neatly wrapped, cloth-covered package. "I saw that you didn't have many things when we unpacked your bag. I thought you might be able to use this. Here, for you." She handed it to Luisa. "Open it."

Luisa smiled as she unfolded the colorful cloth wrapping. She brought a hand up to her mouth to cover a gasp when she saw the gift. Inside was an oval-shaped bar of pastel-green flower-scented soap, a hand-sized mirror, a jar of fragrant aloe, a tiny silver pair of scissors, and a double-edged razor with a neatly wrapped package of shiny new blades. There was also a handful of brightly colored ribbons for her hair.

Luisa bit down on her knuckle as an expression of joy crossed her face. She was unable to find the words to express herself, and her chest heaved up as she swallowed a deep breath. She leaned into Carmen and said softly, "Thank you. Oh, my god! Thank you, Carmen. All my life I've owned very few woman things, and pretty much nothing the last ten years." She held the soap to her nose and inhaled the fragrance. She closed her eyes to savor the sensation.

"You're more than welcome. I like to keep a few 'woman' things around for special occasions, and today is special for the both of us." She turned and watched the children.

Luisa clutched the gifts to her chest and said through watery eyes, "I can hardly believe this is happening, thank you for being so kind to us."

Carmen smiled and looked back to Luisa, "You know what else? I'm going to take these two tadpoles of yours back up to the house, feed them honeyed dates and cream, brush their teeth, and put them to bed in my daughter's room. While there's still some daylight left, I'll leave you here to your shaving. Looks like you might be out of practice. Then, can I make a suggestion?"

"Of course," Luisa looked up, still overwhelmed, clutching the gifts.

"Take a walk over by the beach house. I saw Felix sitting down by the water earlier. That young man cares for you. Go over there and visit with him. It's just a suggestion, woman to woman. He'll only be here another day is all."

"Hmm," Luisa replied. Carmen could see she was thinking it over.

"Good, it's time for you to start living again." She leaned over and placed a kiss on Luisa's forehead.

Luisa's lips parted in a smile, and she brought her hands up over her heart, still holding her precious gifts.

★★★

The previously abandoned Los Dolores Mission was three miles south of Timbabichi, along the beach. It had suffered through more than a dozen hurricanes during the more than two centuries since it'd been built on a dune overlooking the Gulf. Nobody currently alive had any idea why it had ever been built there in the first place. The scattered shacks and lean-tos up the arroyo hardly constituted an actual village, and the few migrant occupants came and went with the different fishing seasons. As the stories went, the mission never had any permanent clergy. Some of the elders in La Paz who falsely claimed knowledge of such matters believed the Mission was built with the intended purpose of attracting settlers who would form a spiritual community in the vicinity of the Los Dolores and Timbabichi arroyos. If that, in fact, was the case, the plan never came to be.

The mission had been built of local stone and imported timbers. The roof collapsed more years ago than anyone could remember, but recently a barge-load of new timbers from the mainland were placed across the openness, and boatloads of fresh, green, fan palm ojas completed the new roof. In its current use, love songs, romantic ballads, and festive folk tunes reverberated off the thick stone walls in place of the intended inspirational harmonies of spiritual choirs.

Leo rode through the low hills above the beach, seldom losing sight of the water in that brief time where late afternoon slowly fades toward evening. From the top of the last rise before the descent into Los Dolores, he heard mariachi music blending with the dull roar of a diesel generator. He was surprised to see a dozen pangas lined up in the shallows along the beach, several of them super-pangas, with dual outboards mounted heavily on their transoms. He nudged the gelding and approached the beach. The pale spotted mare followed faithfully behind with her heavy pack saddle.

"Heh," Leo said as he came upon three fishermen – two middle-aged men and a boy in his teens. He held firmly back on the reins, and the gelding came to a halt.

"Hello there," the older men answered in unison. The boy said nothing and carefully observed Leo with his arms folded across his chest. The boy jerked his head back and to the side in a failed attempt to clear the long hair from over his left eye without using his hand. A belt made of woven hemp baling twine held up a pair of ragged canvas shorts, low on his buttocks. All their feet were bare and hardened.

"My god," Leo started, "looks like Los Dolores has come back to life, but not quite the way the old padres intended!" he chuckled.

The older of the two fishermen smiled and answered, "You're right about that! I like what they've done with the place, but not everyone would agree with me. But then, I like to sip tequila probably more than most. I'd much rather land my panga after a long day fishing and walk into a cantina than I would a church. Holy water doesn't do it for me!"

The boy cracked a smile and swung his head back in a second attempt to clear the hair out of his eyes.

Leo leaned forward in the saddle and swung his right leg back and over the horse's rump and slid to a standing position on the ground in front of the fishermen. He extended his hand and said, "My name's Leonardo. I'm from up in the Gigantas."

"You're a long way from home for a man on horseback. My name's Cayetano, and this is my brother-in-law, German. We fish mostly north of La Paz. We're up this way after shark, but we're not having much luck. I don't like to stay in one place too long, so we travel, looking for new fishing grounds. Never fails. Eventually, we hook up some fish and head back home to sell the catch. What about you? What brings you all the way down here?"

Leo glanced over toward the old mission. "I guess I'm like you, I got the urge to do some riding and see if I could pick up a little cowboy work along the way." Changing the subject, he said, "What's behind the idea of turning the Mission into a cantina out here in the middle of nothing?"

"Crazy, isn't it? But there's a crew building a road from here up the arroyo and out to the La Paz road. They're building an airstrip back over there, too," he pointed beyond the dunes. "Who knows where they come up with all this, but who cares? I'm happy to have a place where I can land my panga, buy a drink and a hot meal, and mix it up with a chica. They've got it all right here." He waved his hand at the Mission.

"Hmm," Leo muttered as he thought it over. "I think I'll walk over that way and have a drink. They friendly to strangers in there?"

"I was a stranger until a few hours ago, and they were happy to take my pesos!"

"Folks usually are, aren't they? Happy to take your pesos."

The old fisherman chuckled to himself and added, "Good luck to you, wherever you end up."

"Nice meeting with you, Cayetano. I hope you find those sharks you're after!"

Leo led the horses across the beach and up a small rise as he approached the Mission. The closer he got, the louder the music. It sounded as if there were some serious festivities inside.

★★★

As the sun was going down, Leo tied his two horses to the fence rail in front of the mission and stepped up to the massive double door. He noted it was four inches thick and hung on heavy hand-forged iron hinges. It was arched at the top and formed a half-circle high above his head as he entered. Once inside, the floor was made of great wide slabs of sandstone, solid as bedrock under his boots. The music blared to the point of irritating him. He realized he preferred the sounds of silence out in the desert. There were a dozen or more occupied tables in the vast room with the towering ceiling.

The first person to see him come through the door was a young woman standing at the bar. She was prettied-up in heavy make-up and wore a tight, low-cut dress that exposed nearly all her smaller-than-average breasts. She promptly walked in Leo's direction with a confident swing in her hips and a broad smile on her face. He saw where she had a deep scar across her left cheek, but it failed to diminish her beauty.

"Buy me a drink?" she asked as she placed her arm under his and turning, walked in unison with him toward an empty table.

"How could I refuse? I just spent a week riding in the desert, and you're the first pretty thing I've seen in all that time! I'll have tequila with a lime, and if that generator is making ice, I'd love a big tall glass full of ice cubes."

"This is your lucky day, Señor. First, you find this cantina in the middle of nowhere, then you by chance run into me, and I happen to know where they got buckets full of ice. What's your name, cowboy? Mine's Flora. Nice to meet you!" she extended her petite hand.

"Name's Leonardo. Happy to meet you, Flora. Truly." He took her hand and noticed the softness, the lack of callous, and the red satin fingernails. He'd always had a soft spot for pretty whores, but nothing at all like his cousin Antonio. Leo more enjoyed just talking to them. He noticed she smelled wonderful, and he thought he must smell a lot like a horse.

She offered him a cigarette, and he declined, but he took the match from her hand and lit it for her. He watched as she placed it between her thick red lips and daintily sucked in the smoke. Just as daintily, she exhaled to the side, careful not to get any smoke in his space. He looked beyond their small table and guessed there to be twenty or more people in the room, mostly men playing cards or simply drinking. He counted five whores flirting with clients at different tables. A three-man mariachi group was providing the entertainment.

"Just what in the world finds you way out here in god-for-sakin' Los Dolores, Flora?"

"Oh, long story, I'm from Michoacan, over south of Sinaloa. I knew people with ties to La Paz, and they offered me a free ride on the ferry and a little pay for starting this place up. I jumped at the chance. You only live once, as they say," she pulled another hit on the cigarette and exhaled toward the ceiling. "It's back to La Paz the day after tomorrow. Then, it's all the way back home a day or two after that. Where you from, Leonardo? Just riding in here from who knows where out there in the great beyond? And for what?" she shrugged her shoulders.

"How about that drink? I haven't had an ice cube in so many years, I can't remember. Can we get someone over here to get it for us?"

"Sure. Juanny. Heh!" she shouted over the music and beckoned a young man with a wave of her hand. He scurried across the floor and took her order.

Leo was impressed with her directness and answered, "I'm from up in a mountain range called Las Gigantas. That's about one hundred miles north of La Paz, as the bird flies, well at least that's where it starts. It goes another hundred miles north from there. Big mountains, more than a kilometer high some of them. One little snake track of a road goes through there. Not much else. I live on a pretty little ranch down on the Cortez coast, at the base of those mountains."

"So, why are you down here in Los Dolores? You're avoiding my question."

"Not avoiding you, as I told a fisherman over on the beach. I like to take off and ride every once in a while, explore new country. As you say, we only live once. I'm out living, just like you, and if I can pick up a little cowboy work along the way, all the better."

"I don't believe you. You're too old for that to be the answer, but it doesn't matter. Here we are, about to have a cold drink and maybe a little more. I'm fine with it, cause you're about the most interesting man that's walked through that door the whole time I've been here. All these other guys like to think they're cowboys, but they're not. Cowboys don't ride to work on the Sinaloa ferry and stay in fancy hotels every chance they get."

Their drinks arrived, and Leo saw where Flora ordered him not only tequila with lime on the rocks, but also a tall glass of ice cubes with a cherry on top. He smiled.

"Here's to the most beautiful woman I've ever laid eyes on in Los Dolores!" Leo raised his glass to hers.

She punched him softly on the arm with her free hand, laughed and said, "I'm the only woman you've met in Los Dolores, as far as I can tell!" She smiled at him, and he noticed how her charcoal colored eyes twinkled in the pale light.

"Doesn't matter, Flora. You are beautiful, and I wouldn't kid you about that."

Two well-dressed cowboys walked through the door and stopped after taking a few steps inside to let their eyes adjust. They looked around and headed directly toward Flora's table. The first one eyed Leonardo with clear resentment. His lips were drawn in a tight straight line below his thin black mustache as he stepped up to their table.

From the expression on his face, his mannerisms, and the glare in his squinted left eye, Leo took an immediate disliking to him.

"I got all cleaned up and thought you'd be in here waiting for me, and here you are drinking with this grubby lookin' stranger." He glanced at Leo with disdain. "I hope you don't intend to make a night of it," he growled.

"Just what if I do, Manny? You don't have anything to say about it. You don't own me."

"I thought we had a date is all. That's the way we left it last night."

"That's the way you might've left it, but I'm a working girl, and I get to choose who it is I work with and when. Right now, I'm choosing to have a drink with Leonardo here, and if we choose to have another, or whatever else it might lead to, well that's entirely up to us."

He wasn't pleased with her answer. He gritted his teeth and his face hardened. He took a step forward and raised his hand to slap her. Leonardo placed both hands flat on the table and rose to his feet so quickly it startled the man, and he stopped. He looked straight at Leo who was glaring at him. He turned left, then right, and muttered something under his breath. Leo nodded almost imperceptibly and slowly sat back down.

The mariachis approached the table but stopped short. They saw the tension, "We'll be back later, Señora," the guitarist said to Flora.

The interruption emboldened the man. He asked Leo with an air of authority. "That spotted mare out there, and that other bay horse. They yours?"

Leo was staring up with his eyes fixed on the man and said, "What's it to you?"

"I haven't seen you around here before. That spotted mare. She has an arrowhead brand on her left hip," he glared right back at Leonardo. "That's the same brand we see on the older cows we've been gathering. Where you from?"

"Not that I really care to discuss anything with you, after how rude you were to the lady." He glanced at Flora. "But I've got nothing to hide. I'm from up in the Gigantas. I'm passing through on my way to somewhere else. I doubt very much you'd even know where the Gigantas are. Where you from? You don't look like you're from around here, all fancied up like a banty rooster," he said it with a smirk, spitting out the words.

"None of your goddamned business where I'm from. I'm gathering up a bunch of scattered out old cows we just bought, and some of them happen to have the same brand as your horse. I find that odd. Where'd you get that horse?"

Flora sat perfectly still, watching and listening. She nearly fell out of her chair when the serving boy dropped a tray of drinks behind her. The two men standing looked at the boy. Leo never flinched.

"I bought her at a sale up in Insurgentes when she was a filly. Had her ever since. She's a damned good animal. In fact, I need to speak with someone in charge. I want to board both horses tonight."

"That'd be me you need to talk to. I'm the foreman here. It'll cost you ten pesos a night for the two horses. There's hay and empty corrals out back."

"That's a pretty stiff price, but here you go, seeing as it will only be for one night. I was going to inquire about some work, but I think I'll just be moving on in the morning. Here's your ten pesos." He tossed a coin across the table.

The man thought for a moment and said, "Yes, I think it would be best if you did that. Just move on in the morning." He picked up the coin and stuffed it in his pocket.

He turned to his partner and said, "Come on, there's plenty of whores who'd be happy to have our business tonight. Let's go find one." They walked away.

"Friendly fella," Leo said as he took a sip of tequila. He put the cherry in his mouth along with a few ice cubes. "Mmm, I forgot what a mouthful of ice felt like. I could get used to that."

"Manny's a jerk, but he is the foreman." She reached for her drink. "He may be in charge of the men, but he's not in charge of me. I work for the boss guy in La Paz, and I did my job getting things ready around here. Like I said, I'm out of here day after tomorrow, and that's none too soon as far as I'm concerned." Her lips curled as she said it. "This isn't my type of place."

"I can understand that." He warmed to her and smiled, "If you're free for the night, can we start with you showing me where I can put my horses, and we can take it from there?"

"I'd be happy to. Thank you for that." She placed her hand over his weathered fist and squeezed. "After we get your horses settled in, I'll give you the grand tour of Los Dolores!"

Leo swallowed what was left of his tequila and said, "Call me 'Leo.' I'm looking forward to the evening, Flora." He rose up from the chair.

In the twilight, Leo and Flora led the horses out behind the old Mission to a mesquite forest, with a recently cleared three-acre flat in the center. Piles of grubbed-out tree roots and loose branches lay well off to the side, waiting for a torch. The tree trunks were cut into fence posts, spaced perfectly apart and planted solidly in the ground across the flat. Between the posts were intricately woven long, finger-thick stems of ocotillo, covered with razor-sharp thorns forming an impenetrable barrier that would hold back the wildest of range cattle. It was an admirable piece of work, most likely accomplished by locals who took great pride in tradition. A wooden water tower stood on thick posts and supplied a steady flow to mortared stone troughs in each corral.

Flora pointed at an empty corral, "Let's put the horses in there."

They got the horses fed and settled in, then they walked, circling all the corrals. Leo counted cattle in his head, and he eyed the surrounding terrain. He saw the mesquite flat extended well beyond the corrals, and steep foothills rose on three sides. The fourth side to the east was composed of sand dunes, miles of them along the beach fronting the ocean. The bone-dry Los Dolores Arroyo crossed the center of the flat and wound its way toward the ocean from its source, many miles west in the higher desert ground. Leo counted more than two hundred head of cattle, and he recognized many of the older animals.

"My God, that's a lot of cattle," Leo said.

"Sure is. You should hear the noise they make when they bring in each new bunch and close the gate. I swear to god, it's hard to sleep. They settle down after they get filled up with that alfalfa there." She gestured over at the hay wagon. "I heard someone say this is about half the herd, and they'd have the other half here in a week or two. That's what they're working on now, but I don't care or pay it much attention."

"How many cowboys are there?"

"Oh, I don't know exactly." They stopped and she paused to think about it. "I'd guess seven or eight. They've got a camp up the arroyo a little bit." She pointed to some tents and a small horse corral on the other side of the flat. They live up there, and they come down to the cantina in the evening, along with the other men who are building the airstrip. That's over that way another quarter mile." She pointed again. "And the road crew comes down to drink in the evenings too. They live in another camp about a mile more up the arroyo. This place can get pretty busy. Tonight, it's a little slow, but it's early, and that will change the later it gets." She looked up at him in the pale twilight. She thought he had kind eyes. She took his hand, and they continued their walk.

"Interesting. Five years ago, I camped right there at the Mission. The only other people were a few fishermen and one family living in a palapa where those corrals are now." He glanced over that way.

"There's two families living back in the mesquite somewhere, now. The women work in the cantina cooking and cleaning."

They came full circle around the corrals and stopped again. Leo said, looking down at her, "I appreciate the tour, Flora. Why don't we go back and have another drink? That ice was awfully good, and I don't get to spend time with a lovely young woman very often. I want to take full advantage of the evening." He placed his arm around her and gave her a kiss on top of her head. Her hair smelled fresh and clean, like the desert after a soaking rain.

She looked up into his eyes and said, “I’d like that. I’m not about to trade you in for one of those Sinaloa boys. Not a one of them knows how to treat a woman.”

They walked hand in hand back to the cantina. Her heart fluttered for the first time in years.

★★★

As midnight approached, Rosario’s 1959 black Chevy pickup continued to weave its way up and along the primitive road through the high Gigantas on its way to Loreto. There was a full case of beer in the back, along with two hundred kilos of marijuana, fresh off a Colombian airplane they’d met earlier in the day on a beach north of La Paz. The occupants of the truck had already finished their first case of beer. They were ready for the second.

“Pull over. I’ve gotta piss so bad I can taste it,” the fat man at the passenger window groaned.

“Okay, okay. I need a beer anyway,” Rosario answered. “I’ll pull over on that flat spot up ahead.”

The road was little more than a primitive, single lane, two-rut trail, and they’d only seen two other vehicles since leaving Insurgentes six hours earlier. Nobody in their right mind would drive through the Gigantas at night, but the occupants of the truck were all lousy drunk, and none of them had ever been on the road to Loreto before. They didn’t know it, but they’d climbed to nearly three thousand feet in elevation from sea level back near Insurgentes. It was so dark in the canyon’s shadows they couldn’t see much past a few feet off to the side of the headlights.

Anna Marie was sitting in the cab with her old “friend” Rosario to her left, the two others to her right. She’d had four or five beers; she hadn’t counted. Between the beer and the late hour, she was groggy. She’d forgotten how crude drunk men could get. The three men in the truck were cracking vulgar jokes throughout the drive, and continually saying offensive, ugly things about women. She tuned them out. Her thoughts kept returning to Antonio, and how she left him standing in the road. She dearly cared for him, long before she’d ever met Felix, but they’d had their share of troubles. She realized now what a good man he was, and how they could easily work things out. She'd decided to go to Loreto with Rosario on a hairbrained whim, and the farther they drove, the more she regretted it. But here she was.

"I'm pulling over," Rosario startled her when he hit the brakes. All three men jumped out, barely taking two steps before draining the beer from their bladders. Anna Marie more modestly stepped behind the pickup and squatted in the pale red glow of the tail lights.

Rosario cracked open a beer and began searching under the driver's seat for a package he'd placed there earlier in the afternoon. "There it is!" he exclaimed as he retrieved a manila envelope. Nobody was paying attention, the other three were chugging beers in front of the headlights.

Rosario turned on the dome light and opened the envelope on the seat. "Look here what I've got," he called to the others. The other two men gathered around to look over his shoulder.

"What you got?" asked one of the men.

"Remember on the beach when the pilot took me off alone to talk?"

"Yeah," answered one of them.

"He made me promise we wouldn't touch a single one of those keys back there. They're all weighed, wrapped up tight and numbered, and that's the way he wants em delivered. In exchange for my promise, he gave me this, look here," he excitedly unfolded a square of aluminum foil. "It's pure uncut cocaine, fresh from the Colombian jungle. He said to go easy with it, cause its killer stuff. Let's see if he knew what he was talking about."

"You son of a bitch," one of them said. "You held out on us? We could've been in heaven all day. Go on, spread out some lines. Let's do it. Here's a bill. You can have the first hit." Rosario rolled up the bill and put it to his nose. He sniffed up the first line and did the same with the second in his other nostril. He raised his head and sucked in fresh air through his nose for good measure, wiping his nose with his forearm.

"Wow, that hits fast. Try that!" he said with a grin, handing the bill to the bearded man next to him.

The other two men repeated exactly what Rosario had done. Five minutes later the three of them were standing in the headlights smiling, spinning around in their heads as if they were free of gravity. Rosario went back to the truck and laid out two lines for Anna. She stepped up. As she leaned into the cab of the truck and snorted the lines off the vinyl driver's seat, Rosario grabbed her ass. She straightened up and pushed his hand off. The coke hit her with a wallop, "Please, not here."

"Coke makes me horny. Let's fuck."

"Don't say that. They'll hear you."

"That's okay. They can watch! Come on, it'd be fun!"

He creeped her out. She curled her lip and pushed him back. She stepped away and picked up her beer off the hood. She joined the other two men in front of the headlights. She was lightheaded and woozy.

They finished their beers and had another round. Rosario had a liter of tequila. They all shared hits on it, draining the bottle. They were seriously messed up and stood in a small circle in front of the headlights. They agreed that it definitely was pure, uncut product. Anna felt Rosario's two unkempt friends staring at her as the conversation wore on. They positioned themselves close up on each side of her. They leaned into her, touching her. She wanted to run, but there was nowhere to go. She stepped away to pee and didn't return. She climbed up in the cab of the truck and waited.

The men might have stood there mindlessly chatting until dawn, except Rosario reminded them they had to be in Loreto later in the day. Having forgotten about Loreto, they focused on getting back to the truck. They swayed and stumbled and groped, but all three managed to find their way up in the truck, where they joined Anna on the bench seat. She'd been snoozing but woke to their blundering efforts.

Their vision of the road ahead in the headlights varied from sharp to hazy. The men were unusually happy as reality slipped away. Rosario felt like a true master of the universe as he steered the truck along the dangerous narrow road with one loose hand draped over the wheel. The short fat man by the passenger window sang folk ballads for a huge adoring audience, or so he thought. The windows were rolled up tight, and poor Anna gagged, inhaling the over-powering sweaty stench dripping off their bodies. The bearded man next to her on the right let off the most disgusting series of loud, foul farts he thought were hilarious.

Rosario continued, steering, swerving, managing to stay on the road.

"Don't. Don't do that!" Anna demanded.

"What's your problem?" the bearded man asked.

"I'm with Rosario. That's what! Get your hands off me!"

"Aww, come on. He doesn't care. He told us you were cool, didn't you, Rosario?"

"Rosario, tell your friend to keep his grubby hands to himself!" she demanded again.

Rosario reached up and turned on the dome light to see what was going on. He saw his friend had his hand up under Anna's blouse. He smiled and said, "Don't worry baby, he's just having some fun," he paused. "In fact, how about a little for me?" he reached over with his free hand and searched under her blouse. He pushed up her bra to free her left breast, "Ahh, there it is!"

"Not now," she squirmed, "You're driving, you fool! One more time. Tell your friend to quit it! I mean it. Tell him to stop," she pulled down on the hand. Nothing she did could get him to stop. His hand went right back. He squeezed hard. He leaned into her. He nuzzled her. His foul breath invaded her flaring nostrils.

Rosario liked what he felt. He stopped the truck in the middle of the road. He put on the parking brake and turned his complete attention to Anna.

"Come on, baby. I can't believe how nice that titty feels." He reached his hand back up and fondled her. Her heart was pounding in her chest. Adrenaline was pumping through her veins. She felt desperate, angry, frantic, trapped, with no way out.

Anna let loose a guttural, terrified, primal scream. Her arms were strong for a small-framed woman. She raised them, making rock-hard fists against the ceiling and brought both arms down with such force she nearly broke them across the arms of the men. Their hands came right back.

"Come on now, baby," Rosario tried to sound romantic. He nuzzled up on her left side. "Let's take that blouse off. I want to see those gorgeous tits of yours out in the open."

"Oh my god, Rosario. Please!" she tried to think clearly. "Babe, you know I'm in love with you. Let's go to Loreto. I want to make love to you there, not here. Only to you. You're my man. My only man. We'll get a room and make love. We can fuck all night. Just you and me. Please! I'll do anything for you. I will. I promise!" She sobbed.

He didn't care. He ripped her blouse off and violently pulled her bra up over her head. "Now look at that! Look at those things hanging there all big and loose like that!"

The bearded man on her right side bent down and began to suck. Rosario leaned in on her left side and did the same.

"Oh my god!" she screamed. She looked desperately around for a weapon. There was nothing within reach. She started to scratch and claw. She growled like a cornered animal. She beat on them with her fists. She pulled on their hair with all the strength she had. She clawed and tried to rip out their eyes. She drew blood. She angered them. The bearded man leaned back and swung a punch so hard to the side of her face there was a terrible ugly cracking sound.

They devoured Anna Marie, trying to climb up and rub themselves on her body in the cramped space. Something in her head caused her brain to scramble. She began to hallucinate. Strange thoughts of other times and places, flashing colorful scenes in her head. She moaned incoherently in a voice not her own. She gave up. She went limp. The third man became entangled. They fought over her. They grunted and snorted like the disgusting miserable pigs they were.

Rosario was pinned between the seat and the steering wheel. He finally had enough. He threw open the driver's side door and pulled Anna out. The other two clamored out past the wheel. They dragged Anna to the front of the truck in the headlights and two of them propped her up, topless, in a peaceful serene trance, her arms dangling down at her sides. The short fat man pulled down her slacks and undies. The bearded man let her sink down to the ground. Fat man slipped the last of her clothing over her ankles and spread her legs there in the center of the road.

Anna Marie's small, compact body was simply unable to process all the poison, withstand the stress and the horrible abuse. She drifted further away, to another place. She felt nothing. She fell into a deep, life-threatening coma.

Each of the men had their way with her. When they were finished, they dragged her lifeless body to the side of the nearby cliff and tossed it over the edge. Anna Marie's severely damaged body landed with a sickening slap on a narrow ledge of rock, thirty feet below, draped precariously above a seven-hundred-foot sheer vertical drop.

The men sat on the tail gate and drank more beer. They finished the rest of the cocaine.

Rosario's head was somewhere in the clouds as he drove away. The other two men made senseless incoherent talk. Anna Marie's name was never mentioned. They never referred to her again. As if she'd never existed.

Less than an hour later, the 1959 black Chevy pickup, with two hundred kilos of Colombian weed in the bed, drove over the cliff on a blind hairpin turn. The three men were ejected as the truck careened off the rocks and floated in the dark air for a timeless moment. They were splattered all over the craggy rocks like a handful of broken eggs half-way down. The truck continued without them. It flipped and tumbled eight hundred feet in all. It bounced off an out-cropping near the bottom causing a fierce firestorm, before coming to rest on the narrow canyon floor, in one final hell-on-earth explosion.

At the Hotel Pescador in Loreto that night, Rosario's reservation was tossed out as a "no-show." Two angry, very dangerous men from Tijuana plotted how they would get even with the double-crossing narcos from Sinaloa, who had cheated them out of more than one hundred thousand pesos worth of Colombian weed.

★★★

Oscar Padilla and eight of his business associates approached the marina in La Paz where his luxurious 120-foot yacht, the "Doña Guadalupe" was docked. A crew of four had been preparing the vessel for a three-week tour of the Cortez islands and an extended stay in the scenic fishing village of Agua Verde. Spirits were high. Oscar had a spring in his step as he anticipated their time in the remote, undeveloped Baja wilderness.

The boat was equipped with all the fishing and diving equipment they'd ever need. They'd be passing through some of the most prolific waters on the planet. The kitchen and the cold storage were fully stocked with far beyond what the group required. The wine closet was full. High on the upper mast the Mexican national flag proudly waved from its perch above the stars and stripes. The ship was licensed in both countries. Two super pangas would launch with the yacht. Each one would carry two heavily armed bodyguards. They would remain within eyesight of the vessel for the duration of the trip.

"Welcome aboard," said the first mate, as Oscar, a fit, agile man in his late sixties, climbed the final few steps of the ramp.

"Thank you, Fernando," he replied through a smile. They shook hands. "I saw the weather report this morning. The extended forecast couldn't be better," he added.

"Yes, sir. I saw it too. Do you have any special instructions for me?" he asked.

"Yes, I thought we might stay at the anchorage I like out on Espiritu Santo this evening. There's no reason to rush ourselves. In fact, let's stop at three or four other islands on our way north and maintain a leisurely pace. I wouldn't care if it took us a week to reach Agua Verde. There are so many beautiful places to stop along the way."

"I'll plan it that way, sir."

"All of our guests are on board. We can depart when you're ready."

"Yes, sir. That will be less than an hour then."

Oscar and his guests gathered on the upper deck, overlooking the Malecón for celebratory drinks served under an elegant canopy. Fresh bouquets of flowers adorned the tables. Redwood easy chairs with thick, forest-green cushions surrounded the tables and matching chaise lounges lined the railings surrounding the deck. Oscar led the toast.

★★★

Felix was in a melancholy mood as he sat back in an old chair next to a small fire in front of the beach house. The soft rhythmic spell of the three-inch waves mesmerized him and helped him think. Although he'd known it for days already, he admitted to himself all things with Anna Marie were over. Her cold hard stare as he left her at the door in Insurgentes should have been enough, but it took time to sink in. It wasn't meant to be.

He serenely watched a brilliant moon rise, inch by steady inch, from the depths of the darkness out over the sea. It caused a sparkling lightshow that made the water seem like it was dancing. It reminded him how Pedro always used to say, "We're lucky to be alive." He rose from the chair and retired to his bed in the beach house, feeling at complete ease with himself and the world. He inhaled the night air and thought how the sea smelled rich and fertile. Such a contrast with the desert world he was born into.

Luisa finished soaking and shaving her body in the glorious warm water of the hot pool. As she spread the aloe paste over her neglected skin, she felt alive again. She couldn't recall ever feeling as alive as she did at that moment. She too watched as the moon rose out over the sea, the dancing lights on the water, the soft gentle lapping of the three-inch waves. She knew what she wanted, what it was she needed.

He didn't hear her come in. He smelled the fragrance as he was fading away into the early stages of sleep. He thought surely, he was dreaming. He felt her hand as she placed it on his cheek and caressed him there. She placed a kiss there, soft as a feather.

"Are you awake?"

"Mmm, hmm. I think so."

"Can I lay with you?"

"Mmm, hmm," he murmured, turned toward her, opened his arms.

She slipped out of the light cotton smock. She was naked under it. She laid down next to him and found him naked under a thin sheet. Their bodies merged in an embrace. Mysteries unfolded as they touched in that way for the first time. There was no hurry. They were slow, deliberate, respectful and gentle in their movements.

He found her lips in the dark, and they kissed as deeply as only two people in love can. There was no hesitation, only a long, slow, deep kiss where their tongues caressed and tasted. Neither of them could believe it was happening. She pressed her breasts against his hard-muscled chest, and she felt truly at peace for the first time in recent memory. Ever since he was a young boy, he had thought of her as an untouchable goddess. Unbelievably, here she was in his arms. Her mouth covered his, and he felt her hips pressing against him. The sweet smell of the aloe on her skin was overpowering.

They spent the night together. They made love three times. They clung to one another. Without a word passing between them, they understood the commitment they'd just made. They would be together. They'd been in love in a different sort of way before this night. This precious moment would stay with them for life.

★★★

Leo never slept. At three a.m. he quietly rose in the pale candlelight from the bed he shared that night with Flora. He slipped into his clothes, as she lay peacefully under the sheets. She stirred and rolled, but never woke.

He gathered his belongings. He paused to look down on her and whispered, "Muchisimas gracias, Floracita." He bent down and placed a soft, delicate kiss on top of her head, careful not to wake her. He turned around and slipped out the door, without making a sound.

Outside the night air was brisk, and the moon was fading away in the west. Leo kept to the shadows and found his two horses content and asleep in the corral where he left them. He quietly saddled them and spoke softly to keep them calm. On foot, he led them away from the corrals to the edge of what was left standing of the mesquite forest, avoiding the cowboy camp and their corral full of horses. He was out of sight up the arroyo in less than three minutes, where he mounted the gelding and pointed the horse toward Insurgentes.

Leo had no choice. He needed help. He decided to ride for two days without stopping up to Insurgentes. He wasn't quite sure how he was going to recover all the cattle, but he was thankful that Osuna's cowboys had already done the largest share of the work by gathering them in one place. He had ninety miles of country ahead of him, but he would follow the road the whole way. He was glad the horses were rested and fed up full on the alfalfa. They'd need it.

A mile up the Los Dolores Arroyo, Leo came upon the camp used by the road crew. He swung the horses wide around the camp and circled back after he was past. He was encouraged to find a new graded road up the arroyo that would cut his time in half. He set the gelding to a trot and followed the road easily in what was left of the moon's waning light.

Leo kept up his pace through the pre-dawn hours and surprised himself at how quickly he put the miles behind him. By daylight he was much farther along than he'd expected. He recalled his conversation with Antonio about truck traffic on the La Paz road. Instead of riding the seventy or so miles to Insurgentes, perhaps he could catch a ride, he thought. He'd find a place to board the horses, and they could take life easy until he was able to get back to them. Feeling energized, he kicked up the pace.

★★★

Flora rolled out of bed at daybreak and realized Leo had left. Not that many good men passed through her life. She sighed. She glanced at the nightstand next to the bed. There was a one-hundred-peso bill. Her regular charge was ten. She would have stayed with him for free. She smiled.

She was startled out of her thoughts by someone pounding on the door. Manny and three of his men didn't wait for her to respond. They barged in. They were heavily armed.

"What do you want? What do you mean by coming in here? I'm not even dressed." She covered herself with the bed sheet.

"Since when are you so modest?" Manny gruffly asked, staring at her with his squinted eye.

"Where's he hiding?" he questioned her, scanning the small room.

"Who you talking about?"

"You know who I'm talking about. Where is he? The man with the horses last night. A few of the local fishermen know who he is. They were kind enough to fill me in. He's down here after our cows, and I'm gonna set him straight." He kept looking left then right, expecting Leo to come at him out of thin air.

"Oh, him. I didn't know who he was, other than his name's Leonardo. He's from somewhere up north. He had a quick one and went on his way. I'm not sure where he was going from here."

"He gave me ten pesos to board the horses last night. A man wouldn't do that if he was just gonna come in for a quickie!" He yanked the door back and looked behind it. "You're lying to me, Flor. This is serious. Our employer won't be too happy if your friend messes up our plans for the cattle." He ordered one of his men to look under the bed. The man got down on his knees, peered under and stood back up shaking his head.

"You're fooling around where you shouldn't be sticking your pretty little nose." He pointed at her menacingly. "You're just a whore, Flor. Don't cover up for him. You might never make it back to Michoacan!"

"Don't threaten me, Manny. Don't you dare threaten me!" she spit out the words. "I told you. He's long gone. He got his rocks off and hardly said goodbye."

Manny eyed the one-hundred-peso bill on the nightstand. "You always leave one hundred pesos laying around like that? It's not like your bedroom isn't a public place. I think your friend left you that money cause you fucked his brains silly. Nobody pays one hundred pesos for a quick piece of your ass. I'll warn you – don't you be lying to me you little slut. Where is he?" he kept demanding. She saw he was about to get physical.

"Go fuck yourself, Manny," she snarled as she reached for the bill on the nightstand but pulled a pistol out of the drawer below it. She took two steps forward, the sheet she was using for cover fell to the floor. She pointed the gun squarely at his face. "If you don't turn around and walk out that door, I'll splatter your brains all over the wall! I mean it! Get out and don't you dare threaten me again. I'll do it, I'll blow your fucking head off. Don't doubt me, I've done it before, you ugly fuck!"

With all of her one hundred twelve pounds, she stepped up closer. The gun barrel was only three feet from his face. She cocked the trigger and held the pistol rock-hard steady. He and his three men backed-stepped slowly. He stopped outside the door and said, "I shoulda whipped your ugly little ass soon as I came through the door. You'll get what's coming to you, bitch!"

"I'll be gone real soon. You leave me out of it. All I did was fuck a cowboy who was passing through here. It's what I do. You know that. Just get the fuck out!"

"You think you're real smart, don't you? You better hope your friend never shows his face around here again. I'll put a bullet through it. I swear!"

"Get going, you asshole! Now!" She continued to hold the gun, pointing it at the open door after they left. She heard their angry cussing as they walked away. She wanted out of Los Dolores. The sooner the better.

★★★

As the sun beat down and the rocks around her radiated heat, Anna Marie raised her head. She had no idea where she was, or even who she was. She only knew she was alive. Throughout her life, she'd learned how to survive – the orphanage, the nuns, the streets, the cruel men. Draped over a pile of jagged rocks on the narrow ledge, her only comfort was the warm rays of the sun bearing down on her battered, naked body. She absorbed the heat.

She told herself to think. She trained herself to breathe. Steady, deep calm breaths. Think. Breathe. Steady. Breathe. She repeated the words in her head.

Breathe. Think. Steady. Deep.

Ninety percent of her body was covered with dry-crusted blood, including her matted, tangled hair. Her face was a grotesque mass of ugly gashes and purple bruises. Only one eye would open. Her head, swelled and distorted, pounded from multiple concussions. Ragged open wounds covered her scalp. Dagger-like pains coursed up and down her spine. Perhaps it was a blessing she felt nothing from the waist down.

Breathe. Steady. Deep. Breathe. Think.

She looked down through her one functioning eye and saw the sheer vertical drop, less than twelve inches in front of her. She twisted her head left and glanced over her shoulder. She saw an escape if only she could pull her body thirty feet up and over the layered rock steps.

She placed her hands on the rock in front of her and pushed. Her arms were fine. Her life depended on them now. She dragged her body up and over the first rock, only to collapse, but she'd made it. Her breathing was strained and shallow.

Breathe. Steady. Deep. Breathe. Think.

The splintered ribs in her back pinched the soft muscle tissue along her spine when she pushed and pulled with her arms. She convulsed each time she moved. She was so entirely dehydrated no tears would form in her eyes.

She rested. Breathe. Steady. Deep. Breathe. Think.

Two dreadful, agonizing, near-miraculous hours later, Anna Marie dragged herself over the last rock. She was on flat ground. The mid-day sun, hours before a blessing, became her enemy. She tried to crawl, but there was no controlling her legs. There was nothing down there. She found enough energy to whimper, dry-eyed. It gave her comfort. She curled into a fetal position the best she could. She hugged herself. She drifted into unconsciousness, then a coma, not knowing she'd reached the side of the road.

★★★

Pablo Sandoval and his large extended family were returning during late afternoon to their small farm in the village of San Javier from a fruit and vegetable delivery down in Loreto. A dozen of his children, nieces, and nephews hugged the wooden stakes that rose from the bed of his 1948 Ford flatbed, as the old truck rattled and strained on its way up the steep road. They carried plenty of water and sang folk songs as they poked along in first gear, as fast as the old truck would go up the steep hill.

"Oh, my God," cried Pablo's wife, Lupita, from her perch in the passenger window. "There's a woman on the road! Stop the truck. Stop now!" Pablo didn't have much brake, but he let off the gas, and the tired old truck came to a halt. The children piled off the back, and all five adults in the front cab slid off the seat. Lupe kneeled next to the woman, and everyone gathered around to see. Anna Marie was only a few short shallow breaths away from death.

"Water! Bring me water!" Lupe shouted. One of the boys handed her a tin can full of water. Lupe pried open Anna's clenched jaw and let the water trickle into her mouth. The first container of water went in and spilled out the other side. "Bring me more. More water. Now!"

Lupe was encouraged when, after the third container, Anna coughed as the first drop of water found its way to her throat. Like nursing a newborn, Lupe cradled Anna's head and coaxed a tiny trickle down her throat. Lupe focused with sheer intensity on each precious drop. Anna Marie cracked open her one undamaged eye just a hair's width. Seeing as the day was slipping away from them, Lupe ordered a bed be made for Anna across the front bench seat, leaving only enough space for Pablo to drive. Lupe squeezed her round, ample body in on the passenger side floor and nursed Anna from there. They were three grueling hours from San Javier.

Lupe and her sister spent the night at Anna's side, under the pale light of a flickering kerosene lamp, whispering softly between themselves as they desperately worked to save Anna Marie's life. They delicately cleaned and bandaged her broken body, paying special attention to her gruesome face and head wounds. They cut off her thick matted hair to fully expose, dress, and bandage her scalp. Her jaw and her nose were broken, and one eye was swollen shut, an ugly black color. Drifting in and out of a coma during the night, Lupe saw Anna turn a corner at dawn. She was certain of only one thing that morning. It was going to be a terrible struggle with a questionable outcome for the young woman, whoever she was.

★★★

Surprising himself, Leo made it to the La Paz road by noon, though the longer portion of the journey still lay ahead of him. There was a small ranch outpost at the intersection, and for just a few pesos, the old rancher agreed to board the horses for as long as necessary. The old man noticed Leo's sense of urgency and figured him to be a man on the run. He suspected Leo would never be back, and the two horses would bring him a huge profit. He'd give Leo thirty days, no more.

An hour later, Leo flagged down a truck carrying a load of empty chili crates up to Insurgentes. The driver told Leo he'd be in Insurgentes in eight or ten hours if all went well. Leo settled in for the drive and started thinking about a plan. Three hours later, the old truck's engine quit, and Leo spent much of the afternoon helping the trucker repair it.

Close to midnight, the truck carrying Leo and the chili crates came to a stop along El Centro in Insurgentes. By this time, Leo could barely hold his head up. He gave the trucker a thirty-peso tip, picked up his saddlebag, and found a place to lay down on a patch of grass under a giant eucalyptus tree in the town square. Before he could count to twenty, he fell off into a deep sleep. He hadn't slept well the previous two nights, one of them lying next to Flora.

Leo stirred at the sound of a few pre-dawn trucks passing by, hauling farm workers on their way to the fields. He massaged his forehead and willed away a headache. He sat up and stretched his aching muscles and sore joints. He'd ridden more than twenty-five hard miles the day before, between Los Dolores and the La Paz road, and he felt it in his bones. He stood up and limped over to the trunk of a big tree and took a leak. By this time, the faint rays of early light showed in the eastern sky, and he walked stiffly down the street to Sammy's office. It was locked up tight, and he took a seat on the front steps. Fifteen minutes later, Sammy pulled up in a 1965 Ford pickup truck.

"Who'd ever believe this?" Sammy asked with a confused look, walking up to the bottom of the steps. "Hardly recognized you, that long hair! Quite a bit of gray in it too. Thought there was another bum lookin for work, sittin on my steps. Happens all the time. Leo, good to see you!" He extended his hand.

Leo rose from the step, shook hands and squeezed Sammy's shoulder with his free hand. "Five years, Sammy. Long time," he said through a smile.

Sammy looked around, puzzled, "No horse? How'd you get here? What?" he was at a loss for words.

"We need to talk, Sammy." He got serious. "I just came in from Los Dolores. There's big trouble down there. Can we go in and talk over coffee? I need some coffee, bad."

"Yeah sure. Let me open the place up. Just what I need, more problems." He turned the key in the lock. "I think I know what it's about." He opened the door, and they went in.

Leo looked around the office. He spotted a jug of drinking water in a dispenser and served himself a glass of water. He splashed some on his face and wiped it clean with his bandanna. Sammy made the coffee. They settled in around the government-issued metal desk.

"Before we go any further, here, read this," Sammy handed Leo the letter from Osuna's attorney declaring ownership of the ranches and the cattle.

"I knew most of this already," Leo said. "They got half the cattle already rounded up. They'll have the rest gathered in ten days, ready to drive em' down to La Paz."

"Dammit, this is happening faster than I thought." Sammy wrung his hands. "Antonio left yesterday to drive the cattle up to Santa Marta. You need to catch up with him."

Leo set his empty cup down on the desk, "I'll need two of your best horses trailered out to the end of the road. I'll need three days of provisions."

"Consider it done."

"What a mess," Leo took off his hat and held his throbbing head in his hands.

Sammy lit a Camel. He took a deep pull and held it in. A pained look crossed his face. "I have to ask you to deliver a message to Tonio for me. I'm afraid its bad news. I got a call from Loreto last night. There's a young woman, Anna Marie, she works for me. Antonio is sweet on her."

Leo sat up straight in the chair and forgot about his headache.

"She went off on a lark with a guy up to Loreto. Antonio was angry with me for letting her go. I promised him I'd check up on her." He stood and started pacing back and forth behind the desk.

"And?" Leo said.

"I'm afraid there's been an accident. The truck they were riding in went off a cliff. Someone passing by saw smoke. The vultures and coyotes had body parts scattered everywhere." He choked up. "He cared for that girl. He'll need to know,"

"My God, Sammy, just what I don't need! What the hell was she doing that for, if Antonio was so sweet on her?"

"Who the fuck knows?" he snapped and threw the cigarette on the floor, crushing it with his heel. "Doesn't really matter now, does it?" He looked as if he was about to cry.

"No," Leo said slowly. He looked up at the ceiling. "What'd you say her name was?"

"Anna Marie."

Leo's headache took a turn for the worse. He pinched the bridge of his nose.

★★★

Antonio, Naco, and Benito made it to the cliff camp on the afternoon of the third day. Pepino greeted them with his typical enthusiasm and took charge feeding and watering their horses and mules. Pepe grudgingly served them spicy bean burritos as they waited for the crew to return to camp. Just before dark, one by one, each exhausted, miserable man appeared on the trail from over the rim. Their feet dragged, their heads were down, and their faces were covered with dust.

When they saw the three visitors, their spirits lifted. Except for the night Luisa had been in camp, they'd never had visitors. There promised to be a festive evening of conversation and socializing, anything at all to break the ugly monotony.

Antonio greeted Felix with a handshake.

"Let's take a walk and share a few sips of this. I'd like to have a word with you," he pulled a pint of tequila out of his pocket.

"That tastes good after a long day," Antonio started as he passed the bottle to Felix, who took a pull. They sat down on the rim rock.

"Alonso told me how you put this crew together. I'm proud of you. I wouldn't a had it in me when I was your age." He patted Felix on the back. “I was too busy chasing girls and getting drunk when I was your age.” He chuckled.

“Not many girls, or tequila for that matter, in San Juanico. I don’t deserve too much credit.” He smiled and took off his hat and beat it on his knee to knock the dust loose.

“I hear you on that.” Antonio laughed. “About how much more trail you have to go?”

“We’re doin the last part down near the bottom. Two weeks more at the most, I’d guess.”

“Good, we might need you to pick things up just a bit.” Antonio spit off to the side. “We’re on our way down to Timbabichi to get the cattle. Not sure how long it’ll take to get em’ back up here, but we’ll need to run em’ right up the trail when we do. No waitin around down on the bottom. Think you can get it done in ten days?” he looked up at the orange glow as the sun faded in the west behind the Gigantas.

Felix thought before he answered, “I’ve been pushing the guys pretty hard, but maybe with the end this close in sight I can squeeze a little bit more out of em.”

“Good then. On another subject, Alonso told me you took Luisa down to Santa Marta. I encouraged her to visit Santa Marta when her husband got back.”

“I know, she told me.”

“Then I learned her husband died.” He glanced away. “Just wanted to say, you probably saved her life and the lives of her children, getting them out of that hell-hole back there.” He cocked his head in the direction of San Juanico.

“I know that too. I wanted to help her. I’ve known her my whole life. I care for her in a different way now.” He looked away. “Luisa and I are together now.” He looked back. He saw Antonio smile.

“That’s good. That’s real good.” He offered his hand and they shook. “I saw right away what a fine woman she was. She deserves to be with a smart young man such as yourself. That’s good, that’s real good.” He repeated himself.

“Thanks for saying that.”

Antonio cocked his hat a bit higher on his forehead, still smiling, “On the subject of women, Anna and I have been working things out.

Thought you should know that. Funny how life takes its turns, isn't it?" he took a sip and wiped his mouth with his arm.

"Yes, it sure is." Felix shook his head and smiled.

"So, my next question is why the hell are you camped up here on this dammed old rocky cliff if you could be down below? You hike all that way down to work then back up to camp. Why not have a short walk up to work and a short walk down to camp? That would save a whole lot of time, and that's where Luisa is. Wouldn't you rather be down there with her?" he shrugged as if it was a stupid question.

"I wouldn't want the men to think I was moving the camp so I could be with a Luisa. They all had to leave their women behind."

Antonio glanced away for a moment. "Tell em' I told you to move the camp down to Santa Marta. Tell em' it makes better sense. That's all. We'll help you move in the morning."

The following morning, the men enthusiastically packed up the camp and moved it down to the shady edge of the palm grove, only a short walk from the beach where they could bathe every evening. Things worked out for everyone.

★★★

The next morning, the luxurious Doña Gudalupe sailed into Santa Marta Bay. The super pangas shuttled the passengers ashore, and Carmen walked down to greet her latest guests. She and Oscar embraced, two old friends with a history. For a short moment, he held Carmen at arm's length, admiring her smile and the sparkle in her eye. She looked right back at him, an unspoken understanding.

"My Lord, Oscar," she broke the spell, "would you believe a couple weeks ago I was here by myself, getting lonesome? Now everywhere I turn, there's more people than I've seen around here in years. There's the four guys from Agua Verde hauling ojas; there's Felix and his crew of seventeen back over that way." She pointed. "Antonio just arrived along with two cowboys, and now all of you have unloaded on the beach. And I forgot to mention the little family that's moved in with me since the last time I saw you!"

"Don't worry, Carmela," he used his affectionate nick name for her. "We have no plans to stay. We're on our way to Agua Verde, but we're in desperate need of a cook. Our cook became ill." She raised her eyebrows, skeptical of his lie. He cleared his throat and continued, "And we had to leave him behind. I was hoping Leo would let us borrow you. Are you telling me Leo's not here?"

"He went down to Timbabichi to count cows, getting ready for the roundup."

"Hmm, I see," Oscar replied as he thought that over. "Are you cooking for all these people?" he waved his arm toward the ranch house as he asked the question.

"No, the trail crew has their own cook, and he won't let me near his kitchen, not that I'd care to work with him anyway. Luisa and I are mostly cooking for ourselves. I think Antonio and his men will be leaving day after tomorrow."

"Well then," he was careful to word things just right. "If I made you an attractive offer to come along and take charge of our kitchen, would you consider? I'll be hiring a cook's helper in Agua Verde, so there wouldn't be much labor. We'll be out for two weeks. I think you'd enjoy life on the boat. I hope you'll consider." He tried to sound convincing.

Carmen knew what he was up to, but she went along. "I'm flattered you think my cooking is good enough to subject it to your guests, but I'll have to think it over. Like I said, I have a new helper." She glanced up toward the house. "I'd want to ask her how she felt about being here on her own. There's the ranch chores, besides all the work in the kitchen."

"Yes, please speak with her and see how she feels."

"She's in the kitchen. Let's walk up to the house. I'll make you some coffee while I speak with her."

Oscar and his guests settled in around the ironwood table on the veranda, while Carmen went into the kitchen where Luisa was preparing tortillas. She was covered in droplets of sweat but smiled brightly when Carmen entered the room. Her life had turned a corner, and it showed all over her lovely face.

"So, who was out there on the boat?"

"That was Oscar Padilla. He owns this ranch. He asked me to cook on the boat for a couple weeks up in Agua Verde. I'd love to do it, but I told him I had to see how you felt about being here without me."

Luisa placed the tortillas on the table and wiped her hands on her smock. Carmen could see the wheels turning in her pretty head.

"Oh, I almost forgot. There's eight people out on the veranda. Could you make them some coffee?"

"Of course," Luisa replied, and she reached for a bucket of fresh water on the floor. She filled the blue enamel coffee pot and placed it on the burner. She untied the ribbon behind her neck and let her long hair free, lowered her head forward, and threw it back before she re-tied the ribbon. Carmen could see that Luisa was thinking about how to respond and waited.

"If you'd like to cook on the boat, you should. I can take care of things here just fine. Now that Felix is nearby, he can help if I need him to. You should go."

"Are you sure? Unexpected things happen all the time."

"I lived my whole life in a place that was far more primitive than this." She waved her hand around. "I've learned how to deal with what comes at me. Please go and enjoy yourself. You're the one who told me it was time to start living again. An important part of living is not passing up opportunities. Go, Carmen. You owe it to yourself. Go."

"You're right. You can take care of things here. I'll tell Oscar I'll be going. Thank you, Luisa. It was my lucky day when you showed up at Santa Marta. I'm so happy you're here."

Luisa blushed and checked on the coffee. "I'll serve the guests. Join them and make a plan with Señor Padilla. Thank you for the many kindnesses you have shown me and my children. It warms my heart." She hugged Carmen.

Carmen sat down next to Oscar and said, "I've decided to go with you. Let me introduce you to Luisa," she looked over as Luisa was placing the coffee servings on the table. Oscar was immediately struck by the poise and confidence so evident in the woman pouring the coffee.

"So nice to meet you, Luisa." He stood and offered her his hand.

She shook it firmly and asked, "You just arrived on that beautiful boat? I only saw my first panga a month ago. I had no idea there were boats as beautiful as that."

"We'll have to give you a little tour. Maybe while we're waiting for Carmen to pack her things?"

"I'd like that, but I wouldn't want to be any trouble." She looked over at Carmen.

"Don't be silly. I love showing off my boat." He took a sip of coffee. "Let's walk down to the beach and have one of the pangeros take us out to the boat. We'll circle around the reef. Should only take us fifteen or twenty minutes. Carmen should be ready to go by the time we return." He looked to see the children peeking around the corner. "Are those your children? Perhaps they'd like a ride on the boat?"

Luisa smiled. "I'm sure they'd love it." She waved them over.

Luisa didn't know what to think as she stood unsteady on the deck gripping the rail, as they motored out toward the white frothing water off the rocky point. The children seemed fine. Oscar was in his element. She noticed how he balanced when the boat tilted back and forth with the waves. She gripped harder, until her knuckles turned white. Oscar casually waved a hand here and there, gesturing as he talked. He was completely at ease on the water.

"Here, come see the kitchen. I'm very proud of it," he said as he went down a short set of steps into the spacious room. The bright yellow appliances and laminated countertops sparkled under the lights. In the center of the room was a ruggedly handsome teakwood chopping block with an assortment of fine knives built in. All of it took Luisa's breath away.

"Step over here," Oscar invited as he opened a heavy door, causing a rush of frigid air to pass over them. Luisa stepped back and shuddered when the icy blast hit her squarely in the face, by far the coldest air she'd ever felt. The children stepped back warily.

"This is the freezer." He waved his hand at the assortment of shelves. "As you can see, we have enough steaks and frozen vegetables to last us for a month, and that doesn't include the fresh fish and shellfish we'll be adding along the way. Too bad you're not coming with us. I think you'd enjoy it."

"I'm sure I would, but someone needs to stay at the ranch while Carmen is gone. I don't mind. It's all new to me."

"Sounds like you enjoy being at Santa Marta."

"Far more than that. Being at Santa Marta has changed my life. It's a chance to start over."

"I'm curious about where you came from and how you ended up here."

"I'd prefer not to talk about the past just now. It makes me weary. I'm taking my time to enjoy every little pleasure that comes my way. There are so many of them. Let's leave it at that, for now."

Oscar nodded, understanding.

The yacht reached the farthest point of the reef and turned sharply back toward shore.

"We're headed back already, and we have more of the boat to see. Come, follow me. I'll show you the dining room, the lounge, and the various berths. It's really a marvelous vessel."

Luisa was overwhelmed. Fine china in the dining room, exquisite linens on the beds, carpeted bedroom floors, and two bathrooms with flush toilets and showers. She could have never imagined it. Her head swiveled right, then left, trying to see everything as they passed from room to room.

"I'm afraid I'm getting dizzy and a little queasy." Luisa braced herself on the wall.

"Don't be concerned, that's only motion sickness. It happens the first time on a boat."

They stepped through the doorway of the master suite, and Oscar swept his arm at the various features in the decadent bedroom as he spoke. Thick plate-glass portholes surrounded the berth barely above the water's surface. Waves splashed against the glass, only inches away from the stacks of puffy white pillows spread across the bed. Luisa tried to imagine what it would be like to sleep in such a bed. Her mind wandered for a moment.

Luisa suddenly flushed pale as she said, "Thank you for the tour." Her head began to spin, and she held back the vomit with a balled-up fist covering her mouth.

"The pleasure's been mine," Oscar replied as he offered her his hand to help her steady.

Luisa couldn't wait to plant her feet on solid ground.

★★★

Leo was exhausted. He'd had very little sleep over the past many days of traveling. He arrived in Rancho San Juanico late the next day and found his old friend Alonso in a pensive mood; the village was nearly deserted.

"Good to see you, Leo! Where'd you come from?" Alonso looked up the trail where Leo had ridden in.

"Long story. Have any coffee?"

"Come sit down, Leo." He waved his hand at the table.

Leo embraced the chubby old man with the bushy white hair. "We're both getting old, eh, Alonso? I can't ride like I used to. I'm stiff as a fence post." He winced.

"You? How about me? I can't hardly walk anymore." He limped over to the table and pulled out a stool. "It's pretty lonely around here without any men to talk to. Have a seat." He motioned at a stool.

"Where is everyone?" Leo looked in the direction of the village. "They all working on the trail?"

"Yeah, and guess who all the chores fall to with them gone? I'm too old and crippled to be hauling water and chasing goats! I think I'll go to Insurgentes, where I can rest and relax in my old age."

"No offense, Alonso, but I think you're needed here. I'll be spending the night, so let me help you with the chores. You can feed me in return."

The two men worked until an hour after dark, hauling buckets of water and chasing after wild goats. Several young children followed along behind and curiously watched. Over the years, Leo had forgotten what a pathetic life his closest neighbors were forced to live.

★★★

"This is turning into quite the gathering," Antonio said as he watched Charro and Christian ride into Santa Marta on their two lively cow ponies. The ponies had silver medallions on their bridles and handmade saddles on their backs. Christian was wearing Paco's clothes and riding Paco's pony. The two boys both had brightly colored bandannas around their necks, sombreros on their heads, matching long-sleeved shirts, and heavy leather chaps from their waists, down their legs, to the top of their handmade boots. They'd ridden for two days on old goat trails down through the coastal canyons from Agua Verde.

Almost at the same moment, Leo reached the lower end of the cliff trail, and the crew was kind enough to take a break from their blasting for him to safely complete the downhill trek. He arrived within minutes of Charro and Christian, and that completed the six-man crew. Next, they were looking at two long, hard days of riding south to Timbabichi, through the rocks and canyons without the benefit of any trails.

Leo looked at Charro and asked, "Where's Paco? I was expecting him to be with you."

Charro looked down and said, "We lost him in the hurricane. Our boat sunk. He drowned."

Leo's chest deflated, and he said, "Sorry to hear that." His voice trailed away. He was lost for words.

Christian watched as the grief came in a wave across Charro's face. "I was there, I'd say we're lucky to have Charro still with us. Gayo pulled him out of the water after the panga sank. He dove back down after Paco, but it was too late. Almost lost Gayo too, and would've, except he was tied to the anchor rope. We had to rebuild the whole village. Every palapa was blown away."

Antonio took off his hat and ran his hand through his hair, "Anyone else die?" he asked.

"No, only Paco. He was my friend." Christian looked down.

Getting ahold of himself, Leo tried to lighten the mood, "A man could get spoiled coming down that new trail!" he looked back over his shoulder at the cliff. He added, "I doubted they could pull it off, but by God, I guess cutting a new trail down through that rockslide wasn't as crazy as I thought. Every once in a while, Sammy surprises me with a good idea. Now, where's that woman of mine?" he looked around. "I was sure after two weeks she'd be anxious to lay her eyes on me," he said, twisting around in his saddle.

"She finally came to her senses, Leo," Antonio answered with a snicker. "She decided to trade you in on a newer model, one that happens to have a great big yacht. The way I heard it, Oscar floated by in the Doña Guadalupe and said they were short of women for their little fishing trip up to Agua Verde. Half the women in Santa Marta signed on to go with him, which, unfortunate for Oscar, only added up to one woman. Luisa, who you haven't met yet, she's living here now. She decided to stay put and run the ranch."

"Hmm, you say Carmen's up in Agua Verde?" he looked at Charro and Christian. "Did you boys happen to see my wife?"

"No," Charro said, "they hadn't arrived yet. We've been riding for two days back through those canyons." He nodded in that direction.

Christian spoke up, "The only big boat in Agua Verde when we left was the old ferry from Santa Rosalia. They shut down the mines for a couple months, and they decided they'd rather anchor in Agua Verde, while they put a new coat of paint on it. We never saw any other big boats, except for the Guaymas shrimpers who brought us our ice."

"Well, she deserves to get away. Hasn't left Santa Marta in five years. Been stuck here with just me for company. She and Oscar go way back. Probably do her some good." He scratched the whiskers on his chin as he thought it over. "Hell. I just had me a nice time of it with a pretty young woman down at the Los Dolores Mission, who am I to talk?"

"Now what kind of a 'nice time' would that of been?" Antonio asked, looking at Leo as if he was crazy. "What'd you do, mix it up with a fisherman's young daughter? Nobody else down there to speak of."

"No, Tonio. You got it wrong this time." He wagged his finger at his cousin. "That old Mission is all fixed up. It's got a brand-new roof a foot or two thick, diesel generators humming away making light and ice, good music, good food, good drinks, and more than a few good-looking whores are living there, all ready to go." He let it sink in for a moment.

"I'll not believe that unless I see it," Antonio quipped.

Leo shook his head at his stubborn cousin. "And that's not all of it, they built three acres of new corrals right there. The last time I last saw em', they had two hundred head of our cattle in there. That's about half the herd, the way I understand it."

"So, they have our cattle corralled at Los Dolores? And they got whores there? I'll be," Antonio muttered as he took off his hat for a second time and thought that over. "Maybe this far-flung fiasco could turn out to be more fun than I thought, and it might not be near as much work as I expected."

"I looked around the place pretty well. I think we can get our animals out without too much trouble." Leo swung his right leg back behind and over the horse's rump and landed with both feet planted firmly on the ground. "There, that feels better," he said mostly to himself. "Coming back up this way is what concerns me. All those canyons with no water. There's never been a cattle drive like it that I know anything of."

"You're right about that, cousin. But you're the one who got us into this dumb mess." He ran his hand through his hair for a second time and put his hat back on. "While you've been laying around getting fat and lazy, you ignored that herd of cattle down there. The way I see it, you're damned lucky to have us here to bail you out of this jam of your own makin."

Leo jabbed his finger in Antonio's direction, "How many times have I bailed your ass out of some dumb mess you got into? At least, this time we got those cows we can sell for a big pile of cash when we're done with it. In your case, all we ever end up with is angry husbands and whores pissed off at us. I don't see where you got any room to get after me."

Antonio cleared his throat and spit off to the side, then shook his head back and forth. "I'm not gonna sit here and argue with you, Leo, but I'll admit, I'm curious to see that old Mission turned cantina."

With the conversation settled, the three of them without horses turned toward the ranch house. Leo, Charro and Christian led their horses to the water trough, talking among themselves about the journey they were about to take.

★★★

The crew spent a long day making final tedious preparations for the cattle drive. As the evening came to an end, Leo and Antonio were the last two people sitting around the fire. They hadn't talked one-on-one that day, as they were far too busy attending to their many chores. During a break in the conversation, Leo glanced up at Antonio across the fire and decided the time had come for him to break the news.

"Before I left Insurgentes, Sammy asked me to speak to you about something. I waited til' we had this quiet time to ourselves before bringing it up, because it's not good news." He looked down at his hands.

Antonio picked up on the mood immediately. "What is it? Be out with it. You know I like to hear things head on. Don't beat around the bush."

Leo had been whittling a mesquite stick, and he threw it on the fire. "Okay. Right to the point. Seems you have a special friend over in Insurgentes. Anna Marie?" he looked up to see Antonio thoughtfully nod his head. His posture stiffened at the sound of her name.

"What about her?"

"I'm afraid there's been an accident. The truck she was traveling in, up to Loreto?"

"Yes?" Antonio stared hard at his cousin.

Leo took off his hat and held it to his chest out of respect. He looked to the fire, searching for words. "It went off a cliff somewhere up in the Gigantas. There was an explosion. Everyone in the truck was killed. I'm sorry, Tonio, I'm really sorry to be the one to tell you this. I wish I knew more, but that's all Sammy was able to tell me. He said you were close to the girl." He looked up and over at Antonio.

"Oh, Jesus. I knew it!" He slammed his fist hard into the ground next to where he was sitting in the dirt. He stood up and looked at the star-studded sky. He turned circles in place as he tried to sort through his feelings. He threw his hat to the ground in anger, and his body stiffened as he balled his fists.

"Yes. We were close. Far more than that." He ran his hands through his hair, still turning in nervous circles. "We'd been seeing each other on and off for months, ever since she came up from La Paz." He placed his fingers on his forehead, as if to stifle a headache. "We were in the process of taking the next step. She was just about as stubborn as I am about such things, but we got beyond it. She saw other people, and God knows I did too, but…" He lost his voice. He kicked his hat. "Fuck." He kicked at his hat again, and it sailed to the other side of the fire.

Leo stood, ready to embrace his cousin if the moment called for it.

"I sensed something like this would happen! She took off to Loreto with those narco assholes. I could've stopped her, but I had too much on my mind with this stupid roundup. I wasn't paying attention. I had the chance to stop her, and I know she would've stopped, but it's not my nature. I looked the other way, and now, this. I'm sick. I'm just sick to my stomach that I'll never lay eyes on that beautiful woman again." His words drifted off in the night air.

Both men respected the silence.

"If you'll excuse me, Leo. I'm going to throw my bedroll down by the hot spring. I need some time to think. I've got to learn to live with the fact that I let that girl slip away. I'll regret it the rest of my days. I'm just too Goddamned set in my ways. Look what it's led to. Like I said, I need some time. Hopefully, I'll be ready to go in the morning."

Leo looked at his cousin in the dim firelight. The shadows highlighted the creases and wrinkles covering his face. Leo had never noticed them quite that way before. His lips were drawn tight in a line. His eyes were wet and sad. "Sure, Tonio. Take your time. We'll give you all the time you need. I wish I'd met her. I'd like to know the woman who finally got through to you."

Antonio laid his bedroll above the high tide line in the sand. He looked up at the thousands of bright flickering stars and wondered which one was Anna Marie, and he cried himself to sleep.

★★★

At a pre-dawn breakfast, Leo spoke in a hushed tone as he told the group about his conversation with Antonio. It was followed by a dead silence around the table. Felix bowed his head, and tears dripped across his face. Luisa noticed and broke the somber mood by saying, "Eat. You won't be having a hot meal for nobody knows how long."

A moment later, Antonio stepped up on the veranda and sat down at the table. Two kerosene lamps flickered softly, providing a pale amber light.

"Morning, boys. I take it Leo has spoken to you?"

Several of them acknowledged.

"I want you to know that I'm committed. I'm alright. We got a job to do, but I gotta change the plan a little. When this is over, I won't be going back to Insurgentes. I'll be staying here. I'm gonna build me a casita over on the other side of the palm grove there." He half-nodded in that direction.

The men around the table were all quiet.

Leo nodded.

Luisa placed a plate covered with refried beans, machaca, sunny fresh eggs, and tortillas in front of Antonio. She leaned forward, put her arms around his neck and kissed him on the top of his head.

"Bless you, Tonio," she whispered.

★★★

They rode hard and long that day. They far out-rode the miles Leonardo had covered two weeks before, crossing that same rugged country. They were all business with Leo and Antonio up front in the lead. They stopped only twice for a short ten minutes each to relieve themselves and pass around burritos. Charro and Christian followed up from behind, each of them leading a packed mule; one with supplies, one with guns and ammunition. Naco and Benito were sandwiched in the middle of the group. There was tension in the air, the men were all on edge.

Only after the sun went down did they stop. They found a flat spot where a few stunted ironwood trees grew, and they made camp. Christian gathered enough deadwood to build a fire, and he made coffee. Christian was the youngest, at seventeen, but he more than carried his weight. A bright, wiry young man, strong as an ox, he took after his father in that way, but weighed one hundred twenty pounds less than Gayo. Christian had an air of confidence about him not seen in many men far older than he.

Naco was the wise, experienced one at fifty-two years old, tough and weathered like the ancient ironwoods growing in their camp. Naco and Antonio had been on a dozen round-ups together high in the Gigantas, and they knew one another like brothers. While in his twenties, Naco lost his young wife to childbirth, and he could never bring himself to re-marry or even bed another woman. Horses, mules, and cattle were his life. He was a quiet thoughtful man who the others all respected.

Around the fire, they spoke among themselves for a short time, mostly about their progress. All the men except for Naco and Benito had been to Timbabichi and had an idea of what to expect. The four men described the place to the other two as best they could, but they all felt unsettled and retired early, prepared to resume their journey at sun-up.

Coco welcomed them to Timbabichi late on the second day of their journey. He fed them an evening meal of greasy lard-soaked fare, and provided them the latest local news. He explained how Osuna's men had all the cattle corralled at Los Dolores, ready for the drive to La Paz. While he had the men gathered around the fire, he took time to warn them about the dangers they faced.

He poured each of them coffee with a splash of tequila and said, "There's some real bad men over there." He went on, "The way I heard one story, the ranch foreman got angry with the gal in charge of the whorehouse, and she turned up dead."

Leo jerked at the news and grew painfully alert, he asked, "The little gal with that nasty scar on her cheek?"

"Uh huh, that's the one. Real pretty girl, even with that big old scar."

Antonio noticed. He studied Leo thoughtfully.

Coco continued, "Not just dead. They tortured the poor girl, bad. Dragged her out to the dunes, spread-eagled her and staked her down. They each of them had their way with her, God only knows how many, then shoved ocotillo stems up her privates. Left her there to bleed out. Fishermen found her in the morning, just as the vultures started in." He spit off to the side in disgust. "Like I said, some bad men over there."

Leo felt a pang of guilt as he pictured Flora's brown eyes dancing, her easy laugh and her delicate hands. He tried to keep it to himself. He was sick inside. Antonio watched as Leo turned his back to the fire and bowed his head.

After only four hours of sleep at Coco's, the six cowboys met the dawn high on the rimrock overlooking Los Dolores. Each man had a pair of binoculars glued to his eyes as they studied the activity below.

Antonio strained to see what he was looking at in the pale light and said, "I can't make out if those cattle are sorted or just thrown together in those corrals. Someone needs to go down there and have a closer look."

"I'll go," Christian volunteered.

"Take one of the mules and act like you're looking for work," Antonio told him. "Take off those boots and that shirt, go in there looking like you're poor. Ride bareback and act like you're hungry. Ask around for work, act desperate. Learn what you can and get back here soon as you can so we can make a plan. Get going now!"

Christian rode a quarter mile down the hill to where it met the beach. He steered the mule in the direction of a dozen pangas anchored in the shallows out in front of the mission. There wasn't a breath of wind, and the water was flat calm as glass. He slid off the mule's bare back and led the animal up to the cantina. All was dead quiet as he tied the mule to the hitching rail and entered the mission through the open front doors. That time of early morning, the place was empty except for a middle-aged bartender cleaning up the mess from the night before.

"Good morning," Christian said respectfully to the older man.

The bartender hadn't seen him come through the door and turned quickly, startled. He studied the handsome, shirtless, barefooted boy as he approached the bar.

Christian inhaled the strange odor of smoke, alcohol and greasy food for the first time in his life. He'd never been in a cantina before.

"Good morning to you, too, young man," the short burly man answered. "What brings you in here this early in the day?" he said, polishing a shot glass.

"I'm looking for work. I'm willing to do anything."

The bartender paused for a moment. “You know how to clean up a mess?” he asked, glancing around the room. “One of the fisherman’s wives helps me some, but she’s the cook and has a big family. She’d probably like some help.”

“I’d work hard.”

“Well you seem polite enough,” he replied, wiping the counter. “Go talk to her. If she’s willing to teach you the work, come back and see me. Her name is Teresa. She lives behind the corrals to the left. A little palapa shack back in the mesquite. Go up there now. She’s there with her kids.”

“Thank you, sir. You won’t be sorry.”

“Fine then,” he placed some glasses on the shelf. “I’ll see you back here.”

Christian couldn’t believe how easy that was. He was just given an invitation to have a look around Los Dolores where it wouldn’t arouse any suspicion. He set off on foot in the direction of the corrals.

★★★

Alberto and Felipe, the two explosive experts from La Paz, carefully placed the dynamite down the prepared holes in the rock, just like they had more than one hundred times on that same cliff face. The fifteen-man San Juanico crew climbed up to a safe location to avoid the blast. The two men lit their fuses simultaneously and ran uphill to join them.

The ancient rock that made the cliff above Santa Marta was fractured and rotten to its core. High above the men, it gave out, unable to withstand the man-made earthquakes any longer. With the latest blast, the cliff collapsed in upon itself. Two hundred feet above the men, it slid. Their ears were still ringing from the force of the blast below them. The dust cloud from the blast was rising mushroom-like in front of them.

Perhaps there is a merciful God, because the slide was deadly and quick. Not one man among them expected it or saw it coming. Death came to them all in the stroke of an instant. Felix, Luisa’s brother Fausto, and thirteen other men and boys from Rancho San Juanico were buried, along with Alberto and Felipe. They never had a hint it was happening. The completed trail where the men were standing was buried in rubble, thirty-some tons of rock found the ground at the bottom of the cliff in a thunderous few seconds.

Pepino sensed it. He was always alert. Something wasn't right. Something was different about the blast. He stepped out from under the canvas shade where he was stir-frying pungent red chilis in a pan. Shading his eyes with his hand, he stared up at the cliff. Thick clouds of dust engulfed the rock wall and prevented him from seeing anything.

"Pepino, get back here and finish this!" Pepe scolded.

For only a second, Pepino froze in place and didn't respond. Something snapped in his head. He started to run toward the cliff. The amount of new rubble at the bottom scared him. With adrenaline pumping and pounding through his veins, he scrambled up through the massive new pile of rocks in his bare feet. The skin on his ankles tore, when his feet slipped between the rocks, but it didn't faze him. He was running, climbing uphill on raw energy. The dust settled just as he reached the site. A man's lifeless arm reached out from the rubble, and Pepino began rolling rocks that weighed more than his own body off to the side. Sobbing, because he was a smart young boy, he knew well the outcome. Yet, he continued moving rocks with desperation in an effort to free the man.

He screamed over and over again, "Help me! Someone, help me!" But there was no response. Nothing.

Pepino limped back through the camp an hour later in a dazed shock. He was covered with blood, his own and that of the three bodies he dug out of the rocks. He knew what he had to do, and he untied Felix's mule. From under the sunshade, Pepe looked up and yelled at him, "Get back to work."

"Go fuck yourself," the twelve-year-old boy swore as he turned the mule toward Santa Marta and kicked it into a full gallop.

Luisa was humming softly to herself in the vegetable garden. She adored her time alone in the garden. She held a basket full of ripe tomatoes in the crook of her arm, as she plucked more of them from the vine. She heard the sound of the mule long before she saw it. It concerned her for a moment.

"Why would Felix be coming home in the middle of the day?" she wondered. Then she smiled when she thought of the possibilities. For the first time since they'd gotten together, the ranch house was empty of other people. Even the children were gone down to the beach. She thought of how she would tear his clothes from his body and ravish him with abandon. She was incredibly horny and ready for him. She stepped out from the garden and turned toward the house with her tomatoes.

To her surprise, it wasn't Felix on the mule, but Pepino. It happened so fast it was a blur. Pepino flew off the back of the mule as if he had wings. He hit the ground with his feet spinning in the dirt and ran straight toward Luisa, who was standing below the veranda. Her mind was unable to process what she was seeing as he raced closer. He was crying from deep within, when he wrapped his arms around her waist and buried his face in her belly. He seemed unable to breathe, he gasped, choking. He was covered in blood. Luisa dropped the tomatoes in the dirt and reached down to hold him.

"Pepino, dear. What's happened? What's wrong? Are you hurt? So much blood …" her voice trailed away as she sensed the seriousness of the moment.

He looked up into her eyes, unable to answer. He again buried his face in her soft belly and sobbed. His entire body was throbbing with convulsions.

She cradled him around the shoulders and led him slowly up the two short steps of the veranda. She placed him in a chair and sat down herself only inches away. She placed her hands on his cheeks and kissed him. She cradled his face. With her eyes just inches from his she calmly said, "Pepino, please talk to me."

He looked up directly into her dark eyes. Tears flooded his eyes. His small body shaking uncontrollably.

"They're gone. They're all gone. Every one of them. Felix, too."

From the absolute depths of her body, Luisa didn't need to be told anything more. She'd been there before. She could read Pepino's eyes. She reached forward and pulled him over to her lap. She hugged him relentlessly. She cradled his face and kissed him on the head as she began to cry along with him.

After some unknown amount of time, such dreadful moments cannot be measured, she spoke.

"Pepino, please tell me what happened. What do you mean they're all gone? Where did they go?"

He looked up in her eyes again and pleaded, "Please, hold me. Please, Luisa, don't let go."

She obliged him and said not another word. He would answer when he was able. She looked up at the blue sky, clenched her jaw, and cussed under her breath.

"They're gone. The cliff caved in above them. It buried them. I dug three out, but I'm not strong enough to move those rocks by myself. I couldn't find most of them. Felix was one of the three I dug out. He's laying up there in the sun. His head, his whole body, was crushed. Oh, Luisa. It scares me."

Through the pure horror of what she heard, Luisa gathered her wits and took a moment to examine Pepino. Most of the blood must have been from the bodies he dug out, but she saw his torn, mangled ankles.

"Let me get something to clean you up with. I'll be right back, don't you move. We'll talk about what comes next. Wait right here."

As soon as she was alone, she collapsed on her bed. She buried her face in the pillow and screamed. She made a fist and slammed it over and over again into the bed. After she vented her anger, she rose up and took deep calming breaths, dozens of them, to settle herself. Pepino needed her to be strong.

★★★

The Doña Gudalupe was anchored in a sheltered cove along a white sand beach within the larger bay of Agua Verde. Across the bay, also on anchor, was the ferry boat from Santa Rosalia, known as El Toro. It was being painted and tuned up for the upcoming grueling schedule of shuttling people, vehicles, and cargo between the Santa Rosalia mines and Guaymas, just across the Sea of Cortez. All of Oscar's guests were on land, taking a stroll through the newly re-built village of Agua Verde. His entourage of bodyguards were tasked with finding a few young women from the village willing to help out on the boat.

"Carmela. Come sit with me. Would you, please?"

"Certainly, Oscar. Just as soon as I finish preparing your lunch."

"This is just like old times, isn't it?"

She looked up and wiped her hands on a dish cloth. She crossed the room and sat next to him, close. Nearly touching. She placed her hand on his chin and fixed her face right in front of his. His eyes were soft and warm. She had him in her grasp.

"No, Oscar. This isn't just like old times. We are old. I'm forty-five years old. I have three grown children. You're nearly sixty-eight! Those things happened to us when I was a teenager, but I've never forgotten. More than once, I've wondered what might have become of us, but I married Leo and never regretted it for a moment. Though you always had a special place in here." She placed her hand over her heart.

Oscar stroked her cheek. He brought a finger to her upper lip and touched it, feather-like. He melted under her closeness.

"When you asked me to come on this vacation with you, I knew you were lying about your sick cook. My God, Oscar. You could have hired a dozen cooks in La Paz. You think I'm stupid enough to fall for that one? I wanted to come, because I knew we would have a private time like this. I wanted to be with you one more time before the time came where we couldn't. You see, I can be as devious as you. I promise you this, though. This is it. This is that 'one more time,' and there won't be another." She took his hand and led him to the master suite, where she threw back the covers.

★★★

Christian tried counting more than once, but he always lost track when the cows started moving around. He guessed there to be more than four hundred animals. The bulls were off in one row of corrals, separate from the mother cows. The heifers and calves were together in another section. There were no steers, because Leo had never cut the bull calves. Everything was sorted perfectly.

"What are you up to, son?" a cowboy walked up and asked.

"I've never seen so many cows in one place. I'm curious. What are you doing with all these cows?"

The cowboy chuckled and thought he'd amuse the poor boy.

"We brought them all over on a boat from Mexico. You see, the man I work for decided the people of Baja California don't eat enough meat. They eat too much fish. Fish aren't good for you. If you eat too much fish, it won't build any muscle. Look at yourself. I can tell you eat too much fish, cause your skinny as an ocotillo stem. You must eat fish all the time. Am I right?"

Christian decided it would be in his best interest to play along. He shrugged his shoulders and nodded.

"So, where you from, boy?" He placed his hands on his hips as he waited for a response.

"It's called Agua Verde. Way north of here. I'm looking for work to help my family," Christian tried to play upon his sympathy.

"Hmm, never heard of it. But then, I'm not from here. I'm from Mexico." He gestured in that direction as if the boy wouldn't know which way Mexico was.

"It's a small village, up north of here. Not many people ever heard of it." He looked down and ran the bare toes on one of his feet through the deep pulverized dirt left to right.

"Well, no matter. These cattle are headed for La Paz. We're going to do the hard part first and move those bulls out in the morning." He turned to look at the corrals holding the bulls. "You know how to ride? We could use an extra hand."

"I can ride, but I'm on an old mule. Don't think it'd be much good at herding."

"We got horses. Leave your mule over there." He pointed at the horse corrals.

Christian kept running his toes through the dirt. "I've an offer to work in the cantina. Think I'll do that."

"Fine with me," the cowboy said as he tossed some alfalfa over the fence to the cows.

★★★

After nearly two weeks, Anna Marie was sitting up in bed, confused. Lupita told her they'd found her on the side of the road in the mountains, but she had no idea how she got there or where that was.

She could hear the bell ring in the San Javier Mission and the sounds of burro hooves clacking along down the cobblestone road outside the window. That confused her as well. Everything confused her. Worse, she didn't recall her own name or anything about where she came from. Lupe tried not to press her very hard in the beginning, as her physical recovery was far more important.

"I see you're awake, dear," Lupe said as she stepped into the bright, airy room with a tray in her hands. She placed it on the bedside table. Anna looked up and cracked a faint smile. The smile caused a sharp pain in her swollen jaw. She grimaced, and her head jerked back. Her left eye remained a black-purple color, swollen shut, and her head was shaved bare, and heavily stitched under the cloth wrappings. Lupe hid her mirror away in a drawer.

"I brought you chicken broth and scrambled eggs. There's a straw. Here, let's sip some broth first." She held the cup forward and brought the straw up to Anna's swollen, cracked lips. Anna Marie was famished and sucked up the full cup of broth.

"Good, good. Now, let's try the eggs. They're soft-scrambled, you won't have to chew. Can you manage to swallow them?" She placed a baby spoon of eggs in Anna's mouth. She swallowed each spoonful and finished the entire bowl of bright, fresh, yellow eggs in short order.

"Good, good. Now, if we can keep this up for a few more days, I think your strength will start to come back. When it does, we'll get you out of bed, but I don't want to rush it. You're still very weak, and you're just fine where you're at for now. Do you remember anything at all that will help us know who you are?"

"No," Anna replied in a soft whisper.

"Well then, let me start by giving you some hints." Lupe sat down on the edge of the bed. The bed springs squeaked and sagged under her two hundred pounds. "When we found you, you were on the only road there is through these mountains." She pointed to the mountain outside the window. "On this end of the road, pretty much the only thing there is the small fishing town of Loreto. People from all over, mostly the United States, fly in small airplanes to go sport fishing there. There's a beautiful old mission in the town square about two streets back from the water. We call it the sister of our mission here in San Javier. Loreto has several tourist hotels right on the water and a short but very pretty Malecón. Does any of that sound familiar?"

"No," she whispered again.

"Hmm," Lupe thought for a moment. She straightened the blanket covering Anna's legs. "I've never been down the road the other way. That would be south, but I've seen maps, and I've read things about it. After you drop down out of the mountains there's a farming town called Insurgentes. They call it the Magdalena Plain. There's a lot of farms there. That's where we get all of our chilis. That mean anything to you?"

"No," with a slight shake of her head and a wince. She brought her hand up and touched her swollen jaw.

"Okay then, Baja California is a long skinny peninsula about a thousand miles long. We are in the bottom half," Lupe thought back to the little bit of geography she learned in school. "I'm sorry, would you like a sip of water?"

"Yes please," Anna answered, barely audible.

Lupe stood and waddled across the room to a well-worn chest of drawers. She poured a small cup full of water from a glass pitcher and picked up the straw she'd used for the chicken broth. She waddled back across the room. Anna watched and would have smiled at the big round woman if it wouldn't have hurt her jaw to do so. Lupe brought the straw to Anna's mouth. The cool fresh spring water felt soothing in her throat.

"Now, back to our lesson," Lupe sat down on the bed and the springs groaned again. "I wish I had a map to show you. I'll just have to explain things best I can." She smiled at Anna. Lupe had a front tooth missing.

Anna smiled back, by winking her good eye.

"There's only one road down the peninsula," Lupe thought hard how best to describe what she wanted to say. "Well, let's just say it this way, if you got on an auto-bus here in San Javier and went that way for two days." She pointed south. "You'd end up in the only city in this half of Baja California. It's called La Paz," Lupe was proud of herself and gained confidence after such a clear explanation.

Anna's eyebrow rose just a bit.

"I've seen in magazines La Paz has a large port where ships come in from Mexico, and other places all over the world. There's a ferry too, it carries people across the Sea of Cortez over to Mexico. Sinaloa, I think," Lupe paused and looked at Anna's eye. "Anything?"

Anna didn't respond. Something Lupe said triggered a thought, but she couldn't quite put two and two together. Lupe noticed.

Following a long silence, while Lupe patiently watched and waited, the girl whispered, "Anna. Anna Marie," and placed the flat of her hand on her chest.

Lupe's eyes turned wet and a smile crossed her pleasant, round face. She leaned over and kissed Anna's cheek on her good side.

"Wonderful! So nice to meet you, Anna Marie. That's a beautiful name. What made you think of your name? Something I said?"

"La Paz."

Lupe thought for a moment, got up from the bed and said, "Excuse me. I have something I want you to look at. I'll be right back." Anna Marie watched her waddle through the door and felt grateful for the woman's kindness.

Anna tried to sort things out while Lupe was gone. She looked around the room as if seeing it for the first time. White lace curtains were pulled back neatly to the side of the single window. She could see a towering mountain and large birds soaring in a thermal. Fluffy white clouds passed lazily above them. She became lost in her thoughts.

Five minutes later, Lupe came in with an old, tattered copy of a tourist magazine that must have been ten or more years old. It was full of beautiful color photos, mostly advertisements, for La Paz and the south cape region. Lupe pulled a chair up to the side of the bed and sat down. She laid the magazine on Anna's lap.

"Here, I'll turn the pages for you. Let's see if you recognize anything in here," she turned the first page, and there was an immediate reaction. Lupe saw it in Anna's body language and what little facial expression she was able to show. Lupe looked at the inside cover, at what caught Anna's attention. There was a full-page color ad for the Hotel Los Arcos on the Malecón in La Paz, with a beautiful photo of the gardens surrounding the dozen or so quaint little bungalows sitting next to the historic ninety-room hotel.

"Do you know this place? The Hotel Los Arcos, on the Malecón in La Paz?"

"Yes," she whispered.

Lupe was beside herself, she never expected it to happen so quickly. "Did you live in La Paz, Anna Marie? It looks like such a beautiful city!"

"Worked there." She touched the photo of the garden with her finger.

Do you have family there?"

"No."

"Okay," Lupe thought. "We're making progress. Anything else about the Hotel Los Arcos?"

"Flowers, music."

"Friends? Do you have friends there? In La Paz? At Hotel Los Arcos?"

"Oscar."

"This is wonderful, Anna Marie! Let's look at more pictures and see what happens," she said through her joy.

★★★

Luisa lost her devoted lover, her brother, and thirteen others she had known, loved, and lived among her entire life. They were an extended family, nearly all of them blood related. The entire male population of San Juanico was gone, with the exception of Pepe, Pepino, Alonso, and a scattering of young boys. Life in San Juanico would be difficult, if not impossible, without the men. Terrible thoughts – desperation, fear, anxiety, and the unknown, threatened to overwhelm her, just as they had when she lost Pedro. She was grateful for Pepino. The young boy, wise beyond his years, kept her grounded, for the moment.

"How's that? Am I hurting you?" she asked as she cleaned Pepino's bloody feet with a small cloth soaked in rubbing alcohol.

He grimaced but answered, "No, it's alright."

"Pepino, I need to ask you to do something for me," Luisa said as she looked up from his feet into his pained eyes. Her forehead wrinkled with worry.

"I'll do anything you want me to," the boy answered. He worshiped Luisa.

"We have a terrible problem," her lip trembled. She placed a hand on his knee. "Leo, Antonio, and the others are trailing hundreds of cattle up here. We can't let them do that with no way out. They'll need to make a new plan or forget the whole thing."

Pepino nodded, unsure of what that meant.

"You are a far better rider than I am." Her face became distraught. "I have two young children I need to care for." She looked into his eyes. "Do you think you can ride the mule down to Timbabichi and tell the men what happened?"

A frightened look flashed across the boy's face, "Santa Marta is the farthest I've ever been from San Juanico. I might get lost."

Luisa was fighting tears when she said, "I know. This is the farthest I've been from San Juanico too, but you and I are the only ones left. I think Timbabichi is two or three days that way," she pointed to the south, "and it's right on the beach, just like Santa Marta. If you stay as close as you can to the ocean and don't wander back away, you should find it."

"I can try," he said with uncertainty, he couldn't hold the tears back. He was frightened.

"I've seen you ride that mule, Pepino. I know you can do it."

He sucked up a deep breath, straightened his posture, and said, "I'll do it. I'll ride Felix's mule to Timbabichi! I can do it!"

"Thank God for you, Pepino. I'm so grateful to have such a strong boy with me at a time like this. Please go find your boots and put a saddle on the mule. I'll prepare you some food and a medical kit, so you can dress those feet. They'll be easy to infect."

"Okay, Luisa." He stood and hugged her for all he was worth.

★★★

"Let them have the bulls," Antonio stated flatly as the six men huddled together on the rimrock. Christian had just returned with his report after scouting Los Dolores. "They'd be nothing but trouble anyhow. Look at it this way – most of those cowboys will be off herding the bulls to La Paz. It'll be the perfect time to cut the rest of the cows loose."

"I agree," Leo responded. He patted Christian on the back, "Nice job. I knew it was a good idea to send you down there."

Antonio took charge, "Everything needs to be in place when the sun comes up. I want every man to have a rifle and at least one pistol. Each of you are to have as much ammunition as you can carry," he looked down at Los Dolores and the cattle pens, then back at the men. He noticed them fidgeting and looking at one another. He suspected other than himself, Leo, and perhaps Naco, none of the other three had ever shot anyone before.

Charro spoke up nervously, "I haven't shot a gun for so long, I can't remember."

"Then, we'll just have to get back up to Coco's place and practice up before the sun goes down. We're about finished here anyway. I just wanted to get the lay of the place. We've done that."

"I'd feel better if we could do some shooting before we go down there," Charro answered. He looked worried.

Antonio paid no attention, but he went on. "We'll give them two hours to get up the road with the bulls, then we'll move in. Without the bulls, there's nine corrals full of cows, heifers, and calves. We'll need to get them all pointed in this direction, up and over this ridge as quickly as we can move them," he spit off to the side and looked around again at his men.

Benito looked at Charro as if to thank him for speaking up. He never owned a gun and didn't know how to shoot.

"Good then. We spend as little time as possible within gun range of them. We move fast. In and out. I promise you, they'll have a lot of guns. Our job is to get those cows and us out of their gun range as quick as we can."

Naco nodded. His right hand dropped to his hip and felt for the Colt that was holstered there.

★★★

Luisa went in the house and began to cry, a continuous series of heart-breaking, gut-wrenching sobs. Through her tears, she went to

Carmen's room and found an old pair of dungarees. She stripped off her smock, threw it on the floor, and pulled on the pants. She cuffed up the legs and cinched a piece of twine around her narrow waist. She laced a pair of heavy work boots over her bare feet and pulled a flimsy cotton t-shirt over her head. She walked down to the beach and found the children playing in the hot pool. She instructed Juan Carlos to return to the house and wait for her there.

She walked a mile through the palm grove to the bottom of the cliff, where she saw the mountain of fresh rubble. She started to climb through the rocks. The first part was hand-over-hand, because the pile was so enormous. She worked her way up through the rubble, until she came to the old trail. The crew hadn't widened it there, yet.

She climbed up the trail and thought of the day Felix led them down it on their journey to Santa Marta. She'd fallen deeply in love with him that day. He was the most self-confident, sensitive, and kindest man she'd ever known. Now she was climbing up the same trail to bury him. Her heart was heavier than she'd ever known it to be. She felt as if she was only getting to know this wonderful man. She knew there was so much more about him for her to discover. The emotions were so overpowering that she felt sick to her stomach. Her head began to spin in circles, she kneeled, and vomited in the dirt.

After she steadied herself, she resumed climbing until she came upon the buried section of new trail. She saw the first body Pepino had uncovered. Although his skull was crushed and shredded, she recognized one of her San Juanico neighbors. The man's vacant face and neck were twisted in a horrible contortion that haunted her, yet she dropped down on her knees beside the body.

For nearly an hour, she carefully placed rocks over the corpse. She tried not to look, but she could see two more bodies above her. She tried to prepare herself for the moment she would lay eyes on Felix.

She cried when she knelt next to him, surprising herself that she had any tears left to shed. She took his broken, shattered hands in her own. They felt cold and clammy, even in the hot sun. She removed the wedding band that Pedro had given her fourteen years before from her finger and tried but failed to slide it past the knuckle on his smallest finger. She placed the thin brass band in the palm of his bloodied hand, folded it, and laid both hands over his heart. She was meticulous about which rocks she chose and where she placed them on his body. When she had it perfectly covered, so no vultures or coyotes could harm him, she moved on to the third body. It was her brother-in-law, Nora's husband.

★★★

The sun rose in a fiery ball to the east over the Mexican mainland. The six men were in place behind the rocks on the ridge looking down on Los Dolores through their binoculars. They could see a bustling of activity in the vicinity of the corrals far below them. Six horses were saddled and tied to a section of corral that held many dozens of frustrated restless bulls.

"I'm glad we decided to let them have the bulls. I don't envy those boys having to trail 'em all the way to La Paz," Antonio commented as he spied through his binoculars.

Leo chuckled, "Good riddance."

"Alright, everybody double-check your guns. Make sure they're fully loaded and you have quick access to them at all times. Remember, don't shoot unless you absolutely have to, and if you do, shoot to kill. They'll darn sure kill you if they get the chance." He lowered the binoculars and studied his men.

Christian was crouched and steady on his toes, ready to go. Benito and Charro looked nervous and uncomfortable. Naco was standing, stroking his horse's nose. Leo was studying the scene below through his glasses, working the muscles in his jaw back and forth.

"Look, they're opening the first corral," Leo exclaimed. "There go the bulls. Look at that." They all peered down at the scene through their binoculars.

The bulls broke away in their long-sought freedom under a cloud of dust and chaos, but the cowboys were well prepared to steer them up the arroyo along the road. The corrals were designed perfectly to control the direction of the herd once they'd been released. Two cowboys blocked them from going the wrong way out the gate, the other four kept them from straying side-to-side once they got moving. Someone opened the second gate and dozens more animals repeated exactly what the first bunch had done, and followed the others right up the arroyo. Finally, a third, fourth, fifth and a sixth corral were emptied. The bull drive was on.

Many of the bulls wanted to run, and the cowboys let them go, just as long as they headed in the right direction. Any animals that veered left or right were immediately caught up with and whipped back in line. Antonio was impressed the Sinaloa cowboys knew so well what they were doing. They didn't appear to be the amateurs he'd assumed they were.

"They handled that nicely. I'll have to admit," Antonio said to Leo, still watching through the glasses.

"They did. Surprised me," Leo added.

Two hours passed quickly. The men waited and observed the goings-on down below, but since the bulls had departed, it was mostly still. Two cow hands were tossing hay to the remaining cattle and fussing with the water. They wandered back over to their camp, and all was quiet at the corrals.

"Let's go. Time's up," Antonio commanded. "We'll ride down along the beach. When we come to the arroyo, we'll head straight up and over to the corrals. When we get to the corrals, go straight to your assigned positions. Let's go. No reason to dally. Let's throw open those gates and show those two boys down there how to move a herd of cattle in a big hurry. Check your pistols one last time … Go! Let's go now," he spurred his horse as he said it.

In single file, they came down off the ridge on the water's side of the hill, where they couldn't be seen by anyone in Los Dolores. They galloped along the beach and turned up the arroyo toward the corrals. They never looked back. Each of them had a bandanna tied over his face as they rode through the thick choking clouds of dust. Christian blocked the lane that headed in the wrong direction. Charro started opening corral gates. The cracking of their vicious bull whips terrified the cattle, and they came out running. Leo, Antonio, Naco, and Benito were out the other way, ready to keep the cattle in line, headed north toward the ridge.

Just like when the Sinaloa boys released the bulls two hours earlier, what appeared at first to be a chaotic mess was a very well-executed release of the entire herd. They were out of shooting range in under three minutes. Only then, did the two Osuna cowboys walk out of the cow camp, not at all expecting to see the empty abandoned corrals. Not a shot was fired.

In less than an hour, the herd dropped over the ridge on a trail leading north to Timbabichi. The men eased their pace. The thundering sound of pounding hooves slowed to a dull monotonous thudding. The dust settled. The animal's frantic breathing and frothing calmed. Mother cows bawled for their lost calves. The men yipped, shouted and whistled, cracking their whips and lariats if an animal got out of line. Following the trail to Timbabichi would be easiest part of their journey.

The trail ended at Timbabichi, and they would start traveling cross-country. Antonio and Leo guessed it would take five days to reach Santa Marta, if all went well, much longer if they had trouble steering the herd. Timbabichi was the last water before they reached Santa Marta. The men were nervous. Cattle need water every day. That wasn't going to happen.

Once the herd reached flat ground, Leo and Antonio dropped back and had Naco and Benito take the lead. They checked on Charro and Christian, who were following up behind the herd, pushing stragglers along. When all looked well, Antonio and Leo backtracked up the ridge. They tied their horses below the ridgeline and crept up behind the rock-strewn rim. They each had a lever-action Winchester Model 94. They were both experienced marksmen.

As soon as they raised their field glasses and peered down the other side, they saw four cowboys rapidly climbing the hill on horseback, heading directly at them. All four men were heavily armed, with rifles at the ready.

"They're gonna ride right into us," Antonio whispered. "Lay low. Take em down at twenty-five yards."

"Twenty," Leo responded. "Cleaner shot."

"Good enough. Two on the right are mine."

The four Osuna cowboys didn't know what hit them. It happened so fast – four quick shots, three men hit the ground. The fourth one got hung by his foot in the stirrup and was dragged downhill through the rocks by his frantic horse. The three rider-less horses followed it back to the cow camp.

"Nice shooting," Antonio smiled.

"Darn. That one got away," Leo muttered.

"I promise, he's deader than a fence post. What do you care if he got dragged off by his own horse?"

"I wanted to see who they were. I met a few of them the night I was in Los Dolores. There's one of em I want dead. I'm gonna look at the three on the ground there. Be right back," he climbed around the rocks.

"I'll go with you." Antonio stood up. "I'll pick their pockets."

Kicking the third one over on his back, Leo said, "Nope, I've not seen these men before. I'm gonna guess the one dragged down the hill wasn't my man either. I bet he's off with that herd of bulls."

"What? You got a grudge against the guy?"

"Might say that. Enough said." He sliced his hand through the air, ending the discussion.

"I know when to leave well enough alone. You know that. There'll be no more questions out of me."

Antonio gathered up the pesos out of the men's pockets, and they walked back over the rimrock to their horses. They left the three dead men on the ground where they fell.

★★★

Young Pepino rode well past dark, aided by the glow of the moonlight. He trotted the mule and made far better time than he would've on a horse. The mule was sure-footed and skillfully maneuvered through the rocks. Much later, in the middle of the night, as the moonlight began to fade, he stopped in a wide flat arroyo, tied the mule, and threw down his bedroll.

Never in his young life had he felt so alone. Memories of the gruesome dead bodies, buried in the rocks, haunted him and flashed by in his head when he closed his eyes. He stopped closing them. He lay awake there watching the stars. Coyotes howled in the distance. He felt his lip quivering. He tried again, closing his eyes. The bodies returned.

All three of them. There was no getting away from them if he closed his eyes.

The boy laid there, suffering through the night. He waited for dawn. With the first hint of it, he was on the mule. He promised himself he'd not stop riding until he reached Timbabichi.

★★★

The six cowboys pushed the herd hard all day. They arrived in Timbabichi in the late dusky light. The two mules, with their supplies and extra firearms, were waiting for them in Coco's corral. Coco prepared them a meal of mesquite-broiled trigger fish, deep-fried clams in lard with flaming hot chilis, and flour tortillas. Antonio passed a bottle around. Groups of cattle came and went, drinking at the three long tin troughs during the night. The men snored in their bedrolls, except for Leo. He sat on a rock high on the hill with his Winchester and watched.

Before the sun had fully risen, they were off across the rock-strewn desert, climbing up and out of canyons, draws and arroyos too numerous to count. The land was so dry the cactus struggled to survive. The only life they saw were occasional groups of sea birds soaring high overhead on heated thermals. They had trouble holding the herd together, and it was only the afternoon of their first day. The cattle were scattering across the landscape, searching for food and water. Antonio and Leo rode off by themselves to talk.

"This isn't good," Antonio said.

"I can see that," Leo took off his hat and wiped his brow with a bandanna. "This could turn into a week, ten days, longer. I'm not sure they'll survive. I had no idea they'd be this hard to move."

"I agree," Antonio paused, about to add something when his eye noticed movement high on the ridgeline, a half mile away.

"Look there," Antonio said, pointing at the ridge. "Looks like a boy on a mule. Look how fast he's moving."

"Hmm, looks like that kid Pepino from San Juanico. What the hell…" Leo's voice faded off.

They kicked their horses and got moving up and across the hill toward the boy. As they closed the gap, they saw clear as day it was Pepino. The three of them met on the sidehill.

"Pepino, what brings you way in the hell down here?" Leo asked.

Antonio wiped the sweat out of his eyes and waited for a response from the boy.

"Luisa sent me. You can't take the cows to Santa Marta. There was a rockslide. It killed everyone. It buried the trail," he blurted, bravely holding back tears.

Leo stared at the boy with a stunned look on his face.

"Take it easy, son. Go slow with it," Antonio clearly didn't believe what he heard. "Now, what the hell all happened?"

"Everyone's buried. The mountain slid down. There's no trail. Everyone's dead." He broke down and cried.

"Oh, by God. What next?" Antonio muttered. He slapped his hat down hard on his knee. He looked up at the cloudless sky and shook his head. He looked back at the boy on the mule, crying his heart out. He was at a loss for words.

Leo spoke up, "All of them? All the men were buried?"

Pepino nodded. His face looked like a red chili pepper, not just from the sunburn.

Antonio sat for a moment in thought, "If we can't go to Santa Marta, we'd better get back to the herd and figure what's next." He turned his horse. The other two followed.

The six cowboys and Pepino gathered up, and Antonio explained their dilemma, saving the boy from telling the story again.

"Simple as that," Antonio said. "We can't go to Santa Marta. We can't go inland. The cows would be dead before we reached water that way. We can't swim em' out. We don't have a choice. We have to herd em back through Los Dolores and fight our way past Osuna's men. I see no other way out."

Christian was standing next to his pony, quietly stroking the animal's muzzle.

Charro asked, "What? What you thinking?"

"I've seen cows swim. Gayo and I swam a herd around Punta Aguja once. Saved us a day's time pushing them over the mountain. We swam them right up to the beach on the Agua Verde side. Only took us an hour."

Antonio looked at Christian, "Where we gonna swim them? Over to Mexico?"

"Out to a boat. Gayo took a cow to Loreto in his panga once. Sold it up there."

Antonio rolled his eyes, Leo glanced at the sprawling herd.

"One cow in a panga?" Leo turned to Christian, "We got two hundred fifty animals right there, if you hadn't noticed," he cocked his head in the direction of the cattle.

"Not in a panga. El Toro, the Guaymas ferry. It's in Agua Verde. It hauls cars and trucks. Why not cows?"

Leo asked, "How would that work? One of us rides up to Agua Verde and talks to the folks with the ferry? That'd take a week just to get there. We'd be right here with all the cows waiting for Osuna's men to come get us."

Christian answered, "No, trail the cows to Cajón Bonito. Its over that way, not too far." He pointed. "I know the people who live there. We bring them tortillas when we dive for scallops on their reef."

Leo looked at Christian and said, "I've been to that place. The cows can be corralled on the beach, and there's a freshwater spring, but that doesn't get us the ferry."

"That's the easy part. I'll steal one of the pangas at Los Dolores. I'd be in Agua Verde three hours later if I took one of the big ones. You move the herd over to Cajón, and I'll be there tomorrow with the ferry. I'll bring Gayo. He'll know how to load the cows in the ferry."

Leo looked at Antonio who raised his eyebrows and nodded in agreement. The other four looked at Christian, amazed, and smiled at his ingenious plan.

They started moving. Antonio stepped off to the side and beckoned Christian and Pepino.

"Pepino, who's at the ranch? Just Luisa and the children?" he asked.

"Yeah, well Pepe's back there, but he's no help. Luisa won't speak to him. She's there alone with the children, far as I know."

Antonio turned to Christian, "When you get to Agua Verde, after you line things up with the ferry, look to see if Oscar's yacht is there. If it is, ask Oscar to bring Carmen to the ranch. Luisa shouldn't be alone. Tell them what happened."

"I can do that."

Antonio added, "Take Pepino with you. Drop him at Santa Marta. Leave him with Luisa."

Christian responded, "I'll pick him up at Timbabichi after I steal the boat. I don't want him there for that."

"He'll be with Coco, waiting for you on the beach," Antonio answered.

Without another word, the plan was set.

★★★

Christian rode the mule back to Los Dolores. When he approached the beach, he cut the animal loose and slithered through the shallows like a sea snake to where the pangas were anchored. He spotted a twenty-three-footer with side-by-side, nearly-new 55 Johnsons. He looked left and right, and he scanned the beach. Nobody in sight. His heart was pounding hard in his chest. Adrenaline took over. He slipped over the side and down to the floor where he checked the fuel. The five-gallon tank was full. There was a full spare. More than enough to get him to Agua Verde.

He kneeled low in the boat, set the chokes, and pulled the starter rope on the first motor. It roared to life. The second motor did the same. Using the knife on his belt he sliced through the anchor line. He took the single tiller handle in his hand and turned the boat as it was idling toward open water. He stood, and twisted the tiller to full throttle. The bow of the powerful panga rose four feet as it sliced through the air. The massive thrust nearly caused him to fall over backward, but he gripped the tiller hard and regained his balance as the boat planed level. The wonderful blast of wind and the salt spray in his face felt like freedom. He turned the boat in a half-circle at full break-neck speed and pointed it north toward Timbabichi, Santa Marta, and Agua Verde. He looked back over his shoulder and saw that not a soul in Los Dolores had seen the boat leave. He yelled, "Yes!" pumping his fist.

★★★

Three hours later, Christian steered the panga into Agua Verde Bay. The only time he'd backed off the throttle since leaving Los Dolores was when he stopped to pick up Pepino at Timbabichi, and when he dropped him off two hours later at Santa Marta. As he crossed the bay, he saw El Toro to the left and the Doña Guadalupe anchored in a quiet little cove off by itself to the right. He slowed the panga and idled up alongside El Toro, tied his bow line to the towering ship and climbed up the ladder.

In less than fifteen minutes, Christian convinced the four-man ferry crew to join the Timbabichi cattle drive. They were bored painting the rusty old vessel and were always interested in supplementing their pathetic wages. Christian promised to pay all expenses and two hundred pesos to each of the crew. They agreed to leave that evening and were fine with traveling all night. They hoped to arrive at Cajón Bonito sometime the next morning. The ferry was much slower than the panga.

Christian next motored across the bay to the Doña Guadalupe. He came up alongside the luxurious yacht and was greeted by two men in a panga. Two more men dressed identically in black, skin-tight clothing, looked down at him angrily from the deck. One of the men above pointed a pistol squarely at the center of Christian's chest. Christian held his hands up in a surrendering position.

"Who are you? What do want, pulling alongside like that? Stay in your boat. We're coming aboard." One of the men from the other panga stepped across onto Christian's bow. The man looked Christian up and down, then at the powerful dual motors. He ordered, "Keep those hands up!"

The man frisked Christian and removed the knife from the sheath on his waist. He tossed the knife in the water and said for the second time, "Who are you? What do you want?"

"My name is Christian. I live here in Agua Verde. I have a message for Señor Padilla from Leo and Antonio. They're on a cattle drive down south. There's trouble at Santa Marta."

"What trouble would that be?" the man with the gun asked from up above.

Christian looked up, "The seventeen men building the trail on the mountain were buried in a landslide. Antonio asked to please have Señor Padilla take Señora Carmen back to the ranch. She's needed there."

The bodyguard thought for a moment, "I'll ask Señor Padilla to hear this for himself. Wait right there. Don't move." He stepped away.

Christian tried to smile but the best he could do was make a nervous twisted expression, "Thank you, señor."

When the man returned, he asked Christian to climb up a rope ladder, then escorted him to the steps leading to the upper deck. There were tables and chairs up above under a sunshade, where Christian saw a distinguished-looking older gentleman sitting with Carmen at one of the tables, sipping what appeared to be red wine. The bodyguard gestured toward Oscar and said, "Please, sit down." The guard slid out a chair, and Christian sat.

Christian had no idea who Oscar was, other than he owned this incredible yacht and he kept a lot of scary bodyguards around. He'd met Carmen some years back at Santa Marta with Gayo but he was a young boy. He was sure she didn't recognize him now.

"Hello, my name is Oscar Padilla. I understand you'd like to speak with me. Something about Santa Marta? I own that ranch. Carmen here," he gestured politely in Carmen's direction, "and her husband run it for me. So, what is it that brings you here?"

"My name is Christian. I live there on the beach," he pointed, "I was helping Leo and Antonio with the cattle drive at Timbabichi. A young boy from San Juanico rode down there from Santa Marta to tell us there'd been a landslide. The seventeen men working on the trail were all buried. Luisa and her children are at the ranch alone. Antonio asked if Señora Carmen would please return to be with Luisa." He studied their expressions as he waited for a response.

Oscar was immediately concerned. Carmen was horrified.

"They were all buried?" she asked.

"Yes. That's what we were told." He looked down at his hands resting on the table in front of him.

"Oh, my God," she gasped. "Felix was the foreman. Was he killed?"

"I was told they all perished, Señora."

"Oh, Oscar," she turned toward him. "I must to go back to Santa Marta to be with Luisa, please." Her eyes pleaded with him.

"Of course. Of course, we can go. This is terrible. Those men were on my payroll. I saw them up there working when we stopped there last week. This is terrible," he said, shaking his head, letting it sink in.

Oscar turned to Christian and asked, "You say you were with Leo and Antonio on the cattle drive?"

"Yes, Señor."

"They planned to move the cattle up that trail to our feedlot in Insurgentes. What is the plan now?"

"I've arranged for the old ferry on the other side of the bay there," he pointed, "to leave this evening. We'll load the herd on the ferry at Timbabichi tomorrow. I'm not sure where they're going to take them from there."

Oscar thought for a moment, then said, "I know where they'll be taking them. My family owns a feedlot in Sinaloa a few miles inland from the ferry dock at Topolabampo, along the road to Los Mochis. That's where the cattle need to go. Tell that to Leo and Antonio, if they haven't figured it out by themselves already. It's only twelve hours across the gulf."

"I'll tell them. Is there anything else, Señor?"

"No, nothing I can think of. Thank you for your trouble, son. We'll be leaving for Santa Marta shortly." He extended his hand across the small table.

"Thank you, Señor. Señora," Christian stood and nodded with appreciation. As he turned to go, he saw the tears in Carmen's eyes.

★★★

Oscar and Carmen had one of the bodyguards take them to Santa Marta in the panga. They arrived at dusk. The setting sun was displaying its magical shadows up on the Giganta cliffs, but they didn't notice. They saw not a soul as they rushed across the beach on their way up to the house. They stepped in the door to see Luisa standing at the kitchen table, feeding Pepino and the children their dinners. Luisa appeared to be completely and utterly spent. Her hair was wild and dirty, her face was covered with grime, and her jaw was clenched. Her eyes were vacant and cold. She was dripping with sweat after working over the hot burner. There was a rancid greasy smell in the stuffy air. Luisa looked up at Carmen with an expression of relief on her tired face, and she dropped the plateful of food on the floor. She ran across the small room toward Carmen.

The two women embraced and cried. Luisa's body was trembling. The children were frightened and failed to understand what was happening. They watched with big round eyes, expecting Felix to walk through the door behind Carmen. He always arrived at dark for dinner. Oscar observed the heartbreaking scene from the doorway.

"Let's go to my room," Carmen said. "Pepino, please watch the children for a few minutes. I'll be right back. Oscar, please excuse us." She led Luisa by the hand.

Oscar nodded, "Certainly, take all the time you need."

Carmen was heartbroken for Luisa. Such a tragic turn from the week before. She found it hard to even imagine. She closed the bedroom curtain behind them and sat Luisa down on the bed. She lit a candle on the night table and draped one arm over Luisa's shoulders. She could feel the woman's body trembling. With her free hand, she drew Luisa to her bosom.

"We need to clean you up, but we can do that later. I'm so sorry, Luisa. Everything was going so well with you and Felix. I could see it. Everyone saw it. You adored one another. You were perfect together. I'm so, so sorry." She stroked the side of Luisa's cheek.

"I can't stay here, Carmen. I had to go up there to bury him. He was crushed, every bone in his body was crushed. Even his beautiful face. All I think about is what might have been. It's torture. I look up at that Goddamn mountain every time I step outside. I don't know if I'm ever going to heal from this. It's far worse than when I lost Pedro. I haven't been able to eat. I can't stop shaking, and I haven't slept. I'm sick. I'm sick down in the depths of my soul."

"I'm here now. You'll be sleeping here tonight, with me in my bed. Let's lie you down, now. Here, lay back. Put your head on the pillow. There you go." She cleared the loose hair from over Luisa's face.

Carmen rubbed Luisa's shoulders and did her best to relieve the tension. The trembling slowed, but it didn't stop.

"Just try to relax, dear. Lay back. Close your eyes, concentrate on breathing. Just think about breathing. Try to put everything else out. Just throw it out the window. Breathe deep. I'm going to see the children are fed. I'll wash them up and settle them in bed. I'll be back, and we'll go down to the hot spring to soak. Just you and me. Then, I'm going to make you something very special to eat before we come back here to bed. I want you to just lay there and think about breathing. There you go. Relax, Luisa. I'm here now."

Carmen remained by her side for several minutes, stroking her cheek, as Luisa passed into a trance-like state. Carmen's presence was the relief she sought. For the first time in three days, she rested.

Completely distraught, Carmen rose from the bed and quietly left the room.

★★★

Gayo and Christian joined the four-man crew on the ferry and set out for Cajón Bonito that evening. The going was steady but slow. They chugged along through the night. While the ferry spewed thick, black, foul-smelling fumes from its sooty stack, the men took advantage of the onboard kitchen and the bar. They passed beers around freely and made a party of their voyage.

The ferry arrived at Cajón Bonito mid-morning. Christian and Gayo immediately launched a small dinghy and rowed to shore. They could hear cattle bellowing and cowboys whooping it up, as they pushed the herd down through the narrow canyon. The father and son hiked up the canyon until they met Leo and Antonio, who were explaining the plan to Mondo.

"The ferry's here," Christian said as he walked up.

"Good, good. Perfect," Antonio replied. He was energized, light on his feet, ready for anything. "We should have the herd all down on the beach later this evening."

"Ok, we'll position the ferry as close to shore as we can, but we need sixteen feet of water to float, so we'll be out there a ways," Christian explained.

Gayo spoke up, "Don't worry about that. You'll be surprised how well those cows can swim when they have to. They'll swim right up on that ramp and walk right into the boat. I'll be out there nudging them along."

"You have that right, Señor," Antonio said to Gayo. "You're formally in charge, the minute the first cow steps in the water. I'm not much for swimming and neither is Leo, so we're naming you foreman of this operation until every single one of those animals are in the belly of that boat. So, you all know, soon as we get the last cow down to the beach, Leo and I will be going back up the canyon to make sure there's no undesirables following along behind. If you hear any shooting, it'll be us attending to things."

Christian spoke up, looking to Antonio, "Carmen is at Santa Marta with Luisa."

"Thank you. I take it you found the Doña Guadalupe?"

"I did, and I told Señor Padilla about the trail and the ferry, he said we should take the cattle to his feedlot at Topolabampo."

"Good. I was about to head up to Guaymas with them. I had no way of knowing if Padilla's feedlot was still in business. You just saved us a week's time."

The group of men all turned at once to see the first of the cattle herd coming down the canyon from around the corner, with more than two hundred others not far behind. They smelled the spring water and the sparse greenery at the spring pool's edge. The thirsty old cows broke into a trot, headed for the water.

★★★

Osuna's men had no trouble following the tracks of two hundred fifty head of cattle and a half-dozen horses. There were six of them, four roughnecks from the road crew and two of Osuna's cowboys. They stopped for the night in Timbabichi where Coco, who did his best to remain neutral, fed them and made them comfortable. They expected to easily catch up with the herd they assumed was slowly making its way across the forbidden desert toward Santa Marta. They were in no hurry, and Coco volunteered nothing about the ferry and the change of plans.

The last of the cattle reached the beach an hour before dark. They were crowded, pressing up against one another taking their turns drinking at the spring. One by one, Naco and Benito led them down the beach to where Christian and Charro would be herding them into the water in the morning. Gayo watched the operation from off-shore, floating serenely in his dinghy with a beer in his hand. The ferry was on a one-ton anchor, three hundred-fifty feet out from the beach in eighteen feet of water. The massive corrugated steel truck ramp was lowered down in the water held in place by a set of four-inch-thick, rusty steel cables. The ferry crew was enjoying the peaceful evening over cold beers on the upper deck.

With darkness approaching, Antonio and Leo rode back up the canyon to the narrowest part of the gorge, just above Mondo's camp, where they stopped and studied the vertical rock walls.

"Right up there," Antonio pointed over his shoulder. "I'll climb up this side. You go up the other," he nodded his head in that direction. "We'll find us a place in the rocks where we can look right down on the trail. Anyone trying to reach Cajón Bonito will have to ride right through this trap. We'll sit tight, until such time as they have all the cattle loaded up. If anyone happens in on us, hold your fire until one or the other of us takes off his hat. That's when we cut loose. Watch the hats. If my hat comes off, shoot."

The two men tied their horses down at Mondo's camp and instructed the little family that nobody was to venture up the canyon. They might be shot dead if they did. They re-checked the ammunition in their saddle bags and draped them over their shoulders. They slipped the Winchesters out of their scabbards and walked up the canyon around the corner. Up the rock walls they went, settling in for the night on well concealed ledges, with a perfect view of the trail below.

★★★

Carmen packed a woven straw bag with everything they would need and carried it to her bedroom where she found Luisa sitting on the edge of the bed, trembling in the candlelight.

"I see you're up. Let's walk down to the hot pool." She reached out and helped Luisa up with her free hand. Luisa rose slowly without saying a word. They took short baby-steps until Luisa responded to the rhythm. They walked hand-in-hand down the short distance to the beach and turned toward the hot spring. There was a perfect half-moon, which provided just enough light for them to see where they placed their feet. The moonlight sparkled on the surface of the placid water in the bay. A sea turtle, burying her precious clutch of eggs in the sand, paid them no attention.

They stopped at the side of the pool where Carmen reached over and helped Luisa out of her filthy smock. She pulled it up, over Luisa's head. Carmen noticed Luisa's body odor; it was powerfully bad. She hadn't washed in three days, the day of the rockslide.

Carmen slipped out of her own skirt and blouse, then led Luisa out to the center, the deepest part of the pool. They sat, and Carmen gently poured warm water from a small cup over Luisa's back. She rubbed her back gently, slowly massaging it with a bar of scented soap, then she scrubbed with her bare hand. She took her time.

Slowly again, with great care, Carmen laid Luisa gently back in the water and cradled her head on her lap. She poured more water from the cup over Luisa's hair, avoiding her face and her sad weary eyes. Carmen lathered the soap into Luisa's matted, tangled hair and massaged her scalp. Evenly, with both her hands, she worked the lather. Luisa moaned, the first and only sound she made. Carmen thought it a good sign. She kept massaging her scalp, working the fragrant lather. Carmen hummed softly along. Fifteen minutes passed. Carmen rinsed her hair, over and over. The grime, the grease and the salty encrusted sweat all washed away. She continued to hum. She felt Luisa give in. She went pliant. Luisa opened her eyes and looked up at Carmen for the first time. A faint almost imperceptible smile appeared on her face. A small dimple on her chin. Her eyes fluttered.

Much later, perhaps an hour or more, they settled in along the shallow edge of the pool. They talked until after midnight, while Carmen brushed Luisa's long beautiful hair.

★★★

At sun-up, Christian and Charro pushed a half-dozen head of cattle out through the shallows toward the deeper water. The two boys were comically barefoot in the stirrups, sitting up on their saddles barely dressed, in only their underpants and wide-brimmed hats. On opposite sides and to the rear of the small group of cows, they pressed the animals ahead with lariats swinging like whips, in the direction of the ferry, whooping and hollering all the way. They passed into eight feet of water. Their horses started to swim, a strange sensation for the two young men who had been riding all their lives. The horses and cattle floated like buoyant corks bobbing up and down in sync with their paddling hooves. In twelve feet of water, the boys pulled back on the reins. The horses reared and turned back to shore. The cows kept bobbing along and swam on ahead, as Gayo moved in from behind, hollering them on from his dinghy.

"I liked that!" Christian exclaimed through a wide smile when they reached the beach. "Only two hundred and forty more to go. This is fun!"

Charro, a bit more reserved, "Long as I don't fall off. You know I don't swim."

"Not to worry, I'm right there next to you. Just hang on to the horse. They're good swimmers, aren't they? Had no idea!"

"Need to be careful out there."

Christian, still smiling, having a good time, looked over to see Naco and Benito herding eight more head to the water's edge. "Let's go, here comes eight more. Get in behind them there!"

Gayo's first group of six animals swam closer to the ferry in front of the little dinghy. He whistled and yelled them on. Their eyes were rolling around, bulging from their sockets. Long stringy strands of snot, from their snorting flared nostrils covered their faces and foreheads. Tongues hung out the side of their wailing mouths as they frantically worked their hooves through the water, closing in on the floating island in front of them. When their front feet touched the submerged ramp, they blundered up like wet elephants into the quiet dark confines of the boat. They coughed, snorted, and bellowed as they awkwardly tried to shake the water off their furry backs. Gayo laughed and yelled at them one last time. He loved the thrill of it. He watched them settle in the front corner of the cavernous boat and smiled. He floated the dinghy over to his ready position halfway back to shore and waited for the next bunch. He was sure they'd have all two hundred fifty head loaded up by noon.

★★★

Carmen rose early, from her and Leo's bed, next to Luisa who was snoring, so she'd be up ahead of the children. She brewed coffee, squeezed orange juice, scrambled eggs, and heated refried beans. Tortillas warmed on the shelf above the burners. Oscar was next to rise. He'd slept down in the beach house, sharing it with the bodyguard. He quietly stepped into the kitchen and took a seat at the small kitchen table.

"Good morning," he said to Carmen.

She turned sharply when she heard his voice. "Good morning, Oscar. Sorry, I didn't hear you come in. Would you like some coffee? Orange juice?"

"Coffee please. How was last night?"

"A little better. Luisa calmed down. We had a long talk. The sad part is she doesn't want to stay here. She was traumatized. She climbed up the trail and buried Felix. He was crushed almost beyond recognition. After she explained what it was like, I understood how she felt, as hard as that is for me. I love having her and the children here."

"I see," Oscar replied. "Where will she go?"

Carmen placed a cup in front of him, "I'm not sure. We didn't discuss that."

"Thank you," he sipped the coffee.

"She also told me Antonio won't be returning to Insurgentes. As hard as I find it to believe, she said he'd fallen in love with a young woman who worked for Sammy. The girl died in a car accident about the time he left on the cattle drive. Luisa said he was devastated and wanted to stay here and be done with it up there. I'd heard him talk of doing that, but I never took him to be serious. Maybe he did fall hard for the girl."

"Hmm, wonder who that might've been. Tonio's got a good eye for the women," he thought out loud. "I'll ask Sammy next time we talk. We'll miss him up there. Please wish him my best if you speak with him before I do…" he trailed off.

"I will," She paused over the stove. "If you're passing by here on your way back to La Paz, would you stop in for a minute? I'd like to send a letter back with you. To Sammy."

He looked up, curious, "A letter to Sammy?"

"Yes," she set down the spoon she was using to stir the beans and turned to face him. "The widows and children in San Juanico will be needing his help. Sammy needs to move them to Insurgentes, find them somewhere to live, help them settle into new lives. They won't survive long in that village on their own."

"I hadn't thought of that."

"I wouldn't expect you to. You've never seen San Juanico; you've never been there."

"You're correct, I've only flown over it, at five thousand feet," he felt a twinge of guilt. He paused and thought before he spoke, "I'll not only see he gets the letter, I'll cover the moving expenses and whatever else it takes. The men were working for me."

"Thank you, Oscar," she stepped across the room. "And for the time on your boat. I'll never forget." He stood, and their eyes met.

He opened his arms, and she stepped into them. He pulled her close and kissed the top of her head. They held the embrace for a long moment.

"I think I'd better be getting back to my guests. I'll stop by for the letter. Please, wish Luisa well for me." He pecked her on the forehead and turned away.

Oscar went through the open door, Carmen turned back to the stove. Juan Carlos came in, yawned, stretched his arms above his head, and sat down at the table, hungry for breakfast.

★★★

Shortly after Osuna's men left Coco's ranch the next morning, they came to the place where the cattle tracks made an abrupt turn toward the coast, away from the direction of Santa Marta. The men were both confused and pleased. The herd would be trapped somewhere down in the coastal canyons. There'd be no way out. The cattle thieves would be easy to pick off one by one at their leisure. They kicked up their pace and spurred their horses into a trot as best they could through the rocks.

By early afternoon, Charro and Christian were swimming the last of the herd out to the ferry. Gayo was proud of himself. They'd loaded all two hundred fifty head of cattle in the boat without so much as a single stray or casualty. The herd, usually loud and raucous with their bellowing and blustering, went eerily quiet once they were confined within the dark shadows inside the boat.

As the last animal stumbled up the ramp, Gayo rowed the dinghy back to the beach. Charro, Christian, Naco, and Benito were huddled together talking. Gayo yelled at them, "Swim your horses out and up the ramp. Let's go!"

"I'll get Antonio." Naco turned his horse back toward the mouth of the canyon.

At that same exact moment, Leonardo glimpsed some movement two hundred yards away, up near the head of the canyon, just above where it dropped from the flat arroyo down into the narrows. He whistled at Antonio, caught his attention, and pointed up in that direction. Antonio looked up from his perch high on the ledge opposite Leo, in time to catch a glimpse of the six men before they dropped out of sight down between the high rock walls.

"Okay, this is it," he thought. He waved acknowledgment back over at Leo. He held up five fingers on his left hand, his index finger on his right – "Six". Leo nodded.

Both men tensed. Sixteen long boring hours up on the cliff had dulled their senses and cramped their muscles. Each of them laid their rifle barrels on the rocks in front of them. Adrenaline pulsed through their veins. Jaws clenched. Eyes focused like lasers on what they could see of the narrow trail below. They each laid their index fingers gently on the triggers of their Winchester 94's.

Below and behind Antonio and Leo, Naco dismounted at Mondo's camp. He untied Antonio and Leonardo's horses. They'd been tethered there for sixteen hours. They were anxious to move. He started leading them on foot up the canyon.

Leo saw a flock of white-wing doves flush up out of the canyon one hundred yards in front of them. He was sure they were scared up by the six riders. He whistled at Antonio, who turned to see Leo point down and nod. Antonio nodded. He adjusted his rifle barrel. Leo went from a sitting position to his knees. He lined up his sights on the trail where it went around the blind corner. He wiped the sweat back from his eyes. The sun was directly overhead. It reflected off the canyon walls with a hot dull glare.

Two abreast, the six men came in pairs from around the corner. One pair after the other. Their rifles in place, gripped tightly in their right hands, across their laps, left hands on the reins. They rode slow and quiet, tense and ready. But they weren't ready for the moment Antonio took off his hat; his signal to Leo.

Shots rang out, seemingly out of nowhere. They pierced the dead silence like a knife. They echoed and ricocheted off the canyon walls. Naco, Mondo and his family all stopped and listened. At sixty yards, it wasn't the cleanest of kills.

Four of the riders took more than one shot to drop. Two of them, who were only grazed, turned quickly on their horses back up-canyon. They never made it around the corner. Both were shot squarely in the back and dropped from their horses to the dirt. The two rider-less animals continued in a frenzied gallop up the canyon with empty saddles. The other four horses, frantic when they lost their riders, ran down-canyon around the corner. All six men lay dead or wounded on the trail. Leo looked across at Antonio. He sliced the palm of his flat hand through the air from left to right to say "finished." He pointed below, and they started climbing down.

The four rider-less horses galloped down-canyon around another sharp turn and ran directly into Naco. He had no time to lead his three horses out of their path. All three of Naco's horses reared up. He held tight to the reins. The four horses coming down-canyon were running blind with fear. The first three passed by, so close they grazed Naco, nearly knocking him to the ground. His three horses came down off their hind legs in a cloud of dust. One of them tripped up the fourth horse coming down-canyon. The horse let out the most god-awful, bloodcurdling scream as it stumbled and shattered its front leg in the rocks. Its body skidded and spun in the rock-strewn dirt. It tried desperately to get back up, but the front left leg flopped loosely on the ground. On its second attempt, the horse rose up on three legs but quickly fell. It was pathetic. The animal's chest was heaving. It was gasping for air through flared nostrils. All Naco could see were the whites of its eyes rolled up in its head. Naco slipped the Colt pistol out of his holster, stepped up, and put a single bullet through the animal's skull. The sight of it brought him to tears.

Leo and Antonio climbed stiffly down the canyon walls. They walked among the victims. One of the men was only wounded, he sneered and cussed at them. Leo put a bullet in his forehead. "Well, that's taken care of, cousin," he said flatly, as Naco came around the corner with their horses.

"We should be on our way," Antonio said in summary. He holstered his pistol.

The three of them rode down the canyon, passing by Mondo's camp on their way to the beach. Leo stopped to thank Mondo, while Antonio and Naco watered their horses at the spring. Reaching into his saddle bag, Leo found what he was looking for, and climbed down from his horse.

"Here you go Mondo, for all the trouble we caused you." He handed Mondo three dozen tortillas, a jar of chili salsa, and a bottle of tequila.

"I'd like to ask you a favor?"

"Anything," Mondo replied, his hands shaking as he reached for the offerings. The pleasure in his eyes was unmistakable. He gazed with the wonderment of a young child at the tortillas.

"There's six dead men up there." He nodded his head that way. "Would you drag em down to the beach, float em out to the reef, and sink em for me? Oh, there's a dead horse too. Not sure what to do with that."

"We'll think of something. Don't want to smell up the canyon any more than it is," he chuckled and sniffed the air.

"Good." Leo reached out and patted him on the shoulder. "I'd keep an eye out for a while. There'll be more men down here looking for us, I'm sure. Play ignorant. Tell them we floated the cattle on out. Tell them you never laid eyes on us before. Didn't know us, nothing about us."

"That's easy."

"I'll be seeing you then, Mondo. I'll be sure to bring you more tortillas. Give my best to your family," he glanced over at them lounging in the shade under the overhang. Sorry for all the trouble." He squeezed the man's shoulder.

"No trouble at all, Señor!"

Leo tipped his hat and walked his horse over to the spring for a drink, then followed Antonio and Naco down to the beach.

★★★

They saw the ferry had fired its engines. Thick plumes of jet-black smoke rose from the stack. Gayo met them on the beach, where his dinghy was lying in the sand just above the waterline.

"Time to swim. Don't be shy, Señor," Gayo chuckled at Antonio.

"I don't care for this at all. It hadn't occurred to me we'd have to swim out to the boat," Antonio said, as he looked with uncertainty across the water.

"Don't worry about a thing. The horses know how to swim. You just need to be firm with them. Point them that way," he gestured toward the boat. "Once they're off their feet, they'll know what to do. Keep em moving toward the ramp. If two hundred and fifty dumb old cows can do it, your horses can. They're a lot smarter than a cow. I'll be right behind you in the boat. Let's get moving!"

With fearful looks on their faces, the three old cowboys gritted their teeth, and walked their horses into the water. None of them had ever swum a horse before. As they stepped out further, the water got deeper, up to the horse's bellies.

"Shit!" Antonio muttered. "My boots are filling up!" he looked over at the others to see if they were having the same problem. Right then his horse stepped off the sand bar and dropped into deeper water. They became buoyant. Antonio's stomach spun around in his gut. He dry-heaved and grabbed the saddle horn with both hands, so hard his old weathered knuckles went white. "Whoaaa, easy now. Don't run." The horse was paddling madly forward. "Slow down." He didn't think to pull back on the reins. The horse was closing the distance between them and the ferry. It saw Christian's horse watching from inside the boat. It whinnied at them. Antonio could take no more. He closed his eyes.

All three of them reached the ramp in quick succession. Antonio's horse was first. When its front hooves touched down on the ramp, the animal lurched forward, "Whoa, now!" he yelled. He thought he was about to be thrown. Instead he felt the solidness underneath the horse. They were in the boat. He opened his eyes and looked around. He nearly found religion at that exact moment but forgot all about it after he slid down off the horse and his feet landed on the floor.

Gayo about split his gut, laughing as he dragged the dinghy up the ramp. "You did good there, Señor!"

Antonio was in no mood for jokes. He sat down and tried to pull off his boot. The suction inside made it impossible. "Don't just stand there, make yourself useful, pull on that boot," he demanded. He raised his foot up.

Gayo grabbed the boot, and with his thick massive arms, he dragged Antonio, on his butt, three feet across the floor through the fresh, sticky cow manure, before the boot popped off with a loud sucking sound. Gayo found it incredibly funny and kept laughing. He pulled off the other one, laughing so hard it bent him over forward.

The ferry crew hit the winch lever. The rusty corroded cables wrapped on their spools. The ramp gate slowly rose from the water. The cables rubbing against themselves on the spools made a sickening sound, like fingernails on a chalkboard. The heavy steel door closed tight, sealing them off from the ocean. Their eyes adjusted to the dim light. They tasted the dank air and smelled the fresh manure and urine now trapped in the depths of the dark, windowless space. Christian stepped down a narrow metal staircase with a kerosene lantern. He stopped near the bottom.

"Follow me. Up here!" They didn't need to be told twice.

With boots in hand, they climbed the stairs. They felt the heave and tremendous thrust, as the engines engaged the propeller. The old ship creaked, groaned, and shuddered as it gained speed. They were on their way to Topolobampo.

★★★

Manny and his men returned to Los Dolores from their bull drive down to La Paz to find the corrals empty and the entire herd of cattle gone. Also gone were the cowboys he'd left behind. The cow camp was empty, and most of the horses were missing. Without dismounting, he and his men followed the cattle tracks north up and over the ridge. They descended the opposite side of the ridge and saw where the herd met up with the Timbabichi trail. They continued until they rode into Timbabichi. Coco limped out to greet them.

"This has sure been a busy place the last few weeks," Coco croaked as Manny and his men came to a halt in front of him. "First, your men passed through here moving cows down to Los Dolores. Next, all those cowboys from up north came by on their way to Los Dolores. Then they came back through, headed north with all the cows, probably a couple hundred of them! Not far behind them came six of your cowboys, going after the cows that way." He nodded his head to the north. It's been quiet ever since. No more cowboys or cows. Until you that is. Wonder where they all went."

Manny was angry. His face turned a bright crimson color under the sunburn and a week's worth of ugly black stubble. He looked around at the surrounding hills and ridges with his squinted sinister eyes and said, "What the fuck? You mean that's all you have to say? You never saw any of them again?"

"Nope, it's been just me here alone ever since. I'm as curious as you about where they went. A dozen cowboys and two hundred cows. They all just disappeared. I swear!"

Manny thought that over. He looked around at the men on horseback to his left and right and said, "You two," waving his hand at two men on his left side. "Get you some food and water from Coco here. Follow the tracks until you find what happened. I need to get back to Los Dolores. I'll be waiting for you there. Be quick about it, but don't come back until you have me some answers. You hear? I'm losing my patience. I'm tired of fucking around!" He gritted his teeth and worked his jaw after he said it.

The two men got off their horses and started filling their canteens at the trough. Some of the other men offered them their spare ammunition. Coco turned toward his palapa to retrieve some food for the two men. He was glad to get away from Manny. The man was pure evil.

★★★

The Doña Guadalupe anchored offshore at Santa Marta. Oscar's guests watched from the open deck as he was motored to shore in one of the pangas. His khaki pants were rolled up below his knees. He stepped out of the boat in his bare feet and touched down in the shallows. Carmen heard the motor and walked down from the house to greet him. She was wearing a pair of light cotton shorts and a loose-fitting, white t-shirt. Her letter to Sammy was folded in her hand. They met near the water's edge, where they stopped to talk. The conversation took a serious turn, and they sat in the sand. There were frequent hand gestures, and Carmen turned to look up toward the house several times. Oscar did the same.

Luisa was sitting by herself on the steps of the veranda, forlorn, watching them. The children were in the garden, busying themselves. The mid-day sun was directly overhead, beating down hard on her head. She wanted to escape. She decided to take a siesta. She stood and walked into the house, scuffing and dragging the heels of her flip-flops along the way.

An hour later, Oscar and Carmen rose and walked slowly up to the house, talking softly and seriously as they went along. They stepped up in the shade under the veranda and Oscar took a seat at the ironwood table. Carmen went in search of Luisa. Five minutes later, Carmen and Luisa stepped out from the house, hand in hand. Luisa appeared disheveled, sleep wrinkles and creases on her face. They sat opposite Oscar at the table.

"Oscar and I just had a long talk, as you probably saw," Carmen started, looking Luisa in the eye, holding her hand.

"Yes," Luisa nodded. Her eyes were sad. She brushed loose hair back away from her face.

"Oscar?" Carmen asked, looking at him across the table, a request for him to speak.

"Hello, Luisa. Nice to see you, again. I'm so sorry for your loss. Carmen has told me some about your life in San Juanico, and I am sadly aware of what happened here." He folded his hands in front of him on the table and paused. Luisa watched his every gesture for a clue.

"I have a proposal I'd like to make, if you might be open to one?"

Luisa thought before replying, the wheels in her head spinning, "Yes?"

"As you know, we've lost our cook," Oscar said, glancing at Carmen. He turned back to Luisa adding, "We've decided to spend a week on the islands before we return to La Paz. We'll be anchored in a sandy cove out on Monserrate for three or four days, then on to Santa Catalina. It's not only beautiful out there, but it's a very peaceful place, good for the soul, as they say. I would be delighted if you would join us. We have a cook's helper from Agua Verde, but she is young. We could use someone with a little more experience to work with her."

Luisa looked at Oscar, then her dark charcoal colored eyes darted to Carmen. Her lip quivered. She squeezed Carmen's hand. She was lost for words.

"That's not all," he continued. "After our time on the islands, I'd like you to stay on when we return to La Paz. I have a hacienda in a place called La Ventana, about fifty miles south of La Paz. I spend time there when I'm able to get away. It's perched high on a bluff, overlooking the bay and miles of sandy beach. The home is surrounded by magnificent gardens, and the couple who have been caring for them are elderly. They would like to retire and move to La Paz. They live in a small bungalow there on the grounds. It's really quite nice," he paused for emphasis. "I'd like to offer you the home, along with a fair wage, if you'd be willing to care for the gardens."

The corners of her mouth rose. Her tight, straight lips parted, revealing her perfect white teeth. Tiny wrinkles appeared next to her eyes; the ones caused by smiles. She gripped Carmen's hand more tightly.

"I'm not finished," Oscar added. "A short ten-minute walk down the road from the house, is a small private school where the local children attend classes. I know most of the teachers. It's a truly wonderful school. Your little ones would love it."

Luisa burst out crying. She hugged Carmen and pulled up her blouse to wipe away the tears. She tried to catch her breath. "Yes, Señor. Yes! You have answered my prayers. I promise you won't be sorry. I'll care for your garden, and anything else that needs done. Anything! You won't be sorry! How can I ever thank you?"

Oscar smiled, "Very good, then. One thing I should add. As Carmen knows well, I've become fond of sleeping in the open air on the upper deck, under the stars. The only place we have for you and the children on the boat is my suite down below. That would be fine with you for the week?"

Luisa thought about the bed with the fluffy pillows and the portholes with the waves splashing up against them. She couldn't believe what she'd heard over the last several minutes, "Yes, Señor. Yes!"

"One last thing. You must call me Oscar from now on. No more 'Señor,' please? All my friends call me Oscar."

She nodded and smiled through her tears.

"Well then, take your time and gather your things. Prepare the children. Carmen and I have more to talk about. We'll leave for the islands when you're ready. There's no rush."

Luisa leaned over and hugged Carmen again, so hard it took the wind out of her. She stepped around the table and hugged Oscar. She kissed him on the cheek. He blushed. She was like a young teenager in her joyousness, "I need to find the children. I won't be long!" she skipped away on her toes.

Carmen looked across the table and mouthed a thank you to Oscar. The tears were dripping from her bright, sparkling eyes.

★★★

A day later, as Pepino was finishing breakfast, Carmen asked, "Would you come with me out to the garden?"

"When?" he looked up.

"Soon as you're finished."

"I'm ready," he rose from the table.

As they walked behind the house, Carmen said, "I'm afraid the garden's gotten out of control. I could use some help trimming things back, picking the fruit and vegetables. Look," she waved her hand, "the mangos and oranges are falling off the trees. It's a shame."

She opened the gate. They walked over to the two side-by-side mango trees and started picking the ripest fruit. There was a sweet fragrance rising from the fruit that laid rotting on the ground. The early morning air was crisp and clean. Quail called from the cholla thickets, chuck-wacca, chuck-wacca.

Carmen thought, "What a refreshing, beautiful morning." She inhaled a deep, satisfying breath. Carmen turned back and saw the boy already picking fruit off the tree. It reminded her of something.

She said "Pepino, I was thinking this morning, we're living under the same roof, and I hardly know you. We haven't had much of a chance to talk. Do you have plans to return to San Juanico?" she asked, placing a mango in the basket at his feet.

"No reason to go back there. Nothing for me there." He reached up among the branches.

"No family?"

"No, I never had a father, and my mother, she died a year ago. She got sick and stopped eating. Something wrong with her stomach. Nobody could help her. She withered away." He dropped an armful of mangoes in the bushel-basket. "One day she was fine, a month later, she was gone. My little sister went to live with the neighbors, but I stayed living in our palapa. I know how to take care of myself." He stopped and straightened his posture to make a point.

"You're only twelve, Pepino. You need someone in your life."

"The neighbors shared meals with me, but I like being on my own. I herded goats for the village. Had all the milk I could drink. It was easy."

"You can't live on goat's milk." She stopped and watched him. He lifted himself up on a branch where he could reach more fruit.

"Get below me, I'll hand them down to you. Anyway, there won't be a San Juanico to go back to, not without the men."

She stood under him, reached up. He passed her a mango. "I know, Luisa and I talked about that. Oscar is going to help the women move to Insurgentes."

"I wouldn't want to do that. I'm not sure what I'll do," he paused. "Haven't thought about it. Things happened fast. One day, everything changed."

Carmen watched him up in the tree. She saw the independent streak in him. She also saw a twelve-year old boy.

"With Luisa gone, I'll be needing some help around here. Pepino," she started to say, but paused when she saw him watching her from above.

He was looking down at her with a questioning expression.

"I could use a hard-working boy like you here on the ranch. I like you, Pepino. I like you a lot. Would you like to live here at Santa Marta? Stay here? Be part of our family? You could have my son's room, all to yourself."

"Do you really mean that?" he asked with a broad smile on his face. "I love it here. If I lived here, I'd never want to leave!"

Carmen laughed, "Well, that was easy! As of today, then, this will be your home." She said it in motherly way, and she meant it.

He jumped down from the tree and gave her a big hug. He lifted the basketful of mangoes and set it on the worktable. He turned back to her and said, "There's one thing I need to do before too long though. It's very important to me," he seemed worried about whatever it was.

"What might that be?"

"After Leo and Antonio return, so you're not alone here, I need to walk back to San Juanico. I have some things hidden in a cave there. I want to get them and have them here with me."

"You would walk all that way?"

"Have to. Can't get a burro or a mule up the trail anymore. It's really not that far. I could be there in two days. It wouldn't hurt me to sleep on the trail for a night. I did that going to Timbabichi, didn't I?" he thought back to the terrible night he spent having nightmares in the arroyo.

"You are really an amazing boy, Pepino. I think it's going to be wonderful to have you here. I hope you stay for a long time."

"I already told you, I won't be leaving," he laughed and lifted the basket. "I'll carry these to the house, and I'll be right back with an empty basket."

Carmen turned her attention to the orange tree and smiled.

★★★

"What's with you wanting to go back to Timbabichi?" Antonio asked.

"I've got serious business there, that's why," Leo answered gruffly as they stood in the breeze on the open deck of the empty ferry as it chugged its way back across the Gulf toward Timbabichi. They were making good time after unloading more than one hundred thousand pounds of cattle.

"We could've had them drop us off at Santa Marta and been done with it at Timbabichi. I'm sure that Charro and Christian will be taking the ferry back to Agua Verde. That'll save them days of hard riding through the rocks."

"I didn't say you had to get off at Timbabichi, did I? I don't recall telling you that!" Leo snipped.

"Well I have a pretty good idea what that serious business of yours in Los Dolores is, and I don't intend to let you deal with it on your own. You know better than anyone I'm able to put two and two together. You and that woman they killed had something going, didn't you?"

A burst of wind crossed the bow and blew off Antonio's hat. He nimbly caught it in the air with his right hand, just before losing it over the railing. He held it as the wind blew his hair about.

"No, we didn't have something going," Leo turned away and looked out across the choppy water. He turned back to face Antonio, "We were friends, that's all. She was a good woman with a fine spirit. You don't run across many like her." A hard, steely expression filled his eyes when he added, "I'm going to make the man pay for what he did. Simple as that."

"That's why I'm going with you on this. Never hurts to have backup. You know that as well as I do," he turned to see Christian walking toward them across the deck.

"Why are we going back to Timbabichi?" Christian asked when he stopped in front of them.

Antonio looked at Leo, who was uncomfortable with the question. It was a personal matter, and Leo didn't care to share it with the others. Antonio was bad enough.

"Well, I'm not one for game playing," Antonio replied as he glanced at Leo. "Recall that woman they tortured to death over at Los Dolores?" he looked to Christian.

A confused expression crossed Christian's face as he thought, "Yeah, I think I remember Coco telling the story." He looked to Leo, then back at Antonio, questioning.

"She was a friend of Leo's. We're going to pay a little visit over to Los Dolores and settle up with the guy who did that."

Christian turned to Leo, "I'm sorry."

Leo looked out on the water again, without responding.

Christian looked to Antonio, "We four – me, Charro, Naco, and Benito – we decided we'd get off the ferry at Santa Marta. We want to help you build your new palapa. We could have that finished in a week, a nice big one at that."

"That's good of you, I won't turn down the help. Thank you." He patted Christian on the back.

Christian spoke back up, "Seeing as you're going to Los Dolores, no reason we can't stick together and help with that too."

Leo shifted, uncomfortable. He looked at Christian, "No need for that, Antonio and I can handle it well enough."

"There's quite a number of men in Los Dolores. I'm sure they're not very happy about having their cattle stolen and ten of their friends dead. No, we came all this way together, we'll finish up that way. I'll tell the others we'll be getting off at Timbabichi. Don't argue with me, it won't do you any good."

"He's right, and you know it, Leo," Antonio added as he spit over the side.

Leo sighed with resignation. He thought about Flora, her lovely smile, her life cut short.

★★★

"You're the last ones I expected to see coming back through Timbabichi! Are you out of your minds? That Osuna bunch would like nothing more than to lynch the whole lot of you," Coco said after Antonio, Leo and the other four rode up.

"Leo remembered he had some unfinished business over in Los Dolores. We thought it better if he didn't go back there alone. Do you know if those boys who pushed that herd of bulls down to La Paz ever got back?" Antonio asked, still in the saddle.

"They did," he shifted off his bad knee to the other. He looked over his shoulder in the direction of Los Dolores, as if to be sure nobody from over there was listening, "In fact, they followed the cattle tracks from the corrals back to here." He pointed at the ground close to where he was standing. It was covered with old cattle tracks. "I talked to them day before yesterday, right in this exact spot where we're standing now."

Antonio and the five other men on horseback all looked around at the cattle tracks.

Coco continued, "Manuel, he's the foreman, he was angry as a tomcat in a dog fight, I swear," he spit with the reference to Manny. "He's a mean son of a bitch anyway. He sent two men down the trail that way," he waved, "to find out where the cattle went. Like the six men before that, they haven't come back, least not yet. You get your cows over to Topolobampo?"

The moment Leo heard Manuel's name, he tensed. "You say Manny was here day before yesterday?"

"Right there, where you're sitting on that horse," Coco replied. "He went back to Los Dolores."

Antonio smiled, "To answer your question. The cattle are fat and happy, over in the feedlot at Topolobampo. Quite the cattle drive." He chuckled as he recalled it.

Coco shook his head, "I'll be. The older I get, the stranger things get," he mumbled to himself.

"How many men Manny have with him?" Leo asked.

"Hmmm, let's see, he sent two that way to follow the tracks." He nodded over his left shoulder. He scratched the sparse white whiskers on his chin, adding, "I think he had five other men with him."

Leo glanced south in the direction of Los Dolores, then up at the late afternoon sun. "We have just enough daylight left to get over to Los Dolores before dark. We can stop on the ridge in the rimrock and make a plan," he said, turning to Antonio.

"Let's be going then," Antonio said.

Leo looked back at Coco and cracked a smile. "Get your things ready, I promised to take you to Insurgentes, for a look around the chili patch. I'll be ready to go tomorrow, once my business with Manny is finished with, if that's something you still want to do."

"Dammed right, I thought maybe you were just kidding about that. I'll be ready. I'll make burritos for the trail."

Confused, Antonio asked, "Insurgentes? Chili patch? What?"

Leo smiled, "Coco wanted to see the chili patch before he got too old to travel. I promised to show him around. I'll be a couple weeks behind you getting back to Santa Marta."

"Whatever," Antonio shrugged.

With that, they turned their horses toward Los Dolores, and they were on their way to even the score.

★★★

"I see the road crew's finished up," Antonio said as he peered down at Los Dolores through his binoculars. "The road's done right up to the corrals. The heavy equipment's still there. There's about a dozen horses in the corral. There's one, two, three, hmm, looks like eight men right there around the equipment."

"I see that," Leo replied, scanning the area with his glasses. "I say we stay put here until well after dark. Let things get busy in the cantina. Let them do some drinking."

"Good idea," Antonio said, "We should send Naco in first. Make sure the man you want is there. If he's the foreman, Naco could inquire about work, and get the lay of the place for us. Nobody would suspect an old man like Naco being one of us," Antonio schemed.

"I agree," Leo said. "I say we wait two hours after dark. Let them get good and tipsy."

Antonio snickered, "I like that. Then we move in fast, before they know what hit em."

"Uh huh," Leo answered.

"Boys, listen up," Antonio lowered his binoculars. "We go in with pistols. If you have a spare, load it up and slip it under your belt. Better to have two. No rifles, too confined a space. We'll send Naco in ahead for a look-see. He'll tell us what we'll see when we walk through the door, we'll finish the plan then. For now, rest up. Take a snooze if you can. I want everyone alert and at their best."

The boys went through their saddle bags looking for extra pistols and ammunition. They checked and re-checked the pistols strapped to their legs in their holsters. They were quiet. There was none of the typical back-and-forth chatter.

The sun faded pink and purple to the west, and all the men except Antonio were stretched out on the ground among the rocks with their hats covering their faces. There were grunts and snores as the they relaxed, or at least tried to. Antonio watched several men slip into the cantina in the dusky light. Leo woke first and crawled over next to Antonio.

"See anything interesting?"

"Not much. Three men entered the place, a couple of whores."

Leo scanned down at the cantina in the dim light. "Getting too dark to see much," he muttered. "Let's give it two more hours."

"We'll start down in an hour. We'll wait on the beach, and we'll send Naco in."

★★★

Naco heard the mariachis long before he passed under the wide-spanning archway and through the open doors of the old mission. The three-man ensemble, two guitars and a stand-up bass, were serenading two men with whores on their laps at a corner table in the far end of the expansive room. He glanced at the thick stone walls and up at the heavy timbers supporting the high ceiling. The music bounced and echoed off the stone. The air was thick with cigarette smoke and the smell of beer.

Naco stepped across the sandstone floor, the heels of his boots clacking on the solidness. Dodging tables full of men as he crossed the room, he found his way up to the bar. He said to the busy bartender, "Tequila with a lime," he noticed the bar was built around what had once been the altar in the church. He set two pesos down in front of him.

"In a sec, let me finish up with the lady there," he nodded toward a pretty whore in a low-cut, flower-patterned, red dress at the end of the bar, "She's working tonight." The girl smiled and gave Naco a cute little wave. He tipped his hat.

A moment later, as the bartender passed Naco his drink, he asked, "Where you from? Haven't seen you in here before."

"I'm looking for work. Got a place in the desert to the west of here that's not paying its way. Need to pick up a few extra pesos. Is there a foreman here tonight I could talk to?"

"Sure, he's in that card game over there," he pointed. "First table to the right of the door. "He's the one with his back to us. The one with the hat." The other three men around the table were bare-headed. "His name's Manny, but I'm sure he's not doing any hiring. There's no more cattle on the place, and the road crew's mostly finished up, but you can ask him."

"Won't hurt," Naco said as he swished the drink around in his mouth. The tart lime and the ice-cold tequila tasted good on his tongue. He looked around the room. There were sixteen men, counting the four at Manny's table. The other twelve were scattered in pairs and threes at different tables around the room. He counted five whores, two pairs sitting at two tables each with two men, and the pretty girl in the red dress who was walking over to another table, about to sit down.

"Thanks for the drink," Naco told the bartender as he started for Manny's table.

"Sure thing, Señor. Come back any time."

Naco stepped up to the table and looked around the card game. His gaze held on Manny for a moment, as he sized the man up. He was a huge, ugly sort of brute with a commanding presence. The other three men clearly deferred to him, though they all appeared to be rough characters in their own right.

"Excuse me," Naco started. Manny looked up and over his right shoulder, irritated at having been distracted from his game.

"What do you want, old man?" he questioned as he pulled his cards close, not wanting to share his hand with Naco.

"Sorry to bother you during your card game, but I was told you're the man to see about work around here."

Manny peered at Naco through squinted eyes, "Even if I had any work, which I don't, I don't make it a habit of hiring old codgers like you. There's plenty enough young studs in this country with good strong backs. You'd best turn around and get where you came from. I have no work for you." He laid his hand down on the table. He looked back up at Naco. "You didn't hear me? Get out, don't be bothering me!" he snarled.

Naco smiled, took a look around the room one more time, and walked out the door.

★★★

"Seventeen men, counting the bartender, and five women in there. Manny's at the first table to the left after you walk in the door. He's playing cards with three other men. He's the only one at the table wearing a hat. His back is to the door. The other twelve men are scattered around at different tables, all to the left past where Manny is. The girls are sitting around with the men," Naco explained.

They were in the dark shadows on the beach, one hundred yards downhill from the mission. The five men listened closely to every word, as if their lives depended on it. The six-inch waves lapped peacefully up near their feet.

"Alright, here's how it works," Antonio stated, "Leo and I will take Manny's table. I'll come at him from behind and put a choke hold on him. Leo," he said turning to him, "do what you need to subdue the other three at the table, then Manny's all yours. That make sense?"

"It does."

"Christian, you cover the bartender," he turned to Christian. "He likely has a gun behind the bar. If he reaches under the bar for anything, take him down, put a bullet in his head. You might warn him not to try it. Good with that?"

"I'm fine."

"Benito and Charro, you two come in fast right behind Leo and myself. Go right past us with your pistols out and ready. Cover the other tables with the twelve men. Yell at them, make them place their hands flat on the table. Shoot any one of them that doesn't do what they're told. Be fast and firm about it."

Benito and Charro nodded in tight-lipped agreement.

"Naco, I want you to cover the door. The last thing we need are any surprises coming up behind us. If we do this right, we'll be in and out of there in less than a minute. Any questions?"

There were no questions.

"Alright, let's go!"

They led their horses up to the cantina and tied them loosely to the hitching rail. They stopped just outside the open double doors, while Leo and Antonio stepped to the front of the group. Charro, Benito, and Christian, stood side by side by side, directly behind the first two. They glanced nervously at one another. Naco hung back, to cover the door.

"Let's do it!" Antonio ordered.

Antonio stepped into the room, moving across the sandstone floor as if he were a man twenty years younger. Leo was there at his side with his gun drawn. Before Manny knew what hit him, Antonio had him standing next to the table in a choke hold with the barrel of his pistol forced up into his open mouth.

For good measure, Leo fired a round into the center of the table and screamed, "Don't you fuckin' move! Put your hands flat out on the table or you're dead. Now!" he scanned the pistol across the table from man to man. They placed their hands on the table, shock on their suddenly pale faces, muscles in their jaws quivering, pure fright in their eyes.

The entire cantina went dead silent with the gunshot and the sight of Manny with a pistol in his mouth. Everyone in the room was dumbfounded. The mariachis stood paralyzed, holding their silenced instruments.

Benito and Charro, with a pistol in each hand, covered the other twelve men at their tables, "Hands flat on the table! Now!" Charro screamed. With that, he shot rounds through three or four tables to make his point. All twelve men placed their hands on the tables.

Christian walked up to the bar and pointed his pistol at the bartender's face. He screamed, "Hands flat on the bar, or I'll splatter your brains!" The man placed his hands on the bar.

Leo turned toward Manny as he pulled a razor-sharp skinning knife from a sheath on his belt, his eyes hard, cold, and determined. He sliced through Manny's leather belt as if it were nothing more than a kite string. He reached with his other hand and pulled on Manny's pants where the belt had been and sliced them open clear down along the fly. He pulled down the pants to mid-thigh, exposing his privates. The three men around the table watched in horror.

Leo reached up with his freehand and grabbed Manny by the balls. He growled, "This is for Flora, you ugly fuck!"

His knife sliced through Manny's scrotum as if it were a stick of warm butter. He tossed the handful of testicle and tissue on the table, splattering the cards and the three men behind them with blood and body fluids.

Antonio smiled as he let go of Manny, who dropped to his knees. Manny reached across the table with one hand for the scrotum, as if he could repair the problem. He stared at the mucky mess in his hand and brought it down between his legs and held it tight against the place it came from. He let go a bloodcurdling wail that reverberated throughout the cavernous room, right before he curled down on the floor in a fetal position, whimpering like a punished child, his hand still tight up against his crotch.

All eyes in the crowded room fixed on Leo and Antonio.

Leo screamed, "Pay attention, you assholes! This is what we do to men who treat women badly. Any of you remember Flora? Now, you'll never forget her!"

Antonio followed up, yelling, waving his pistol, "All you men be advised to leave Los Dolores, and don't come back. Be gone tomorrow, or we'll shoot you dead! This is and always has been our ranch. You're lucky we didn't kill the whole lot of you! Torturing women and stealing cattle won't be tolerated!"

The six of them backstepped to the door, guns waving left then right across the room. The only sound was Manny whimpering on the floor and the dull hum of the generator outside behind the building. The whole thing took only a minute.

Outside the mission, they mounted their horses. Before they rode off, Leo looked from one man to the next and said, "Thank you for that." They then turned their horses in the direction of Timbabichi.

★★★

The following morning, they woke at Coco's ranch. Around the campfire, over coffee, Leo thanked the men one more time. He was parting with them, setting out with Coco for the chili patch. Antonio and the others were leaving on their two-day journey across the rocks, canyons, and arroyos for Santa Marta.

Christian and Charro eventually found their way back to Agua Verde where they teamed up together and resumed their lives as fishermen. They sold one of the two fifty-five horsepower Johnson engines off the stolen super panga, in Ensenada Blanca on the black market for a handsome sum. They re-painted the boat and inscribed the name "Paloma," after Christian's mother, on the bow.

Naco and Benito went along to Agua Verde, because they could no longer climb the old trail up and out of Santa Marta with their horses. They traveled on a long round-about series of trails, working their way back up and across the Gigantas. A week later, Naco settled in back home, on the El Coronado Ranch up in the high country. Benito rested there for a few days before finding his way down to Insurgentes.

Two weeks later, Leo rode his bay gelding, followed by the pale spotted mare with the arrowhead brand on her left hip, into Santa Marta. He arrived during the early evening, as the sun was setting behind the Giganta cliffs. He looked up at the magical colors and thought "How beautiful!" He and Carmen had a joyous reunion that night in the hot spring, just the two of them, under a thick blanket of stars.

★★★

"Señor Padilla, there's a call for you," Oscar's office assistant said as she stuck her head through the crack in his door. "The connection is bad, but I think the man said his name was Pablo Sandoval. Calling from Loreto, something about a friend? Anna Marie?"

Oscar paused, "I'll take the call," he replied, thinking, his hand on the phone, not picking up.

"Yes, this is Oscar Padilla. Who am I speaking with? I'm sorry, the connection's very bad, can you speak up, please? San Javier, you say? Yes, I know where…" He stood with the phone to his ear.

Confused, he asked, "You say she's? I see … I was told. All these months? Yes. When? No, let me think for a moment." He reached for a pencil and scribbled something down.

"I have an airplane. I'll fly up to Ensenada Blanca tomorrow. Twelve noon. Yes, the airstrip. On the beach. Thank you, thank you so much." He slowly brought the phone down to its cradle.

He took three steps to the window behind his desk. It looked down on the Malecón. He placed his hands on the sill for balance.

"Sofia, would you come in please?" he called to his assistant.

She came through the door and paused, "Yes?"

He turned to speak, "Please cancel my appointments for tomorrow. Something's come up."

"You only had the two, I'll take care of them. Anything else?"

"Yes, please get Sergio on the phone. I'll be needing the airplane."

He picked up the phone, "We'll be flying up to Ensenada Blanca tomorrow morning. Nine a.m. The 206, yes. No, one passenger. Stop-over at Playa Aguja, the new strip there. We may be on the ground for several hours. Yes, thank you. See you in the morning."

★★★

The 206 circled twice. Oscar saw the old Ford flatbed parked at the south end of the strip.

"Approach from the north. I see the party we're meeting there, under those palm trees on the south end," he pointed.

The plane taxied to the south end of the strip. Both doors opened on the Ford. A man got out on the driver's side, two women on the passenger side. The older woman assisted the younger one down. Oscar waited for the propeller to stop spinning. He climbed down and walked toward the truck, stopping half-way. Anna came around the rear end of the bed. She stopped, leaned on a cane. They were twenty feet apart.

A bright flowered scarf covered her head. She smiled, in spite of the deep-red scars on her face, she was lovely. Oscar stepped forward with open arms. She fell into them and began to cry.

He held her away, in front, so he could look at her, "You're the most beautiful girl I've ever laid my eyes on! His eyes were watering. He couldn't stop smiling. He pulled her to him for another hug, "Anna, this is the most wonderful thing to have ever happened. We all thought you were gone!"

"I was. For a long time," she sniffed.

"You're back, you're back! You're right here in front of me!"

"I want to go home, but I don't know where that is."

"Please, don't let it worry you. I'll be taking you to your new home. Today. He has no idea, but Antonio is waiting there for you. I had no way of contacting him. He's living on the beach at Santa Marta. You remember me talking about the place, don't you?"

She shook her head, "I'm sorry, so many things I don't remember."

"No matter," he gestured with his hands and shrugged to reassure her. "I'll be taking you there."

She looked away, with a worried expression, "Do you think he's going to want me, I mean, the way I look?" she brought her hand up to cover the worst of the scars.

"He's going to feel the same as I do, that you are one of the most beautiful miracles on earth. You truly are, Anna. You're a beautiful miracle. I can't believe you're standing here in front of me." He placed his hands gently on her shoulders. He kissed her on the forehead. "You're a miracle! I can't stop saying it, it's true."

She sniffed, "I don't know how this happened." Her eyes looked up at him, uncertain.

He draped his arm around her. "Don't worry about any of that, you're back. That's all that matters." He glanced at Pablo and Lupe who were watching the reunion. "I'd like to thank these people for all they've done." He took her free hand, and they walked to where Lupe and Pablo were standing. Anna limped and pushed herself along with the cane.

Anna embraced Lupe as Oscar shook Pablo's hand, "Señor Sandoval, I'll never be able to thank you. You and your wife have saved Anna's life." He reached into his pocket for a small envelope. "Please, take this for your family." He handed Pablo the envelope. "For the kindness you've shown Anna. The least I can do." He squeezed Pablo's shoulder with his hand.

Pablo, a poor humble man, responded, "That's not necessary, Señor. We feel blessed we could help. She was on the road for a reason, waiting for us. She is one of our children who needed our help." He tried to hand the envelope back to Oscar.

Oscar studied Pablo, dressed in the ragged clothing of a dirt farmer, with genuine kindness in his eyes and in his words. He said, "Please, that is from me, for your family. I have more than enough, I'd like to share it with you, please."

Pablo looked down at the envelope in his hand, "May God bless you, Señor."

After teary good-byes, Anna glanced one more time back at Lupe as she limped toward the plane. She broke down crying all over again. Lupe was the closest thing to "family" she'd ever known.

★★★

Thirty minutes later, Oscar ordered through the headphones, "Fly over Agua Verde. Buzz Gayo's palapa."

The plane circled several times over the bay, to lose altitude, it dropped to one hundred feet along the beach. Gayo stepped out from the palapa, waving his arms. The plane buzzed him a second time, dipped a wing, and flew low over the water, around the corner past Solitaire Rock, toward Playa Aguja. It landed on the new strip. Gayo met them fifteen minutes later. Following a short discussion, Oscar, Anna, and Gayo were on their way to Santa Marta. Gayo's panga sliced through the choppy afternoon waves with ease under the bright, cloud-free sky. Anna's flowery scarf fluttered in the wind, and her eyes watered because of it.

The panga coasted toward the beach. Oscar removed his shoes, and Anna took off her sandals. She was wearing a bright yellow sundress. She pulled it up over her knees as she stepped out of the boat into the water, leaning on her cane for balance. Leo and Carmen crossed the beach to greet them.

"Oscar?" Carmen exclaimed. "We didn't expect you," she curiously looked at Anna.

"Please, allow me to introduce you. Anna Marie, meet Carmen and Leo." Oscar gestured toward each of them. "Leo, Carmen, meet Anna Marie. Anna is a close friend of Antonio's. Is he here?"

A shocked look appeared on Leo's face. His jaw dropped. He was afraid to speak, to say the wrong thing. He tried to add things up. He'd broken the news of Anna Marie's death to Antonio. It shattered Tonio's life, but here she was.

"You mean?" he looked at Oscar.

"Yes," Oscar replied, he smiled, he placed his arm around Anna.

Carmen looked back and forth between the two men, then at Anna. As she put things together, she raised a hand up over her mouth and gasped, "He's at his palapa. Follow me, I'll walk you there."

They followed a well-worn path through the palm grove and came out the other side. Antonio was sitting in a chair at a small rustic table under the front awning, eating a bowl of fruit. His hand stopped in mid-air on the way to his mouth with a chunk of mango, when he saw them coming. He rose to his feet when he recognized Oscar, then Anna Marie. He placed his hand over his forehead. He shook his head and visibly blinked, as if he was seeing a mirage. She was still there. She smiled at him. It was her! The other three stopped as Anna limped forward three more steps. She dropped the cane and opened her arms. Antonio stumbled, he knocked over the table as he rushed toward her. He started to cry.

"Anna?" he wrapped her fragile body with his muscled arms. He lifted her off the ground.

"It's me, Tonio. I've come back. Will you have me?" They were both crying.

Carmen dabbed her eyes with the corner of her t-shirt. Oscar and Leo couldn't release their gaze from the dramatic scene playing out in front of them.

Antonio placed one hand on each of her tiny shoulders and gently pushed her six inches back so he could see her eyes.

"It really is you. My Anna! My Anna Marie, what do you ever mean, will I have you? I'll never let you out of my sight! You're the most beautiful woman I've ever known. Where did you come from?"

"Let's not speak of that right now."

She stood up on her toes. He leaned down, and they experienced the longest, deepest, most wonderful kiss of their lives. He thought, "She smells like flowers."

★★★

Pepino slept on the ground along the trail, five miles from San Juanico. He woke at dawn to a stiff wind, as a cool front passed over the high rimrock, a thousand feet above. He continued his walk, through parched cactus forests, impenetrable thickets of catclaw, and the endless sea of twisted, thorny mesquite. The small palm grove came into view, miles in the distance, and he picked up his pace. The pulverized gray dust on the beaten-down trail rose in clouds with each of his steps. His nostrils were ringed with it, his eyes watered from it, his ears were caked with it. Small dust devils hurled it at him. He covered his lower face with a ragged, sweat-stained bandanna. Later, he turned from the trail behind some low-lying rimrock, no higher than him. The black lava rocks formed a half circle, cove-like. Within the cove were the graves, scattered across the ground in no particular order. Many of the graves were marked by small piles of hand-sized stones. Most of the them were tiny.

The boy stepped carefully between and through the graves. He came to the one he sought. He kneeled and placed his hand on the center of the low mound. He held his hand there as his eyes watered.

"Hola, Mama. Te quiero," he whispered.

Pepino remained there for a long time. He rested his cheek on the mound, and he cried. Before he stood, he balled his small hand in a fist. He slammed it into the mound of dirt.

"Porque?"

A small puff of dust rose from the grave. It disappeared with the breeze.

Brisk winds kicked up as the boy walked through the forlorn, abandoned village. Dark ominous clouds rolled over the rimrock, threatening rain. He looked about for any sign of life. He pictured the men, his friends, toiling along the trail with buckets of water. Two stray goats frightened him when they darted out from the shadows of a collapsed palapa. They pranced away, wild and feral. They were the only living creatures he saw until he reached the waterhole, where a covey of quail fluttered off to the scrubby space that had once been a garden. He lowered the rusty tin bucket down the well and raised it, full of brackish green water. He drank thirstily.

He stepped through the doorless opening of his palapa. The dirt floor resembled a sandy beach where small dunes of dirt had blown in and formed waves, because nobody was there to sweep. Some of the palm fronds had blown from the roof and from two of the walls. He could see the clouds passing above, and the neighbor's palapa through the wall. The wind rattled the fronds, some of them flapped loosely. A vacant feeling engulfed him.

He passed Alonso's palapa, the largest in the village. It too was empty. Not a pot, not a pan, hung from the ceiling. The corral was empty. Even the mule turds were dried out, covered in a layer of gray dust. Beyond there, he walked past Juan Pedro and Luisa's palapa. A wall had collapsed. The entire structure, if it could be called that, was falling in on itself, down in the dirt.

San Juanico was in a state of decay. It was rotting away in front of him. He shuddered. It scared him. He thought of the men, buried in the rockslide. He felt their spirits here. He was frightened by them. They were all his friends.

He hustled up the hill trail that led to the caves. He crept in through the cave, in its darkness. It smelled like the bowels of the earth. Musty and dank. The pungent aroma of bat shit. He got down on his knees. He crawled into a pitch-dark narrow crevice. Without the aid of light or sight, he felt for and placed his hand on a small, tightly-bound canvas package. It contained his most precious possessions – a small rubber ball, a handful of metal jacks, dominos, a frayed comic book, a whistle, and a stick doll. Most of all, there was his mother's necklace, made of cheap multi-colored plastic beads. She'd had two. She left one to each of her children. They were the only things she owned worth leaving them when she died.

THE END